Eyes of Horus

"During the last twenty years, seven books of mine have been published as historical novels which to me are biographies of previous lives I have known."

Joan Grant

Joan Grant Books

Far Memory Books
Winged Pharaoh (1937)
Life as Carola (1939)
Eyes of Horus (1942)
Lord of the Horizon (1943)
Scarlet Feather (1945)
Return to Elysium (1947)
So Moses was Born (1952)

Fiction
The Laird and the Lady (1949)

For Children
The Scarlet Fish and Other Stories (1942)
Redskin Morning (1944)

Travel
Vague Vacation (1947)
A Lot to Remember (1962)

Autobiography
Time out of Mind [UK]/Far Memory [USA] (1956)

Non-Fiction
Many Lifetimes [with Denis Kelsey] (1967)
Joan Grant: Speaking from the Heart (2007)

JOAN GRANT

Eyes of Horus

a far memory book

DAWN
CHORUS PRESS

Reprint, retypeset edition, 2009
First edition, Methuen & Co., 1942

For information, address:
Dawn Chorus Press, P.O. Box 151011
San Rafael, California 94915, USA

Library of Congress Cataloging-in-Publication Data

.

Grant, Joan Marshall, 1907–1989
Eyes of Horus / Joan Grant.—1st Dawn Chorus retypeset ed.

p. cm.
Originally published: London: Methuen & Co., 1942.
ISBN 978-1-59731-357-5 (pbk.: alk. paper)
ISBN 978-1-59731-382-7 (hardback: alk. paper)
1. Egypt—Fiction. I. Title.
PR6013.R2737E9 2009
823'.912—dc22   2009025074

Cover image:
The god Ra-Harakhty (Ra merged with the god Horus) and Amentet,
goddess of the West, detail from the burial chamber of Nefertari,
c. 1298–12345 BCE

CONTENTS

PART I

Ra's Messenger

BY THE TIME I was seven I could not remember my mother very clearly; though sometimes, just before I went to sleep, came a memory of her voice, telling me small comfortable stories before she carried the lamp out of my room, or the sound of her laughter when she and my father had played with me as though they too were children. I remembered Niyahm, my nurse, telling me I had a sister and Mother not coming to my room any more, as part of the same vague unhappiness. I learned that even grown-up people cried, and the house seemed full of whispers which stopped when I tried to hear what they were saying.

The last thing I really remember about her happened soon after my second birthday. I had been told I might go into her room, but must be very quiet because she was ill. She smiled and let me kiss her, and said that she would soon be well again, long before my sister was old enough to join in our games. I noticed she had grown very thin, and seemed too tired to raise her head from the pillow. Her bed was so high that my head was on the same level as hers; and I whispered to the long wooden leopards, which made the sides of it, to guard her well.

Sometimes I saw the baby in the arms of another woman who came to help Niyahm look after it, and I knew Niyahm was jealous because she had no milk to give it. The baby was named Kiyas. At first I was disappointed because it couldn't talk to me, and only cried or made pigeon noises. My father seemed to like it, for I often saw him coming out of the room it lived in.

Then I was sent away to Roidahn's house, and when I came back, Mother wasn't there anymore. Nekht-Ra told me she had gone ahead of us to the land where the Gods live. I asked where that land was, and he said, "Beyond the sunset; the land Ra loves so much that he is always hurrying through the day to get home."

I thought the land where Ra lived would be very hot, for he is the sun as well as a God; but Nekht-Ra said it was a beautiful country, where all the trees and plants are without blemish, and animals never try to hurt each other, or get ill. He said it was only

1

while we were human that we saw Ra as the sun—he was too shining for us to see with ordinary eyes. After I was dead I might see him, and he would be like a man only more perfect than I could imagine. Then I asked Nekht-Ra if one had to be dead to get to the Land beyond the Sunset. And he said people usually had to wait until then, though some, if Ra had a special love for them, might go there when they were asleep.

After that I used to pray very hard that Ra would remember how much he loved my father, and take him to where my mother was, and let him remember all about it in the morning so that he would stop being unhappy. I wanted to ask Father if he remembered, but for a long time I didn't, because I knew it hurt him to speak about her. I didn't tell him I'd prayed to Ra about it, I just asked him if he ever went to see Mother in the Land beyond the Sunset. He had let me be in the room with him while he was scribing—quite often he made his own writing-signs although he was the Nomarch and had two scribes who worked only for him.

I thought he hadn't heard what I said, for he went on sharpening a reed without answering. Then he said very slowly, "No, Ra-ab, I've never been there. When Ra shall judge me worthy he will send a messenger to take me to her."

"Will I see the messenger when he comes for you?"

"Nobody sees him save the one whom he comes to fetch.

"Always remember, Ra-ab, that when he comes to you he is only Ra's messenger come to bring you home."

"How shall I know him? What will he look like?"

"Ra has many messengers, and their robes are as many-colored as the clouds which hide his land from ours. Some are in green, gentle as the quiet morning, and others wear the Warrior Scarlet."

"Is the messenger's name Death? Niyahm told me that Death had come to take Mother away. I thought he was an old man in a black robe, with a kind of hood hiding his face. That's why I cried so much when I knew she had to go away with him. I only stopped being unhappy when Nekht-Ra told me about the country she was living in. Can I tell Niyahm that Death isn't an old man in black?"

Instead of answering my question, Father said, "Come and look at this picture; I don't think you've seen it before."

He took a papyrus from one of the shelves and unrolled it on the table. It was of wild geese, flying over a very blue pool at which two gazelles were drinking.

"The colors are bright, aren't they, Ra-ab?" I nodded. "Shut your eyes — what do you see now?"

I was puzzled. "What do I see now? Nothing, it's all dark!"

"And what color is dark?"

"Well, dark's black."

He picked me up and set me on his knees with his arm round me. "That's why Niyahm thought Death wore a black robe; it's only the people who shut their eyes against him who don't know of the bright colors he wears. Smile at Death and watch for his coming; then you will always recognize him as Ra's messenger."

The Story of Oyahbe

I ALWAYS FELT that even though my mother was dead she was nearer to my father than either Kiyas or I. He was always kind and gentle to us, but even when he was trying his hardest to be understanding we were still remote from his heart. It was Nekht-Ra who told me about Mother. He used to call her Oyahbe, the moon-flower, and this is her story, as it was told to me by Nekht-Ra when I was nearly eight years old:

I knew your mother since she was a child, for I was a priest of the Temple of Ra in the town where her parents lived. It was a very small temple, little more than a sanctuary set in a wide courtyard which also enclosed the priest's dwelling-house. When I came into authority I tried to follow the old traditions of my office, making the temple not only a place where tribute to the Gods was received, but the house of a man to whom people could bring their sorrows. The one who had preceded me, though not a true priest, was a kindly man, and so I found no wall of suspicion or fear between me and those under my protection.

Because I am not a seer, I could not know which of the children who came to me were set in the way of the priest, so I would not accept any of them as pupils; even when the parents brought them to me, hoping to gain favor with the Gods by giving one of their family as a temple virgin. Though I had had little experience of the temples of the new religion, I had seen enough to know that they were not training places of true priests.

When your mother was brought to me she was twelve years old, and I told her father that it were better she should continue to live in his house, following in the way of life I tried to teach, than seeking to gain knowledge of the mysteries. I saw that both man and daughter were deeply distressed, and he said he wished to talk to me alone. I learned that both he and his wife were frightened of their daughter because she had strange visions. At first they thought she was deluded by demons; they had beaten and starved her, shut her in a dark room and sewn magical amulets into her clothes, to try to make her like other children. When they saw that instead of being frightened of them she was compassionate, their awe of her grew, until they thought she must be a child of the Gods, sent to test the fidelity of their faith. Knowing that at my temple no more than the tribute of the tenth part was accepted, they tried to propitiate the Gods whom they thought had set this child to spy upon them, by taking gifts to the new temple three days' journey downriver. It was the girl herself who said she must live in my temple because it was her destiny to become a priest. Her parents rejoiced, thinking they need live no longer under this eye of the Gods, but could rest content in the honor she would do them.

After hearing the father's story, I talked alone with the girl: and instead of child and priest, it was as though two carvers talked of their calling. She must have heard so many harsh answers when she spoke of her reality, yet she accepted my understanding without question; neither trying to heighten her story with mystery nor belittling its significance. In the past she must have been an initiate of Anubis, for in the memory of her dreams and of her far journey there was nothing tenuous. She talked of forgotten centuries as though they were yesterday, making them live so that I could almost share her sight. She knew her parents were strangers to her, yet she had hoped that in time they would have accepted her as a friend; it must have been bitter for her to realize that the more she opened windows to reality the more they shut themselves away from her.

As she spoke, so greatly did I respect the authority in her voice that I forgot she was a child and I a man of forty years.

4

"I belong here with you, Nekht-Ra. There is no work for me in my father's house, but here is much that I can do. In the days when all temples were the house of Truth, there were many who could do much more than is within my little power; but now even I can help you. I know, for I dreamed it last night, that Yeki, the wife of a stoneworker, will come to you today, carrying her sick baby for which she will beseech the pity of the Gods. She will tell you that the child is growing thin, though it has no fever and this is the cold weather; that it wails, and is restless even when it sleeps. She will ask you to give her an amulet to protect it from the demons which she thinks are drawing on its strength. But she will not tell you the child sickens because her milk is starving it; nor will she tell you that her breasts grow empty because her husband ill-treats her. She told me only because she was asleep and not bound by a false loyalty to him. You must tell her to send her husband to you; and you with words must break the rod with which he beats her."

We had been standing at the entrance to the sanctuary, now she went down the steps into the brilliant sunlight of the courtyard. For a moment Oyahbe the priest was again the child of twelve years old, "You will let me stay here? Don't send me back to my father's house. . . . I'm so tired of always being a stranger."

There was no longer any decision for me to take. "You have no Father save Ra. How could you go forth again from his house now that you have returned to it?"

A woman carrying a baby came through the gateway of the courtyard. Instinctively I knew she was the wife of the stoneworker. Oyahbe had told me why she had come, and what it was I must tell her.

My fellow priest smiled up at me. "I'm so glad you believed me *before* she came. If truth is shining it doesn't need to be proved, and I have prayed so hard to make people see my truth."

Oyahbe's powers increased as she grew older, and the door of my own memory, though never so vital as hers, swung wider on its hinges. Where one had come for comfort, now did ten come, though we could accomplish so little compared with what we wished to do. Once there would have been seers and healers, priests of Ma-at and of Ptah, and many pupils learning to become

the wearers of the Golden Sandals, by which men cross the Causeway of the Gods.

The fame of Oyahbe came to the ears of those who saw in her a
way of increasing their own power. A messenger from the high
priest of the new temple of a city down river came to summon us
to audience with him. I answered that though our work was of
small importance we could not leave it to go on a journey. For
more than a month no other message came, and we began to
think they had forgotten to disturb our peace. But they sent
another priest to take my place, and he told me I must take
Oyahbe with me when I took up the office he had vacated.

Oyahbe wanted us to ignore the command, saying, "The
stranger priest can live in the sanctuary, and we will find somewhere else to live. The people will come to us there, for surely
we are nearer the Gods than is a statue."

I had to answer, "The power of these priests is not our power; it
is the Flail of Pharaoh. If we disobey the order soldiers will come
to punish those who follow us. They who love us most will suffer
most. Would you have them prove their loyalty with death?"

Seeing my distress she tried to comfort me, "For six years we
have found peace, surely we have also found a strength that will
sustain us?"

The town sorrowed at our going, and many of our people followed us a long way on the road to the North, beseeching us not
to abandon them.

I will not describe the temple to you, Ra-ab, for when you are
older you can see it, or others like it. In the setting of stones on
each other, or the spacing of columns, there is little to show
whether a building is to the glory of Ra or furthers the dark
dominion of Set.

I had the memories of my own youth to forewarn me of that
temple, and of the priests I should find there; but so familiar had I
become with the old teaching, through the recordings of Oyahbe,
that I was not fully prepared for their tawdry spirit. Their rituals
were rich in pageantry, and the offering vessels of precious metals;
yet the seers were men who wore the ephod only as a sign of
office and possessed no more than ordinary sight, and if those
who went to the healers found better health for their going, it was

6

because the illness had been a product of their own thoughts and not due to a lack of the Life of Ptah.

Among the looking-girls there were a few who had kept a trace of the ancient faculty, and so could tell what was happening at a distant place. But because they were afraid of the priestess in authority over them, they used to invent some incident to satisfy her rather than admit they had seen nothing. Each time they thus betrayed their power, a little more of it was lost to them. When it was decided they had become useless, they were driven from the temple, to wander as outcasts from village to village. Many were the devices they employed to try to gain credence for the vision they claimed.

On every third day petitioners might enter any of the three outer courts. The looking-girls were not strictly segregated though they might not speak to any one who did not belong to the temple. They would find an excuse to pass through one of the most crowded courts, hoping to hear of something to lend color to the stories they were driven to invent. It might be that a man grumbled at his harvest, and said a kinsman in another Nome suffered worse than he; or a woman might speak of her sister who had taken the fever which raged in a distant town. The girl who overheard such things was fortunate, for she could make it seem as though she had seen them in her looking-bowl.

It was among these girls that Oyahbe had to live. Had it not been for her I should have refused to stay there, but as I thought that helping her was more important than anything else, I played my part in rituals whose meaning had been distorted or forgotten. Some of the priests were men of good heart, trying to do the best that was within their narrow compass. Others were less than ordinary men; they were cold, neither lit by the flame of the spirit nor warmed by the embers of humanity. They intoned ritual prayers as a singer might follow the words of a song in an unknown language. They were celibate both in flesh and spirit, having renounced the love of women and being unable to attain the love of Ra. Cut off from the streams of all affection, they resembled men only as dead trees still hold something of the likeness of those in which the sap still rises.

At first Oyahbe tried to teach the other girls, but because

her powers were genuine their awe soon turned to jealousy; and jealousy grew from fear to hatred. Though she followed Anubis and so was not a rival to the looking-girls, they knew she could see through the veil of their deceits. They tried to increase her loneliness, turning away when she spoke to them, and running from the pool when she went there to bathe.

When she realized that her powers were being used to increase the awe in which ignorant people held false priests, awe that drew forth their gold more easily than the overseer's flail, she pretended to have lost her sleep-memory. For a time they gave her only sufficient food to keep her alive, saying that fasting sharpened magical faculties. I think they may have brought other pains to her, though she would not admit this even to me.

It was a year before they turned her from the temple and because I followed her I also became an outcast. By my shaven head all who saw me knew that I had been a priest, and because I had only a loin-cloth instead of a white robe bordered with purple, they knew I had been degraded from my office. Oyahbe had to wear the tunic which marked her as a woman driven from a temple, for she had no other; and in the minds of the people a temple outcast is lower than she who hires her body to a foreigner.

Often people threw filth at us as we passed, and women by a well would upset the full water-jar rather than we should drink from it. So that Oyahbe should not starve I was driven to steal. I would leave her in some field near a village, and then go back to snatch onions or lettuce from the gardens of people who had refused us charity. I became liar as well as thief, for I told her I had met someone who had given them to us out of kindliness. After five days we came to the Oryx, your father's Nome, and there we found that though people stared at us with curiosity they showed no hostility. When we begged for food it was given, though without the customary greeting.

We had been two days under the protection of the Oryx, when your mother had the dream which changed the course of our lives. I remember there was a full moon and we were sleeping on the edge of a bean field. . . .

In her dream she saw a child, a boy of about five years, lying in some reeds near the bank of the river. She saw he was hidden from any one going down the path which led from the track between the village we had just passed and the town we could see in the distance; and though he had cried out no one had heard him. She saw he had a broken leg, so she comforted him and told him to lie quiet until she came to take him home. He said he lived in a white house standing away from the others, and that his father was the overseer of three villages.

Dawn was touching the eastern cliffs when Oyahbe woke. She told me her dream, and said we must hurry to find the child. I followed her down the dusty road, as she searched for the track she knew would turn off towards the river. At last she found it, though it was almost hidden by standing corn. We thrust through high reeds fringing the river until we came to a small clearing, where a sleeping child lay with his leg twisted under him. He whimpered as I picked him up, but when he saw Oyahbe bending over him he patted her cheek and smiled, saying, "You will take me back to my father as you promised? I called and called, but nobody heard me except you."

The child's father, whose name was Benoat, was so overjoyed to see his son that instead of treating us as outcasts he himself served us food and wine. He asked how we had found the boy, and Oyahbe said she had heard him calling and gone to help him. We might have left the house and gone on our way, had not the boy's nurse come to tell us that he cried for Oyahbe. The woman stared at her, and then said deliberately, "He says he did not call out to you. He prayed to Ra, as I had taught him, and then he saw you in a dream and you promised to come to find him. He says he told you exactly where he was lying, even how the path turns off through the cornfield and that he was hidden by the reeds. I should not have believed him unless I knew he often had strange dreams. Is it true, what he says?"

"Yes," said Oyahbe, "it is quite true."

The woman nodded, neither disbelieving nor surprised, and said, "As soon as I saw you I knew he had had a true dream."

Then Benoat said we must remain as his guests, and I knew he would have accepted us without question even if I had not told him our story. He asked by what road we had come from the North, and then inquired earnestly if we had been better treated since we had entered the Nome of the Oryx. When I answered that we had both noticed at once that the people were more kindly than any we had met before, I could see he was well satisfied.

Then he told Oyahbe that a room had been prepared for her and in it she would find fresh clothes and other things she might need. Turning to me he said, "Our priests wear a yellow robe, and I will have one ready for you by sunset."

He paused, "But I go too fast; I am making plans before asking if you both wish to stay here to live within the Oryx. There is work here for both of you, and we shall be grateful for the help that you can give us."

I answered, "We came as outcasts, and you have treated us as honored guests; our work was taken away, and you have given it back. Do you need to ask if we will accept so great a gift?"

"Tomorrow I will take you to the Nomarch. Though he is still young he is wise, as was his father before him. He does not himself wear the Golden Sandals, but he knows how to lead men to their happiness. He knows his Nome as an ordinary man knows his garden, and all who dwell therein are his kinsmen. His father and his grandfather were great scholars. In the Great House there is a room of hundreds of papyri; some of them I have seen, old, so very old, yet though the color of the writing-signs may fade, the truth is brilliant as the day when it was scribed. He says I should not honor him for ruling as he does because he only follows the pattern of the old laws. When I was a little boy his father told me, it was after I had heard for the first time the Reading of the Laws, 'You have heard a lot of long, solemn words today, Benoat. But these are all you need to remember, for their magic is as strong as all the rest together — "Sow the seed you wish to harvest, and remember that he who sows love reaps joy."'"

When on the next day we approached the entrance pylon of the house of Nomarch, I expected that soon we should see a man seated in audience, legendary as an ancient Pharaoh. Crossing a wide forecourt, we followed Benoat up seven shallow steps into a hall, whose high roof was supported by a double row of square pillars. He looked into a room which opened off it; this was empty, but before he turned back I saw that the walls were lined with shelves, and on a long table were the reeds and palette of a scribe.

Beyond the hall there was another doorway, closed by a blue curtain. Benoat held it aside, for us to pass through into a walled garden, which was of formal design with trimmed acacia trees at the four corners of a fishpool. The garden also was deserted, and we crossed it to an opening in the wall on the far side.

Now we were in a vineyard, bordered by narrow water-channels. From the fields beyond, the scent of flowering beans joined with the warmth of ripening grapes. A man wearing only a loincloth, was working among the vines. He was much younger than I, not more than thirty, perhaps less. The sun had burnished his skin to the likeness of carnelian, and there was a sheen of the same warm color in his dark hair. Benoat gave him the greeting between kinsmen, and then told him our names. When Oyahbe returned his greeting there was a tone in her voice I had not heard before: once I had heard a child speak like a priest, and now the priest spoke as a woman. I wondered if the man was the overseer of the vineyard. I knew Oyahbe was lonely, and sometimes, when I felt the weight of my years, I dreaded the death that would leave her without my protection. It would be well if she found a husband who belonged to her heart. . . .

The man said he had done enough work for the day, and led us to a stone bench, shaded by vines which had been trained over wooden bars jutting out from the mud wall. He sat between her and Benoat, and while he listened to our story, which he had asked her to tell, he seemed to forget the two of them were not alone. Again I wondered who he was. . . . If he were only a gardener his wife would have to work hard: and it is not good for the memory if the day is too full of things which clamor to be done. Then I thought of how he said he had done enough work; surely he would only have said that if he had been the overseer?

Then I thought he must have even wider authority, for when Oyahbe had finished telling him all that had befallen us he told Benoat to take me to the wine-store to try the first jar of the vintage pressed five years ago, which had been opened that morning. I glanced back before following Benoat through the square archway which led towards the house; and from the way they were looking at each other I knew I was content to leave the two of them together — even if he was only a gardener. The wine was better than any I had drunk before, and until Benoat had finished praising it I forgot to ask the name of the man with whom I had left Oyahbe. . . .

Nekht-Ra stopped talking. I saw there were tears in his eyes, and I slipped my hand into his. I waited for a long time, but still he didn't speak. So I asked, "What was the name of the man? You never told me; you stopped just when Benoat was going to tell you."

He put his arm round me and drew me close to him. "His name? Do you need to be told your father's name, little Ra-ab?"

I realized I had been very stupid not to have understood before, though I was still puzzled. "But you said the man in the vineyard was much younger than you, more than twenty years younger; and my father is an old man, as old as you are." Then I thought I might have hurt him, so I said, "Not that you're *really* old, dear Nekht-Ra."

But Nekht-Ra didn't seem to be offended, though his voice was sad. "So Khnum-hotep seems old to you? Yes, a child must see him like that. To me he is still a young man, so alive with the happiness of your mother. . . . But of course he must seem old now; a man is as young as his heart, and his was buried in her tomb — to live with her's beyond the sunset."

Poyok the Wild-Cat

WHEN I TOLD KIYAS all that Nekht-Ra told me about our mother, she was interested, but more as though it were a story than something that had happened to a real person. She said, "Poor Oyahbe! She did have an awfully horrid life, and Nekht-Ra didn't tell you about the nice part, the part with Father and you and me in it. It must have been so dull living in a little temple with only an old man to talk to, even if he was a nice old man like Nekht-Ra. The other temple must have been just as bad, not so dull, but more horrid. I hope all the other girls who were nasty to her came out all over spots and died quite soon."

"It couldn't have been a *dull* life, Kiyas, at least not after she had got away from her stupid parents; because she must have remembered doing much more exciting things than we do even on our most adventuring days. She could walk backwards and forwards through the centuries as though the years were the trees of an avenue. That *couldn't* have been dull."

"It all depends," said Kiyas, "on what the centuries were like, and how much trouble it was to remember them. Nekht-Ra told me it was very difficult to remember, worse than learning writing-signs."

"I think remembering is so much the most important thing to do that when I've learned how, I don't suppose I'll bother to do anything else. I shall just wake up enough to write down what I've dreamed and then go to sleep again."

"I think that's a silly idea. You would be so dull for everybody else, and then your dreams would be dull too and no one would want to read them. Your legs and arms would get all flabby if you never ran about or went swimming, and you'd be almost sure to get fat. I'd hate to have a fat brother, even if other people thought he was full of magic — not that they would!"

"Mother wasn't fat, she was the most beautiful person that ever happened, much more beautiful than you'll ever be! And Nekht-Ra says she was a fully initiated priest. He said she followed in the way of Anubis, and that's what I'm going to do . . . when I've remembered how."

"I know all about Anubis," said Kiyas. "He's the god that looks like a jackal, and one that's in Father's little sanctuary which Niyahm told me he had had built for Mother. I always like Anubis the best of the Gods; he reminds me of Anilops."

I knew she was trying to make me annoyed, because Anilops was a kind of wooden lion that was her favorite toy. She was always making up stories about it and expecting me to believe in them. "I know you're only six, Kiyas, but if you tried hard I don't think you could be *quite* so stupid."

"If you tried hard I don't think you could go on trying to be quite so clever. Even Niyahm says you are sometimes as solemn as an old man. She's quite right, and it's the very old mumbly kind, so you'd better stop, before it becomes such a habit that you can't."

"Sometimes I think it is very unfair you were born a girl. If only you hadn't been, or I'd been a girl too, I could give you a really *hard* slap."

13

She giggled. "You try! And I'll yell, and then Niyahm will come, and then she'll slap *you*, and I'll laugh. Come on smack me!" She bent over and pulled up her tunic. "Come on, smack me if you want to!"

How I wanted to slap her! And I was so angry it wouldn't have been a small slap either. Then I saw she had bent so far forward that she was watching me through her legs. And her face was so funny upside down that I laughed too.

She wasn't very often in that sort of mood: I should have realized she was having what Niyahm called "one of her difficult days." When she had them they were difficult for everybody, sometimes even for Father. It usually began with her having a nightmare and waking up screaming. I would go into her room to see what was the matter, but she never seemed to remember much, only something vague about people or things chasing her through mud, which clutched at her feet when she tried to run away. She would wriggle when Niyahm was trying to comb her hair; and make as much fuss as a duck might if it was being plucked before anyone had taken the trouble to kill it. Then she'd say the milk was sour, and when another bowl was brought she would find another excuse for not drinking it. She was very good at excuses; once she almost made Niyahm believe that the reason she wouldn't drink it was because the goat had been so unhappy at its kid being taken away that it had left its unhappiness in the milk . . . she said she could see blobs of unhappiness floating on the top as clearly as if they were drowning flies.

I always tried to argue her into a better temper, but it never did much good, though she was always better with me than with other people. Probably next day she'd wake up friendly again and if any one referred to how unpleasant she'd been the day before she'd say disarmingly, "I know. The moment I woke up yesterday I said to myself, 'This is going to be a difficult day!' And I was right, wasn't I!"

She became nice again as soon as we had both laughed after I hadn't quite slapped her. She said, "The trouble with most people is that they're a little bit cross every day, and no one notices it; the trouble with me is that after I've been solidly nice for days, and days, and *days*, all the crossness that I haven't let myself have for

14

all that time piles up into a great big mountain. And then the most extraordinary thing happens: the mountain turns into a wild-cat and the wild-cat turns into me! How can I help being cross when I'm not me at all but a horrid fierce wild-cat?"

"I think I'll call you by a different name on your wild-cat days: Poyok, the clawed-one."

"That's a *very* good idea."

"Are you going on being Poyok all day?"

"Well, the extraordinary thing is," she said solemnly, "when I woke up this morning I was almost sure I was — though I didn't make up the fly in the milk, there really was one there; I knew perfectly well that Niyahm had only taken the bowl out of the room and then come back again and pretended it was a fresh lot . . . but now I'm almost sure I'm not Poyok anymore." She flung her arms round me. "Dear, dear, Ra-ab, I've been so horrid to you! You did know it was really Poyok and not me, didn't you? I've decided I hate being Poyok. I wish Anilops had snarly teeth instead of smiling all the time, for a lion could eat a wild-cat right up, even if it was a specially fierce wild-cat called Poyok. I've just had a lovely idea! We'll *pretend* Anilops has eaten Poyok, and then I can be nice all the time. Don't you think that's a lovely idea?"

"Yes I do. You didn't really mean what you said about me getting fat if I tried to remember properly?. . . I don't think I would have dull things to remember, for the bits I do wake up with are usually very exciting."

"*Course* I didn't mean it! It wasn't me who said it, it was that horrid Poyok, and she's dead now." She picked up Anilops and patted his stomach. "Look how full up he is. He's busy digesting the whole of a wild-cat that's never going to be a trouble to us anymore."

"Then will you help me to remember?"

"*Course* I'll help you. What shall I do?"

"Ask me first thing every morning what I've dreamed about . . . and pretend you're interested even if you're not. And when I come to see you before I go to bed say, 'Dream well' instead of 'Sleep well' — that'll help remind me to remember. You'll have to do it for weeks, and months — and perhaps even years, because Nekht-Ra said that was how Mother practiced; and it must have been much more difficult for her because no one in her horrid family would help her. She had to do it all by herself without any one understanding how difficult it was, and how dull sometimes."

"You said remembering couldn't be dull."

"Well, Nekht-Ra said the making-yourself-remember part was dull sometimes. It means always waking up suddenly instead of having the nice comfortable time before you open your eyes — not being woken up but waking yourself up. He said it is rather like trying to catch a fish in your hand, and if you're not very quick the dream wriggles back into forgetfulness and you've lost it. Then there's lots of little things that are important to remember even though they are not at all exciting . . . same as it's important to hit the target gazelle even though it's only painted on linen. They're both part of the practicing you have to do."

"What kind of unexciting things?"

"If in a dream you're walking down an avenue you've got to try to notice exactly how many trees there are and how widely apart they are spaced, and the shape and color of the leaves. And if something attacks you, you mustn't just run away, unless you know *why* you're running."

"I shouldn't like that part," said Kiyas. "When I see something that *should* be run away from I just run; and if it's going to catch me I scream to myself to wake up. I *do* think it's brave of you to want to follow Anubis if he's going to lead you into places you can't run away from however frightening they are."

"Father says fear is the only real enemy. I suppose he's right really . . . he says Set and Fear are two names of the God of Evil."

"Could Anubis show you how to kill Fear?"

"I don't know. . . . He hasn't accepted me yet, and perhaps he never will. But I think if I follow him long enough he'll teach me not to run away from things. And perhaps when you're not running away nothing is so very frightening. You will promise to remind me to tell you my dreams every morning?"

"I promise," said Kiyas.

Anilops

KIYAS ALWAYS took Anilops to bed with her. She said that since he had eaten Poyok he had learned to tell stories to make her go to sleep. I asked her to let me borrow it, but she wouldn't. So one night I hid in her room to see if I could hear what it said; but Anilops just went on being a toy and the only thing I heard was Kiyas talking to it.

Because of her believing in Anilops I minded because she wouldn't believe in my dreams. She liked me telling her about them, but she never thought they were things I had really done. She used to say, "Of course I understand about those sorts of things. Anilops and I have adventures too!"

One day when I was trying to make her understand that mine were different, she said, "Last night, just before my bath, two crocodiles came out of the water-jar. They were very fierce, and their teeth were five cubits long! They would have eaten me right up if Anilops hadn't roared at them. Then he bit their tails so that they grew as small as mice with fright, and scuttled away down the drain in the floor."

"Kiyas, you know that's not true. What I told you about really happened, it wasn't just a silly story I'd imagined."

"I don't think it's a silly story, I think it's a lovely story. Did I tell you what Anilops did only the day before yesterday?"

I was tired of hearing about Anilops, but I knew it was no use trying to stop Kiyas when she had made up her mind. "Well," she said, trying to speak very impressively, "this is what happened. I got up very early in the morning, when it was still dark, and I went for a long walk till I came to a big lake in the middle of nothing — at least the nothing must have been there although I didn't notice what kind of something it was. And in the middle of the lake there was a big hippopotamus. I think it was the King Hippopotamus because it had purple wings. It was very polite and asked if I would like to ride on it and go to visit the great fish that lived in a cave far under the water. Anilops didn't like it and growled a little, but I smacked him till he was good. Then we both got on to the hippo's back. He was as large as the Royal Barge and soft as goose-feathers, though rather damp. For a little

17

bit he flew and for a little bit he swam. Then suddenly he dived right under the water, and I might have got washed off if I hadn't been holding on by Anilop's tail and he hadn't been holding the hippo's wing with his teeth. We went a long way, and quite soon the water became as comfortable as air—it was wet, but not at all unusual. Then we saw something as big and silver as a cloud, and from its front end colored moons were rising, one after another, like the beads of a necklace. I didn't know what it was, until suddenly I saw it was a huge enormous fish. It looked very old, and very, very wise—not a bit like the eating kind of fish or even the ones who live in our pool. It was singing to itself in a kind, bubbly voice, 'I am older than the sun, and younger than the moon. I knew the sky before there were any stars, and the mountains when they were small as grains of sand. . . .' I wanted to hear some more of the song, but Anilops growled and the great fish shut its mouth and looked very fierce. It said, 'Very small girl, what are you doing in my cave? Do you know the Answer to the Question? Because if you *don't* know the answer I shall have to eat you for coming here.' I didn't remember the answer—any more than I can remember writing-signs. Then the fish began to lash its tail, and the water became dark, darker than a room when the lamp is pinched out and the shutters are closed. Now I found myself swimming and swimming through the dark, and very, very frightened. Then I felt something pulling me out on to the bank by the back of my tunic. And I saw Anilops shaking the water from his coat and looking cross—he hates getting wet. I couldn't see the hippopotamus anywhere, not even a purple feather from its wing. So Anilops and I went home; and he turned to wood again and I went to sleep. . . .

"So you see I *do* understand your stories, Ra-ab, because the same sort of thing happens to me!"

"You *don't* understand—I thought you would, but you don't. My dreams aren't just things I made up. I don't behave like a silly child when I go to sleep. I do very important grown-up kind of things, not ordinary six-year-old everyday adventures."

"My adventures *aren't* ordinary. You're jealous because you never even thought of dreaming about a hippopotamus with wings!"

18

I tried to think which of all the things I remembered doing would impress her most. "Well, I can fly when I'm asleep. I don't need a silly hippopotamus to ride on. I can fly like a bird without any wings!"

"A bird without any wings couldn't fly!"

"Don't be silly. I mean I can fly without wings like a bird with wings. You're only trying to be tiresome."

"Really, Ra-ab, I'm not! You try to take me into your dreams, and I'll try to take you into mine, and then we'll know whose are the most real. Try, Ra-ab, *promise* you'll try—the very next moment we're both asleep."

It would be nice to have Kiyas in my dreams. It wouldn't be so lonely if I had her to talk to about them. Even Nekht-Ra didn't really understand, though he used long words to explain what I did when I was free of my body. But it wasn't the same as having somebody who knew exactly what it felt like.

"I'll try to take you with me, but you'll have to try too."

"I'll knock on the wall as soon as I'm in bed."

"I'll knock on the wall too."

"Then you must say, 'I'll go with Ra-ab into his dream. I *will* go with Ra-ab into his dream.' Say it over and over again—very loud inside your head."

When I heard her knock on the wall I began, "Let me take Kiyas with me and remember. Let me take Kiyas with me and remember. . . ."

She was standing beside me and I thought she had come into the room to ask me something. I got out of bed to take her back, and was just going to tell her she mustn't interrupt, when I saw that my body was lying on the bed, asleep. I took Kiyas by the hand and led her back to her room and pointed to her own body lying there, with the wooden lion beside it on the pillow.

She nodded. "That's only the daytime Anilops—I can't think where he's gone to; it's naughty of him to run away.

Why, there he is!"

Beside her there was a strange animal; something like a lion but stiff in its joints. Kiyas patted him and he purred, a small, comfortable sound, more like a cat than a lion.

"How did Anilops come alive?" I asked her.

"It was soon after I had him. Someone made him to look after me; I look after him when I'm awake and he looks after me when I'm asleep. Sometimes I get tangled up in a story I have told myself before I go to sleep, and until I had Anilops I used to get very frightened. After Niyahm told me that if I went down to the river alone I should be eaten by a crocodile, I wanted to find out if what she said was true or if she was only trying to frighten me. So I used to imagine myself going down by the little path through the reeds and finding nice shallow water to paddle in. But sometimes the reeds rustled, and a crocodile waddled slowly out of them. I was so frightened that I couldn't even run away. When its mouth was opening to bite me in half I could run, but it was always just behind me; and the path had turned to thick mud which caught at my feet as though I were a fly in honey. It was so frightening, being asleep, that I used to try holding my eye-lids open." She sighed contentedly. "Then Anilops happened, and now I'm never frightened, for if a dream gets too exciting he comes to rescue me and I know I'm safe."

In the morning I went to Kiyas's room to find her already awake. I asked her, "Did you remember? Did you remember being with me, and telling me about Anilops?"

She yawned. "Of course I can remember telling you about Anilops, but that wasn't in a dream; it was yesterday."

"No, Kiyas. I don't mean your telling me about him down here, I mean when we were both asleep. Can't you even remember seeing yourself lying in bed? Or *anything*?"

She shook her head. "No, Ra-ab. I'm very sorry, but I don't remember. I didn't even have an Anilops adventure last night. I did try most awfully hard, just as you told me; and then it was morning, and you came in, and that was everything that happened."

I was so disappointed I wanted to shake her; but she looked so small and worried I couldn't go on being cross with her for long.

"It's all right, Kiyas," I said, "let's go and bathe; and if the moment you're dry you forget we've been swimming—I don't mind."

Maker of Amulets

KIYAS AND I often went to stay with Roidahn, whose estate on the northern boundary of the Nome was called Hotep-Ra. He was our kinsman, and after Father the most important noble of the Oryx. His wife had died before Kiyas was born, and he had a son called Hanuk, who was four years older than me, and a daughter who thought herself too grown up to join in our games. In spite of having a dead wife, Roidahn was not solemn like my father. He was so full of vitality that everyone felt twice as alive when they were in his company; yet he was very wise and could always answer questions even when they were the kind that most people didn't understand.

Kiyas always took Anilops with her when she went away from home, but one day when we went to Hotep-Ra Niyahm forgot to pack him, and when Kiyas found he wasn't there she made a tremendous fuss and refused to go to bed. I was cross with her because I was afraid that if Hanuk saw her behaving like that he might think we were both too young for him to play with. I was trying to make her be quiet when Hanuk came into the room.

Kiyas was saying despairingly, "I *won't* go to bed without Anilops! Something horrid might happen to me, and he would be at home and not know anything about it."

To my surprise, instead of being scornful, Hanuk sat down on the bed and got her to tell him all about Anilops. When she had finished he said:

"I used to have an Anilops too. Only mine was alive in the daytime as well. She was a puppy when she first started being magical and coming with me into my dreams; now she's old, and when she barks in her sleep I think it's usually because she is chasing water-rats or having a different sort of adventure that I don't remember being in too."

"Oh, I'm so glad you understand," said Kiyas. "Ra-ab sometimes thinks I'm silly about Anilops."

"I will explain to Father about him and he will send someone to bring him here tomorrow."

Kiyas began to look more cheerful. "But what shall I do tonight?"

"I'll lend you *my* Anilops. She can sleep on your bed if you like. She snores rather, but it's quite a comforting sort of noise when you've got used to it."

He went and fetched the dog, which was a black hound bitch, and Kiyas curled up quite happily as soon as it settled itself at her feet.

Hanuk was my favorite person after Kiyas, and he and Roidahn were much more like brothers than father and son. He didn't have to divide everything into those that grown-ups must never be told, and those which they can be allowed to know about. He never seemed to worry about what an idea would sound like when it got into words, and just said whatever occurred to him. So when we met Roidahn, soon after leaving Kiyas, Hanuk told him all about Anilops. Roidahn, didn't seem to think it was silly either, and said that of course he would send a messenger to fetch the lion first thing in the morning.

The three of us went and sat on the wall of the vineyard; swinging our legs and talking and eating grapes.

"It is awfully kind to take so much trouble about Anilops," I said to Roidahn.

"How could I possibly have done anything else?" he answered in a surprised voice. "Anilops is a very important person to Kiyas."

I suddenly thought he might be thinking that Anilops was a real lion that was pining for Kiyas, so I said diffidently:

"Anilops is only a *wooden* lion, you know. Kiyas only *thinks* he is real."

"Everything is real if you think it is; and every one's reality is what they make it."

"But he's only wooden and she thinks he's alive. Her thinking can't make any difference to his woodenness," I objected.

Hanuk said firmly, "She doesn't think he's alive when he's only wood; she told me herself that it is only when she is asleep that he becomes the real Anilops."

"I wonder what made the dream Anilops come alive," I said.

"I did," replied Roidahn unexpectedly. "You have probably forgotten that the last time she had a really bad nightmare was when she was here nearly two years ago. I knew how horrid it was for her because the same kind of thing used to happen to me when I was a child; and it happened to Hanuk too."

"Why did it?"

"A child is only young away from Earth for a part of each night . . . that is if you've gone quite a long way on the far journey. The rest of the time you can live in your real self, which isn't affected by the temporary inconvenience of being born, and dying, and being born again. In your real self you can do lots of important things: you remember them sometimes, don't you Raab?" I nodded, and he went on, "Our real selves have enemies as well as friends, and those enemies often try to attack us while we are using our child sleep-body, for we are more vulnerable then, having for the moment forgotten how to use our full powers. That's why in a nightmare you are usually trying desperately to escape; you either want to get back into your real self where you can cope with the attacker, or else into your down-here body where it can't reach you."

He pointed across the vineyard to where a man was picking some of the ripest grapes, "Suppose you were here alone, and that man suddenly ran at you with a knife to try to stab you. And suppose you knew that though I was out of sight I was near enough to hear if you shouted for me. What would you do?"

"I'd yell for you to come and help me."

"Exactly: and that's what you should do if you are attacked in sleep by something too strong for you to tackle alone . . . call to a friend to come and help you. I made Anilops as a sort of permanent answer to such a call. Anilops has the instincts of a highly developed dog, who would protect the one he loves from every kind of attack. He is quite strong enough to deal with most things which might try to harm Kiyas, but if something comes along that is too strong for him to tackle he will let me know about it . . . just like a dog who barks for his master when he scents a leopard."

"Are nightmares always because an enemy is attacking you?"

"No. In sleep, even more than when you are awake, your thoughts create the surroundings in which you live. Those surroundings are made of what you hope for and what you fear; that's one of the reasons why it's so important not to be afraid of things. Many of children's fears are born of stories told by ignorant grown-ups; these stories are intended to frighten them away from dangers, but often instead of protecting them they lead to troubles much more serious. For instance, Kiyas was often told by Niyahm not to climb the high wall beyond your garden. She disobeyed; so Niyahm told her that if she did it again she would be bound to fall off and then would be a cripple and would have to spend the rest of her life in bed. Kiyas didn't climb on the wall again while she was awake; but she wanted to even more because it was forbidden, so she *did* climb on it when she was asleep. When she was walking along it she suddenly remembered what Niyahm had said; she was frightened of falling, so she did fall. She had been told that if she fell she would be a cripple, so she was a cripple. I found her lying at the bottom of the wall, with her legs twisted under her: she thought she couldn't walk, so she couldn't. I went to her and showed her how that thought could be broken; and she was well again at once. It was after this I made her an amulet in my name, so that when she was in trouble, I would be called to help her."

"What would have happened if you hadn't found her?"

"Another of her friends would have gone to her."

"But suppose they hadn't?"

"Well, either the thought would have lost its power as soon as she woke up, and she would have suffered nothing worse than a most unpleasant nightmare; or else—though this would only happen to a person who had deliberately cut himself off from every one with whom he had a link of true affection—Kiyas would have been so sure that she couldn't move her legs that her earth-body would have been just as paralyzed as her sleep-body."

"Why did you make her protector in the shape of Anilops?"

"The shape of that kind of amulet isn't important, nor does it much matter whether it has a physical counterpart or not. But with children it is usually better to choose a shape they associate with going to sleep. Hanuk had a dog which always slept in his room, so I made his protection amulet to look as much as possible like the dog. Kiyas loved Anilops, so I made her amulet in the shape of a wooden lion; I deliberately made him rather stiff in the joints so that she wouldn't confuse him with any real lions she might meet in her dreams."

"I thought amulets were things like beads, or little ornaments

24

made like some of the priests' symbols; an Eye of Horus or an Ankh or a Tet."

"They often are; but the value of an amulet is not in its shape but in the power which is stored in it. You can store power almost as you store wine; sealed in an amulet until you need it."

I said, "Niyahm's sister, the one with a mole on her cheek, can put her hand on your forehead if you've got a headache and the pain goes away almost at once. Is her hand a kind of amulet?"

"We are all in some degree a channel for the Life of Ptah, for if that channel were cut off we should die; but some of us have been trained how to cause more life to flow through us than we need for the use of our own body. Niyahm's sister must have had some of this training, though not as much as a fully initiated healer-priest."

"If healer-priests stored up their power in lots and lots of amulets would that be enough to last forever?"

"No, for while the source of life open to a true priest is inexhaustible, an amulet can hold only so much power as was stored up in it. The making of real amulets is a difficult magic and in these days rare."

"Can you have killing amulets as well as healing ones?" asked Hanuk.

"Of course. No one has ever made a papyrus with only one side, and no force has been created which has no opposite. A papyrus can be used to scribe a blessing or a curse; so can power be used to heal or to destroy. Neither the papyrus nor the power is in itself good or evil; it is the means for which they are used which decides whether they are dedicated to Ra or to Set."

Hanuk suddenly remembered he had promised to help a friend of his make a fish-trap, so he went off towards the river and left me alone with Roidahn.

"I wish I'd thought of talking to you about these kind of things before," I said. "Ever since Nekht-Ra told me about Mother, I've wanted to be like her and follow Anubis. She went into a temple, but I don't think Father would let me be a priest, do you? I'm not really at all sure I want to be a priest, and anyway I've soon got to go to the House of the Captains and learn to be a soldier. Do you think it's wrong of me not wanting to be a priest?"

"You can train your memory sufficiently not to be cut off from the source of your own wisdom, and learn to be a soldier at the same time. But you couldn't lead the Oryx into battle if you'd lived in a temple all your life. Your father has no other son, and when he joins your mother you will be the Nomarch. One day you will know how important that is going to be; for the Oryx is different to the rest of Egypt, because we are building for the future on the wisdom of the past."

The Asiatics

BY THE TIME Kiyas was nine she could beguile people even when they tried to be cross with her. She had always been able to be much naughtier than me before Niyahm got angry, and even then there had been a kind of pride in Niyahm's anger, like Hanuk felt when the leopard cub he was trying to tame bit his aunt, the one whom he'd never liked, in the ankle. I wanted to have a leopard cub too, and I think Father would have let me if Niyahm hadn't told him it might hurt Kiyas. When he said I couldn't have the cub and I knew the reason, I was quite cross with Kiyas for two days—which was unfair because it wasn't her fault, and she had wanted it more than I had, and had even made Hanuk promise to catch one for me. In fact the cub would really have been her's, but she said it must be called mine as there was a better chance of my being allowed to keep it.

"That's one of the good things about being a boy," she said. "People think you are cleverer about looking after yourself, and they let you do the things that grown-ups call dangerous without making so much fuss."

"Well, boys *are* cleverer," I said firmly. I was always trying to be firm with Kiyas, and make her realize that she was nearly two years younger than me, but I never had much success.

"Nonsense! It's much more difficult for me to get my own way than it is for you. You're allowed to do more, but I have to do things without being allowed."

"What about the day we both got lost?"

"If I hadn't thought of making up that useful story we might have both been scolded, even by Father, and perhaps made to go to bed early for three or four days."

I didn't like being reminded about that day, and ever since had felt rather uncomfortable when I thought about it.

Kiyas and I had decided to play at being an army sent against the Asiatics. I lent her one of my bows—she could use it quite well because I'd taught her privately. We took food and my hunting-knife, and two of the hunting-dogs in a double leash. We tied parcels on their backs so they could be the pack animals, but they didn't like it much so we soon let them go home.

Everybody except us were Asiatics, which made it a very exciting game, and we had to crawl on our hands and knees a lot of the time to keep from being seen. The big water-channel beyond the vineyard was the Narrow Sea, and the marsh was the Great Lake.

On the way we saw one of the gardeners, the only one we didn't like, squatting down to weed the lettuces. He was a fat man, and his behind looked very large and round. Just as I noticed it Kiyas nudged me and whispered, "You needn't think he's a gardener. He's really the King of the Asiatics come to spy on us. Asiatics are covered with scales under their clothes, and the only way to kill things that are covered with scales is to find their soft place. With crocodiles it's their tummies and with Asiatics it's their bottoms. Go on, Ra-ab, see if you can shoot him! He'd never find us if we hide in the beanfield, and we could stalk him from there."

"No, Kiyas, we mustn't." I tried to pull her away, but she stood firm, notching an arrow carefully to her bowstring.

"Poor Ra-ab's frightened!" she said as if to an imaginary companion. "He's frightened because when he set out to fight the Asiatics he found one right in his own garden. He's too frightened to kill it. But *I'm* not frightened, I only suggested he should have the first shot because he's still a little better at arrows than I am. If he's too frightened to shoot Asiatics it won't be long before he's too frightened to shoot anything. I expect that if he had to kill even a very small hippo he'd run all the way home to Niyahm and say the hippo was chasing him."

The very last time that Kiyas had dared me I'd promised myself not to be taken in again. But almost before I knew what was happening I saw the Asiatic—I mean the gardener—jump up with a roar. And then I realized it was *my* arrow that had hit him.

Kiyas plucked at my kilt and whispered urgently, "Don't stand there, Ra-ab. You've killed one of the enemy, now we must go and find some more of them."

We crept away between two rows of beans, and after we'd gone what Kiyas thought was a safe distance, I parted the stalks and looked back. The gardener was going on with his work. We listened, and could hear him muttering to himself. He had stuck the arrow through his belt, so I knew he had recognized it as one of ours—they had blunt tips—and he would probably betray us to Niyahm, and she'd tell Father.

We were out of the beans now, on the edge of a cornfield. We crouched down in an irrigation ditch which ran between the two fields, and as there was no one in sight we no longer had to whisper.

"What are you looking gloomy about?" asked Kiyas. "I'm wondering if Niyahm is bound to tell Father about us shooting the gardener, or if you'll be able to persuade her not to. I don't suppose you'll really have a chance to try, because she'll have told him before we get home. Us shooting gardeners is one of the sort of things he really minds about."

"Why will you always spoil things by wondering what's going to happen afterwards? It's like not eating too much honey in case you get a pain."

"Well if you *did* think of the pain you wouldn't eat too much honey and then you wouldn't have one." This was a reference to what had happened to Kiyas a few days before: she never got cross at being reminded of things like that.

"What you don't understand, Ra-ab, is that I liked eating the honey, that's why I ate such a lot of it; because I *liked* it. And I'll always remember that, though I forgot the pain as soon as I'd finished having it. If I'd been like you I wouldn't have eaten too much, and I wouldn't have had the pain, but then I wouldn't have had anything nice to remember. I think the most important thing to do with a day is to fill it as full as possible with nice things to remember."

I sighed. "I know you do, Kiyas. It's a pity though that your kind of nice things do seem to lead us into troubles, almost always."

"You'll be glad of me one day, Ra-ab; when you're very old and your legs have gone wobbly and you can't go looking for any more adventures. You'll be able to sit in the sun—or in the shade if it's too hot—and smile to yourself about all the interesting things you did when you were young. Even when you're very old, so old that your children are beginning to worry in case the wall-paintings of your tomb get too faded before they can shut you up in it, I'll only have to say to you—of course I'll be very old too by then—'Do you remember how your arrow hit the gardener's bottom when he was being an Asiatic among the lettuces?' and you'll smile, quite probably you'll laugh, and you'll be thinking of bean-fields instead of bitumen. It is bitumen they do mummies with isn't it?"

"Kiyas, you know people aren't made into mummies in the Oryx."

"Yes, but they do everywhere else in Egypt, and before I die I'm going to ask people to do me too. Then in hundreds and hundreds of years somebody may unwrap me to see what the people of our time looked like. I shall look as thin, and much more beautiful, even than I do now. And the man who unwraps me will be young—I think he can have hair the same color as Father's—and he will have a very rich fat wife, who he has always hated living with without realizing it. Then when he sees me looking so young and beautiful he'll know how horrid his wife is, and he'll wrap me up again, very carefully so I shan't get spoiled, and go away and live all by himself and think about me. And he'll be happy when he's thinking—like I am." She sighed contentedly. "It will be very splendid to have someone fall in love with you after you've been dead a thousand years."

Thinking of her being turned into a mummy made me feel cold down my back. I thought she had done it on purpose, so I said dampingly, "A moment ago you were laughing at the gardener's bottom when we were both about eighty years old. You'll have to make up your mind which of those two stories you like best, because if you're going to grow very, very old so that we can enjoy remembering what fun we had as children, if anyone ever does unwrap your mummy—even if he is a handsome young man and not a dull old scribe—he'd take one look at you and go home and tell his wife how beautiful *she* is, even if he had noticed that very morning that she was getting fat!"

Kiyas was not at all disconcerted. "Poor Ra-ab! The trouble with you is that you haven't learned yet how to imagine four things at once, all opposite, and believe in them at the same time. It must be so dull for you—worse than if we had to eat the same things every day."

Then, before I could answer, she pulled me down into the bottom of the ditch. It was much muddier than it looked.

"There's a whole army of Asiatics coming this way, very fierce ones with curly beards! You can look now, but take care they don't see you."

A group of women carrying baskets and sickles were coming along the path leading to the cornfield. "Look!" she whispered excitedly, "they're coming to cut off the heads of the Egyptians! We must go and collect more of our army. We'll need about a hundred; then we shall only be outnumbered ten to one—that's about fair between Egyptians and Asiatics, but enough on our side to make sure of us winning."

We crawled the whole length of the irrigation ditch, and by the time we reached the end of it Kiyas was mostly covered with thick, black mud; it had even matted her hair. When I told her what she looked like she said she couldn't look any muddier than I did because there wasn't enough mud in the Nome. She agreed that mud was one of the things that Niyahm really did mind about and that we'd better go and wash it off somewhere.

We couldn't go to our bathing pool because someone would be sure to notice us and tell Niyahm. Before now we'd washed in one of the shallow pits, made of baked brick, where the cattle drank, but there was no way of getting to one without being seen, and Kiyas wouldn't stop believing in Asiatics. So we decided to go down to the river. It was a long way, and for us to go there alone was very forbidden.

"Even if anyone does see us they won't recognize us," said Kiyas comfortingly. "I don't think even Niyahm could unless she was quite close."

I decided that as Niyahm was bound to be very cross if she saw us like this, it was worth risking an extra crossness that would come from us being caught beyond the places where we were allowed to go alone. The reeds were very high, it was just before they were due to be cut, and there wasn't a proper path through them, only a narrow track where gazelles and small animals went down to drink. I thought I saw leopard spoor, but was not sure so I didn't tell Kiyas.

We came out of the reeds where the river made a kind of little bay, and the bank shelved steeply enough for us to swim without having to go far out. I kept a good watch for crocodiles but didn't see any, and there were none of their tracks in the mud. We got ourselves fairly clean, though our clothes still looked dirty even after we had washed them and dried them in the sun. The pleats had come out of the kilts and they looked rather queer.

We didn't realize how late it was until the sun was very low. Then we thought we should get home quicker if, instead of taking the path we had come by, we went back along the river and found another way through the reeds. But the reeds went on much further than I thought they did, and we couldn't find another track through them. I began to wonder if the spoor really had been a leopard's, and almost at the same moment Kiyas said, in a firm, brisk voice, like Niyahm uses when she says it is time for bed, "I won't think of crocodiles. I *won't* think of crocodiles. I *can't* think of crocodiles even if I try to!"

I tried to reassure her, "There aren't any crocodiles here: where they live is a long way off."

"I know it is," said Kiyas, but her voice didn't sound quite so firm. "Of *course* I know it is. If there were crocodiles here I should *have* to think about them. . . . Still, I do wish this was a dream with Anilops in it."

"If it was a dream you'd forget about it in the morning; and this will be awfully exciting to remember when we've got home."

Now it was quite dark. We could see a little way right down by the river, but it was no use trying to push our way through the reeds. Kiyas's hand in mine was cold, and I felt her shiver. She knew I had, and said, "It wasn't a frightened kind of shiver, only the cold kind."

I had begun to think how nice it would be to hear Niyahm scolding us, when Kiyas said, "I wonder if they have started to look for us yet. I suppose they wouldn't think of looking down here . . . or do you think they will, just because it's so specially not allowed? I rather hope the gardener has taken the arrow to Father, then perhaps he'll know this is one of our days for doing specially not allowed things; and then he might look here first."

The stars were very bright though the moon was too young to be much help. The bank shelved unexpectedly; I stumbled and hit my shin on a stone. It didn't feel like a deep cut, but I could feel the blood trickling down though it was too dark to see it. Suddenly we saw a light a little way ahead of us, like a torch reflected in the water. We ran forward shouting. It was a man holding a torch, with a fish-spear in his other hand. He said he had been after eels in the shallows. We both knew him, though not very well, but when we told him who we were he didn't believe us until he had whirled the torch round his head to make a better light in which to see us.

He walked ahead of us to show the way. I whispered to Kiyas, "It's rather a shaming end to an adventure, having to be taken home."

"No, it isn't," she answered comfortably, "not if you've captured one of the enemy and made him guide you by the secret way into their stronghold; specially if you've killed as many Asiatics as we have. Poor things, I'm quite sorry for them: we've left so few of them alive!"

Niyahm was so worried about us that she was in tears when we got back—at least she was sniffing as though she had been crying. The fisherman had left us outside the entrance to the courtyard— I had asked him to come in, but he said that he wanted to get back to his eels, so Niyahm thought we had found our own way home. She was so relieved to see us that she forgot to ask exactly where we'd been. Kiyas put on her special look which she kept for occasions like this—it made her seem very small and pathetic, while she told Niyahm we had both got so tired playing that we had fallen asleep . . . "and when we woke up it was all dark. And then poor Ra-ab fell and cut his leg and he has been so brave about it." I made a face at her behind Niyahm's back, but she went on, "And Ra-ab was so good at looking after me. He held my hand all the way home and didn't let me get frightened at all. Dear Niyahm, it's so nice to be home again!" She put her arms round Niyahm's neck and hugged her; which flattered her so much that she forgot to scold us, and only made small disapproving noises at the state of our clothes. Kiyas explained the mud by saying we had fallen into an irrigation ditch in the dark.

On our way to bed I said to Kiyas, "Niyahm can't have known about the arrow, or even you wouldn't have been able to get round her so easily." Kiyas agreed, and admitted that perhaps the gardener wasn't an Asiatic after all.

When I went in to say good night to her, she said sleepily, "It *has* been a lovely day, hasn't it, Ra-ab? And wasn't I right in not worrying about unpleasantnesses which never even happened?"

"Yes, I suppose you were," I said rather grudgingly, "but you mightn't have been. It was lucky for us that Father has gone to Roidahn's house, for you couldn't have taken him in like you did Niyahm. If he'd asked where we'd been we would have *had* to tell him."

"I wish Father *had* been here. I'd got such a lovely story to tell him. . . . I made it up all the way home."

"What story?"

"Oh, a story to explain why we'd been down by the river. I knew we'd have to tell him where we'd been. It was about how we'd seen a poor little hare in the corn that had hurt one of its paws. It was its right front paw. We wanted to bring it home and make it well again. But it made for the river, and of course we had to follow it . . . we couldn't leave the poor little thing to be eaten by something it couldn't run away from. But it went on and on, and several times we almost caught it . . . and then it got suddenly dark and of course we were rather lost. Nobody could be cross with us just for trying to help a poor little hurt hare."

"Kiyas, you mustn't tell lies like that, especially to Father."

"Well, I told him about Anilops and he thought I had made it up; so why shouldn't I make up a hare that he would believe in, just to make it fair? Anyway I think it would be a very kind thing to do. He'd be happier, thinking what kind children he'd got, and we'd be happier thinking what a nice believing Father we'd got. And if I give him practice in believing things I tell him, he'll soon be able to believe in real things like Anilops."

She yawned. "And I like making people happy," said Kiyas.

PART II

The Voice of Anubis

FATHER USUALLY TOOK Kiyas and me with him when he traveled within the Oryx, so I had been several times to the soldiers' village before I went to live there soon after my thirteenth birthday. It was the tradition for either the Nomarch or his son to be Captain of the Nome, so I was not surprised when Father told me the time had come to begin my warrior training.

Egypt had three armies under the direct command of Pharaoh; the Royal Bodyguard, most of whom were drawn from the three Royal Nomes which divided the North from the South, and the two great garrisons. Of these the one in the North protected Egypt from the Asiatics, and the other, below the second cataract, was held in readiness to put down rebellions either in the Land of Gold or Southern Nubia. In addition, each Nome had its own soldiers, maintained by the Nomarch and the principal nobles. Their chief duties were to keep order within their own boundaries, but they must go to the aid of Pharaoh if he should call on them to repel invasion.

Since my grandfather's time, the Oryx could always muster a thousand fully trained men between the ages of sixteen and thirty: all of whom knew how to use javelin, mace and bow, and must have special skill in one of the three. Their training lasted for two years, after which time they went back to their own villages save for two months every year; only four hundred remained permanently at the soldier's village.

These four hundred saw that the laws of the Nome were upheld, and in addition protected the community from dangers such as floods and marauding animals. They also supervised the building of roads and irrigation channels and collected the tribute of the tenth part. Their families lived with them, and, if they wished, they could have land of their own to cultivate, though their food and clothing, both for themselves and their dependents, was provided by the Nomarch. The men were divided into Hundreds; to each of these there was a Leader of a Hundred, who was usually a noble by birth, and to three leaders of a Hundred

34

there was a captain, the highest rank except the Captain of the Nome.

Hanuk had been made a captain the year before I began my training, and had then returned to Hotep-Ra, leaving Sebek, a nephew of Roidahn's in command. I wished that I had been going to train under Hanuk, for ever since he had been so sympathetic about Anilops I had been able to talk to him about things at which I knew Sebek might laugh. I had known Sebek all my life, but our friendship was of a different quality. He had always been tall for his age and very strong, and so he seemed more than five years older than me. In spite of this he had never been too grand to play with Kiyas, nor did he seem to mind when she was tiresome. When I told her that I was to be trained by him, she said:

"If he's ever horrid to you, tell him I'll bully him if he does it again, and then he'll stop."

"Kiyas, do try to understand that I've got to learn how to be a soldier. A soldier can't tell his captain to stop being horrid; he's got to do what he's told without arguing."

"You must never do that," said Kiyas emphatically. "It sometimes happens that you are told to do something you think is a good idea; then of course you are obedient. But quite often one has to argue, or disobey, and sometimes both."

"It would be a silly kind of army if all the soldiers argued among themselves instead of doing what they are told.

Soldiers quite often *are* silly. I expect it's from having to be obedient so often. Sebek isn't nearly so much fun as he used to be— though I'm fond of him in spite of his being so pompous." She sighed. "Oh, Ra-ab, I never thought I should want to be a boy, but I do now, for then I could come with you! It's going to be so very lonely without you. Father says I can sit with him in audience and things like that, but half the time he forgets I'm here. Will you be able to come home often?"

"I don't know. It depends on Sebek; but from what Father says I'm afraid I shall be away nearly all the time. There are such a lot of things I've got to learn . . . javelin throwing, and wrestling, and swinging a mace—which isn't nearly so easy as it looks. And I shall have to learn how to lead men across unfamiliar country on a cloudy night; and lots of really dull things, like how many men are needed to carry the supplies required for a battle after a five days journey, and how much a pack donkey can carry, and how much food and water are needed for each Hundred when they can't live on the country. Then there is the men's food and clothes and all the rest of their equipment to learn about; and I shall have to give judgment if they quarrel among themselves or their wives get jealous of each other."

"I should like that part," said Kiyas. "I should be bad at remembering how many arrows to take, or how many mace-heads a donkey can carry, but I'm good at sorting out people's quarrels. I suppose there's *no* chance of Father letting me come with you?"

"I'm sure there isn't," I said gloomily. "You'll be here being lonely, and I'll be there being more lonely still."

"We'd learn much quicker if we were together, we always do. We could remind each other of the things we'd forgotten. It's so *silly* of Father to make me stay here without you. I would look nice as a soldier; I tried your new things on this morning, so I know."

Three days later I was wearing the clothes which Kiyas had tried on. They were the same as those of a Leader of a Hundred, though without the gold armlet; the kilt was striped in white and yellow, like the sphinx head-dress of stiff linen. We went naked to the waist except in cold weather, and then we wore cloaks of white wool clasped at the neck by a gold oryx. I was glad that I had inherited Father's easy sighting of an arrow, for because of it the others didn't seem to notice that a mace was still too heavy for me to swing freely or that I couldn't throw a javelin as far as they did.

I soon found it much more difficult to train myself to remember, for we were awakened very early and the fragile bridge by which sleep-memory can join the record of the waking day was broken before more than a fragment had passed over it. I tried to wake before the others, but was usually so tired that even if I succeeded it was to drowse in the peace of relaxed muscles, reluctant of unnecessary effort.

I tried to make myself believe that it was enough for a man to be skilled with arrows. Dreams were for priests, or sometimes perhaps for women—if it were not so why did I fear the laughter of the others if they knew of my secret ambition?

I pictured myself in many roles. My favorite was one in which I led a victorious army against Pharaoh's enemies. When I returned from the final battle of which peace was born, I spoke of Anubis to the multitude who acclaimed my leadership: and because I had triumphed in their cause they believed in mine. I would teach them to see the jackal tracks clear on the path they must follow, and looking back to the land of the old peace they would make their future in its image: knowing that only a fool cries pity on the past while the wise man learns of it. I would say to them, "Man has not changed, though cities fall to sand and Pharaohs are forgotten. The past man is yourself, and your far sons unborn till the last obelisk is lost. So let Anubis teach you of the past, that you may know yourself and judge what course to set on future seas—to lands beyond your dreams."

But even imagination seemed to desert me through the monotony of long, hot days. My shoulders and the muscles of my back ached with long effort, while the voice of the Master of Javelins endlessly repeated the same small pattern of words which to him were the magic from which came the rhythm of body and spear. "Swing your body further round. Poise with the hand well back, level with the ear, weight on the right foot, now swing back. Now forward in a single movement, body and shoulder and arm must be one with the shaft. . . ." Even my thoughts are clumsy. How many javelins have I thrown? Fifty? A hundred? And there are always more! It looks so easy when Sebek does it, as though the javelin were as light as a child's throwing-stick. . . . The wood of this shaft is rough, and a splinter has broken the blister on my thumb. Each javelin feels twice as heavy as the last, even the lines which space the throwing-ground flicker in the heat. If I were at home I could be asleep, or swimming with Kiyas. I haven't any home; there's no water to swim in, nor any coolness anywhere. There's only the pain in my hand and sweat trickling down my back; and the voice of the Master of Javelins, who will not say— will surely *never* say, "The practice is finished."

Then, just when the days seemed most crowded with dull necessities; eating to stave off hunger, sleeping only because one was too tired to do anything else, I had a dream unlike any I had had before:

I was walking over long, gray fields. Mist was rising from the sodden ground, closing in on me like the wings of sorrow. Then, ahead of me though hidden by the mist, I heard a bird calling, and though it was born of the mist there was no melancholy in its cry, which seemed to promise that it would guide me to the clear air wherein it flew. I hurried forward over the dark, wet earth, through the stubble of corn long harvested. Again I heard the bird call, and beyond it the sound of flowing water.

I came to the brink of a cliff; down which led a narrow path cut in the rock. I followed the path; still the mist clung to me, and the narrow steps were slimy with moisture. The steps grew narrower; now they were only footholds. The mist swirled aside, and showed me a river so far below me that if I slipped I must hurtle to my death.

I gained the ledge where I could stand firmly; and saw that beyond it the track widened, until again there were steps. The mist closed in again, and with it came the crying of the bird. Now there were words in its cry, "A man may walk down, but only a winged one can fly. There are steps in the rock, but there are wings in the mist—my wings. Trust to the mist. Are you still so heavy that you need rock to hold you? Fly to the boat that knows the River. There is no boat to be found by the way of the steps."

I thought, If I follow the steps I shall be safe. Only a bird can fly. Again the voice, "The mist shall be your wings. Believe in my wings, and I will not betray you."

I stood poised on the narrow ledge: then stretched out my hands and stepped forward. . . . The mist was buoyant as water; softly it carried me down, quiet as a bird that glides upon the air.

Now I was standing on a rocky beach. A boat waited there, a narrow boat without a sail. The figurehead was familiar. Where had I seen it before? It was the Anubis of my mother's sanctuary.

The steering oar was in the likeness of a feather. It spoke to me, "Give me my name and I will steer you."

And I answered, "Your name is the voice of the bird of whose wing you are a feather."

"Name the prow, and we will take you to the far side."

"It is He whom I follow, the Timeless One."

Then did the boat tell me that I might enter it. I saw the mist close in upon the cliff by which I had come. Ahead the mist was no longer gray; it was white, as though beyond it the moon had risen. When the boat reached the far side of the River I saw the light came from neither sun nor moon, but lived in everything I saw there, for it was the Land without Shadows. Even the leaves were lucent with warm silver, and before me stretched an avenue of trees, mighty in stature.

I walked far down the avenue, and could no longer hear the sound of the River. Under the great trees the light was pale, but ahead of me I saw that it grew brighter.

Someone was waiting for me at the end of the avenue, someone whom I had always known, and for whom I had always been lonely. I felt her hands, cool and narrow, within mine; and I heard her voice. In it there was an echo of the cry of the bird that had led me there, but also there was warmth, humanity, laughter. "I have waited for you such a long time. Why did it take you so long to learn to fly?"

"I came as fast as I could. It was difficult to find the way; the mist was so close—but I followed the bird. Did you send the bird to bring me here?"

"No, but I knew the boat had gone to fetch you. They told me someone was crossing the River, and I knew that at last it would be you."

"How did you know?"

"Because I am alive—because I dream. My heart told me, and I have learned to listen to the voice of my heart. . . . We mustn't wait here any more: we must go on. *He* is waiting for me to take you to him."

The trees had vanished, and now we stood together in a flowery meadow which surrounded a temple of soaring columns. She took my hand and led me up the steps of the great entrance.

"Where are you taking me? Who is *he*?"

She pulled me by the hand to make me hurry. "Don't you want to see him? You have asked for so long that he would let you come here. This is the first time you've been able to cross the River; but I've been here before, many times. The woman who brought me here told me she knew you."

"Who is she?"

"I don't know: she called herself Oyahbe."

"Oyahbe is my mother!"

She looked a little puzzled. "I don't think so: the woman I mean is more than only asleep.

"My mother is dead."

"Then perhaps she was your mother. I wonder if she remembers?"

For a moment I was frightened. "Are *you* dead?"

She laughed. "No, like you I'm only asleep. It's more difficult to get here when you're only asleep. That's why I told you to hurry; in case after you've got so far someone wakes you up."

We were in a great hall; though the roof was closed and there were no lamps, it was silver with light, and the soul of the light was perfect serenity. I knew there were words in the light, born of the peace of all great harmony. "You have returned to me, Ra-ab, my son, after many days. You went Forth from my house, and now you have found your way again across the River. My daughter has brought you here. She too is a child again, and soon you will see her, for you Follow the same path. . . ."

I heard myself crying out, "Anubis! Anubis! . . ."

Like the blow of a mace, sound shattered my dream. I felt myself being shaken by the shoulder. Sebek stood over me. "Wake up, Ra-ab! Stop shouting for Anubis in your sleep."

I hit out at him in a fury of despair "You fool, you blind, ignorant fool! You dragged me back before I found out how to return there." I buried my face in my arms and tried to Force myself to remember.

But I only heard the voice of Sebek, sharp-edged though still good-humored. "Stop behaving like a child Ra-ab! They're waiting for you down at the practice ground."

Crocodile!

SOON AFTER I went to live at the House of the Captains, a fisherman came to ask help for his village against crocodiles. He said it was no longer safe to bathe even in the shallows, for one old crocodile of great size had taken a little girl while she was playing by the river, and now the women were too frightened to leave their children unguarded even near the huts.

Sebek told the fisherman, whose name was Dardas, to spend the night in the soldiers' quarters and promised that in the morning he would return with him to his village. Sebek said that I was to go too, and that with us we should take forty men, most of whom were already familiar with what we would have to do.

When we set off, soon after dawn, I saw that the men were carrying several things whose purpose I did not understand. There was a huge net, made of rope as thick as my wrist and measuring about six by fifteen paces; some heavy stakes sharpened at both ends; a stone mallet such as butchers use for slaughtering large cattle; a pointed rod sheathed with metal at the tip; and a quantity of stones, rather larger than maceheads, with a hole bored through them; together with several coils of strong rope. I could not make out how all these things were going to be used in the catching of crocodiles, but I did not like to ask Sebek to explain them as he thought I had been on a similar expedition with Father the year before—as I should have been if I had not had a fever.

There were no reeds at the part of the river we came to, and the bank rose steeply above the shelving mud beach. Dardas led us along the top of the bank, cautioning us to move quietly, and a little further on we saw below us six crocodiles basking in the sun. Sebek asked Dardas if this was the most likely place, and he answered:

"Yes, but if the 'old one' doesn't come here we may find him further down, below the village."

"But you have seen him here?"

"Three times. He cannot be mistaken; for he who took the child is the greatest of all crocodiles. We can drive the others away, but he is too cunning, he waits and comes back against our children."

"You have the bait ready?"

"Two goats have been bloating in the sun since the day before yesterday."

Then Dardas went to fetch the goats while we made our preparations. At a word from Sebek, four soldiers crawled forward to the edge of the bank and began to throw clods of earth at the sleeping crocodiles. Sebek told me, "They are doing it well. Notice how they throw everything near enough to disturb them

41

and make them slide back into the river, but not so near that they will seek another place to bask. Crocodiles usually come back to the same place every day. It's lucky for us they do, or it wouldn't be nearly so easy to trap them."

When the last evil head had sunk under the water we all climbed down the bank to the mud flat. The long net so heavy that it took twenty men to carry it, was spread out at the water's edge. The half nearest to the bank was pegged down on three sides by stakes, driven far into the mud but leaving part of them, about half the height of a man, sticking up. Four ropes were attached to the further side of the net, one at each corner and two others spaced between them. These ropes were threaded through stones, which held them in place and so prevented them from crossing the part of the net held down by the stakes. Then they were led up the bank out of sight of the beach. Other pierced stones were lashed to the far edge of the net, and I realized that this loose part would be dragged over the half that was secured so as to trap anything which came between the two. Only the further part of the net was in the shallows; the rest was now carefully concealed by mud and a litter of dead reeds which had been brought from further upstream.

This had just been finished when Dardas returned, followed by two men carrying the dead goats slung on a pole between them. These were so far putrefied as to be swollen almost beyond recognition, and were now dragged several times over the concealed net to hide the smell of humans.

While the bait was being pegged down on the quarter of the net nearest to the stakes, Sebek told me that although crocodiles will attack a man in the water, most of them try to avoid people when on land.

It was now nearly sunset, and Sebek said it was unlikely the crocodiles would return before the next day as this was the place where they usually came to bask. He posted two men to watch for the return of the crocodiles, and the rest of us went a little distance beyond the bank where we should be out of sight and hearing of the river. We lit a fire and sat round it to eat the food we had brought with us, which was only bread and radishes. I was very hungry and wondered what Sebek and I would have been eating if we had gone to the village as Dardas had suggested. . . . Fish certainly, and probably wild duck or other game, and several kinds of vegetables.

Every hour two other men went to take the place of the lookouts. As we had to sleep out, each man had brought his cloak, rolled up between his shoulders. It was a warm night, but I was glad of mine for the ground was very hard and I was too excited to sleep soundly. Soon after sunrise, two girls, the eldest of whom was the daughter of Dardas, brought a jar of milk for Sebek and me, and, tied up in a blue cloth, sufficient hardboiled duck eggs for everyone. I asked them to stay and eat with us, but though they smiled they seemed a little shy, and the younger girl said they must go back as her father was waiting for her.

The morning was very long and hot, and I began to disbelieve in the crocodiles' return. I was half asleep wondering what Kiyas was doing and how long it would be before I saw her again, when we heard the long awaited signal.

Ten men ran to each of the ropes that had been led up the bank, those in front crouching to conceal themselves so as not to alarm our prey before the right moment. I crawled forward beside Sebek until I could look over the edge of the bank. The longest crocodile I had ever seen was lumbering towards one of the goats. He moved his head from side to side as he tried to find the source of the smell that was attracting him; I was near enough to see the wrinkled eyelids opening and closing over his wicked little eyes. Then he must have got a strong stench of goat, for he quickened into a kind of clumsy run. But before he reached the bait we saw another, smaller crocodile follow in his tracks and make to contest the prize. Almost at the same moment the two pairs of great jaws crunched into the swollen carcass. Like a sudden puff of black smoke the flies that had been interrupted at their feast swirled angrily upwards, and hovered for a few seconds before settling on the other goat.

At first, instead of attacking each other, both crocodiles tried to tug the goat away from their rival. Sebek shouted to the men who had been standing braced to take the sudden strain. They flung their weight back, and half the great net rose, dripping with mud, out of the water. It doubled over on itself, until, when suddenly released, the weight of the stones on the bottom edge brought it sharply down so that the stakes drove up through the meshes and held it fast. For a moment the crocodiles were too startled to move and lay motionless as floating logs. Then, finding themselves trapped, they began to struggle. They threshed their tails, but instead of freeing themselves only became more firmly entangled.

Blood began to ooze out over the mud. "They must be attacking each other," said Sebek," that quite often happens when two are caught at the same time. It's a good thing it does, for two are much more difficult to kill than one. Sometimes they even break the net and get free."

"What happens then?"

He laughed. "The man who jumps fastest lives longest."

"How soon can we kill them?"

"We'll let them fight a bit longer until they are more tired." Then, pointing to the blood, he went on, "Why interfere when they're doing our work for us?"

It seemed the net was bound to be broken by the fury it contained; but it must have been even stronger than it looked, for though three of the stakes were wrenched out of the mud at no time had the crocodiles a chance to free themselves.

Sebek had been watching them intently. "The smaller one is done for! Look, he's turning on his back. Now watch, we'll finish him off: a javelin can pierce through the belly."

He shouted the names of the two men who had first seen the crocodile come out of the river. "He is yours! Javelins at five paces, and wine to the man who kills it!"

Four shafts stuck out of the thick yellow skin before the smaller crocodile was dead. The other still writhed with tireless ferocity. Sebek wasn't going to let me see he was excited; he was still young enough to be afraid of losing dignity if he showed too much enthusiasm. But I knew what he was feeling by the sound of his voice.

"The big one's still moving too fast for us to crush his head in with the mallet—that's only possible when they've got their jaws tangled in the net and can't turn quick enough to snap. And he's not tired enough to open his mouth to gasp . . . sometimes if you're quick you can thrust a spear down the throat. I've seen it done often enough, and done it myself more than once. It's a risky job, though, and a hand pays forfeit for clumsiness. We'll have to net this one tighter and try to turn him on his back."

One of the forelegs was thrust through the mesh, which through struggling had become so tightly constricted that the leg might have been held in a noose. This prevented the crocodile reaching the far side of the net, which was now released from its stakes and more ropes attached to it. These ropes were carried round the heavy net and then jerked into a position where a pull on them would again double the net over on itself. The slack was drawn in, and with a tremendous effort, in which we all joined, the crocodile was turned over on its back.

This time no men were singled out to attack it, and ten launched their javelins together. Dark blood flowed out in glistening rivulets, but even then Sebek would not let me touch it until the long metal-sheathed rod had been driven into its head by heavy blows of the mallet.

"Never go near a wounded crocodile, Ra-ab, however dead it looks, unless you prepare for it still being alive. They'll sham dead and get you when you come to skin them. Even a child could see they are Set's animals, no one else would have made anything so evil."

"Are we going to lay the net again?"

"I'll know that when I've opened them up. The missing child was wearing a copper bracelet with a rough turquoise set in it."

He took out his hunting knife and ripped the soft and horrid belly of the great crocodile. The things he dragged out through the slit made me feel rather sick. They were mostly viscera with a ghastly putrid stench. He spread them out on the mud and turned them over with his knife. I saw him pick something up. It was a child's bracelet, bent but still recognizable. I could even see the hole that once had held a turquoise.

"No, we needn't set the net again," he said. 'We've got the right crocodile.'

Dardas the Fisherman

AS IT WAS ALREADY late afternoon, Sebek said that we should all spend the night at the village. Until we reached it I did not realize that Dardas was the village headsman. His house, built of unplastered mudbrick, was larger than the others, and had four rooms opening on a small walled garden. Jars of warm water for us to wash in had been set ready in the room I was to share with Sebek. There was clean matting on the floor and a fresh cover on each of the two bedplaces; someone had even put a shallow dish filled with trails of blue convolvulus on the high window sill.

Dardas' elder daughter ate with us, but when the meal was finished she left us alone with her father. At first he had been a little diffident, but soon he began to talk more freely. I saw that to him the rest of Egypt was an alien country, even those who lived in the adjoining Nomes of the Hare and the Jackal might have been Asiatics. Listening to him made me realize that for all I knew of the rest of the Two Lands, they might indeed be alien. I was nearly fourteen yet had never been outside the boundaries of the Oryx. Sebek had been outside them, but why did he never speak of it? I had supposed it was because everything he had seen on those brief journeys was too familiar to be of interest. Why was the Oryx different? Why did even Father so seldom go beyond his own lands?

Sebek was tired; only courtesy held back his yawns, and when he went to bed I stayed and talked to Dardas. A boy, and a fisherman who was already growing old, talking together on the night a crocodile was killed. . . . I wonder if a man who wore the Double Crown cried out in his sleep at an echo from the future?

This is the story which Dardas told me:

I was born in a village downriver, but though it was less than five days' journey from the boundary of the Oryx it might have been among foreigners that I grew up, so different is their way of life to ours. The priests taught us that the Gods must be propitiated by gifts, and that if these were considered unworthy, a plague or a famine would be sent as punishment. So when—it was more than twelve years ago—the river fell lower than in living memory, it was easy for us to believe it was a sign of Nut's anger that the water stank and the mud flats grew wider every day.

My brother and I took our last possession of any value—it was a necklace which had belonged to my mother, five turquoise beads on a knotted cord, and added it to what was being collected from the four other villages which paid tribute to the same temple. Our spokesman took these offerings to the town, exchanging them for gold, which, before being taken to the temple, was made into the form of a fish. Still the river did not rise; and when the spokesman went again to the temple, he was told that Nut would not relent until one of us had been made sacrifice to the river.

There were some brave enough to speak against this command, but they were soon silenced, for the people were beginning to fear that the river had forever forsaken us—and fear breeds faster than lice in a foreigner's beard. Until the sacrifice was chosen no one knew ease. Whispers crept like thieves from house to house. . . . Who shall it be? Which of us has angered Nut and made us suffer?

Because of their ignorance they chose the one who was least like themselves. She was a woman named Hayab, who though blind since birth, had shown herself to have a sight which is not possessed by ordinary people. The others found it easy to forget how she had always been gentle and had given them cause to honor her. But I could not forget how when I was a child she had saved me from becoming a cripple. I had been lame for a long time, and Hayab had come to my mother and asked if she might be allowed to look for the cause of my hurt. My leg was swollen and I could not sleep for pain. Hayab took the foot between her hands and put it against her forehead. Then she said, "There is a thorn, small and curved, deep in the soft flesh under the instep. It is the seed of the pain and must be cut out." She marked my foot with quail's blood where the cut must be made. The thorn was found and the wound soon healed. Because of Hayab I was not lame any more.

Yet to my shame I made no open protest when they bound her hands and told her she must die. She walked serenely between the men who took her, smiling as though she were the captive of a children's game. They made her prisoner in a little hut, where no one would live since a woman had died there in childbirth; and through the thin mud walls I could hear her singing to the river as a girl sings to her young lover.

It was five days to the dark of the moon, the time appointed for the sacrifice. Her songs brought a new fear to the village. Why was she not afraid of death? What knowledge had she which was hidden from them? No one was willing to bring her death, yet none dared question the priest's authority.

When I said that I and my brother would drown her from my boat the others rejoiced and praised our courage—for they thought that at the moment of death she might make her sins fall upon us and condemn us to join her in the Caverns of the Underworld.

No one watched us take her from the hut—I think they feared she might cast a spell on them. My brother had asked where we should take her, but I had told him she would tell us when the time came. Even the boat seemed changed when we gained steerage way; there was life in the mast and the sail was eager for the wind. Until we were well out from the bank I dared not tell her that we were going to set her free, lest by her joy she would betray herself to a spy lurking in the reeds. But when I did she showed no surprise, and said, "I know. You told me yesterday."

I saw my brother's hand tighten on the steering oar, for he knew no one had had speech with her since she was in the hut. She turned to him, "Why are you surprised that I should know of it before Dardas told me? Had you forgotten the thorn which made him lame?"

I asked where she wished us to take her, and she said, "Follow in the wake of the white barge."

When I did not answer, she pointed up the empty river, "Surely you can see it too?"

"There is no other boat within sound or hearing; and it is a dark night with few stars."

She smiled, "Forgive me. I forgot that sometimes I see what is hidden from other people. Keep on upriver, until I see the helmsman of the barge change course or he tells me to land."

The wind held steady from the north, and dawn found us between unfamiliar banks. During the next two days we passed barges heavy laden with stone from the southern quarries, and once a war galley of forty oars. I had brought food with us, but she ate little though she had had only water and uncooked meal for five days.

It was evening when we came in sight of a large village on the west bank. Then she said, "The helmsman of the white barge tells me it is here we shall find the house I have seen in my dreams. It stands alone, the most southerly of the houses. There is a white wall round it, and a fig tree grows by the gate in the wall. Take me there, and I shall remember the name of him who told me to come."

I remember that three boats were tied up to the landing-stage; and a child was playing with a white kid beside the path up to the village. At first I did not know why the people seemed strange; then I realized it was because the women were singing as they carried brimming water jars from the well, and the men who tilled the fields looked strong and content.

Beyond the village we came to a wide road bordered with sycamores, and at the end of it there was the long wall with a fig tree growing by the door, even as she had said. I knocked, and the door was opened by a woman with a child on her shoulder.

Hayab said to her, "This is the house of Roidahn, and I am Hayab the blind woman, to whom he spoke in a dream, bidding me come here."

The woman did not seem surprised to see us. She smiled and said, "He is waiting to greet you in the name of the Watchers of the Horizon."

She led us into a garden, and beside a fish pool sat a man who, by his clothes, we knew to be of noble rank. When we would have prostrated ourselves before him he shook his head and gave us the greeting used between equals. He called Hayab by her name and spoke to her as though they were friends long parted.

When I said that my brother and I must get back to our boat, Roidahn said that a room had been prepared for us and that we must rest and eat before deciding whether we wished to return to our own village. The room to which he took us was finer than any we had seen before. On a table there was food, fruit and wild duck and cold roast kid, and wine in alabaster cups.

It was the first time we had drunk wine; it was smooth and dark, strong as sunlight. Suddenly my brother began to laugh as though he were a child again. He stood up, swaying a little. "Since our father died I have feared Death, and now I know that I was a quail chick fearing even the shadow of the bird scarer. Death was so insignificant that I cannot remember what he looked like. Can you remember us falling out of the boat, Dardas, when we were drowned? Who is he whom we call Roidahn? Is he Ra or one of his brothers? I drink a toast to Death, who steered us here and waited not for thanks!"

The next morning I left my brother to sleep, for he seemed reluctant to wake, perhaps fearing to find the dream had vanished. I went in search of Roidahn, and found him sitting under a vine trellis beyond the fish pool. He asked me how my brother and I had fared, and then spoke of Hayab, saying she would stay on in his household and learn the harp strings which should accompany her singing.

Then he said, "You are wondering why you are not afraid of me, for since a child you have been taught to fear what you do not fully understand. You have been told to accept authority without questioning its source; but I will answer your questions and demand no allegiance."

"Why have we come here? How did Hayab know that your house was near this village? I know that she has never been more than a little way from the place where she was born. She has never seen you, for she has always been blind, yet you greeted each other as friends. . . ."

"Even *your* priests must have told you that we are born many times. Is it then so strange to meet a friend whose face is unfamiliar? And what is more natural than to turn to a friend when you are in trouble?"

"But how did she know of you?"

"Are your priests so ignorant they have not taught you that dreams may be a surer messenger than the swiftest runner?"

"I know nothing of magic; I'm a fisherman, not a priest."

"Yet you followed a helmsman you could not see; was that the action of a man heavy with Earth? No, you came here because you recognized the wisdom of Hayab, and loving it you ceased to fear the shadow."

"Why are the people of your village different to ours, even the children are not afraid to see a stranger?"

"Because they know that the God of Fear rules only in the Underworld, unless men give him power by setting his image in their hearts. It is to Ra or his brothers that my people address their prayers, and so they live in peace. There is an empty house in my village; live there for a month, and only then decide whether you will return to your own people or live on in the Oryx."

"That is the end of my story—and the beginning of my life," said Dardas. "For I learned happiness in the Oryx."

Fear Over Egypt

SINCE HEARING from Dardas of Egypt beyond the Oryx, I waited eagerly for an opportunity to see Roidahn. This came within a month, for Sebek told me to stay the night at Hotep-Ra on my way, with ten soldiers, to a village in the north of the Nome.

The Roidahn I knew was as different to the man of whom Dardas had told me, as was Sebek the Captain to the boy whom Kiyas had sometimes teased until he almost wept. It was the Roidahn who had said to Hayab, "I greet you in the name of the Watchers of the Horizon," I wished to know, and somehow I must convince him that he could talk to me as though I were not bounded by the Oryx or by my fourteen years. He had welcomed Hayab because he had seen her in a dream. Could I not use the same key to unlock the door of his speech? But what if I dreamed of him and he did not remember?

I tried very hard to meet him away from Earth, and I did so on the night before I reached his house. Though I brought back only a fragment of what must have been a long conversation, I remember him saying, "Yes, I shall remember this meeting, and to prove it, when we go into the garden I shall point to the pool and say, 'Yesterday there were five lotus, how many are there today?' And you must answer, 'Another bud has opened, there are six.'"

I was so afraid of forgetting his exact words that I wrote them with a burnt stick on the linen of my second kilt; I had nothing else with which to scribe, for we were sleeping out.

I reached his house late that afternoon. The gate in the wall was open. The fig tree which grew beside it was very old; and I thought of Dardas standing under it with the blind woman beside him. Had she doubted the strength of her dream as already I had begun to doubt in mine?

I went straight to the garden of the pool. No one was there, and I stood staring down into the water, half expecting to see more than the shadows with which lotus leaves patterned the tiles. I heard footsteps behind me, and turned to see Roidahn coming through the opening in the wall beyond the pool.

He gave me the greeting between father and son, and standing with his arm round my shoulders, said, "There were six lotus in the pool yesterday, how many are there today?"

"No, you should have said 'Five lotus yesterday,' and I should answer, 'Six today, for another bud has opened.'"

He swung me round so that he could look at me, excited as a boy. "You did remember! I was so afraid you wouldn't that I only asked the question to convince myself that Ra-ab was not a dreamer of true dreams. But I was wrong! Never has a man been so glad to prove himself a fool. How your mother would have rejoiced to hear my question and your answer . . . or perhaps she did hear them."

"Can you really see her?" I asked eagerly. "I have never seen her, even in a dream."

He sighed. "Only once since she died; and that was to tell me to try to raise your father from his grief. I made him remember the Oryx, though I could not give him back joy, for he had given it into her keeping and would take it from no other hand."

That night Roidahn talked to me until it was nearly dawn. I learned that other Nomes were not as ours, and that I might go from temple to temple across Egypt and not meet another priest such as those the Oryx knew.

I shall always remember Roidahn saying, "When the Two Lands were known as Kam, and the stone from which the Great Pyramids were raised still slept in the quarries, the Oryx would have been a province of little wisdom; for then were temples torches in the land and even the fear of Set had been forgotten. The Pharaohs who built the 'Two who Remember' were wise in their power; yet those who came after them saw only the shadows cast by these great pyramids and were blind to the light which is reflected from them. Gradually the reason for their building was forgotten, and in its stead came worship of a mighty achievement: they were made enduring so that they should be landmarks for the soul through many journeys; but now they symbolize not power on Earth, but power of Earth.

"Since their time many temples have been built; yet men have forgotten that a building has no virtue save that of the dweller therein, even as the body is carrion save for the spirit which houses in it. The stone of these new temples is dead stone, and the clay of the priest's houses is the dust of the tomb. The priests follow a ritual they do not understand, and those few among them who have power use it only for their own aggrandizement; because they know so little they must make mysteries; having no real authority they must keep themselves apart. Even if they can go beyond the three measurements of Earth, they seldom understand the forces they evoke. The unknown is always feared; so it is to fear they make their sacrifices—even those of them who call on the name of Ra *direct* their prayer to Set, the Lord of Fear. There is fear over Egypt! From Set to his priests, from priests to Pharaoh; spreading through all the channels which lead from them, Nomarch to overseer, village headman to the youngest child who cries in terror of the dark. The power of Ra is his own power, but Set must draw his power from others. It is from those who acknowledge fear that Set and his consort Sekmet derive their strength."

"How then has Set no power over the Oryx?"

"Your father, as you know, is the fourth of the direct line to be Nomarch. Until you grandfather's time, this Nome was no different to any other, but he was a man of wisdom though he had no temple training. When he succeeded his father he saw that those who used to be his friends now feared him because he held authority. He knew that true authority can inspire only love, and that authority which gives birth to fear derives from force and has no virtue.

"At first it was difficult for him to cut down the rotten framework which the Oryx shared with the rest of Egypt; but gradually he replaced dead wood by strong new growth. The overseers of his towns were chosen not because they were feared, but because they were beloved; and any man who abused his power found that it was taken from him, even though his family had held office for ten generations.

"Because he became worthy to be a friend he made many enemies. The neighboring Nomarchs were jealous of him, seeing that his lands prospered even in a time of famine. He told them that they too should build more granaries, so that good harvests could be stored against lean years. But they would not listen to him, seeing only the gold and ivory, purple and cedarwood, for which they bartered their surplus grain.

"Your grandfather built no temples; he was intolerant of false priests, and saw temples as the chief breeding ground of fear. He maintained the ritual observances of the old temples only because he knew that by doing otherwise he would give an excuse for the adjoining Nomarchs to demand of Pharaoh that his lands should be ceded to them.

"Yet the laws by which he governed were good laws, for he had in his possession a collection of old papyri, many of them dating from the time before the Pyramids, and through them he found that the Pharaohs of the Old Kingdom held the secret by which they ruled in peace. It was from the past, for instance, that he made the law by which orphans and old people, the sick and the lame, are the care of him who owns the land on which they live.

"Then, as now, it was the law that those who could not pay the tribute of the tenth part should work for Pharaoh four months in every year; but, except in the Oryx, this law was abused. If Pharaoh wished to build a city too rapidly, the labor must be found without consideration for the source; if Pharaoh coveted monuments of stone, fields had to lie barren because there were no men left to plow them; and if Nomarchs were idle, dykes decayed and irrigation channels fell in so that the limits of fertility were often reduced to the point of famine. Men were judged by rank instead of by character: they could abuse their office and still retain it. Pharaoh could hold the Crook and Flail and betray them both; tyrant or weakling, either were accepted if he wore the Double Crown.

"In the fullness of years your grandfather died, having brought that peace to the Oryx in which you have grown. Your father is not so strong a man as your grandfather: he is content to continue with a pattern which is already set on the loom, and does not wish to change the color of a single thread.

"The body of the Oryx was strong and clean, but they who brought to it the peace of Ra were your mother and Nekht-Ra. During the five years that she ruled she caused your father to see with her eyes. The ritual priests were sent away and in their place came our high priest, Neferankh—who also came to the Oryx seemingly by chance. It is sixteen years since his first pupils began their temple training, and soon we shall no longer lack for priests, nor will there be a village without its temple counselor.

"In the days of the Old Kingdom, Pharaoh was High Priest; the unity of temporal and divine power. For five years your father and mother achieved together this dual authority; but at her death he became a man whose sight is failing and he could see only that which was near to him. Because the priests were *her* priests he protected them and did them honor, but he was a man acting without initiative. One day, Ra-ab, you will rule the Oryx. In the far past you have known temple courts and held authority; and through you the peace of the Oryx will spread beyond its boundaries, in the name of the Watchers of the Horizon."

The lamp flickered, and Roidahn got up to replenish it with oil.

"Roidahn, who are the Watchers of the Horizon? I had never heard of them until Dardas told me that it was in their name you greeted Hayab, the blind woman, when he brought her here."

He smiled. "So you have been talking to Dardas? He is the head-man of a village now, and I am sure the people prosper under his care. He married Hayab after she had been a year in my house. They were very happy together, but she is dead now. She gave him two daughters, and I think he is content."

"But who are the Watchers?"

"People like me, who know there is a shadow over Egypt. When shadows gather together it is night; but when many turn to watch for the dawn it will surely come. Your father and grandfather both held that it was sufficient there should be peace within the Oryx, that it should keep itself apart from Egypt. But it is not enough to store grain in granaries, it must be sown when the new fields are ready, so as to stave off famine from others. For many years I have brought those whom I term the 'Watchers' into the Oryx; plowmen and fisher people, herdsmen and linenweavers, goldsmiths and scribes: one thing only they had in common, their resolve to banish Fear from the Two Lands. When the time comes they will go forth from the Oryx, and what they have learned here will run through Egypt like fire through dry straw. Those who gave fear shall know it, and those who misused power shall lose it; those whose greatness was a mask shall see themselves pitiful, and those who were humble shall be empowered."

"But Pharaoh will send his army against you!"

"Soldiers cannot hear the voice of the dead."

When, the following morning, I left Hotep-Ra, I felt so different from the boy who had arrived here the day before that I was almost surprised my soldiers recognized me. I was no longer a boy, I was a man who knew what his work was to be. I had always known that one day I should succeed my father, but it had always seemed I should only substitute one routine for another. Now I belonged to the Watchers of the Horizon, who were pledged to drive out Fear.

I was still not sure if I had understood Roidahn correctly when he had said, "Soldiers cannot hear the voice of the dead." Pharaoh had been raised almost to divinity; indeed there were many who held him to be divine. Yet if his power was of Set and not of Ra then it were right that he should be killed. Roidahn had said that *all* who inspire fear are evil.

I knew that to speak against Pharaoh was to die . . . and by a slow death. So Roidahn had not needed to tell me I must repeat nothing of what he had told me, even to Kiyas. I knew I was only Ra-ab, a boy of fourteen walking along a narrow, dusty road at the head of ten soldiers who were going to collect grain from a northern village. But I thought of myself as Ra-ab, the Captain of the Oryx, leading the Watchers against the Royal City; to free the land of Egypt from the shadow of Fear.

Sebek

A FEW DAYS AFTER my return to the House of the Captains, I found an opportunity to tell Sebek that I had become a Watcher. We had taken our throwing-sticks down to the marsh at dawn, to wait for the wild-fowl to come back from their feeding grounds.

Sebek was more skilled than I, but that morning he only got seven birds, five of them wild duck, to my six. It was three months before the Inundation, and it was already warm enough to be pleasant in the early morning, so we decided not to go home for the first meal.

By ourselves, in a clearing among the reeds, it was easy to forget that he was the captain in authority over me. I thought of him only as the Sebek with whom Kiyas and I had played since we were children; the Sebek from whom I need not conceal my thoughts.

He was lying on his back, chewing a stem of grass, when I said, "Roidahn has made me a Watcher, he told me to tell you."

"I'm glad. I told him a year ago that you should join us, but he said the sign must come from you, not from him."

"*You* told him? Why? What had I done to make you think I was a Watcher?"

"Quite a lot of things, but I think the first was when you woke up shouting 'Anubis!' —and abused me as though I were a kennel boy who had forgotten to feed your favorite dog. There are not many soldiers who can be so rude to their captain, and yet make the captain feel he is to blame! Then from what Dardas said about you, the morning after we stayed in his house, I was sure you should join us—Dardas is a Watcher, of course."

"You didn't know I was trying to follow Anubis, though, did you?"

"Oh yes, I knew that. It must be nearly five years since Kiyas told me about it."

"*Kiyas* told you?"

He must have heard the incredulity in my voice, for he sat up and said emphatically, "Yes, Kiyas—and why shouldn't she?"

"It was a secret between us. She promised never to tell anyone; she knew they'd only laugh."

"Well, if that's the reason you made her promise, she didn't break it. I'd give a lot to be able to dream; but I never do, though I've tried hard enough."

"*You* want to dream?" Then I wished I hadn't put it quite like that because I saw I'd hurt him.

"Yes, funny, isn't it? I'm a captain and I talk like a temple pupil. I suppose you think it's odd that a captain should want to know what he's fighting for; to see something of the pattern, instead of being so occupied with keeping the little threads from getting raveled that he can't see beyond them. I suppose you think that keeping a Hundred working in harmony together, and making the lazy ones sweat until they can throw a javelin as well as I know they can if they try, and bringing in an occasional law-breaker, and seeing that each village gets its fair allowance from the granaries in a lean year, should be sufficient interest for a mere soldier! And think of the excitement he gets—netting crocodiles when they make a nuisance of themselves or killing an old lion that has come down on the herds. Oh yes, that's plenty to fill my life. Dreams! What are dreams to a captain!"

"Sorry, Sebek, I'm a fool! You know I didn't mean that, but I thought Kiyas was the only person except Roidahn who knew I was trying to dream true. She thought it was rather nonsense; she only helped me because—well, we always have tried to help each other. She always said dreams were for old men or for priests; and that's why I was afraid of your knowing what I was trying to do."

He lay back and pulled another grass stem to chew. "Well, that's one misunderstanding cleared up. You don't think I've got only one idea, like the Master of the Javelins, and I don't think you are any less good a soldier because you'd like to follow the standard of Anubis. You mustn't be cross with Kiyas for telling me what you were doing."

"That's all very well, but I *am* cross. I know she tells lies to other people—she says it's their fault because they make it necessary. But I didn't think she'd break a promise to me."

"If she hadn't loved you she wouldn't have done so; and to break a promise out of love is much better than being bound a prisoner of words. When she broke that promise she had more knowledge than when she made it, and the knowledge told her it should be broken. Why did you make her promise, anyhow? Because you were frightened of being laughed at. Well, she knew I wouldn't laugh. She knew that my knowing would strengthen the link between you and me—and that's the only way to judge the merits of speaking or keeping silent; whether anything you say can strengthen affection between two people or weaken it."

"Do you think Kiyas will ever be a Watcher?"

"I don't *think*; I know she will."

"But she's only a child."

"Her body may be, but she isn't. Don't you remember how we always did what she wanted us to when we were playing together? She led us into adventures far more often than we led her—and usually she got us out of them too, for she was always quicker witted than either of us. Since you've been here she sits beside your father when he gives judgment. He told Roidahn himself that she was a better judge between two petitioners than he was. She doesn't remember her dreams, but she told me she often wakes wiser than when she went to sleep. It doesn't matter *how* she finds her knowledge so long as the result is true. Haven't you noticed how she always seems to know if anyone on your father's estate is in trouble or needs help? She's interested in people as a priest is interested in magic or a captain in his men. That's how she gets her wisdom; from knowing people's hearts and understanding why they behave as they do. She may not be able to judge if a man has acted for good or evil, but she'll always know *why* he's acted."

"Yes, you're right about Kiyas. I never realized it before."

"No, you wouldn't. You're only her brother!"

I thought how pleased Kiyas would have been to hear that note in Sebek's voice. Dear, naughty little Kiyas; whom I loved and Sebek seemed to think so wise! How she would have enjoyed listening to our conversation!

He went on, still rather heated. "You wait till Kiyas has an opportunity to show her strength. Then you'll realize she's more than the child who teases you—and teases me often enough. Roidahn has known her all her life, and he says if there were more people like her there'd be no need for the Watchers. It doesn't sound much when you put it into words—just being the sort of person to whom people tell their troubles without trying to hide anything. But think what a lot it means—to have someone to talk to like that. Nearly everyone has something of which they're ashamed; and shame is like a statue of Sekmet set up in a hidden sanctuary. A statue they are always trying to propitiate by little lies, little evasions. They are terrified that someone will find them out, but alone they haven't got the courage to destroy it. It's far worse outside the Oryx; people are crippled by the thongs of little false laws they have made themselves. They pretend to be richer than they are; to be cleverer; to be a united family when they would be much better apart; to love their children when there is no real link between them. They pretend to be faithful to the Gods when they believe only in Death. Shame, like a fungus, grows best in the dark; and if spoken about it is as though the room which kept it alive were broken down."

He paused, I think he was embarrassed by his own vehemence, and said, "We must go back, I didn't realize it was so late."

Then, as he stopped to pick up his string of wild-fowl, he said over his shoulder, "So you won't be surprised, will you, Ra-ab, when Kiyas is a Watcher? She can open the mouths of the dumb—and that is a magic worthy of any priest."

The Blue Death

THE SUMMER of the following year was the hottest I had ever known. I did not see Kiyas very often, but I noticed that even she, who loved the heat, had lost a little of her intense vitality. A pestilence, born of the heat and the stagnant river, had broken out in many parts of Egypt. As yet it had passed by the Oryx, but daily it grew nearer. When I heard there were thirty dead in a village less than a day's journey from the northern boundary, I decided to go to consult Father as to what preparation we should make against its onslaught.

In the old days it would have been the priests who combated this enemy of Egypt; they would have given healing to the sick, and to their temples people who had no one to care for them would have been taken. But now, except in the Oryx, temples held no comfort for the afflicted. I had heard that the false priests were telling their followers that the pestilence had come as a sign of Set's anger, and that divine favor could only be regained by still heavier tribute—and the promise of yet more. I had heard also that human sacrifice was being made to the river; and though the priests still pretended that it was being done without their sanction this was believed only by the most credulous.

I thought of what Dardas had told me, and knew how fear must be increasing from village to village. I tried by every means in my power to cross the River beyond the mist, so that I might ask the voice of Anubis how I could protect the Oryx; but I woke with no clear memory except a strong desire to talk it over with Kiyas.

When I reached home I found that Father was working with his scribe, so without disturbing him I went to find her. Before I told her she knew I had come about the pestilence. She said, "Roidahn sends news of the pestilence every day. The people on his estates seem to have relations in almost every Nome, that's why he knows so much of what goes on outside the Oryx. At first he hoped that it was only a very severe form of the summer fever; but there is a terror in this death, Ra-ab; the bowels issue with blood, and blue marks like bruises appear on the stomach, as though the body had begun to putrefy before the soul was free. Father spends all day with his scribes searching through the papyri to find a magical ritual, or even a formula of herbs, that can be used to protect us. He is trying to make himself believe that the Oryx will be spared; but I think he knows it will come here, or why does he search so desperately?"

"Have you seen Nefer-ankh?"

"Yes, and so has Nekht-Ra. Nefer-ankh says it might take two hundred healers to give us full protection, and he has only ten fully trained."

"The fear will be worse than the pestilence. Until now the Oryx has been stronger than fear, but it may break through the barriers we have built against it."

"Roidahn sent Hanuk to the nearest town where it is raging and he returned yesterday with terrible stories of what he had seen. The dead are lying unburied in the streets; people who have been struck down are being abandoned by their families and left to die alone. No one was allowed into the temple unless they first stripped off their clothes to prove that the fingermarks of Set were not yet on them. Hanuk heard that children are being sacrificed to the river; and the blood of a newborn child had been poured on the road leading into one village he passed through, to try to keep out the death."

"Does Roidahn think it will come here?"

"I'm not sure. He is telling his people that it may be sent to test their mastery of fear."

"Roidahn is apt to judge others too much as himself. He thinks his people are strong in their own strength, he doesn't realize how much it is his own which protects them. We mustn't over-judge our people's strength. Has Father a plan?"

"He is looking for one. He knows that Nefer-ankh and the other healers will do everything that's possible, but there are so few of them. Father is still looking to the past, the written past, to find a way. He won't talk about it to me any more, he thinks I'm too young to understand. But I'm not too young, Ra-ab. I've learned a lot in the last year. I don't wish I were as priest as you do, and I don't want to be a scholar like Father . . . perhaps it's because I *am* ordinary that I can understand what ordinary people feel. I think Nefer-ankh will stop the people who are near him being afraid, even if they have to see the ones they love die terri-bly. But I'm thinking about the people who won't have any one to give them courage. Those who are strong in love or who have acquired real bravery will forget about their own danger when they have someone to look after. I suppose there are some who are cowards through their own fault: perhaps it doesn't really matter what happens to them. It's the people between those extremes who I am thinking of people who want to be brave but who have to be led into it. You don't call your soldiers cowards, Ra-ab, when they have to be led into battle. In every village there should be someone to show them what to do. It doesn't matter if they are not priests, nor very wise. They must be people who are used to having to do things they'd like to be frightened of, and from whom the others would take orders."

"You mean the soldiers?"

"Yes, of course. I tried to tell Father about the idea but he wouldn't listen. He said it wasn't the work of soldiers to nurse the sick; that was for women or priests."

"Could I persuade Father?"

She shook her head. "No, he'd only think I'd asked you to try to make him change his mind. Once he thinks an idea's mine nothing will make him believe it's yours too."

"It is Sebek's turn to command the captains, and he can act without Father's seal."

She jumped up. "We'll start now, and I'll come with you. We won't tell Father anything about it until everything's arranged; if he'd thought of a better idea he would be doing something about it instead of shutting himself up with a lot of old records."

"Don't you think you'd better stay here, Kiyas?"

"No. I can make Sebek see that we're right much sooner than you could. He always listens to me."

There was such confident authority in her voice that I realized how right Sebek had been in saying that she was much more than a girl of thirteen. He would listen to her better than he would listen to me, so it was necessary for her to come with me.

"All right, Kiyas, we'll both go, and at once."

As Roidahn and Father were both in the north of the Nome; the temple of Nefer-ankh was near the center, Kiyas and I went to the largest town in the south. I was still a little bewildered by the speed with which Kiyas had convinced Sebek. Now her idea had become a reality, and it was only noon of the day following our arrival at the House of the Captains.

A Leader of a Hundred with fifty men had gone to each town, and five soldiers were posted to every village. These five were under the village headman, but were to report to their captain on the first suspicion that the enemy was within our boundaries. Each captain was to act in conformity with a general plan, so what Kiyas and I did must have been much the same as what was done all over the Oryx.

We went to the overseer of the town and told him all we knew of the pestilence, sparing him nothing that would convince him how necessary it was to prepare every possible weapon against its assault. His house was the largest in the town and stood away from the others, on the east side. As it was so well suited to our scheme I told him that we should have to take it over, to which he agreed willingly. There were three large rooms and two smaller ones, as well as a storeroom, opening off a large central hall. At the back of the house there were servants' quarters and kitchens, built round their own courtyard; and the surrounding garden was enclosed by a high wall.

I told the overseer he could share the house with us, but he said that as he had two young children he was afraid to let them remain where they would come in contact with the sick, and that with my permission he would take them to his wife's mother, who had a small country estate. He said, reluctantly, that as soon as he had taken them there he would return to help us; but I saw he was as much afraid for himself as for his family, and I told him we should have no further need of him after he had seen to the collection of the various things we required.

His storerooms were well stocked with both food and wine; and there was an abundance of fruit and vegetables in his garden. Kiyas said that the sick would need milk more than any other food, so I had a herd of ten milch goats driven into the field behind the house. Then I sent for bales of coarse linen and a quantity of clean straw, to make mattresses that could be burnt after use; and a large number of bowls and drinking vessels, so that each person should have his own, which could be broken when he no longer needed it.

Nefer-ankh had told Kiyas that when Set sends a pestilence he infects water with his evil power, so we knew that every source at which people drank must be protected. Nefer-ankh had carefully instructed her in the method of protection: "Only certain wells must be used and these put in charge of one who is pure in heart, preferably a girl under twenty who was born at the full moon. She must suffer no one else to draw water, so that if the community is large there should be two girls in charge of each well. Her hands and feet must be washed morning and evening in raw wine, and each day she must wear a fresh tunic of white linen which has bleached for six hours in the sun. She must eat only well-baked bread and fruit with a skin which she herself removes, and she must drink nothing but wine, or water she has drawn. Only new water jars must be brought within ten paces of the well, nor must any unclean person approach within twenty paces, or animal within thirty. Fever demons sent by Set may also assume the form of flies, mice or bats; so food and water, and as far as possible dwelling houses and outbuildings as well, must be protected from their contamination."

This order was proclaimed in every street, and in the market-place, at dawn, noon and sunset. Yet though Nefer-ankh had told us that such laws would help to guard us against Set, he had said that we must expect some of our people to be afflicted by the evil onslaught. So it was also proclaimed that any who took the new sickness must immediately notify me, and that those who could not be properly cared for in their homes should be brought to the Overseer's House where they would be tended by every means in the power of the Oryx.

I had been anxious as to what Father would think of our plan or if he would be angry that we had carried it out without first consulting him. Kiyas didn't let this worry her, she only laughed and said that he should be glad his children were not afraid of accepting authority. Still, I was relieved when Sebek came to see us, on his way to the town where he was commanding, to say that our plan had received commendation from both Father and Roidahn.

Sebek added, "I wanted to tell them that Kiyas had thought of it all, but as she had made me promise not to, I told them Ra-ab had conceived the idea and developed it in collaboration with myself and the other captains."

"Did he mind my being here with Ra-ab?" asked Kiyas.

"He said at first that you were too young and that Ra-ab ought not to have taken you with him. But I think he was proud you had gone without his permission—anyway he didn't tell me to send you back. I saw Nefer-ankh on my way here. He is keeping two of the healer-priests with him, and sending the others to the principal towns. One of them should reach you either tonight or tomorrow morning."

"Did Nefer-ankh send any other message?"

"He said that the bodies of any who die of the pestilence should be burnt, because when Set had poisoned the flesh it must be cleansed with fire before burial."

Kiyas turned to me. "We ought to have thought of that. We must have wood collected at once. It had better be outside the town, but not too far from here because if the pestilence gathers force there will be more for the pyre from this house than from any other."

Sebek only stayed long enough to have some food with us as he was in a hurry to get on to his own town. We told him everything we had done and he said he could think of nothing we had forgotten. I noticed that his manner toward me had changed and wondered if it was because of our conversation in the marsh; whatever the reason he seemed to have forgotten his superior rank and treated me as though we had equal authority. To Kiyas he spoke with deference, and as each point came under discussion he waited for her opinion before stating his own and only differed from her when he had some special knowledge not available to her.

There were only two wells in the town and it had been easy to find suitable women to guard them. Some of the townspeople were puzzled at not being allowed nearer than twenty paces, but they set down their water jars obediently and waited for them to be filled.

The healer-priest arrived the evening that Sebek left, his name was Ptah-aru, and though young he was fully initiate. He helped us to make everything ready, and after the first three days there was little for Kiyas and me to do except visit the wells twice a day to see that our orders were being carried out.

For seven days nothing occurred to break the monotony of heat. I had been with Kiyas to the East well, and we were returning through the fields on the edge of the town when I saw a woman carrying a child coming along the path toward us. She was young, and wore a blue tunic that left her right shoulder bare. I noticed the child was wrapped in a cloak, as though it were the cold weather.

Kiyas caught me by the arm, "Look, Ra-ab! She's so tired she can hardly walk. We must help her."

I ran on toward the woman with Kiyas beside me. The woman stood still and watched us coming. She swayed, as though she were going to fall, and I put my arm round her shoulders to support her, saying to Kiyas, "Take the child or she'll drop it."

But the woman held the child closer, and said in a hard unnatural voice, "Don't uncover him. I don't want you to see him. If you want to help me, show me the way to the house where they are fighting Set. I demand the protection of the Oryx for my son. I denied Set because they told me to; now they must protect my son. They said Ra was stronger than Set; now they must prove it. If my son dies I shall know the new religion is no better than the old."

She was talking to herself more than to us; I don't think that after the first few words she even realized we were beside her.

Kiyas spoke to her, pronouncing each word slowly and distinctly as though she were talking to one who was deaf. "We have come to take your son to the house where we will fight for him against Set. You must come too; and we will show you how best to help him. You are tired and you have walked a long way in the heat. Let me carry your son; if he cries I will give him back to you."

I broke in, "No, Kiyas, let me take it." She frowned at me. I knew it was useless to protest, but I said again, "No, Kiyas, let me carry him."

The woman was staring at Kiyas, and her eyes had lost a little of their dull despair. "You look kind," she said slowly, "You are not tired as I am; he will be safer with you. But I will come too. I won't let him out of my sight. You won't try to keep me away from him?"

"No, of course not. We'll only try to show you how best to help him."

The woman nodded, several times as though trying to convince herself, "Yes, he will be better with you. He cried all night and I could not comfort him or quench the fever. Then I saw the blood, and the mark of Set's fingers. I knew I could not fight alone against Set."

She held out the child, still hidden in the heavy cloak, to Kiyas. "Take him." In a flat voice without emotion she went on, "If you try to keep him away from me I shall kill you." Then her voice rose, "You don't believe me? I'll show you the knife; it's very sharp; it was my husband's."

The knife was of the kind used to cut hides; the blade slightly curved and polished to a keen edge. She held it on her palm and stroked it with the forefinger of the other hand. "This knife and my son are the two things I love; the knife brings death if anything should take him from me."

Kiyas seemed indifferent to what the woman was saying. She drew back a corner of the cloak. The face of the sick child was shiny with sweat so I knew it was not already dead. Kiyas settled it more comfortably in her arms and then walked swiftly down the path ahead of us.

The child lived three days. Ptah-aru fought hard for it; but though it rallied a little each time he charged its feeble Ka the fever had gained too strong a hold thus to be vanquished. The first night and day the mother would not leave it, and even then, though she was so exhausted she was almost blind with sleep, she would not rest until Kiyas had promised not to leave the child until she returned. Kiyas had told me to let the woman sleep in her room, and whispered that she would be given the poppy drink that brings deep sleep.

Kiyas would not rest until I told her that this child might be only the first of many for whom she must guard her strength, and she made me promise to call her if he showed any change while I watched by him. The little boy's skin felt cold in spite of the oppressive heat. Sometimes his eyes were open, in them there was the bright terror of an injured bird, yet they did not seem to see me, either as a source of fear or as a friend. I asked if he wanted his mother, but he kept on saying, "Dodi, dodi, dodi." I thought dodi must be the name of a toy, so I twisted some rags into the rough shape of a doll, and this seemed to comfort him. I tried to give him some milk, but even a few drops brought on the black vomit, and it was the same after a sip of wine or of water. The sickness left him so exhausted I could do nothing to answer his cry of "Thirsty! Thirsty!" Each time I replaced the soiled cloths with fresh ones I saw the livid marks were spreading over his body; they were a deeper blue and seemed almost as though pitted into the flesh.

One of the soldiers shared my watch, taking away the cloths, sodden with blood and filth, to burn them. On the second day the child was less restless, and I saw his mother believed he would get well. He was drowsy and seemed content to lie in her arms. When we tried to feed him with milk he turned his head away, and it dripped out of the side of his mouth for he was too weak to swallow. The mother wanted to be alone with him, so Kiyas and I left her for a little while, telling her to call if she needed us.

I think we all believed we were winning this battle against Set, for it was the first time we had seen the pestilence. Twice Kiyas went into the room, and the woman whispered the child was sleeping quietly. Suddenly we heard a scream: so inhuman that for a moment we thought it must be an animal. We rushed toward the sound. . . .

A crazed woman was standing by the bedplace, on which lay the grotesque body of a child that had died and grown rigid while she thought it slept. She had been holding it close to her, and in death it was curved to the cradle of her arms.

Twenty-seven people in our town became victims of the Blue Death, and of these nineteen came under the care of Kiyas and me. Eleven were healed by Ptah-aru before the blue marks showed on the skin, and though the pestilence followed the same course as it had with the child, the onslaught was never so terrible. The black vomit and the issue of blood grew less on the third day and ceased on the fifth, before the one struck down had lost the strength to fight his way back to health. But even in those who recovered the battle was arduous.

For thirty days Kiyas only slept when she was too tired to work any longer, and ate only when I told her she would not be able to go on unless she did. She grew so thin that there were shadows under her cheek bones, and the bones of her wrists and shoulders were sharp under the skin. Every day I thought she would take the pestilence, but though her eyes were bright with lack of sleep they did not show the glitter of fever.

Because of her the soldiers worked tirelessly. There were seven with us in the house, as well as those who prepared food, carried away soiled bedding, and heated the water, in which the sick were frequently washed to cool the fever and cleanse the filthy stench which clung to them.

It was not till afterwards I learned that one of the men who burned the dead had himself contracted the pestilence. Rather than add himself to the burden of the sick he crept away, after having sworn a comrade to secrecy, to an empty hut on the outskirts of the town. I think that even Set must have quailed before such courage, for he fought the filth alone, and lived.

The ordered sequence of the days before the pestilence seemed as remote as though they belonged to another century. Sleep and food were snatched when they became necessities; our horizon had narrowed to the three largest rooms in the Overseer's House, where the sick and dying lay in rows. I think we were too tired to realize we were winning our battle, winning because no new victims had been brought to us for nine days.

I was awakened from a brief sleep by the noise of a distant crowd. I got up and opened the shutters; it was noon and the sunlight was searing as hot metal. I leaned out, trying to hear the words that ran like a ripple through the distant muttering. As it grew nearer, I heard, "The river! The river is rising, rising. . . ."

For a moment I did not realize all that this meant. The start of the Inundation was always a time of rejoicing, but this year the river would bring us even more than the promise of future harvests. Set had no power over the new river, only over stagnant waters which had lost the power of their own vitality. It would wash the earth free of the pestilence, as we had tried to wash clean the bodies of the afflicted. "The river is rising! A cubit since dawn, and mounting as we watch. . . ."

Already the air seemed to have gained freshness from the new water. The nine we still had in our care felt new life flowing into them: even the weakest of them, a young woman, raised herself on her arm and drank from the cup I gave her without needing to be supported.

I went to Kiyas's room. She was putting on a clean tunic; at Ptah-aru's advice we changed our clothes three times a day.

"We've won, Kiyas! The pestilence is losing its strength, and now the Inundation will drive it out of the Oryx, out of all Egypt." She didn't answer and I thought she didn't understand. "The river's rising! They say it's risen more than a cubit since dawn!"

She sat on the edge of the narrow bed and pushed her heavy hair back from her forehead. Her lips were pale, and there was sweat on her forehead and in the hollow of her upper lip. "I'm sorry I'm stupid today, Ra-ab: it's the heat, it seems to press down on me. There's anger in the air, I think there's going to be a storm."

"Have you been sick?" I tried to make my voice sound casual, while I sent out a desperate call, "Don't let Kiyas take it. Don't let her; not now when she's done so much. . . ."

She knew what I was thinking. "No, Ra-ab, it's not that. I know I'm not going to get it. At the beginning I wasn't sure. When the smell made me sick—did you know I was sick?" I nodded, and she went on, "I thought that was the beginning of it; but now I know I'm not going to get it, so I don't have to pretend to be brave. Were you frightened too?"

"Yes, very—at least I was when I had time to think about it. Usually I was too tired, or too busy, to think."

"Yes, I know," she said. "You thought I was brave because I wanted to go on without resting. That wasn't brave, it was only because I was frightened of having time to think. Sometimes I thought I saw the blue spots on myself and sometimes on you—I don't know which was the worst. Then I used to dream about it, and so I dreaded going to sleep. Even Anilops couldn't help me."

"Yes, I know what you mean. I had dreams too. The worst one was when we both had it and we were on the opposite sides of a long room. We were the only people there, and we were both terribly thirsty and crying out for water. We were each too weak to crawl to the other, yet neither of us was sure why the other didn't come."

"I remember that too; there was a jar of water in the middle of the room, too far for either of us to reach."

I put my hands on her shoulders and shook her gently, "Don't think about that, Kiyas—not yet, we're too near it. It's a good thing we dare speak about it, because that shows we're not frightened any longer. You daren't admit to being frightened when you really are."

She laughed, a little shakily. "Dear Ra-ab, I am a fool. I thought that if I was ever sure of not getting the Blue Death I should never worry about anything again. But now that I am sure—though I don't know why I am, I deliberately try to frighten myself with the memory of a nightmare."

Flood Water

EIGHT DAYS after the news of the Inundation the last of the afflicted were well enough to return home. Sebek came to tell us that he had had no new victim for twenty days and so there seemed no need for us to continue to stand armed against the pestilence. I decided that I would go with Kiyas to see Father before returning to the House of the Captains, and Sebek was to go part of the way with us on the following day.

Everything used by the sick had been burnt; or, as in the case of food and drinking vessels, broken and buried. The three main rooms were empty, the walls still streaked with damp where they had been scrubbed, and tomorrow the herbs which Nefer-ankh had sent would be burned in each room as a final purification before the Overseer returned.

The town was near the river, and already the outlying fields were covered by the Inundation. Villages on the higher ground stood like islands, and roads were causeways between flooded fields. By dusk the wind was rising; loose shutters banged in the wind and drafts sighed under the doors. We went outside, down the entrance steps whose edges were blurred with dust.

"The wind is against the water," said Sebek. "If it increases there will be danger."

I did not take his warning seriously: the pestilence was still too near to accept the possibility of another source of danger. It was too windy for a pleasant walk, so we went back to the house. Sebek was sharing my room and we were soon asleep.

I woke with the crash that had brought me back still sounding in my ears. Cold air was pouring down on me from above. The door swung open: Kiyas stood there shading a lamp with her hand and Sebek jumped up, blinking at the light. There was a big hole in the roof over my bed, and I knew that the tree which grew close to the house must have been blown down and crashed through the thin mudbrick.

"It has been getting worse for a long time," said Kiyas. "You had better get dressed. There's water in the garden, but it's too dark to see how far it extends."

The wind was so loud she had to shout to make us hear, and our shadows leaped and flickered on the wall as she tried to shield the lamp from the wind. We heard voices coming from the room at the end of the house, and found the soldiers had come in from the servants' quarters where they usually slept. They told us their roof had been blown away, and that water had been lapping over the doorsill before they left. There were fifteen of them, for I had sent the others back to their own village as soon as I heard from

72

Sebek that he had sent his own men home.

"We can't do anything until it's light," said Sebek. "So we had better try to get some sleep."

I nodded. "I'll fetch our bedding and take it into Kiyas's room."

The fury of the wind was held back in the central hall, and the flame of the lamp Kiyas still carried burned clearly as she went ahead of us. Suddenly she stopped and pointed to something hidden by the shadows at the end of the hall. For a moment I thought it was a snake, crawling toward us from under the closed door. But it was water, narrow and dark on the smooth stone of the floor, winding toward us, alive, in search of prey. It was only water; yet fear was borne on it, as tangible an enemy as a fleet of alien war galleys.

The fear I felt was echoed in Kiyas's voice. "We shall have to go out to meet it . . . now. We had forgotten that this house stands higher than the rest of the town. People may have been calling for us to tell them what to do, and the storm has made us deaf to their voices."

I knew that the room in which the soldiers had taken shelter was on a higher ground than the rest of the house; it was there that the injured must be taken. "Kiyas, we'll take ten men with us and leave five with you. There is still some unused linen in the storeroom; have it torn into strips for bandages and get everything ready. There may be a lot of people badly hurt. Tell them to. . . ."

Kiyas interrupted. "I know what to do; and I shall only need three men to help me. The kitchen is higher than the rest of the servants' quarters, and I'll tell one of them to get a fire going, so as to have some hot food ready for the people you bring here. There's some bedding that was not used so I'll get that laid out. And there are four jars of wine with the seals still unbroken. You just get the people here and I'll look after them."

Sebek had gone to fetch the men. Kiyas put her hand on my arm. "Ra protected us from the pestilence; he'll protect us from Set again now. It's only while the darkness lasts that I'm afraid for you, until Ra returns and sees what Set has done to us. If Sebek thinks you should wait until it is light, do what he tells you. You mustn't let yourself be drowned . . . it wouldn't be brave, it would be betraying the Oryx. You won't forget it's silly being brave sometimes, will you?"

Sebek came back, and I saw he had found a coil of rope. He said, "If the water is too deep we can rope ourselves together, it will save any one of us being swept away. And if we don't need it I expect we shall find some who do."

He swung from its socket the heavy wooden bar that held the door closed. Although he had his weight against it, the door swept him aside and crashed against the wall. Thin water flowed across the floor; the wind raged into the sanctuary made by the thick walls of the hall and plucked the light from the lamp.

I had to shout to make Kiyas hear. "We'll get this door shut and go out the other way."

It took eight men to force the door back, but the cedar planks were thick and well seasoned so they held. It was easier at the back of the house, which was sheltered by the servants' quarters, and the water was only ankle deep. A soldier splashed past me toward the kitchen, a bag of meal slung across his back.

The men were told to keep a hand on the shoulder of the man in front. We went in two files, Sebek and I leading, which were to keep as near to each other as possible until we got into the town.

The wind plucked at the palm trees as though they were slack harp-strings. Now the water was up to our knees. . . . The clouds which had made the night so dark were rent, and the sudden moon seemed bright as torches in a shuttered room. I saw then the power of Set's new onslaught: this was no steady rising of the river; the Great Aqueduct had broken and the two mighty walls which last year had made a new arm of the river, carrying water beyond the previous limits of the Inundation, had failed. Was the river angry that we had tried to change its course? Had Ra refused to accept as his child this bridge of water although it was dedicated in his name?

The water was flowing as a wide river toward the town. It was waist deep, flowing with us, but faster than we could move. A drowned ass swept past, like a leaf washed down a gutter when a sluice is opened.

Now it was dark again; but we could go faster than before because we knew we had to follow the course of the water. Something washed against me; I thought one of the men had stumbled, and put out a hand to steady him. He seemed to be swimming, trying to cling to me. I lifted him up; the body was inert and I held it in my arms above the water. . . . Which of our soldiers was so small? I shouted, "Sebek! Wait, one of them is hurt!"

The moon shone out for a moment as he struggled toward me. His voice was sharp above the noise of the wind, "It's no good carrying her. She's dead. Look at the wound in her head."

There was terror in me. . . . Was it Kiyas that I held? "Ra! don't let this be Kiyas! It *can't* be Kiyas, she is safe inside the house. . . ." I found the courage to look down at the woman in my arms. And I could hear Sebek's voice again, for she was a stranger. "We've got to look after the living, we've no time for the dead. Drop her, Ra-ab, we'll have to leave her to the water."

I tried to speak loudly to myself inside my head, "Don't be a fool! She's not the only corpse you'll see tonight, and none of them will be Kiyas. Kiyas is safe, safe, safe. You're frightened! You *must* be frightened, otherwise you wouldn't have picked up a dead woman. Put her down, you fool! Quick!"

My arms fell to my sides. For a moment the water covered her disfigured face; and then she floated, staring up at the moon. She swept ahead, her hair streaming out like weed in the current; as though to lead us.

Sebek was a little ways ahead of me and when I reached the first house he had already broken down the door. Part of the wall had been crushed in by the water and the moon shone down into the only room. It seemed empty; or, if they who lived there had been trapped, the water held them down.

There was no one there still living and we must not be concerned with the dead.

The second house was empty, and the third. But the next was built higher than the others, and as I got into the shelter of the wall I heard a woman screaming, the thin sound shattered by the wind. The walls were strong and still held against the assault of the water, and as the door faced west it was protected from the full force of the current. I flung myself against it until the bones of my shoulder felt as though they would pierce through the skin. I shouted to the woman to unbolt it but she must have been deaf with fear.

The window was high up and I could only reach it by climbing on the shoulders of the man next to me. The shutters were fastened but I forced them easily, and before climbing into the house I told the men to go on to help the others under Sebek's orders.

There was an upper story to the large single room, from which a ladder led down. The room above was lighted, and I could see that the water, smooth as black oil, was creeping up toward it. I let myself down by my hands, to find, as I had expected, that the floor of the lower room was a cubit below ground level. I had to swim to the ladder; and closed in from the wind I could hear that the screaming was a stream of words.

"Set, forgive me my betrayal of you! It is not my sin; it is the priests who have betrayed you. It was they who told me to put Ra in my sanctuary. They told me Ra had mastered Set, and that you, the Lord of the Dark Moon, ruled only in the Caverns. But now I have come to your kingdom, O Dark Master. Protect me! You took my son. You took my husband. I saw the print of your hand on their bodies. Have you forgotten that when I saw your seal on them I denied Ra? I knew Ra could not protect them. I kept them here, hidden away. I beseeched you not to punish them for my sin. It was I who sinned; I who told them to follow Ra, I who led them to the Oryx and told them to forget the dark hours of your rule and make their offering only to Ra of the High Noon. Why have you sent the water to punish me? My second son went out at sunset and has not returned. He has joined his brother and his father; they wait for me in your Caverns. Bind me with your thongs, but let them go free on your dark water."

The woman was not old in years, but fear and grief had scarred her face with the claws of age. She had made an altar; a square block, covered with linen; stiff, dark red. On it there was a statue of Set, about a cubit high, in his female form of Sekmet the cat-headed. He was false even in his likeness, clay smeared with bitumen in pretense of basalt. A lamp burned in front of the statue, a wick floating in a clay dish which was shaped like a scarab beetle on its back; the sacred beetle, dead and defiled. The oil filled the room with a heavy, pungent scent that sought to cloy a heavier, darker, stench.

The woman flung herself down, cringing before the altar. I

wondered if she were mad. I said, "Get up! I've come to take you to where you will be safe. You'll be drowned if you stay here."

She got slowly to her feet, her sweat-sodden tunic clinging to her body like the wrappings of a mummy. Her eyes were wide and unseeing. "So you have come! Or are you his son? You are too young for so old a God, so strong a God. I am ready. I knew you would come when the water reached the top of the ladder."

She pushed back the hair that hung down over her face in greasy strands. Her eyes had lost their blank stare. "You are the Lord of Fear, yet I am not afraid of you. You have come as an honored guest. See, I have made all preparation, though I am a poor woman, too poor to make your vessels of gold. I will pay your price, but you must pledge in the Name of Set that you will release my husband and my sons when I have paid. They wait for you, hidden by the linen they darkened at your command with the blood of their bowels. The priests of the Oryx would have burned their hearts, their lungs, their bowels, or sealed them in canopic jars with spells you could not break. But the bodies I buried in the ground behind this house were empty; so the ones you took to the Caverns are cold as a clay figurine. You cannot hold their spirits in your world, nor I their flesh in mine. I am a woman, old and poor, with but a little barrier to keep out death. Yet I will barter with you! Their souls against their flesh; my soul, if you will let their spirits free."

She made the sign of the sealed lips. "Do not answer before you have seen my offerings. I am not a fool; I do not try to barter with Set in gold, I know his scales."

She backed toward the crude altar, stooped down and picked up two jars concealed there. They were of clay and a shape common in the market-place, perhaps they had once held myrrh or spices.

I wanted to stop her, but I stared, held in the grip of an awful fascination. She began to pick at the sealings of the jars with the dirty forefinger of a hand that must have once been beautiful. I seemed to hear Nefer-ankh's voice, "You must never run from fear. To fear Set is to acknowledge him. See his works and know them; then shall your eyes be open to seek a weapon that shall break his power. That is the wisdom you must seek, to know what weapon to use against each snare. Courage without wisdom can never be enough." I knew Nefer-ankh was right. What weapon can I use to sever her thongs?

She had broken the sealings, and now drew out the plugs of wax which closed the jars. A stench, heavy as oil, flowed into the room. Her voice sank to a whisper, harsh as brittle bones which grate together. "Incense to your nostrils, O Lordly Son of the Dark Moon. Can you deny your Master so rich a gift? What use has he for the spirits of two poor Egyptians—spirits who will flutter round his Caverns like birds lost at the spring migration? How could he feast on the sighing of their wings? But here he has food, food that he loves; the savor beyond all incense burnt to Ra. And he shall see my soul laboring in the Caverns, to make him smile when he has feasted well!"

I tried to break the circle of her fear. "I am not Set; I am a child of Ra."

It was the first time I had seen terror walk unmasked. She cringed away from me, and stood against the wall, her head thrown back, her mouth wide open. Then she screamed: and I knew what a prisoner of Set would hear in the Underworld.

There was a voice behind me, a warm, soldier's voice. Benik looked up through the opening in the floor. "I came back to see if you wanted any help." He seemed quite undisturbed by the screams and went on, "She's gone mad. There's only one thing to do when they scream like that; throw water over them or give them a good hard slap." He grinned. "One thing we *have* got is plenty of water! Shall I look after her, Captain?"

I nodded. He picked up a crock, bent down and scooped up water and flung it over the screaming woman. The water streamed down her face and ran out of the corners of her mouth; but she did not stop screaming. He looked at me, and without waiting for orders hit her hard on the neck below the ear with the side of his open hand . . . a blow Sebek had taught me. He picked her up and slung her over his shoulder, saying apologetically, "It's the first time I've ever hit a woman. My grandmother's sister went off just like that every time she saw a snake; but we didn't have a flood at the same time so I could argue with her. Better hurry, Captain. The water's halfway up the window."

"Yes," I said, "we'd better hurry. I shouldn't have stayed here so long."

He went ahead of me down the ladder, carrying the woman carefully in his arms. Before I followed him I knocked the statue off the altar. It was only clay smeared with bitumen; only clay smeared with bitumen—nothing to be afraid of. The head snapped off and rolled into a corner. The light caught the eyes; it seemed as though they blinked, lazily, like a cat content to wait.

I overturned the lamp; and the burning oil lapped at the matting with which the floor was covered. As I climbed down the ladder I looked back; the altar was already ringed with fire, the darkened line curling in the heat. "Ra has beaten you, Set! Fire is stronger than you are! You can't even make your shadows except by our light!"

My voice echoed back against the storm. "Ra . . . Set! Ra . . . Set! Ra . . . Set!"

As I climbed down the ladder I saw that Benik had already swum across the room. With the woman over his shoulder he slid down outside the window which was by now half covered in water. The woman's eyes were open, turned up under the lids.

The square of smooth water between me and the window was brilliantly lit by the fire above. A crack like black lightening ran down the wall in front of me. I was still holding on to the ladder. The wall pressed inwards, divided, swung open like a water-gate. The roar of the flood drowned the sharp crackling of the fire. I was plucked from the rung, sucked down into the roaring darkness. . . .

I seemed to see the eyes of Sekmet blinking at me in leisurely enjoyment. A hand, whose fingers were three cubits long, was crushing my ribs. . . . The light is above me; I must fight upwards towards it. Give me strength! Ra is stronger than Set!

I seemed to fight for a year against dark water. . . .I can breathe! I can breathe! Set has not sealed my nostrils with his clay!

The water had found its level. I was floating, staring up at the floor above me on which fire was scoring lines. The heat thrust down on me, trying to push me under the water. . . . I must get out where the water came in. There must be a hole in the wall through which I can escape. But it's under water. I can't go under water; the hand is there; it's waiting for me.

You will be burned to death if you are a coward. Do you want to be burned as a coward? The hand is not stronger than Ra. Set is not stronger than you unless you fear him. Dive, you fool! Swim against the current. You know that is the only way to freedom. You must always swim against the current.

I tried to fill my lungs. Oh, for one long breath of clear air! The heavy smoke is drowning me like water. You must not drown or you betray the Oryx! You will betray Ra if Set conquers you! . . . Down! Down! Swim against the current. . . .

The deep water is quiet as the tomb of the Ancient Ones. The pain is on the surface, where water fights with fire. But in the depths there is quiet and peace. Why should you go on struggling when you are so tired? My hand is not your enemy; rest in its strength and you need fight no longer.

"Don't listen to Sekmet! Swim against the current, and you will be free, free. . . ."

I felt the rough bricks of the outer wall and thrust against them with my feet. The water was solid as a wall of earth, yet it could not hold me. . . . I can breathe! The air is clear! . . .

I opened my eyes, and saw the moon serene between the clouds. The stream was carrying me away from a house that burned against the dark.

It must have been several minutes before I tried to find if the water was too deep for me to stand. I thought it would have got much deeper while I was in the house of Set, but I found that my arms were above the surface when I stood upright. Ahead of me I could see torches streaming out in the wind. As I drew nearer I saw that the flat roofs of all the larger houses were well above the level of the water and were crowded with people. Three men waded toward me pushing in front of them a raft made of two doors roughly lashed together. I realized that the flow of water was much slower than it had been earlier. A woman lay on the raft; she was unconscious, one arm trailed in the water and the other was in a position which showed that it had been broken above the elbow. Beside her was a child about a year old. It was screaming angrily, and pummeling the air with small clenched fists.

One of the men pushing the raft was a soldier and I shouted to him to ask where was Sebek. He told me that he had last seen him in the center of the town, where the people were being assembled in the market-place as the water was shallower there than in the adjoining streets.

I wondered if the storm was really abating or if I had merely grown accustomed to incessant noise. I passed two more parties of men pushing rafts on which lay injured people. I knew that Sebek would have been to every house I passed so did not stop at any of them.

The ground sloped up toward the market-place, and when I reached it the water was only to my knees. By the light of torches, Sebek was directing people how to salvage their possessions. Goats had been herded within the shelter of the garden of the largest house, and sacks of grain were being carried up on the flat roofs.

I reached Sebek. "What can I do to help? I stayed behind in one of the first houses; a woman there had gone mad, but I shouldn't have stayed so long. Benik came back to look for me. Then the wall broke just after he got out. Is he all right?"

"I haven't seen him. Was the woman hurt?"

"We had to hit her before we could get her out."

"Then Benik will have taken her to Kiyas. You'd better go back to Kiyas too, she'll need your help. The water's not rising any more; either it's found its own level or the aqueduct has broken again further down. The worst of the danger is past, and I'm trying to save as many of their possessions as I can. They may panic if there's no one here to tell them what to do, but you'd better go back to Kiyas. Several people have been hurt—I don't yet know how many have been drowned. I can send Sayak with you."

Sayak had a torch; he led and I was glad to have him to follow. The current had lost its violence and we could make our way against it without much effort. We were nearly home before I realized the wind had dropped. Light was showing between the shutters and the water had receded below the second step of the entrance opposite the servants' quarters.

Kiyas was coming out of the storeroom. She ran to me, "Oh, Ra-ab, I've been so frightened about you. Benik told me he last saw you in the house from where he brought the woman. He said he looked back when he got her part of the way here and saw the house was on fire. He thought it might have been the one you had been in, and when he realized he hadn't seen you come out of it he nearly dropped her and went back to look for you. Was it the house you were in?"

"Yes, but I'm all right. I got out before the fire got properly started. I set it alight myself; I'll tell you why tomorrow. How many people are here?"

"Only twelve who are hurt. There are quite a lot of women and children, but they are looking after each other. I've managed to give them some hot food. I got it ready before the first of them reached here."

"Where did you put them?"

"They're in the two big rooms at the other end of the hall. As soon as you'd gone I burned the herbs that Nefer-ankh sent us. We didn't have time to do it for as long as he told us to, but I had to take the risk of putting people in there. There was no room for them anywhere else. When you got here I was looking for some rags and a narrow piece of wood to set a broken arm. Have you ever set an arm? I haven't; I do wish Ptah-aru hadn't gone back to the temple."

"Are many of them badly hurt?"

"No, there's only the woman with the broken arm and a man who was crushed under a falling beam. He says there is a terrible pain in his stomach, and he's badly bruised over his ribs, but I don't think any bones are broken."

"Have you given him a sleep-drink?"

"Yes, but it doesn't seem to have done much good. He's still moaning. Benik is putting hot cloths on him and that seems to help."

She looked tired and very young; yet she was strong in her own authority. "Do you think I'd better set the arm, Ra-ab, or would you like to try it first?"

"You'll do it better than I could, but I'll come and help."

"It's going to hurt her a lot. The sleep-drink doesn't seem to have done her much good either; it doesn't seem to work as well as it did with the pain of the pestilence."

82

The woman was lying on the mattress nearest the door. I recognized her as the woman I had seen unconscious on the raft. The bone of the upper arm had not pierced the skin, but it was pressing against it and looked like a second elbow. Kiyas knelt beside her. The woman tried to smile; she reminded me of when my favorite hound had licked my face while I was cutting a poisoned thorn out of its pad.

"You hold her other hand, Ra-ab."

Gently Kiyas tried to straighten the arm; the blood drained from the woman's face and her thin fingers dug into my palm.

"This is going to hurt a lot," Kiyas told her. "You are very brave. I wish I was as brave as you are." She gave a sudden strong, steady pull at the hand and forearm. The woman shuddered, and I saw that the teeth clenched on her lip to keep back a cry were stained with blood. But the arm was straight, and there was no longer a projection under the bruised flesh.

I helped Kiyas to set the splint in position; a pad of soft rags in the armpit and another above the elbow before it was closely bandaged. I sat with her while Kiyas fetched her a bowl of broth. I smelt the drowsy scent of poppies as I fed her with it.

"You will soon be asleep," said Kiyas. "Soon be asleep, asleep...."

The woman nodded. Already her eyelids were heavy. "Yes, I shall soon be asleep. The Oryx has protected me: I shall soon be asleep...."

Benik joined Kiyas and me as we left the sleeping woman. "The injured man is drowsy now," he said. "I don't think there is anything else we can do for him. He says the pain's much easier. Couldn't you rest? I'll call you if anyone needs you.

"Yes, Benik, I'll leave them in your care. But call me at once if you need me."

Kiyas led me to the storeroom. "We'll have to sleep in here; there's a woman and three children in my room."

We spread our sleeping-mats side by side. There was no window, only a grating high in the wall. I took off my sodden clothes, and was just rolling myself up in the woollen cover to try to get warm, when I suddenly remembered the woman of the house of Set.

"Kiyas, where's the woman that Benik brought here? She's not in with the others?"

"I'll tell you about her in the morning."

"No, I want to know now."

"Please, Ra-ab, wait until the morning. You can't do anything now."

I sat up, no longer sleepy. "You've got to tell me, Kiyas. Did Benik hit her too hard? Is she dead?"

"Oh, Ra-ab, I *do* wish you wouldn't worry about her tonight. She's not dead—at least her body isn't. Her eyes are open but they don't seem to see anything, though she's not blind. She doesn't hear when I speak to her, yet she begins to scream and cringes away from something I can't see. They are terrible screams, Ra-ab. I think even Benik is frightened of them, though he tried to make me believe that one of his relations sometimes behaved just the same. He says it's because she was so frightened of the flood, but I don't think he believes that any more than I do."

"Where have you put her?"

"She's in the little room where the wine used to be kept, next to the kitchen quarters. I couldn't keep her here because she frightened the others too much. I tried to give her a strong poppy drink, but she thought I was Sekmet trying to poison her and I couldn't make her swallow it. What's happened to her, Ra-ab? I've never seen anyone like that, in terror beyond terror."

"You shouldn't have left her alone without someone to guard her. She might kill herself before we could find out how to protect her from Set."

"I thought of that. I had to tie her hands to her sides because she was trying to bite open the vein in her wrist. She said she was making Set impatient because he was thirsty for her blood. I was frightened of her. So frightened I almost wanted to kill her. I've never felt like that except about snakes."

"She sold herself to Set and we've got to get her back again. We've *got* to prove that we can protect our people."

"Ra-ab, she's *mad*. It's not Set, she's just gone mad."

"That's only a word for something we don't really understand. Listen, and I'll tell you what I know about her. . . ."

As I spoke it seemed as though I was back in the little fetid room. The water was pressing down on me, and still I could hear the echo. . . . "Ra . . . Set." "Ra . . . Set."

"Don't, Ra-ab! Don't remember any more! She belongs to Set, not to us. She deserves the Caverns for having tried to bring filth into the Oryx."

"That's not true. Fear is her only sin. We were not strong enough to break her fear, and that is why she turned to Set. She knew of the Caverns, and yet she was ready to suffer them for eternity if the spirits of her son and her husband might go free. Would you call me a coward if I would go to the Caverns to free your soul? Don't you realize that for her we must fight as Ra's children against *his* enemy?"

"I don't know any magic. What *can* we do?"

"We've both got to learn about magic, or how can the Oryx be a *real* protection? We must take her to Nefer-ankh as soon as possible—as soon as Sebek comes back. He'll be able to look after the people here, but we've got to learn to deal with people like her."

Invocation to Ra

BY THE TIME I was awake Kiyas had already seen Sebek, who had come back soon after dawn, and arranged that we were to take the mad woman to Nefer-ankh without delay. Sebek told us that the water was receding rapidly, and as the Temple of Ra was to the northwest I knew we should be able to reach it without having to cross that part of the country most severely affected by the flood. A messenger had been sent to the first town on the higher ground telling the overseer to have litters, each with four litter-bearers, waiting to take us to the temple. Until we reached them Kiyas and I would walk while two soldiers carried the mad woman in an improvised litter.

The journey was fairly easy; the sky was cloudless and the water slept under the power of Ra. We reached the temple just after sunset to find that Nefer-ankh was expecting us, for we had previously arranged to see him on our way back to the House of the Nomarch. He had more news of the flood than we had, and told us that the only other town seriously damaged had suffered less than ours.

One of the houses within the temple enclosure was still occupied by three men who were slowly regaining their strength after the pestilence; but another house was empty, and it was there that the woman was taken. We were to sleep in one of the priest's rooms behind the temple.

Nefer-ankh sent one of the younger initiates to bring sleep to the woman, and then said he wished to hear all we could tell him about her before deciding on a method of treatment.

After hearing our story, Nefer-ankh said that as she was sleeping quietly he would watch her while he too was asleep, so as to discover whether her madness was due to terror or whether she was possessed by the spirit of one who had become a slave of Set.

I tried to remember if I saw Nefer-ankh while I was asleep that night, but I must have been too tired to bring back a true record, and only a few minutes seemed to pass before I woke to see one of the temple pupils standing beside me. He was a boy of about my own age, wearing the white tunic bordered with yellow of one who is soon to take his first initiation.

He said, "Nefer-ankh asks that you and your sister will join him in the sanctuary as soon as you are prepared."

I followed the morning ritual of the temple. After the three prayers of the Eastern Horizon I swam in the temple pool whose water is under the protection of Nut. Then I put on a tunic of white linen and the sandals of they who follow the way of the priest. With my head uncovered I went to the Sanctuary of Ra to stand before his statue, bathed in the shaft of light which shone from his sky through the sacred opening in the temple roof. Here Kiyas joined me, and when she too had made her invocation we waited in silence for Nefer-ankh.

He came through the doorway behind the statue, followed by two young priests who carried between them a litter on which lay the woman. They put the litter down before the altar, and then at her head and feet they set canopic jars of oil in which burned wicks of violet linen.

Nefer-ankh, standing with his head upraised toward the light, made invocation to Ra. "Lord of the High Noon, by whose power all things have life. Let thy force, which is in the winds of the air, and in the earth, and in the seed of the grain below the earth; in the source of all rivers, and in the coming forth of leaves, and in the animals with which they share their strength; and in all mankind who live by thy divinity; give to this son of thy son until the thousandth generation; who am of men called Nefer-ankh, thy strength; by which I may bring forth into thy light this one whose spirit you have not yet named. Let there be your life in my fingers, so that I may make your sign living upon her forehead, so that the shadow is lifted and fear is a stranger unto her. Let thy seal be upon her mouth, so that no echo of the underworld cometh forth from between her lips. Let thy seal be upon her ears, so that the whispers of the unclean cannot enter therein. Let thy seal be upon her eyes so that they can see beyond the shadows to the beneficence of thy high noon. Let thy seal be upon her nostrils, so that myrrh and spikenard, coram and septes oil, are not so eager to them as is the incense of thy sanctuary. Let thy seal be upon her head and upon the palms of her hands, upon her breasts and upon her navel, upon the dividing of her loins, upon her knees and upon the soles of her feet. So that in her going forth and in her waking, in her nurture and in her breathing, in her seeing and her hearing, in her eating and her conceiving, in her traveling and her returning, she may know that she is no longer a nameless one, but a child of a child to the ten-thousandth generation of the Lord of the High Noon."

The light gathered into an intensity of light until it seemed that Nefer-ankh himself was born of it. Then the young priests lifted up the litter, on which the woman still lay as the dead. And Nefer-ankh touched her upon her head and upon her eyes, upon her ears, upon her mouth, and upon her nostrils. Then did he make the sign of Ra upon her breasts and her navel, upon the knees and the dividing of her loins and upon the soles of her feet.

Then did he say, "Set, I challenge you to come forth from your Caverns to do battle against the name of Ra for this child, Katani, who is new-born out of the womb of the earth under the sun, no longer nameless but pledged by Ra's name to our company.

"Come forth, Set! Come forth, Sekmet and your shadowed host! Or judge yourself that this your link is broken. Come forth to my challenge in the name of Ra!"

The woman stirred and put her hand to her forehead like a sleeper waking. She sat up; slowly her eyes opened. They were fixed on the great statue of He in whose name she had been dedicated; and there was no fear in them, nor any madness, nor any evil.

Slowly she stood up. She was no longer old, though her face was still in the pattern of many years. Slowly she lifted her hands, the palms upstretched to the Lord of the High Noon.

Then did she say to him, "I was in the Caverns, and I am free. . . . I set up the Lord of Fear, but Ra has taken me under his protection. I was the dead in the dark night, and now I am born again of the High Noon."

Nefer-ankh told us to wait for him in his room behind the sanctuary, for he wished to speak alone with the woman. I saw that Kiyas was deeply moved. She said, "I never realized that Nefer-ankh was so great a magician. I knew he was very wise, much wiser even than Nekht-Ra, but I didn't know a man could have so much power. Did you see what I saw, Ra-ab? How at first he was only a man standing in a shaft of light before a statue; and then the light seemed to flow into him, as though it were living water soaking into dry earth? And the statue wasn't only stone carved in the likeness of a god; it was part of Ra, as was Nefer-ankh."

It was the first time I had ever heard awe in Kiyas's voice. She had always said she didn't want to know about magic, that it was dull and only for scholars or for priests. When I reminded her of this, she said, "I didn't realize what it was like then, Ra-ab. I don't think I really believed anything happened, any more than all the scrolls Father reads really make any difference. But this was *alive*, more alive than I am. I don't think I believed that Ptah-aru did people much good when he healed them. I saw that they got better quicker than the others did, but I thought that was because they were stronger or not so frightened of Set. I thought I was being much more useful than he was with poppy-drinks and hot cloths and all the things I tried to do. Yet what could I do for that woman? Tie her hands so that she couldn't kill herself! I might have left her tied up like that for years, bound as a prisoner in Set's anteroom. However much we tried to help her we couldn't have *done* anything. I can't understand quite how Nefer-ankh made her safe, but I know we've seen something as great as if she had been dead and he had brought her to life again; for she was much more than dead. How did he do it, Ra-ab? How did he know?" Before I could say anything in reply, Nefer-ankh came into the room; and this is what he told us:

"You, Ra-ab, while asleep have seen others who are also free of their bodies going on with the same things that fill their waking day; the fisherman who is still casting his net although his boat is drawn up on the bank and his body sleeps in the hut beside the river; the husbandman who drives his plow, still singing to his oxen though they stand drowsing in their stall. You have seen also how each finds what he loves or sees his fear take shape. The singing plowman watches his grain spring from the earth in a single night, the stalks standing strong under their heavy yield; but the nets of a man of gloomy heart break when he draws them in, so that his great catch of fish is lost. Of such are the young in spirit who sleep to another Earth, as like to the one they know on waking as is a papyrus reed to its reflection in clear water.

"Gradually they become aware that the limitations of this other Earth are made by themselves. They find when they are asleep that they no longer need to walk from their house to the next village, for as their thought grows stronger it will obediently carry them, just as when the wing feathers of a fledgling are strong enough it learns to fly.

"But some there are who are resentful of their growing wings; perhaps they find that a jar of beer does not satisfy them as it did when they were awake. They think, 'This is not real beer. It tastes, it smells, it looks like beer, but if I think it is water I might as well have filled the jar at the pool where the cattle drink. Oh, that I were on Earth again, where beer is beer, and cannot be changed by speculation!' Or again he may say, 'Oh that I were on Earth, where my wife is the aging woman with whom I have lived in comfortable habit for thirty years, instead of turning into the young woman who says she is the girl I knew before our first son was born . . . and who expects to be flattered. I want to sit in the shade and drink my beer that no one can change to water!'

"When such as he comes to die, unless his body in age had given him pain which made him glad to be free for a time of such discomforts, he may well ask Khnum the Potter to set the clay of a new body on the wheel without delay. And if Khnum answers that he must wait his turn, then he will find the voice of a child of

Set sweeter than honey, when it whispers, 'Khnum the Potter is growing old, and his wheel turns slowly. What a pity that you must wait so long where all the joys of Earth are beyond your reach! I know of a young woman, her body ripe as a fig before the Inundation. It might have been you who enjoyed her . . . but you are only a soul now, a thing of no substance! If you tried to woo her with all your vigor, even if you were a most impetuous ghost, she would continue to listen for the footsteps of the young man from the next village.'

"The man may hear many such stories; each designed to increase those desires which can only be gratified through a physical body. Perhaps the voice will say, 'Khnum the Potter is *very* old, his wheel may stop before your turn comes. But you need not wait so long; and my way will be easier than his. You need not be born, to see your parents loom over your cradle, seeming to your infant eyes as large as hippopotami. No, you can choose your body and your place. Do you want to be rich? Then seek out a man whose storerooms are ranked with jars of gold-dust. Take *his* body and use it as your own: eat his rich food, feel smooth wine on your tongue, and enjoy the welcome of his concubines!'

"The man will ask, 'How can I do this?' And he will be told, 'Some people have barred themselves against unlawful entry, but the clever man can always find a door which the owner has been too lazy to bolt. Should he resist, then seek another house — or ask me again what you shall do. Remember that when the door is shut fast no one can open it save the owner of the house; but when the door is open you can go in without challenge, and the owner must give all he possesses into your care and cannot return without your permission. In his body you may eat beyond satisfaction . . . then go, so that he returns in time to feel the torment in his belly. And, if it pleases you, you may kill with the dagger in his hand . . . but you will have gone when the soldiers come to take him. All these pleasures you may have, and a thousand others. The price is so small: one can hardly call it a price, just a pledge on a bargain between friends.'

"If the man is still distrustful, and asks what will be required of him as his part of the bargain, then does the voice tell him, 'If Khnum should after all make you a new body of your own, you must make ready for us many Houses of the Open Door. There are many ways in which you can prevent bolts being made fast against us. Drunkards are easy to persuade, and some women when they are told that malachite no longer makes their eyes seem young, would open their door to any peddler who said he had youth for sale. Never disturb a lazy man, let him sit in the shade until even the bolting of his door against an uninvited guest seems too great an effort. *Never* tell a rich man that even if his gold is put with him in the tomb his soul will not find the value of its barter. Never tell him that gold and sand have the same weight in the Scales of Tahuti: let him sit among his treasures and forget the sky, and soon he too will forget to set a watch at his gate.'"

Nefer-ankh paused in his discourse, and smiled at Kiyas. "You wonder why I talk in parables when you want to know how Khatani, for that is her new name, has been made safe from Set? You cannot place the lintel on a new door to knowledge until the pylons are built; and before you could understand what I did to Khatani it was necessary for me to tell you how her body might have been possessed by an alien spirit, and how such spirits first come to break that Great Law which has decreed that none shall possess the body of another.

"To enter what is still known as the House of the Open Door is to share in the consequences with him who left the door unbarred. 'Will' is the name of our bolts, and only the weak— deliberately weak because of their own folly—allow entry or themselves enter unlawfully. For he that enters the Open Door will find that in his turn he cannot shut out an intruder. Set does not wish that those who follow in his train should be strong in their own will; it is his desire that they should be without power. They are only channels along which his power may flow at his command.

"From what Ra-ab told me, I knew that Khatani was trying to evoke Set, hoping that by the power he gave her she would be strong enough to take his prisoners from the Caverns. Since coming to the Oryx she had learned that no blood sacrifices are made to Ra, and that his temple tribute, be it of grain or fish, flowers or linen, must all be without blemish, and that only perfumed oils are burned at his festivals. She knew also that what is acceptable to Ra is shunned by Set.

"When she saw the marks of the Blue Death upon her husband and her child, she no longer tried to bring down to them the power of Ra; for to her it was a sign that Ra had been overthrown. There are always those, who when a city is taken try to gain favor by swift obeisance to the conqueror.

"Perhaps she had brought the statue with her into the Oryx—there are many shadows in the land of Egypt and it is not difficult to barter for a likeness of Sekmet. The dark blood of the bowels has long been used in the name of Set; for it is the blood of death, always in conflict with the scarlet of the heart. The oil she burned may have come from a black snake, or from the fat of a black pig or other unclean beast. In the rituals of Sekmet the fuel of the lamps is still more vile, but I think she would have been unable to obtain this further filth. She knew that Ra welcomes to his kingdom the spirit of man; flesh is furthest from the spirit, so it was with flesh she tried to barter for the souls she thought Set had enslaved.

"Away from my body I watched last night while she slept. She was reliving her scenes of terror, in even greater intensity than she had first known them. Her son died a few hours before her husband. She carried the boy's body down to the lower room. Hers was not the practiced skill of the embalmer: with unsure strokes she opened the belly of the child she loved, to drag out the viscera that were already rotting. She had to break the ribs with a heavy stone before she could excise the heart. The boy had died with his eyes open; she thought he stared at her reproachfully as she drove herself to mutilate his wasted body. And all the time she could hear the slow harsh breathing of the husband whom she dearly loved; whom she knew would soon lie dead, his body waiting for her to perform upon it this last rite by which she hoped to save his soul.

"When you saw her, Ra-ab, she had evoked Set many times. She had begun to think she had denied Ra only to find that Set thought her too contemptible to heed. She had a second son, but the boy was with his grandmother in another village when the pestilence came. He had returned home that morning, and she had told him that his father and brother were away on a journey; even from her neighbors she had managed to conceal their illness and their death. Just before the flood came she had sent him down to the market, as an excuse to get him out of the house so that she might make a last desperate evocation of Sekmet before she must hide her ritual away.

"When she saw Ra-ab she thought he had been sent by Set to bargain with her. And when Ra-ab said, 'I am a child of Ra,' was it strange that she knew a terror beyond terror? She worshipped Sekmet, the goddess of Fear; and she thought that Ra had come to punish her for giving allegiance to his enemy. How could she, who had given herself to fear, recognize any other power? She thought her husband and her son were lost to her forever, lost to her also was her dark protector. The lords of the Night and of the Day had both declared against her: there was no rest for her between dawn and sunset, nor till another dawn.

"Fear her ruler cried aloud, until from her past echoed ten thousand voices of all the fears she had ever known. Fear of the first fire she had seen, fear that came with the barking of hyenas, fear born of the eyes of waiting crocodiles, the fear of pain, of death, of separation; fear of being lost and alone, of the child crying in the dark; the fear known by old people that belong to a tribe who bury alive those who are no longer strong enough to work for the common need.

"She thought she crouched on a rock in the midst of a slowly rising tide in which was embodied millennia of fear. I spoke to her, but she could not hear me; and I knew that the power of her fear could be broken only if she summoned up the memory of all she had loved. I called on the name of Ra to let her see what was to her the symbol of her love, even as Sekmet had been the symbol of all her fear. And she saw her son and her husband standing beyond the tide of her fear, holding out their hands toward her. The water between them was turgid with the slow bodies of serpents. Yet when she saw her husband and her son, slowly, very slowly, she stood upright. Between her and them there was a ray of light, narrow as a gold thread. Gradually the serpents sank under the water, and in their place were reflected all the things she had ever loved. Yet they were formless; for the love that is for things of form can build no bridge across a chasm. Then did the golden thread of light grow; until at her feet a narrow causeway stretched between her and those she loved. And on it she crossed over the abyss; by the power of Ra which was the link that joined them.

"So you see, Ra-ab and Kiyas, it was not I who cured her madness. It was her love which drove out fear, and that love brought her into the protection of Ra. All I did was to invoke the power of Ra so that her body might be sealed against any emissary whom Set might send to demand the price which she had offered. In the name of Ra I gave her the new name; for the woman of fear is dead, and she who is Khatani is born again."

Beyond the River

BEFORE KIYAS and I left the temple, a messenger arrived from Sebek to say that the second son of Khatani had not been drowned and was being cared for at the Overseer's House. Sebek himself had gone to see to the work of repairing the breach in the aqueduct. The flood had done even more damage than we had feared, and so he wished me to bring as many soldiers as possible to help him. I persuaded Kiyas not to come with me, for I knew she was very tired; so I sent another messenger to the soldiers' village to summon help, and, telling Kiyas I would return to her as soon as possible, I set off to join Sebek.

For three days we fought to subdue the water into the channel which had been made for it. The soldiers worked in three shifts, at night by the light of torches. The people from the neighboring villages came to help us; bringing food for the men, and carrying baskets of earth which was rammed down behind the great stones after they had been dragged back into their original position.

On the morning of the fourth day all had been made safe, so with Sebek I returned to the soldiers' village where I decided to spend the night before going on to see Kiyas and Father. The weather had been calm since the storm which had come with the rising of the river, but the journey homewards was difficult, for much of the land we had to cross was flooded, and part of the way we had to wade knee-deep through muddy water.

Until we reached the House of the Captains I did not realize how exhausted I was. Even Sebek was so tired that he fumbled with the clasp of his cloak and had to be helped with it. The jar I used for washing had been filled with warm water, and my servant poured it over me to sluice away the mud. I only wanted to be left to sleep, but I was too tired to argue when he said he must first rub me with warm oil to prevent me getting fever.

Gradually I relaxed under his strong hands. For a moment I thought he was Niyahm and I a child again. The sound of water, rising, always rising, was still drumming in my ears. I asked him, "Can you hear the water from here?"

"No, it is quiet: the river is not angry any more. The wind has fallen. There's not a sound save the bark of a jackal."

Yet I could still hear the river when I drifted to sleep. . . .

I was in a boat. The water was quiet; hidden by mist. Then I saw the Anubis of the prow, and knew I was crossing the River, the river I had prayed so hard to find again. I was being taken to the Land without Shadows. . . .

She was standing on the bank waiting for me. She smiled, a little shyly. "This time, in case you couldn't find me, I didn't stay at the top of the avenue. I've been lonely for you: twice I thought I heard your boat coming through the mist; and then it turned back. Why have you been such a long time?"

"You mustn't let me go again without telling me how to get back here. Over there, beyond the mist and the cliff, I have to pretend to be a soldier. They dragged me back when you took me to Anubis: they are always trying to drag me back."

The river had vanished, and we were together in a little valley between gently sloping hills. She sat down on the grass, and I lay with my head in her lap. She said, "I have seen you since the Anubis time. We were somewhere else; not here beyond the river. It is difficult for me to get here sometimes."

I asked her the question which had lived with me since first I saw her, "When am I going to meet you while we're awake?"

"I don't know. Do you think we'll ever meet?"

"We must, we *must*! Tell me your name and make me say it over and over again so that I'll be sure to remember. And tell me the country you live in. . . . Even if it's the other side of the world I'll set out tomorrow to look for you."

She laughed. "How do you know I'm not an Asiatic? Or an old woman in the land of the Dragon People?"

"You're *not*. You mustn't tease me. We *must* belong to the same people and be the same age."

"How old are you?"

"I'm fourteen, Egyptian, and my name's Ra-ab."

"Ra-ab? That's easy to remember. . . . I wonder when you'll hear me say 'Ra-ab' when you're awake."

"What's your name?" I asked her.

"I'll tell you when you see me down there. Anubis said we followed the same path, so you *will* see me."

"You're only making it more difficult, but I shall find you. I'll go to every town in Egypt, to every house in every street until I find you!"

"But, Ra-ab, that wouldn't help you: I don't look like this when I'm awake. I think it's dull to look the same all the time. You'll know me when we meet, but not by what I look like, not by what I'm called. Shall I pretend not to recognize you? I shall recognize you; and I know your name, Ra-ab, and you look here as you do on Earth. What's happening to you over there? Something must be making it difficult for you to get back to this side of the river. Sometimes things get difficult for me too; I get tangled up in little unnecessary things, like a fish in a net."

"I think it's being a soldier, or pretending to be, that's making it difficult. When I was at home with Kiyas it was much easier to dream."

"Who's Kiyas?" she asked quickly.

"She's my sister."

She nodded. "Oh yes, I remember. I've seen her once with you, not here but somewhere else. She had a kind of lion with her she called Anilops—I'm glad she's your sister."

"You're not in love with any one?"

She shook her head. "Not on the other side of the River."

"But you are here; with me?"

"Am I? Perhaps. . . . But I shan't tell you until you see me down there, in case you don't love me then. I may be ugly, with a squint and black stumps of teeth. Or perhaps I'm fat."

"I'd love you even if you were fat; very, very fat."

"Dear Ra-ab! It is unfair you not knowing what I'm going to look like. But it's good for you to love me without knowing, because if we go on living till we're old I may grow ugly but you won't stop loving me. . . . And then we shall never be old on this side of the river."

"How did you know I love you?"

"Because otherwise I shouldn't have been waiting for you when you first came here as Ra-ab. The boat can only be sent to fetch you by one you really love. Oyahbe fetched me. It's curious that she should have made your body for you. I used to think she might be my mother, who died when I was too young to remember her . . . but now I know she couldn't have been."

"Have you ever seen your mother?"

"No, so I think she must have been only someone my father married. I don't really know him very well either. Will you always be a soldier?"

"No, it's only one of the things my father says I'll have to learn. I'm going home soon; when I've become a captain."

"You didn't always hate being a soldier. We both were, not very long ago. We fought in a battle together and drove the Asiatics out of Egypt—they were called 'Zumas' then. You liked being a warrior more than I did in those days—which is funny, as you'll know when you've remembered about that time we were together. I think I'm going to be wakened soon. I'm going on a short journey with my father, and we're starting at dawn. I would have made an excuse not to go with him if I'd known it was tonight we should be together, so we could have stayed here longer."

She bent over me. "Find me again soon, Ra-ab." And I woke with her kiss on my mouth.

PART III

The Gold Armlet

ON MY SIXTEENTH BIRTHDAY, Father gave me the gold armlet of a captain. I thought that now I should be free to begin that
special training which I hoped would enable me to become one
of the Eyes of Horus, the leaders of the Watchers of the Horizon
of Horus. It was difficult to hide my disappointment when I
found that I had only changed one routine for another. I had no
military duties, for though I was the head of the Household
Bodyguard this consisted of only thirty men; in the other Nomes,
whose Nomarchs never traveled without armed escort or left
their courts unguarded, it would have been considerably larger.
One day in every seven I sat beside Father when he gave audience, and after the first month he let me sit alone unless there
was a decision of more than usual importance to be made. Often
I had Kiyas beside me, for when I became Nomarch she would
give judgment in my absence.

There was little for me to do as petitioners were not numerous; only those dissatisfied with the decisions of their headman
came to the Nomarch, and of these there were few. I would have
asked Father to let me go to Hotep-Ra to learn those things for
which I was so eager, had I not seen how greatly he had aged in
the last three years. Perhaps it was not he who had grown heavy
with years so much as my recognition, which had increased;
whatever the cause, I knew that I could not leave him until he
told me I was free to follow my heart.

He no longer hunted lion or went wildfowling in the marshes;
it was seldom that he worked in his vineyards, and weeks went
by without him going beyond his own estate. He withdrew himself still further from human contact, and sometimes for several
days Kiyas and I did not even see him, though through the door
of his papyrus room we could hear him dictating the history he
was compiling, or the monotonous rhythm of the scribe's voice
reading from yet another roll.

One evening, after Kiyas had persuaded him to eat with us
instead of having food sent to his own apartments, I tried again

to make him talk of the Watchers. He saw my eagerness and said:

"Roidahn is the one of whom to ask those questions. He thinks the old Egypt can be born again, and will not listen when I tell him that the Watchers must wait for death to see their dreams become reality."

I asked him if he minded me listening to Roidahn, and he answered, "No, my son. Your mother said he was a wise man—it was me whom she loved, but she knew he was wiser than I. Roidahn should have been Nomarch: he would have been if your grandmother had chosen his father instead of mine."

He was smiling as he got up from the table; it made his face look young, uncertain. "I never wanted to be Nomarch until I married your mother—and then, to make her Queen over Egypt, I wished that I were Pharaoh."

He put his hand on my shoulder and said to Kiyas, "Soon Ra-ab will be Nomarch in my place."

When I would have protested, he went on, "No, Ra-ab, you will not have to wait until I die. Scholars live to be old men, and I shall find contentment in the past while I wait for the future. Roidahn knows of my intention, and he will tell me when you are ready for my office. Roidahn has always been nearer to you than I have been, and that is neither your fault nor mine."

Then, without waiting for me to speak, he went out of the room to join his scribe.

Perhaps this was the first time we realized how very lonely he was. There was a catch in Kiyas's voice as she said, "Sometimes, Ra-ab, we laughed at him, and said he was an old scholar trying to hide from the present in the past. Do you suppose he knew what we were thinking? Could we have made him happy if we had showed we really wanted him?"

I shook my head. "No, I don't believe anyone could have made much difference—but I do wish we had tried."

Kiyas and I both hoped that now Father had once put down his barrier of reserve we should be nearer to him, but the next time we met he was as remote as he had always been . . . like someone smiling at us from the other side of a narrow chasm which neither could cross. Soon after this he told me that I was to go to Roidahn; but it was not until the day I left for Hotep-Ra that he spoke again of his decision to make me Nomarch before his death.

"I am sending you to Roidahn so that from him you may learn what I cannot teach you. Since your mother's death I am only the husk of a man. If I had Roidahn's wisdom I should not be content to wait for death; I should use to the full my days on Earth instead of letting myself drift on the current of the years. Had Roidahn been Nomarch he would have found me a just steward, for though I cannot frame new laws I can see they are administered.

"Were Egypt tranquil, as in those older days which are held like a fly in amber on my scrolls, I should continue to rule; for I can see that a shuttle smoothly threads the loom when the pattern has been already chosen. I believed it was enough to safeguard the Oryx, quiet as an island in a turbulent sea; and until the Blue Death, Roidahn could not make me see this was not so. I thought to keep pestilence from the Oryx in the same way that we reduced the summer fever, by teaching the people to throw open their houses to the sun, to bury all refuse and make sworn enemies of flies and maggots. Our people never have to fear hunger; their bodies are stronger and more beautiful than those in any other province of Egypt. Yet when the pestilence came we could not protect ourselves—if it had not been for you and Kiyas, for Kiyas whose clear eyes saw the Nomarch was an old man, our people would have suffered far more grievously.

"I have tried to shelter the Oryx, but I cannot lead it to victory: that you must do, for you are more Oyahbe's son than mine. I knew that once you hoped to be a priest; I forgot that the wise Pharaohs were priests in more than name, and feared you would shut yourself away in a temple as I shut myself in my papyrus room. That is why I kept you so long in the House of the Captains, and made you work harder than my son need have done. You know our laws, and from the judgments you have already given in my name I know you will keep them wisely. You are a trained soldier, and more skilled with arrow and throwing-stick even than I was at your age. I never let you or Kiyas go beyond our boundaries because I tried to bring you up to be content with my way of life. Now it is Roidahn and not I who will make decisions for your future, and only time will prove whether I have been unwise.

"I should like you to marry when you are seventeen. The

Nomarch of the Hare is a distant kinsman; his daughter is a year younger than you, and when I saw her, though she was only a child then, she held the promise of being beautiful. The Nomes adjoin; and even Roidahn says the Hare is not ill administered. You know I could have appointed Kiyas's husband to rule after me? But I am well content with my son. Tell Roidahn that I should like you to go to see the Daughter of the Hare."

"I know whom I am going to marry, and if she is not the Daughter of the Hare the Houses cannot be united through me."

He was surprised and asked quickly, "Who is she? You have never seen any woman of your own rank who is of suitable age—as far as I know."

"I'm sorry, Father. I can't explain. I can only tell you that I *do* know whom I want to marry. I know her better than I know myself, and I love her. Yet if you ask what she looks like, or even what her name is, I couldn't tell you."

I saw he was getting angry, and I said desperately, *"Please* understand. Nekht-Ra told me that my mother knew she loved you before she knew your name or who you were. Yours was an old love and so is mine."

His face softened. "If you find a woman who is to you what Oyahbe was to me I will take her as my daughter without question. Don't be afraid to tell me who she is. Is she the daughter of one of your soldiers? You never seemed to take any interest in women except Kiyas—does she know about the girl you've chosen?"

"No. Even Kiyas would laugh at me."

"Why? Would Kiyas disapprove of her?"

"I said she'd *laugh*—and who wouldn't, at a man who is in love with a girl he's only met twice, and never except in a dream."

"In a dream?"

"Yes, and I know that I'm going to meet her soon. I'll never be happy until I do. I'm so frightened that she won't remember me—at least sometimes I am, though usually I'm quite sure she will."

With the disillusion of age, he said, as though humoring a child, "Let me know when you find your dream—or when you have decided it is better to have a wife who can bear your children instead of one who disappears when you wake! And then ask Roidahn to send you to the Hare."

Hotep-Ra

BEFORE LEAVING for Hotep-Ra, I decided to tell Kiyas about the girl beyond the river, and explain why it had been necessary to tell Father first. She listened without interrupting while I told her about the two dreams. They were so real to me, and it was only when I spoke of them that I realized how difficult it was going to be to make Father believe I was not free to be betrothed to the Daughter of the Hare.

Since Kiyas had seen Nefer-ankh invoke Ra, she was no longer scornful of dreams. She asked, "Is she very beautiful?"

"I don't know. I feel she must be, but I can't prove it."

Kiyas nodded. "I think you are right. She told you she might be fat; only someone who knew she was beautiful would dare to say that. What kind of person do you think she is? Noble, or just the daughter of ordinary parents?"

"I don't know that either, Kiyas."

"Dear Ra-ab, I never realized what an exciting kind of person you are! I always knew you were the very nicest kind, but not so very *adventuring*. You will be like Isis looking for bits of her husband, only of course you'll find her all in one piece."

I was always a little shocked when Kiyas made jokes about the Gods, but had given up telling her so, as she only laughed at me for being pompous.

"Ra-ab, I should go to the Hare as soon as you can."

"But why? I told you Father will have to give up that idea."

"How do you know she isn't the Hare's daughter? Think how nice it would be if she was, then everyone would be pleased; Father and you, and probably even me—I've heard the Hare's son is very handsome."

"You didn't mind Father choosing me for Nomarch instead of your husband, did you, Kiyas?"

"Of course I didn't, it was my idea just as much as his. I should hate to have a husband who only chose me because he wanted the Oryx. I want to be married for *me*—not that I want to marry any one yet."

"Poor Sebek!"

"So you've noticed he's rather in love with me? I'm glad you didn't realize it sooner, or you wouldn't have been so impressed at the way he listened to my plans against the pestilence. Sometimes I think I shall marry him, and then I think that he'd become a little dull, year after year. Anyway I've decided not to marry anyone until I'm sixteen, even though that is rather old."

Then she changed the subject. "I wish I could be with you at Hotep-Ra, but one of us ought to stay here with Father. I'll often come over to see you, though; Father never really notices if I'm here or not, provided he isn't disturbed to make a decision that I could have made for him."

I had said good-bye to Father the night before, and did not see him again before leaving home. Kiyas came down to the river with me, and watched from the bank until I was out of sight.

It was a very still evening; the only sound was the creak of oars and the water dripping from their blades. At last I could begin my search, not only for the girl beyond the River, though to me she was more important than anything else, but for knowledge to fit me for my role in the plan by which Egypt would find her greatness.

I reached Hotep-Ra by late afternoon, for I had come in Father's boat of twelve oars and made a fast journey. Hanuk was away from home, and as his sister had gone to her husband's family to wait the birth of her second child, I was alone with Roidahn.

"At last we can talk in peace," he said, "without time standing at our elbow to count our words. Your father has told me that when the Watchers have established their rule in Egypt he will make you the Nomarch. His is a wise decision, for when that day comes, the Oryx must be led by one who has the power of our authority."

"Couldn't he appoint *you* Nomarch, Roidahn? He told me himself it would have been better if you had been born to his name."

"Each man must play his own role, and I can do more as the leader of the Hundred of Horus than I could if I were the Oryx. And why should I break one of the Watcher's laws, which says authority shall pass with the blood unless the blood is tainted? That is what the Watchers are for; to see that authority is not abused, and that no member of a family exercises hereditary privilege which is not justified in his own person.

"For many years no one within the Oryx has been oppressed,

and we have continually heightened the contentment of our people. Now the time is nearly come when we must put into wider practice what we have learned, so that our peace extends throughout Egypt. That is why I have gathered together the Watchers who dwell in Hotep-Ra; some have been here for more than fifteen years, and others are but newly arrived. Each is being trained according to the role they can best play in the new pattern. Fear is their common enemy and each has shown that they know love to be stronger than fear. Fear uses a thousand weapons and we must counter all of them. Every Watcher is trained to fight a particular form of attack, and we need Watchers of every rank and calling. A goldsmith, even if he were wise as a high priest, would find no hearing among soldiers; and the wife of a plowman will listen more readily to another woman of the same caste. You who have always lived in the Oryx will find it difficult at first to realize how people in the rest of Egypt are shut away from each other by man-made barriers, of rank and caste and wealth—like grubs in a gigantic honeycomb.

"As well as the five hundred who are living in my villages, there are many Watchers outside the Oryx; nobles, merchants, husbandmen, even officials who hold seal under Pharaoh. Nefer-ankh knows of nearly fifty priests who when the time comes will bring truth to the new temples. Only fifty men of truth in a priesthood of thousands!

"Most of those who now live on my estate originally came to the Oryx for sanctuary. Ask some of them to tell you why they came here, and so learn what you may expect to find when you go beyond our boundaries. Fear is not the only enemy of the Watchers, though it is the most powerful manifestation of Set. He has other ways of keeping men in the shadow: he imprisons them in little false laws; pride of possession that is without generosity, pride of skill that is misused, pride of rank without true nobility. In the rest of Egypt a man is judged by his birth or by the royal favor; but within our ranks, wisdom with character is the seal of authority."

It was usual for Egyptian soldiers of equal rank to treat each other as distant kinsmen. So it had not been difficult for Sebek, and the others who were working with him, to come to know many who lived in other Nomes without arousing suspicion that they had come to talk of more than the arts of war.

Soldiers speak freely among themselves, and so it was easy to suggest that most of their grievances would no longer exist were the Warriors' Code more scrupulously followed. Many of the captains with whom Sebek had discussed mutual problems were eager that the armies should fulfill their old obligations, as practiced in the Oryx. They found it difficult to keep their men contented when they had so little to do, and some of them sighed for the days when a warlike Pharaoh led his armies in search of conquest.

The captains in every Nome were usually kinsmen of the ruling family, and they deeply resented the fact that the Nomarchs frequently had to furnish heavy bribes to those who assessed the tribute due to Pharaoh, so that an excuse would not be found to dispossess them of their lands. So great was the power of corrupt officials that some Nomarchs handed over to them twice the amount which would eventually be recorded on the tallies of the Royal Treasure.

Roidahn told me that even two centuries ago, the royal officials did not abuse their authority, which was then held only by men of personal integrity. Their old title was the Eyes of Pharaoh, and their twice yearly progress through the Two Lands was important less for the collection of tribute than because through them any complaint would be taken direct to the Royal Ear. Now they had degenerated into spies and tax-gatherers, and as such were feared and hated.

Since Pharaoh had built a new capital, now known as the Royal City, where the river divides, he no longer tried to conceal from the people of the South which of the two Crowns ruled Egypt. He valued the South chiefly for the riches which came from it and from the Land of Gold, but he chose most of the powerful officials, and other nobles who comprised his court, from those families on whose loyalty he could depend because they belonged to three Royal Nomes which in their own interest would always support the dynasty.

At the time of the Dawn, which was the name given to the day when secrecy would no longer be necessary, five of the Nomarchs of the South would no longer be allowed to rule. But in each of these Nomes one of the Eyes of Horus had already been chosen from among their kinsmen, whom it was known the people would acclaim and who would assume authority without bloodshed. Three of these Nomarchs were too old to change their ideas, but had agreed to abdicate in favor of their heirs when the time came; another was cruel and could not be trusted with authority; and the fifth was corrupt and in due course would be banished.

Nevertheless these five Nomes would rise with us when the word was given. In addition, the Hare and the Jackal were our friends, and the Leopard would side with us because the Nomarch recognized that the Oryx was better administered than any other Nome. The Tortoise would follow the Leopard, for the two houses were closely united. So the armies of ten Nomes would follow the Watchers. The three powerful Royal Nomes might have to be counted as enemies; but we hoped that our action would be so swift that by the time the news could reach the North the five Nomes which comprised it would not oppose us, even though it might be some time before they were ready to be allowed equal authority with the others.

Every day I learned more of the vast pattern conceived by Roidahn. His position was that of a secondary noble in a small Nome, yet he compassed Egypt with his thought as had the ancient Pharaohs. During the day I talked with different Watchers and in the evening Roidahn discussed with me what I had learned from them.

When I asked him why we had to wait so long before taking action, he said, "As long as there have been tyrants there have been rebellions against them, but the Watchers are going to be sure we open the door to peace, not to war. It would have been easy to persuade the people to rise against their oppressors, and it is easy to depose a man and put another in his place; but it takes time to train the right men to take over authority.

"We shall see that justice is done to everyone according to our laws, which are founded upon those by which the Forty-Two Assessors judge. When a man works a sick ox, he is first told how he should care for his animals, and then, if he does not listen, he may have to carry the yoke on his own shoulders until his field is plowed. That judgment was carried out on my estate three years ago, and your father could show you a papyrus, one of the oldest in his possession, that was scribed long before the pyramids were built, which tells of a similar adjustment. Punishment which is revengeful is always evil: though drastic action may be taken if there is no other means of effecting a cure. In the old days every man had the right to go to Pharaoh for justice; and it was written 'Justice and Pharaoh and Truth are three ways of saying the same thing.' Yet the man who in our time wears the Double Crown is without nobility, though he was born in the line of dynasty; and it is doubtful if either of his sons would purify the blood.

"Egypt has fallen into sorrow because there is too much power in hands that are unworthy of it; so to safeguard our people the authority of the Nomarchs will be increased. Instead of ruling only at Pharaoh's pleasure, henceforward they shall not be deprived of their estates unless it is by the will of their own people. Nor shall Pharaoh make war in a foreign country unless the Nomarchs from whom the armies are levied have given their consent.

"When you rule, Ra-ab, you will have more power than any member of your family has ever held. Unless you agree, your soldiers will not be sent to fight on foreign soil, though Pharaoh may call on you to help defend the boundaries of Egypt. You will be responsible for the tribute of the tenth part, but only half of it will go to Pharaoh, who must use it for building roads, aqueducts, maintaining the level of the granaries or other common needs. The rest will be retained by you for the welfare of your Nome. You will not have to suffer the authority of corrupt officials, or buy your peace from them, for you will be responsible to no one save Pharaoh or his Vizier. Those of your people who pay their yearly tribute by labor, cannot, without your consent, be made to work outside your Nome, though if a Royal Road crosses your land you may have to supply half the labor. In the future, though Pharaoh will still have much wider powers than any Nomarch, he will not be stronger than all of them together and so will not be able to abuse his privileges. I repeat, Ra-ab, it will be your people, not Pharaoh, who shall judge whether you are worthy to rule over them."

"Roidahn, why was a puppet born to rule Egypt? Father has told me so many stories of the old Pharaohs, and you, too, often speak of them; they ruled in peace and wisdom. Why have our Pharaohs changed?"

"Why are there waves on a river—because the wind is blowing! When you know both cause and effect nothing is strange. You should recognize that the puppet Pharaoh is only a symbol of the will of Egypt. When a people see only the Crook and Flail and forget what they symbolize, the man who holds them has less virtue than a statue. They have forgotten that Pharaoh should be High Priest, a link between them and the Gods. Once the royal divinity was more than a legend, for no one ruled who was not fully initiate, a Winged One.

"Later, men saw Pharaoh as a symbol of power on Earth and forgot divinity. They judged him by the monuments he raised in his own honor; and even if the granaries were empty while stone rose on imperishable stone, the people did not cry out against the Royal House, rather did they bow down before it in ecstasy of blind humility.

"Later still, they grew tired of laboring for a royal immortality; they no longer wanted a builder of monuments, or even a warrior to lead them to victorious battle. They were too lazy even to revere divinity, and had found that stone was not worth the carrying. They wanted a Pharaoh whom they could blame for their own faults . . . lazy men always try to avoid responsibility. They wanted to be able to think, 'My corn is choked with weeds, but it is not *my* fault. It is because my son paid tribute of labor during the months of Sowing . . . next year I must bribe the overseer to take his name from the tally, for of course I cannot work my own field.' When you have seen more of Egypt you will not be surprised that, in the person of this Pharaoh, avarice, ignorance, and cruelty have ruled for forty years."

"But how can he be the will of the people? Surely no one *wants* to be oppressed?"

"Of course they don't. Yet they have brought these conditions on themselves, though they are too ignorant to realize it. They find it easier to groan and accept oppression than to change this passive attitude to one which would drive away the shadow which is darkening their lives. That is one reason why the Watchers have taken so long to prepare for the Dawn; we knew that it was no use trying to change the pattern of Egypt until her people were taught that they themselves must demand that Set be sent into exile. Ra does not give a man more power than he asks for, and until the sum of this power is stronger than the power which they have given into the hands of fear they will continue to be ruled by false gods, in the name of ignorant men whom they have put in authority. Something of the divinity of Ra is within every living thing. Use this force constructively and you grow strong; use it for destruction and it will destroy you; allow it to remain idle and it will bind you as its prisoner. Ra gave you the divinity by which you live, but if you refuse to make use of it you are giving it into the service of Set. If you tie a tight thong round your arm, so that the hand is cut off from the scarlet of the heart, it will soon rot off . . . and the poison may spread through your whole body. Cut yourself off from the love of Ra and soon you will be little better than a corpse. Only by remembering your own divinity can you draw on the source of power by which you were created, and so be strong enough to bring about conditions on Earth in which love can flourish and happiness prevail. Remember, Ra-ab, that is the object of the Watchers; to teach people how to open channels which they have allowed to fall into disuse and to make new ones, so that through them love can flow again; bringing them harvests which they can reap in wise tranquility."

Neku the Goldsmith

THE HOUSE of Neku the Goldsmith was quite close to Hotep-Ra, and he was one of the Watchers whom Roidahn suggested I should seek out so as to learn of his story. All I knew about him was that he had lost his right hand before coming to the Oryx, and now had several pupils to whom he was teaching his craft.

When I first saw him he was sitting cross-legged at the door of his house, showing a boy how to beat gold into thin sheets, which, when they covered a wooden statue, would make it seem as though it were of solid gold. He was younger than I expected; about forty, broad of shoulder and with a skin paler than is usual among Egyptians. He greeted me by name, and then took me into a long room where he kept the things on which he and his pupils were working.

He showed me a pectoral in the form of a Horus hawk, its wings inlaid with the three colors of carnelian. It was impressively beautiful; and he must have guessed that I was wondering how he could still do such magnificent work when his right arm was cut off below the elbow, for he said, "This is not the work of my hands, though mine was the thought which has become visible. I can no longer make metal obedient to me, but I can still draw designs which show others what I wish them to create, and so transfer to them the skill which I can no longer practice."

He took a lump of unpolished turquoise from the shelf under the window. "Once I could have brought the color out of this stone, but now I tell my pupils how the matrix must be split so that the fine blue can be freed to make into beads for necklaces. But what does it matter if a man is crippled so long as the beauty he wished to bring down to Earth can find another channel?"

Then he opened a painted chest and took from it sheets of papyrus on which were designs for necklaces and bracelets, pectorals and statuettes. "It took a long time before my left hand could draw as surely as my right, but now it is no longer difficult for me to take the children of my thoughts on that step of their journey down into form."

After he had shown me many more of his treasures, he said, "Come into the other room and I will show you the only thing I have ever made with which I am content."

On a shelf above the bedplace there was a small statue of Ptah; the face of white gold, the body of red. In it there was so much of the spirit of the Great Artificer that it seemed almost as though Ptah himself must have made it; as though if it stretched out a hand the birds frescoed on the walls would fly out of the window toward the sun, or the blue water-lines break into ripples of silver.

Perhaps Neku knew I could find no words to express my admiration, for he said, "My hand is gone, but the statue is its son: Ptah, the Great Artificer, whom one day even little men who must work in metal will know as brother. He made the gold and the silver, the ivory and sardonyx, lapis and turquoise, jasper and

110

chrysoprase—even their names sound a prayer in his honor! Amethyst and chalcedony, onyx and ebony: what rich gifts he gave to us who try to follow him; though we cannot give his life to what we make. My hawks can never spread their wings beyond the span that I allotted them, nor can this silver Oryx know the wind, or that twin cobra lose power beyond its coils. Yet sometimes I think that Ptah will speak to me, not for my skill but for my love of him."

He raised his right arm toward the statue, as though to touch it on the foot with the sign of humility. He did touch it, I was sure of that—yet it was with the hand that he had lost. For a moment there was something of kinship between the face of Neku and that bright reflection of Ptah. It seemed they were already in brotherhood, that the hand I could not see was there, the Life of Ptah flowing from its fingers.

He turned and smiled at me. "You have come to hear why I am a Watcher. Roidahn told me that I could open my heart to you without reservation."

Then, sitting in the doorway, each leaning against one side of the opening to the street, Neku told me his story. And his words were so vivid that as I listened it was not a road bordered with sycamores that I saw, women carrying water jars to the well, a laughing boy with a string of fish in his hand; but the scenes through which Neku had lived.

My father, and his father before him, were sculptors to the Royal Household, and my mother came from a family of Minoan craftsmen. Though she was a foreigner, she brought no household god of her own, but taught me to make my offerings to a statue of Ptah which had been made by my grandfather. She told me that Ptah, and Min, and Ra, were brothers, and that all artificers were their children.

My father taught me his skill, and when he died, though I was only seventeen I was appointed chief sculptor to the Royal Household in his stead. Within ten years I was a rich man; for I worked quickly and there were many who would pay a great price to possess something made by Pharaoh's sculptor, even though they could recognize its quality only by the weight of gold dust which they had bartered for it.

I did not marry, for to me women were only the shadows of the statues I might make of them, and my household was content under my mother's rule. It pleased Pharaoh that people should see the signs of the royal favor; so I was given an estate, larger than that of a minor noble, together with herds, two hundred of both large and small cattle, and permission to plant a vineyard as though I held the rank of the Keeper of a Seal. I also made pectorals and statuettes, and all that I needed for this work was given from the royal treasure-house, and whether it was lapis or malachite, silver or ivory, I had only to ask for it. I made lamps and offering-vessels for the new temples, but they were of traditional pattern and I did not know in whose service they would be used.

Then one day, it was midsummer and very hot, the stillness of my courtyard was broken by the lowing of oxen and the sound of whips. I was annoyed by the disturbance, and left the gallery in which I was working to see what caused the noise. I saw six oxen, yoked to a wooden sledge under which were long rollers, slowly dragging forward a great block of black basalt that was more than three times the height of a man. Though I had worked before on blocks nearly as massive, they had always been sent from the quarries according to my specification, for when Pharaoh had told me for what purpose he wanted a statue he left the choosing of suitable stone to me.

It took several hours, and the strength of forty men, before the block was moved into the place where I could work on it. By its proportions I saw that it was intended for a standing figure, instead of, as was usual, for Pharaoh enthroned. Not until the following day did I find in what form Pharaoh had decreed it should be carved, and to receive this news I was summoned, not to the Palace but to the new temple, then still unfinished.

Save to make the traditional twice yearly offering I had not been to any of the new temples, having never felt a nearer kinship with the Gods through ritual observances. I preferred to pray at dawn and at sunset in the little sanctuary adjoining the gallery in which I worked, where I had placed the statue of Ptah made by my grandfather.

I obeyed the summons to the temple immediately, for it came in the name of Pharaoh and I was his servant. A minor official took me to the sanctuary, not yet completed, and told me to take measurements so that the walls could be built up to the height I judged to be the correct proportion for the statue I was to make. Though the sanctuary was empty, I could see that masons had been working there recently, for the stone dust had not yet been swept from the floor, and the walls were in the process of being covered with thin slabs of basalt, highly polished and uncarved.

From the shape of the block which had been brought to me I thought it probable the statue would be of Ra; certainly it would not be of Anubis or Hathor unless it were to be in human form. Just as I had completed my measurements, a man, who by his dress I judged to be the Temple Overseer, came through the doorway. Such overseers were not priests, though they were responsible for keeping the records of all tributes and the tally of the temple properties.

After a formal greeting, he said, "It is hoped that your statue will be ready to receive the First Offering within three months. We are honored that Pharaoh should appoint his finest craftsmen to work for us; but remember that he whom you depict is greater even than Pharaoh—who has power only on Earth. Let your hands be more cunning than they have ever been; then shall you be as richly rewarded as though you had slaughtered a hundred black bulls to Set at the dark of the moon."

I did not understand him and thought he tried to make a ponderous jest. I said, "This is the first time I ever heard a craftsman bribed with the promise of a curse! If it is Set who will reward me I would cut off my right hand rather than gain his favor."

The man did not answer. Suddenly there was fear in the thick silence of the narrow room: a silence so deep it seemed I must hear the dust motes whirling together in the shaft of sunlight which fell through an opening in the unfinished wall.

"It is not Set whom you will carve, but Sekmet, his female manifestation of boundless power. Sekmet, the power of the Earth, beside whose strength all other Gods recoil in impotence!"

"Is this Pharaoh's order?"

"Who else should command Pharaoh's servant? It is at his command that the new temples are being built all over Egypt. I have seen offering vessels made by you in five new temples. Are you so bound in the narrow way of your craft that you never learned in whose service they are used?"

"Had I known, they should have been made worthy of whom they serve—of misshapen clay from the graves of the unclean, colored with the entrails of a black pig!"

I knew the man was coldly angry, yet as he stared at me his eyes were puzzled. "You blaspheme against Set, yet he lets you live. To speak against him is to wake in his caverns, trying to scream for pity with a mouth that has no tongue. He must have use for you to let you live; for his wrath is more terrible upon those who deny the name of Sekmet even than on those who deny *his* name. To speak against Pharaoh is to die; to speak against his Gods is to find that in death there is no pity."

When I reached home I went straight to my mother's rooms and told her all that had passed between myself and the Temple Overseer. When I asked her if she thought me right to refuse to work for Sekmet, whatever the result might be, she seemed surprised that I could have considered any other course than the one I had taken. The last few years had brought her the brittleness of age, yet she seemed undisturbed by the sudden breaking of the quiet routine of her life, and told me calmly that the best we could hope for was exile.

"Yes, you will be banished," she said. "You will see, we shall be allowed to depart without being molested. We may even be allowed to take with us some of our possessions; not much, but sufficient for our journey. And if we must travel with poverty as our sole attendant, what does it matter to us when it is your hands that are our treasure?"

"We shall be strangers in a foreign country."

"We have lived in your father's country; now we shall go to the island where my father was born. No soil is alien to the children of Ra, for he rules the sky over all the Earth."

I told the three pupils who worked for me that I had incurred the royal displeasure, and that they must return to their homes lest they be associated with me in the decree of banishment. They were reluctant to go, and the youngest of them only consented to leave me after I had promised to let him know where I went, so that he could follow me into exile.

Though our preparations were made no word came from Pharaoh for three days. My mother urged that we should go while we were still free, but I clung to the hope that rather than lose my skill Pharaoh would pretend I had not been commanded to work for the temple or else consider me sufficiently punished by appointing another to be the Royal Sculptor. Almost I began to convince myself that I should be allowed to stay in Egypt, perhaps even retaining my estate, and continue to live among my friends and those who worked for me.

When the decree came it was not banishment. It gave me forty days to make such progress on the statue of Sekmet as would show it to be my finest work. If this command were not carried out, then I should be banished from all the lands of Egypt: after paying the tribute of my right hand to Sekmet.

At the first reading I did not understand the full measure of the sentence. My mother's voice was taut as a drawing-string. "They will cut off your hand, Neku, before we go into exile. I was a fool to hope that Pharaoh would let you work for another master."

It would have been impossible for us to escape even if we had tried, for there were soldiers posted at every gate of the walls which enclosed the house and its surrounding garden, and each soldier was in sight of the next. I had thought to have many years in which to see my thoughts take shape: now the work of years must flower in forty days. Ptah should be made instead of Sekmet; I would work in gold, His metal, while the great block of midnight stone stayed dumb.

I was going to bury the statue, hoping that in the future, when Set had been overthrown, men would find and honor it. But on the twenty-first day my youngest pupil returned to me, having passed the guards disguised as a fisher-boy. He had heard of Roidahn, and had come to tell me that I would find sanctuary in the Oryx—it was the same boy who made the pectoral of the hawk you have just seen. I tried to make my mother go with him to the Oryx; dressed as a servant who was going to market, it would not have been difficult for her to pass the soldiers. But she would not leave me even though I pleaded with her to go. On the thirty-eighth day the statue was finished, and my pupil brought it to the Oryx hidden in the belly of a fish.

Neku paused, his eyes dark with the memory of pain. That is nearly the end of my story . . . the story of how I came to be a Watcher. Then he went on:

I expected to be summoned to the temple, but on the fortieth day the Overseer, a priest, and twelve armed guards came to me. The Overseer asked to see the statue, saying he had heard it was nearly finished. I thought he said it to mock me—I have never been sure. Later, the priest said the plinth on which the unhewn block was standing would be a suitable altar for the sacrifice.

The temple guards advanced toward me, with straps that were to tie me down. I told them they could save themselves the trouble of this formality. The priest told me to kneel, with my right had held steady on the block. . . .

For the last time I flexed my fingers; so swift and supple, so obedient to my thought. As I looked at them, long, and smooth, and eager to obey me, I knew how a mother would feel if she had to watch her child sacrificed.

I saw they made no preparation to stop the bleeding, and realized they expected me to die. . . . I felt the force of the blow. It threw me on my side; and through a red haze I could see the fingers of my severed hand slowly unclench from the edge of the block above me. . . .

When they thought I was dying they let my mother come into the room. Perhaps they did not stay any longer because their order was only for a hand, and Pharaoh is impatient with those who do not carry out his commands exactly. My mother afterwards told me that when she cried out that I was dead they left the house as fast as their dignity would permit.

She managed to stop the bleeding—how, I do not know, for by then I was unconscious. She caused an empty coffin to be carried to our tomb, and the servants of the household put ashes on their heads and wailed for the death of their master.

As soon as my death was proclaimed the guards were removed: had they known I was still alive they would have kept me under surveillance until I had crossed the boundary into exile.

It was a month before I was strong enough to be moved. By then no one took any interest in an old woman who walked slowly beside a curtained litter along the road to the Oryx.

Hanuk's Journeys

ONE DAY about two months later, instead of resting during the noon heat, I took the smallest of Roidahn's sailing boats and drifted lazily downriver. I must have fallen asleep, and only woke when the boat jarred against the bank; at a point where it had been eroded by the water and overhung to form a shallow cave. I decided to stay there until the evening wind instead of rowing back; it was cooler in the shade and I lay down in the bottom of the boat to drowse.

Toward evening I heard someone singing; the tune was familiar though I could not remember where I had heard it before. I roused myself, and saw a boat, very like mine, coming upriver. There was only one man in it, but he was between me and the sun so I could not see him clearly. A net was heaped in the stern, and when he stood up to alter the setting of the sail I saw his loincloth was orange, the color usually worn by fishermen.

There was a hut a little further upstream which I had noted earlier in the day; it appeared to be deserted, though the thatch was new and the door and window shutters were sound and had been recently painted. As there was no cultivated ground near it, nor did the bank shelve sufficiently for a boat to be drawn up, I had wondered why it had been built there. So I was mildly curious when I saw the solitary fisher-man furl his sail and row to the bank below the hut, to make his boat fast to a half submerged post which until then I had not noticed.

Again I heard the tune he was singing, and with the sound came the memory of where I had heard it before. It was Hanuk's favorite tune, which Hayab, the blind woman, had taught him when he was a little boy. Then I realized the fisherman shared more than a tune with Hanuk; they were of the same build and they even moved in the same way. Curiosity was strong enough to make me climb the steep bank and walk along toward the hut.

As I drew level with the door, a voice said, "Well met, Ra-ab! Did Father tell you I was returning today, or did chance send you to welcome me?"

Hanuk came out of the hut, his body glistening with the water he had been sluicing over himself. He laughed. "Why so surprised? Didn't you know this was my hut? It's a magical place, a noble's son changes into a fisherman, and back again. Yes, that door has seen me go through it as an old man, hair smeared with white clay and body crusted with dirt, and come out again as the Hanuk you know."

He must have seen how puzzled I was, though I tried to conceal it. "Did you think I went on my journeys as a noble's son? That would be no use; for the way to find out any abuse of authority is to pretend to be someone who looks easy prey for a bully. I was lucky on this journey, for there was no need to prove a man's heart by tempting him to flog me—but I've not always been so fortunate!"

He turned round to show me his back; and on the smooth brown skin I saw the raised lines of old weals. "Come inside," he said cheerfully, "and I'll show you some of the people I've been."

There were three large chests against one wall, and on the shelf under the window was a copper mirror and some little unguent pots such as women use. The only other furniture was a sleeping-mat and two stools, and at the end of the room, where stood two large water-jars, a square of the floor was tiled and a gutter ran through a hole in the wall to carry off the water.

He opened the chests. There were cloaks and loincloths and kilts, even long robes like those worn by foreign merchants. And there was also many headdresses and wigs—including one of oiled goats' hair as favored by some Asiatics. The third chest was filled with many kinds of small merchandise such as would be carried by a peddler . . . baskets, ointment jars, strings of beads, copper armlets, hair ornaments, bundles of dried herbs, and a quantity of little stoppered jars decorated with magical symbols.

"A lot of old clothes," he said, "but they hold the memory of more than thirty journeys, and four years of my life."

He picked up one of the stoppered jars. "That goes with me when I become a peddler of health. I rub my hair with a mixture of oil and limestone dust, and let it hang round my face in wisps. I walk with a staff, bowed under my cloak, and when I come to a village I put a pebble into the heel of my sandal so that I don't forget to limp. It's a good disguise to use when there has been a lot of sickness, for sick people are eager to talk to anyone they think may have a cure, and then they talk on of other things. They see that I am old and poor, so why should they fear my betrayal of them to the overseer? Sometimes my pots contain unguents to sell to the women servants of large houses; they enjoy flattery even from an old man, and it is easy to get them to speak of how that household treats them. Most of them think I am a little mad, because I tell them I will take no payment until I pass that way again—when I shall ask for a double price as thanksgiving for their cure. I seldom return to the same place twice, for in one visit I usually find as much as a peddler can discover.

"In the big towns I am often a small merchant, and the panniers of my pack animal are well filled with the kinds of things you saw in the third chest. I do very little trade, for I sit in a busy corner of the marketplace with a few wares spread out in front of me, and appear to drowse in the sun. I've learned a lot in market places; other merchants seldom bother to conceal their tricks from one of the same trade, and when I see the barter scales are false or the people are being cheated, it is a sure sign that the overseer of the town is corrupt.

"Sometimes I go as a blind beggar, though this is not an easy role to play. The charity, or lack of it, which people show to a beggar is a good indication of the quality of their headman. If they are treated well they tend to behave in the same way to others, but there are few who learn kindness through receiving cruelty."

He combed back his wet hair, and buckled on a pair of sandals with gold studs, such as I wore. "Bolt the shutters, Ra-ab, for I am ready to be Hanuk again."

He closed the door, and sealed with clay the string threaded through the latch. "If you should need this hut at any time I will give you a copy of my seal. . . . The man who has been my body servant since I was fourteen is the only other person who comes here, and he seals the door after he has been to clean it and fill the water jars. I'll leave my boat for him to collect, and we'll go home in yours."

The wind by now was strong enough to take us against the current, so there was no need to row. I asked him how he had got the weals on his back.

"That was nearly a year ago. We had heard that those working on the new road through the Leopard were being ill-treated, but the man from whom a Watcher heard the news was unreliable, lazy and a grumbler. He bore the marks of a flogging, but in view of his character he might have received them in just punishment. As I was going through the Leopard on my way further south I decided that for a few days the merchant should disappear and a field worker, paying tribute by labor, take his place. The Royal Levy is usually adequately fed, and as this road was Pharaoh's it was not the responsibility of the Nomarch. The men grumbled at their conditions, and I soon found they had good reason. They were not given the noon hour to rest and were fed only at dawn and sunset, and then on bread which was stale and insufficient, with no vegetables, not even garlic, to eat with it. They also complained that on their rest day they had no beer or extra food. Still, their conditions were nothing like so bad as I had seen in the quarries, and for the first few days I saw no one beaten unless they were deliberately slow or clumsy.

"The man working next to me had a poisoned hand, but he was afraid to report it to the overseer, although I told him it was his privilege not to work until it was healed, and that he only owed seventy days' work to Pharaoh in every year and could pay it when he chose. As he was too frightened to state his own case I did it for him. And the overseer had me flogged—for trying to stir up a rebellion by reminding the other laborers of their old rights that are still theirs by the law of Egypt. He said that now there are no laws save the will of Pharaoh. I nearly told him that when the law and Pharaoh were not of equal wisdom Pharaoh was an impostor! It was lucky I kept my temper and took the flogging without speaking my thoughts; or I should have lost my tongue as well as a few strips of skin from my back!"

"Hanuk, when next you go, can I come with you?"

"Have you asked Father?"

"No, he says that when I know enough to be one of the Eyes of Horus he will tell me how I can best help the Watchers. He talks of sending me to the Royal City, not in disguise but as the Son of the Oryx. Surely there is something I can do now, without waiting? Every day I hear stories of how people are being maltreated outside our boundaries; and of what many of the Watchers experienced before they came here. Can't I do something *now,* instead of waiting? When are the Watchers going to rise?"

"When the plan is complete. Perhaps this year, perhaps not for two or three. The oppressors are far fewer in number than the oppressed; but before we can act without bringing war into Egypt we must know the value of *all* who hold authority. In a small village a headman may rule a hundred. *How?* Because they fear him, not only for himself but for what he represents—the chain of authority stretching from him to the overseer, and so to Pharaoh—and to Set. Break that chain and what is the power of the headman? He is no longer a man with the power of the flail, but one man against a hundred. The oppressors have judged their strength by the long shadows they cast, but when the light is round them they will cast no shadow and have no power. They will be the prisoners of the prisoners they once held in bondage."

"Are they to be put to death?"

"Only those whom the Watchers cannot cure need be sent before the Forty-Two Assessors. Already all who are known to us have had their fate decided. Even under the shadow there are some good men in authority and they will retain it. Others will have their land taken from them and instead be given a field to plow, with perhaps a pair of oxen, so that in tilling the earth they may plant again the seed of their forgotten wisdom. A few can learn only from their own punishments, and their backs may have to feel the whips that once they held."

"*Can* I come with you, Hanuk, when next you go?"

"You will have to ask Father. Every one of us has his own work to do, and yours may be different to mine. That's what you must always remember, Ra-ab; so many different kinds of Watchers are needed, every rung in the ladder of authority must be justly held. Perhaps one day all will be Watchers; and then there will be no more darkness at all, after that last sunset when Earth is free of Earth."

Roads to the Horizon

I HAD BEEN to see Neku, and on my way home saw a runner panting up the avenue. He recognized me, and called out, "Where is Roidahn? I have news he must hear at once."

"He won't be back until late this evening. He went to the House of the Nomarch three days ago, but he will have left there by river before noon today."

The man stood still, his hands trembling from prolonged exertion. "Come to Roidahn's house and wait for him there," I said. "Hanuk is also away, but perhaps I can help you."

He followed me into the garden pavilion and drank the cup of mead I gave him, though he would not eat anything until he had told me his story.

"Five of my friends have been killed while we were paying our tribute by labor on Pharaoh's road. I managed to escape. Roidahn cannot know what's happening outside the Oryx, or he would tell us to rise up at once against our oppressors." His eyes stared past me as though he were describing something taking place while he watched, as though I were a blind man with whom he was trying to share his sight.

"I and five others came from a village on the northern boundary of the Jackal. We all belong to the Watchers, but we were told that until the time comes for the new laws we must continue to obey the old. We could not pay our taxes, so although we were free men, we had to work on the Royal Road. We were badly fed, and the huts they gave us to sleep in were filthy and verminous. But we had expected that, and would not have grumbled against it—it is easy not to grumble when you have something to look forward to. That part of the road runs over marshy ground and they are paving it with stone blocks. These are only two thumb-joints in thickness, but the next bargeload brought stones larger than those used before, being three cubits square. The old blocks were small enough to be carried by one man, though even those were a heavy load; but the weaker of us could not even lift these from the ground. There was a new overseer; he did not believe that the quarries had sent this stone by mistake, and that it had been intended as facing-stones for a new wall at the temple near the Old Capital. I don't know whether this is true, it is only what I was told. The overseer had his orders: each man must carry one paving-stone a distance of six thousand paces three times a day. A few of us protested, and for answer were given three strokes each from the whipman. So we tried to obey the orders; a few of the strongest took one block to the appointed place between dawn and noon, but the rest could only manage one between two men, and though they ran all the way back they couldn't make six journeys while the light lasted. We were not given shoulder pads, and the weight of the stones soon cut through nearly to the bone until blood was running down our bodies faster than sweat.

"After four days of it the six of us went to the overseer, saying that we refused to work under such conditions and that we would go back to our village to tell the Nomarch we were being unjustly treated. He told us to come that evening to the house where he was living, which belonged to the headman of a nearby village, and promised that we should be permitted to return to the Jackal and could tell our fellow workers that they would not see us again.

"He had soldiers waiting to greet us. They tied us up, so that the whip-man could work on us uninterrupted. There was a disused storehouse on the far side of the courtyard. We were shut in there after the first flogging and told that each day one of us would be taught how to carry stones for the instruction of the others. I was the last of the six. I had watched the other five staggering up and down, up and down, and whenever they stumbled the whip-man drove them on. Then, when they couldn't get up any more, he stove in their skulls. He was very cruel, and he enjoyed making the next man dig the grave for the one who had provided entertainment the day before."

"How did you escape?"

"When the whip-man brought me food on the last day, he was foolish enough to stay to mock me, saying that as there was no one left to dig *my* grave, I should have to demand the last courtesies from the vultures. I was lying on some dirty straw in the corner. The room was dark, for the only light came through the half-open door. He thought it would be a good jest to throw the swill in my face, and he stooped over me to make sure of his aim. . . . The feel of his neck under my fingers was better than bread to a starving man. His tongue looked as big as a calf's when it came bursting out of his mouth. I bent his head back until I heard the neck snap, to make sure I hadn't bungled it.

"I didn't go back to the Jackal. I don't trust the Nomarch; he would not dare to protect me if he knew I had killed the servant of an overseer. And in my own village Pharaoh's soldiers would be looking for me. But Roidahn will know I did right, won't he? I only took one life in exchange for five. And I gave him a quick death . . . not that I had any choice. It was a good sound, the crack his neck made . . . nearly as loud as the crack of his own whip."

I took him along to the house where people newly arrived at Hotep-Ra lodged until work had been allotted to them. I made him eat two raw eggs beaten up in goat's milk, and then sat with him until he fell asleep.

Then I went down to the landing-stage to see if Roidahn's boat was yet in sight. It was just coming round the bend, and in a few minutes we were exchanging greetings. He had brought a letter from Kiyas and one from Father, but before reading them I told him about the man who had just come to us for protection.

"His name is Ken-han," I said. "He has a kinsman here and once stayed with him for a day or two when he was passing through the Nome. He belongs to the Jackal, but is frightened to return there."

"I am afraid it may be necessary to remove the Jackal," said Roidahn thoughtfully. "He will join us when the time comes, but only because he thinks he will have more power in the Assembly of Nomarchs than he at present commands. His son, if he fully recovers from the injury he received in the lion hunt, may accede; though I hear the loss of his foot has affected his judgment. Hanuk said he was embittered when they last met, and inclined to blame Ra for the shaft of his spear breaking; saying, I *think* it was intended for a joke, that 'Set made better weapons for his followers.' A Nomarch whose people do not come to him when they are in trouble is condemned, as are parents whose children cannot trust them."

"Then you won't send Ken-han away?"

"Not until there is something which he can do better elsewhere. It might have been wiser if he had only rendered the whip-man unconscious without the addition of breaking his neck, but that neither you nor I are yet in a position to judge. It would depend whether the whip-man was obeying orders through ignorance or fear, or whether he enjoyed the power his unsavory office gave him."

"He needn't have thrown the food in Ken-han's face," I said. "Nor need he have said his only grave would be in a vulture's belly."

"You didn't tell me that, Ra-ab. I must impress on you that it is just such details which enable one to form an accurate opinion. The whip-man exceeded his duty, and mocked one whom he thought was helpless. That the other was *not* helpless I consider a most apt example of summary justice."

"I think Ken-han may try to stir up trouble among the others who as yet don't quite understand that we have to wait until the right moment before we take action. He kept on muttering, 'Roidahn must act at once. We can't let things go on any longer.'"

"I will talk to him when he is rested," said Roidahn. "It is impossible to argue with a man who lacks either sleep or food."

A few days later, Roidahn said to me. "You were right in thinking Ken-han would try to spread dissatisfaction. He has collected a following of twenty of the more impatient new arrivals and has even gone so far as to threaten to betray us unless I give the order for immediate action."

"Shall we have to imprison them?"

"I consider that very unlikely, Ra-ab. If the Eyes of Horus are unable to influence those who have already joined the Watchers, it is impossible that we have sufficient wisdom to rule Egypt. Isn't it even more improbable that Ra would let us be betrayed unless we are unworthy to interpret his laws? Tell Ken-han to bring his friends here this evening, so that I can discuss the matter with them."

Roidahn welcomed them most amicably, and insisted that each in turn should tell him exactly why they considered the time for action had come. It became increasingly obvious that while most of them genuinely wanted to better their fellow countrymen as soon as possible, they were also influenced by the trouble of having to learn *how* to be Watchers. Yet their loyalty to Roidahn was sufficiently strong for them not to want to do anything without his consent, and I saw that if he gave them a direct order they would obey him, even though it might be unwillingly.

After the last of them had finished speaking Roidahn began:

"You have come to demand that the Watchers should march

forthwith against the oppressors, saying that men of courage cannot wait for the dawn while blood is crying for retribution. You
are free to make your own choice, for though some of you still
wore shackles when you came to Hotep-Ra you have now grown
strong enough to know yourselves free men, whose old ties have
snapped like twists of withered grass. I have never asked you to
curtail your freedom by making an oath of allegiance to me, nor
shall I ever ask you to make such an oath. Is it necessary for a
man who has walked out of the shadow to declare that the sun
shines upon him? You have had the opportunity to see how people live in the Oryx; if you think you would be happier in another
part of Egypt, go there and dwell in peace."

"It isn't that we don't like it here," said Ken-han. "It's that we
don't like being safe ourselves while we know our friends are still
being oppressed. It's all very well for you to say 'wait' but what
would you feel like if *you* were being flogged every day?"

"Sometimes it is not at all easy to say 'wait.' I can assure you
that I have often wished for the satisfaction which you had when
you broke the neck of the whip-man. But what if I killed a thousand whip-men? Until whip-men are no longer necessary there
would be plenty of others willing to take their place. I am not
training you to fight against men, but against fear. Fear must be
banished from Egypt before there can be peace.

"Let us strike our blow now, before fear grows any stronger."

"You would only make men afraid of *you*; would it make Set
any less strong if you fed him on different blood? Sheep will follow a bell ram even though he leads them to slaughter; you wish
to go and kill the bell ram and leave the flock with nothing to follow. Have you forgotten the story of the sheep who killed their
own bell ram, and then huddled together in terror when they
heard the hunting cough of a leopard? They were afraid because
they were leaderless; and didn't know which way to run. When
they heard the bell with which they were familiar they were eager
to follow it . . . they thought that *this* time it would lead them into
a quiet pasture. You may remember that the bell was tied round
the neck of the leopard who was hunting them. It was a resource-
ful beast, and thought of this simple way of leading them to the
mouth of its cave where it could devour them at leisure.

"You ask me for permission to do what you consider is needed. If you met a man who thought himself blind because his eyes were bandaged, would you lead him by the hand, or would you tell him to take off the bandage and see for himself? Each of you has removed a different bandage, and yet you expect me to say that your eyes belong to me and that you must not use them without asking my permission. Only those who are blind are content to follow a voice they do not understand, but you are free men who must make your own choice. Perhaps I can see further than you, so listen to me a little longer before you come to a decision.

"We will forget such small difficulties as the fact that the army of the Oryx numbers only a thousand men and that the other Southern Nomes are not yet ready to send their soldiers to join us; let us pretend that each of our soldiers has the strength of a thousand and that they are under your command. Would you tell them to kill every official, every overseer, every headman, in Egypt?"

"Not *all* of them," said Ken-han. "Only those who were oppressing the people."

"You consider yourself to be a competent judge of all the thousands who hold authority under Pharaoh? Which of them shall be put to death, which shall be banished, which shall be allowed to continue in office, which shall have his authority reduced?"

"No, of course I don't," said Ken-han uncomfortably. "I've told you about one overseer, though, and my friends have each told you of one or two others."

"I know; that is why you are here. Please do not think I underestimate your help. Each of you has brought me evidence which I needed. Through what you have told me I have been able to make a sound judgment of forty-three men. Some of you look surprised! Do you imagine that I had forgotten your stories and had not taken steps to confirm the wisdom of your judgments? Forty-three names have been added to my list; three of them—I shall not tell you yet which three—will continue to hold office, for the reason that you suffered through them only because they upheld the present laws, and not because they abused authority. When the new laws are in force they will see they are faithfully administered. Of those that remain, five will be banished from

Egypt, twelve will be given positions of a smaller capacity, suitable to their powers, and the others will change place with those who used to work under them.

"If you act now you will only be setting one caste against another; the rulers against the ruled, the rich against the poor, soldiers against field-workers. If this is your plan, had you not better start by killing me? I am a noble and had sufficient treasure to build this village in which you are all living, to own this house in which we are holding this discussion. Or would you prefer to kill Ra-ab who sits beside me? Is he not the son of the Nomarch, who represents Pharaoh?"

Roidahn looked at each man in turn. "Do none of you want to kill me? Are you not being unfaithful to your ideals? Down with the ruling caste! What does it matter what kind of men they are?"

Ken-han flushed, and the others grinned at his embarrassment.

Roidahn turned to me, "It seems, Ra-ab, that we are permitted to live a little longer."

Then to the others. "The dawn will come the moment that the Watchers know sufficient to weigh the hearts of all those who hold authority, and more important still, as soon as they are ready to replace the rotten wood by sound timbers in the house of Egypt. Each of you will then be ready to take your place in the Two Lands according to your individual degrees of wisdom. Thus from chaos shall come order and from tribulation shall come peace. We are here to teach men to see the horizon toward which we are all traveling. When they are no longer blinded by illusion they will know that the roads of Earth are blocked with people trying to go in opposite directions, fighting each other to a standstill, only because they cannot see that all roads lead to the horizon and men who rightly follow them can never come into conflict with each other.

"Those of you who still wish for us to march against the other seventeen Nomes, putting to death all who hold office under Pharaoh, declare it now."

But no one declared such a wish. For Roidahn had shown them that men cannot destroy in the name of creation, nor shed blood in the name of peace.

Goddess of Women

NOT UNTIL several months later did I sleep to find myself on the bank of the River. The boat was waiting for me, and as I stepped on board it put forth on the dark water. Again the mists which obscured the far side curled back to leave a clear channel before the prow.

This time no one waited for me in the luminous country beyond. Instead of the avenue of dark trees, there was a wide plain of turf patterned with small flowers, like a mosaic in a floor of malachite. Then I saw a path on whose smooth, white surface were the hoof-marks of an oryx. I knew that I must follow them, and though I traversed a great distance there was no sense of time to make me weary.

The path led me to a pool of clear water, at which a white oryx was drinking. She lifted her head to watch me as I drew near. I tried to touch her, but she was always just beyond my reach. She pawed at the ground with her forefoot, and I saw that writing-signs had appeared in the dust. Though they seemed familiar I could not read them. The oryx watched me, as though impatient of my stupidity. With all my will I tried to understand what she would say to me. . . .

She galloped off, but now it was easy to keep up with her. The sweet grass flowed faster than water under our swift hooves. I no longer ran with clumsy, human feet. The wind sang past my curving horns, and scents I had not known before were vivid to my nostrils. Now she let me approach, and side by side we nibbled the tender shoots of a young thorn bush. She spoke to me, "At first I thought you were too proud of being human to relinquish it even for a little while."

Startled, I lifted my head from cropping a new leaf. Instead of the oryx, the Girl stood laughing beside me.

She said, "What if you forget how to change back again? Shall I have to spend eternity as shepherd to a solitary antelope? 'Ra-ab' is a funny name for an antelope! I'll be very good to you and find a fresh pasture every day, or shall I gild your horns and make a garland to lead you by?"

She patted me, and then scratched me between my horns—for

a moment it was still pleasant to be an oryx. She laughed, "Poor Ra-ab, he has forgotten how to turn back again! What will they say when you return to Earth? Do you think they will recognize you, or will they shoo you out of the house and wail for Ra-ab?"

I was dumb, frightened and bewildered. I stretched out my forefeet, hoping to find them hands; but they were still hooves, black and pointed. It was no longer fun to gallop, or to snatch at succulent leaves. The Girl must have seen I was frightened, for she knelt down and put her arms round my neck. "Poor little oryx, I was cruel to tease you! It is easy to be Ra-ab again. Do it the same way as you became an antelope. You are a man, how *can* you be an oryx? Think of yourself as Ra-ab. Ra-ab is a man and taller than I am. . . ."

Suddenly she was looking up at me instead of kneeling beside me; and the hands on her shoulders were my hands. She drew away to point at the ground about us, patterned with narrow hoof-prints.

"You didn't like that game, Ra-ab; see, I will make it as though we had never played it." She spread out her hands, and the prints vanished. And the path by which we had come, stretching so far away to where the boat waited to carry me back from my dream, vanished as though the turf were water flowing over a sand-bar.

Then she took me by the hand and told me to close my eyes. When I opened them, we were standing by the door-way of a hut outside a small village. There was the sound of a woman sobbing. Out of the doorway came a man carrying a thin flexible stick, the end frayed, and stained with blood. He seemed not to see us, until the Girl, telling me to watch what she did, stepped forward and pulled the stick from his hand.

Now she was no longer a girl half a head shorter than I. She was a woman more than six cubits tall, wearing the coarse tunic of a worker in the fields. The man cringed away from her, putting up his hands as though to protect his head from a blow. She caught them in one of hers and dragged him back to the hut. It seemed as though his hands were bound together by cords; he struggled but could not free himself. Then she thrust them against the lintel, and they stayed there as though bound fast to the wooden bar.

Calmly and dispassionately she began to flog him, and his back broke open into weals, meticulously placed from neck to thigh. He screamed like a snared animal; yet I found nothing terrible in seeing my love, who was so gentle, deliver such bitter punishment.

The flogging over, she broke the rod into seven pieces and threw them on the ground. Where they fell sprang up seven osiers, each bearing a multiplicity of rods such as he had used. He slumped down in the doorway, staring at the seven trees and at the woman who stood among them.

Then she spoke, "You have used your strength against the woman whom, in the name of the Gods, you made an oath to protect; now you have learned that the goddess of women is stronger than a man. You have felt the pain that was brought by your rod; and in the name of your wife it is broken into seven pieces and from their planting have grown seven trees. Look well upon them, seeing how from their branches spring many rods and that when one is cut two grow in its place. Know also that though I have flogged you I am not weary, and that the rod I use never loses its power, only does it vanish when it is no longer needful. The tears of your wife will make these trees grow fast, and should she cry out because of you then will I answer her voice as surely as an echo. Remember my seven trees, and think well before you give way to the hunger that will be quenched by their fruit—for the lust for power makes bitter eating. Here shall these trees remain, and only when the heart of your wife rejoices shall they go, so that in sleep you may walk unshadowed by them."

I wanted to see her do another magic, but she said it was almost time for us to wake. I thought I would find myself standing in the boat, watching the dark, heavy cliffs approaching as the mist gathered to hide her from me, but she said there was still time for us to talk.

For a moment she disappeared, and then was again beside me. "I'm sorry I had to go away," she said. "Someone opened the shutter; the sunlight was strong on my face and made me open my eyes. But I've pulled up the cover and gone to sleep again."

"How do you change yourself so easily? I think I used to know how, but I've forgotten."

"Of course you did; it's only Ra-ab who is unsure of himself. I know what it feels like, knowing and yet not remembering. They are teaching me to play a harp; I get so cross when my fingers are clumsy, because I know that once the strings obeyed them . . . though the harp I played had four strings instead of five. It's such a nuisance having to learn things one used to know just because one's been born again. Still, it doesn't take nearly as long here as it does down there."

"Do tell me, please, quickly, before you wake up, how can I make myself tall or turn into an antelope?"

"Just by thinking you *are* an antelope. Think yourself into an antelope now."

"No, I'm not going to. You might leave me when I'd forgotten how to undo myself."

"Well, make yourself twice as tall as me."

"How should I know that it wasn't you making yourself shorter?"

"Ra-ab, you're being *very* difficult!"

"I'll practice hard, so that next time we meet I'll be as good at it as you."

"You'd better start on things outside yourself. I think you'll find it easier; I started that way. They used to bolt the door of my room, because I went for walks by myself at night when they wanted me to stay in bed; and there were bars over the window, so I couldn't get out that way either. So I pretended there was a door in the wall which no one knew about except me, and that it would open when I told it to. It became my favorite idea when I was going to sleep. Very soon I could see a thin crack where it fitted into the wall. Then I thought about it even harder, and night by night the crack grew wider till I could walk through it. Then I thought it would be fun if it could open into a garden instead of on the court, and the next time I went through, it did! The water in the pool I made was warm to swim in, even though it was winter and the nights were cold. Then I used to make vines have grapes on them when I knew they were bare; and I made honeysuckle climb up the pillars of the central courtyard and violets cover the limestone floor. I can't remember how long it was before I thought people into different shapes. I had a horrid nurse, at least she is my attendant now but she used to be my nurse, who always pulled my hair when she was polishing it. She was so proud of her own hair that she never wore a wig. I thought her into being bald, not just shaven like a priest but shiny as a duck's egg. At first I thought she was only a person I had invented, but when she began to wail and screech I knew she was real. I am nearly sure she remembered it too, though she pretended not to believe in dreams, for the next morning I heard her repeating a spell against baldness over and over again, and her hair was all greasy with something she had rubbed into it.

"After that I changed lots of people, but none of them into horrid things unless they had been very horrid to me first. There was a little crippled boy who used to sit in the dust outside the coppersmith's, to beg for food. I went to see him when he was asleep, and he was still sitting there. He thought he would always be crippled; so he was, even when he had left his body behind. I made him strong and beautiful, and being happy while he was asleep seemed to make him different even in the daytime. I wanted to bring him to live in our house, but they wouldn't let me.

"Then I thought of making myself different. I started with little things, like the color of my hair or making myself look grown up when I was only eight. Then someone told me other ways of using this kind of magic; and after a time it was as easy to change what I looked like as it is to put on another tunic. I only turned into an antelope to surprise you." She broke off. "You must go back to your boat. I've got to go now. . . ."

And I was alone in my room at Hotep-Ra.

Daughter of the Hare

WHEN I WENT to Roidahn later that morning, I found him studying some plans which a new architect had made for a village to be built to the west of Hotep-Ra. He looked up when I came in. "I have news from your father, Ra-ab. He wishes you to go home for a few days, but you need not leave here until the new moon."

I was surprised, as Father usually sent such messages direct to me. "I wonder why he wants me?"

"I can let you know that, though I think he would prefer to tell you himself."

"Has anything happened?" And then I added, perhaps because I was still thinking of the girl beyond the river, "Has Kiyas decided to get married?"

"No, though the question of his children's marriage seems to be occupying your father's mind."

"You mean—*me*?" He nodded, and I went on, "Well, I needn't go home to discuss it with him again. He brought up the subject before I came here, and I told him that I already knew whom I was going to marry, so it was no use his planning an alliance for me."

"Ra-ab, why did you never tell me you were betrothed? You have become as a son to me, and I should like to welcome her as a daughter."

Then I told him of the Girl, and how we loved each other though we hadn't met on Earth since we were born. It was much easier to put into words than it had been to Father, or even Kiyas. . . . "You do understand, don't you, Roidahn?"

"Of course," he said. "Even the little that Dardas told you should have been enough to show that I find nothing strange in a reunion of friends who may not have met for several centuries."

"Then will you tell Father there is no point in my going to discuss it with him?"

"I'm afraid I can't do that: he had already made his plans before sending for you."

"Well, he'll have to *unmake* them! He married a woman whom he really loved, and I'm not going to betray everything I believe in just because he thinks it would be expedient to have an alliance with an adjoining Nome."

"You told me you didn't know the name of your love, or where she comes from."

"I don't; but I shall recognize her as soon as we meet. I can't prove it. There are very few realities that one *can* prove except in one's own heart. Surely you don't think I ought to betray the woman I love?"

"Have you forgotten the story of the man who dreamed of a gold scarab which had his name on it? In the dream he was told that if he wore the scarab on a thong round his neck he would be eternally young. He left his house and traveled to far countries; but he never found the scarab though he spent a lifetime in search of it. Once he had been rich, but all his wealth was expended on his many journeys, and when at last he returned home his only companion was an old hunting-dog. His house was in ruins, but one room was still standing.

There was some musty straw in one corner, and he crept in there with his dog to sleep. During the night he heard the dog scratching at the mud floor, and he felt something like a smooth pebble roll against his hand. He picked it up, but was too sleepy to open his eyes to look at it.

"The next morning a woman from the neighboring house heard the dog howling and went to see what was the matter. She found the old man had died in his sleep, and in his hand was the scarab he had searched so long to find. For fifty years it had been buried under the floor of his own house. He had never been told that the greatest treasure is often to be found at home."

"You mean I ought to go back to stay with Father, until my love comes to find me? I told her I was going to look for her; she will be waiting for me."

"I never said you shouldn't search if it is necessary," said Roidahn. "I only suggest that it is sometimes wise to look first in the obvious place. Your father wishes you to marry the Daughter of the Hare, and for that purpose has arranged for her to stay with Kiyas, and so give you an opportunity to meet each other without formality. If she is not the girl whom you love you are under no obligation, and if she is—will you then refuse to marry her?"

Except in very hot weather I seldom slept during the day, but when I left Roidahn I went to my room, closed the shutters and lay down on the bed. "I will dream of her," I repeated to myself, over and over again. "She must tell me whether she is the Daughter of the Hare. And I must bring back her answer."

At last I went to sleep, but woke none the wiser. I began to think she was the Daughter of the Hare. How she would tease me when I told her that I had refused to meet her when Father had suggested it nearly a year before! Perhaps she wouldn't believe I had ever dreamed of her. Hadn't she said, "I may pretend not to recognize you?". . . If I had a present made for her before we ever met, she couldn't help but believe me. . . . Nobody makes such beautiful things as Neku; I will go to him at once and ask him to design a necklace such as no other woman can match.

I think my eagerness to see the drawings must have shown him that it was intended for a betrothal gift. The rayed pendants were graduated to the shape of a young crescent moon, and were alternately of red and yellow gold. Each pendant was tipped with a gold oryx, those at the shoulder small as my little fingernail, and in the center perhaps three times as large. It seemed almost impossible that it could be ready in time, even though all Neku's pupils worked on it together; but on the tenth day the necklace was ready to take with me when I returned home.

I had thought that the Daughter of the Hare would not arrive until the following day, yet when Kiyas met me at the landing-stage she told me that our guests were already with us.

"I'm almost sure you'll like her," said Kiyas. "She's not at all fat, and I think she must have been teasing when she said that she might be."

"Then you think she is the girl I dreamed about?"

Kiyas looked surprised. "Isn't she? I thought she must be when I heard you had agreed to come home to meet her."

"I don't know, but I'm sure to recognize her if she is."

"I think she's rather shy about meeting you. She wouldn't come down to the river with me: she said you wouldn't wish to be troubled with visitors when you had only just arrived home."

Kiyas and I went up to the house together, and on the way I showed her the oryx necklace.

"She is lucky to have such a lovely present," said Kiyas, rather enviously. "I wonder if I will ever have a husband who is thoughtful enough to make me something like that before he has even seen me. When are you going to give it to her? This evening, or when you are officially betrothed?"

"I'm not sure whether I'm going to give it to her at all. Only the woman I'm in love with is going to wear it, and if I never meet her it will be buried with me in my tomb."

Late that evening I was again on the same path with Kiyas beside me; but this time I was striding back toward the landing-stage.

"You can't go away like this!" Kiyas was saying. "Father is so angry he has shut himself in the papyrus room and won't come out. And I don't think the Hare really believed your story about an urgent message from Hotep-Ra."

"It was the only excuse I could think of. I'm sorry to spoil your clever little scheme!"

"It wasn't my scheme, it was Father's. He said you were too old to go on being in love with an imaginary woman, and it was only because you had never met anyone suitable to marry, and when you did you would fall in love with her. How could I know she wasn't the woman you wanted? I thought you were going to be so happy; and when you were married there would be lots of banquets and you would come home instead of being at Hotep-Ra, and I wouldn't have to go on living in an enormous house with an old man who is sometimes unreal as a tomb painting. Now everything is spoiled: just because she is not what you imagine she ought to be."

"It's not my fault," I said desperately. "I made it perfectly clear to you and Father that I would find my own wife. Why did you lead Roidahn to believe that no word had been spoken of betrothal, and that she was coming as your guest so that I could meet her casually? How do you think I feel, being put in a position where I've got to behave like an ill-mannered lout? You and Father, and her father, all pretending to be indifferent, yet watching me meet that poor girl like bird-snarers who see two fat wild-fowl walk under the net together!"

"Ra-ab, *do* stop behaving like a fool, and come back to the house. You *can't* run away like this—think how awful she'll feel."

"*You* think how awful she'll feel. It's not *my* fault! Even if her friends *do* know that this was to be a betrothal visit, she will be able to tell them that when she saw what a boorish young man Ra-ab Hotep was she refused to marry him. Of course you'd rather I married her, though it would make us both thoroughly miserable for the rest of our lives."

"I think you're being infuriating!" said Kiyas, who now was having to run to keep up with me. "She is a very nice girl, and much prettier than I expected. You can have a secondary wife if you want to later on."

"I happen to be one of the Eyes of Horus, though you seem to have forgotten it," I said coldly. "We are supposed to set the standard by which other people can find happiness. When I marry—or if I marry—it will only be when I have found the woman with whom I can take the Oath of the New Name. Marriages of expediency may work admirably with many people, but I am not one of them. If you can't see anything higher you will be perfectly justified in letting Father find you a suitable husband. But I *can* see something higher, so if I were to fall in with your clever little plan I should be worse than if I took my pleasures with a foreign concubine who gives the hospitality of her body to any man who pays her."

I heard voices ahead of us, and knew that we were close to the landing-stage. I was glad that my servant had been able to carry out my orders so quickly; evidently the boat was ready.

Kiyas stopped. "It's no good my coming any further. Nothing I can say will make you change your mind?"

Suddenly I wasn't angry with her any more. I put my hands on her shoulders and looked down at her face, pale and anxious in the starlight. "No, Kiyas, I must go: it will be easier for all of us. Make any excuse you like. Say I had to go because of the Watchers; it's true in a way, for I would betray them if I did anything else." I opened the little box I was holding in my hand. "This necklace will go everywhere with me, until I find the only woman who shall ever wear it. Don't ever be satisfied with a lesser love, Kiyas. You and I could be so very happy with the person we really belong to, and there can be no loneliness so terrible as being married to a stranger."

"You're sure she was a stranger?"

"Quite, quite sure!"

"Then I'm glad you are going away. Forgive me for making things so difficult for you."

"I will if you'll promise me something."

"What is it?"

"That you too will wait until you find your love."

"I promise," said Kiyas.

Assignment

THE EYES OF HORUS, who were few in number, had been specially trained in the judgment of character, and in many ways had
been taught how best to cure those who had sinned against the
laws. In nearly every part of Egypt there were Watchers ready to
assume authority when the time came, but in the Royal City
there were still many on whom judgment had not yet been
given. Those who would be Nomarchs of the South after the
Dawn all belonged to the Hundred of Horus, and they, together
with Roidahn, would decide who should be Pharaoh. It seemed
probable that the choice would fall upon the Vizier, Amenemhet.

I was nearly eighteen when Roidahn told me that at last I was
ready to play the part for which he had trained me. He showed
me a list of forty names, saying, "Amenemhet himself has already
judged many of the officials of the Court, but there are some
with whom he cannot become sufficiently intimate to be able to
assess their character. The etiquette of the Court is so rigid that
in the presence of the Vizier men must be as careful of their
speech as they would be in the presence of Pharaoh. He told me
that it would be well if one of us, who had the right by birth to
enter the Court circle, and yet was not sufficiently well known
for people to trouble to conceal from him their thoughts, should
make their acquaintance. That is why I am sending you to the
Royal City, Ra-ab "

I concealed my surprise and elation, saying, "Do you think I,
who have never been beyond the Oryx, will be able to serve you
as ably as Hanuk?"

"If I did not, I should have sent Hanuk instead of you."

"Who shall I pretend to be?"

"Who but yourself?"

"Then how will you arrange for me to meet the people on
whom you want my opinion?"

"That has arranged itself as smoothly as though I had made
the plan myself. The sister of your father's mother married a
Keeper of the Ivory Seal under the late Pharaoh. They had a son
named Heliokios who must now be over sixty. He has no children, and perhaps this has something to do his suddenly

remembering his young kinsman, and sending a messenger to your father suggesting that you go to stay with him at his house in the Royal City. He also is a Keeper of the Ivory Seal, of whom, as you know, there are four who give judgment in the name of Pharaoh. Heliokios is not a Watcher, and he will be one of the forty on whom you must give judgment."

"Am I then to betray my own kinsman?"

"It is not pleasant to accept hospitality when you have been sent as a spy; but should you begin to doubt your justification, think of Neku the Goldsmith, or of Sesu, who cannot walk because when he was a child he was beaten so mercilessly for stealing bread. Think of Benti, blind because she was forced to look at the sun until her eyes burnt out; stretched out like a hide being cured, her eyelids held apart by thorns from dawn till sunset. Ra gives his power to those who reflect the light, but Set is the shadow cast by those who intercept it. Even in the house of your kinsman, whose salt you have eaten and by whose hospitality you are protected, there may be men of the shadow. If light and shadow are born of the same parents there can be no real brotherhood between them: kinship is only valid in the name of Ra."

"May Kiyas come with me?"

"Your father says he cannot spare her until you return; for she discharges many of his duties. And there is another reason: the only women of the household of Heliokios are concubines, and so by the standards of the Royal City, which are in some ways remarkable for their stupidity, it would not be considered correct for her to go there without an elder kinswoman."

"How many servants am I to take with me?"

"It would be usual for a man of your rank to travel with at least four; as well as litter-bearers and perhaps the rowers of a pleasure barge. But I have decided that it would be best if you went with little circumstance. For a long time there have been rumors that the Oryx differs from the other Nomes; but if they see the Nomarch's son with only one servant they will imagine this Nome carries little weight in the affairs of Egypt. When you go to the Palace you will of course take the precedence due to your rank, which is ahead of all officials save they who hold a Royal Seal." He paused and then went on, "I have not yet told you who is to be your servant."

"But I know that," I said, surprised. "Hek has been with me six years."

Roidahn smiled. "But the name of your new servant is Sebek."

"Sebek—but why?"

"As your body-servant he will attend you at whatever house you visit. During formal banquets he will be your cup-bearer; when hunting he will walk behind you to carry your throwing-sticks or spare arrows. Everyone you meet will have a similar attendant, and they will long have had opportunity to make shrewd judgment of their masters. Sebek may well learn more from the cup-bearers of officials than you will have opportunity to find out from the men themselves. You will start in three days, and will travel in your father's barge. Among the rowers there will be four who will stay in a different part of the city, in a house owned by a Watcher. They will act as messengers between us, and by them I shall hear your decree as to who among those forty men shall live, or be banished, or die, for Egypt."

The next day Kiyas came to Hotep-Ra. Sebek and I went along the road to meet her. She told her litter-bearers to go on without her and walked back with us across the fields, which the young grain was just misting with green.

"I knew five days ago where Roidahn was sending you," she said. "For I was there when he talked it over with Father. I think it's a very good idea Sebek going as your servant, though perhaps it will be rather dull for him. And I've got bad news for both of you: I've decided to come with you!"

"But Roidahn told me that Father wouldn't give his permission. What made him change his mind?"

"As far as I know he hasn't changed it," she said airily. "If Roidahn orders me to go, Father will have to let me; there is no higher authority than the leader of the Watchers."

"And why should Roidahn want you to go?" asked Sebek.

"Because I will be able to help you to work for the Watchers. You've both been sent to find out enough about certain people to make a proper judgment of them. So you'll have to make them talk without concealing their real thoughts. Most of them are men, and therefore it will be much easier for me to gain their confidence than for either of you. Some people are foolish enough to think that a girl of sixteen is more guileless than a man; so they would talk to me more freely than they would to Ra-ab. There are all sorts of questions I could ask them, and they'd only be flattered at my interest. But if Ra-ab asked the same questions they would either think he was impertinent or else become suspicious."

"I'm sorry, Kiyas. I'd love to take you with me. I suggested it to Roidahn myself, but it's not only Father; the people of the Royal City have silly ideas. They would think we were barbarians if I took my sister without an older woman to look after her."

"Oh, but I know all that! Father explained it to me himself; he seemed to think it so important that it gave me my idea. I'm not coming as your sister, Ra-ab, but as your concubine!"

How like Kiyas! I said, "I thought you had a serious idea. I didn't know you took it all as a joke."

"It isn't a joke: lots of young men have concubines. I expect Sebek has if he would only admit it."

Sebek looked uncomfortable, and muttered something which sounded like, "I wish you minded whether I had."

Having paused to appreciate his discomfiture, Kiyas went on, "Father told Roidahn that Heliokios had four old concubines living in the women's quarters of the House of the Two Winds. That was why he was so firm about my not going there—Mother would never have been so silly about such things. Still, Heliokios couldn't mind about me. An old man with *four* concubines couldn't grudge a young man having only *one*." She paused. "I've been practicing making my eyes with khol, and you can get me the right kind of clothes as soon as we reach the city. Explain that I have so few with me by saying that one of my traveling-boxes fell overboard.

"Kiyas," said Sebek severely, "you still talk as though you were a child. You must realize that if Ra-ab never marries, you and your husband may rule the Oryx. Do you think it would increase the dignity of our Nome if it were whispered that the co-ruler was once a concubine?"

"Don't listen to him, Ra-ab. He's just deliberately being difficult. You *will* let me come with you, won't you?"

"I'm awfully sorry, Kiyas, but I can't. Honestly, it's not a very good idea; in fact it might quite easily become a very bad idea.

And it would be terribly dull for you, hidden in the women's quarters. If I took you about with me you might so easily be recognized as my sister."

"Do you mean you are *not* going to ask Roidahn to let me go?"

"No, I'm not."

"I think you're being very cruel . . . making me live in this awful dullness when you're going to have exciting adventures."

"The adventures may turn out to be *too* exciting. This isn't a kind of game, Kiyas: if one of us is betrayed we may be very grateful to die. If I made a slip through which I am suspected as a spy—well, Pharaoh is said to have Asiatic torturers, who boast of a thousand ways of making a conspirator betray those who are working with him."

"Do you think I'm frightened because it's dangerous?"

"No, Kiyas, I know you are not. Think what you did during the pestilence. I'm sure Roidahn will find work for you too, and it may be more difficult and dangerous than ours is going to be. Meanwhile you must learn to be patient."

She nodded forlornly. "I suppose I shall have to try; but patient is a thing I'm so very bad at being. I would have been so much cleverer at being a concubine!"

PART IV

Royal City

BY NOON of the fourth day of our river journey we were opposite the Old Capital. I was very interested to catch even so brief a
glimpse of its declining glories, for until Pharaoh had built his
new city, where the river divides, the Two Lands had been ruled
from there for countless generations. Now it's only importance
was as the principal town of the Reed, the most southerly of the
three Royal Nomes.

A little further on I had my first sight of the Great Pyramids.
They were mightier even than I had expected, and though their
temples, and the causeway which led down from them to the
river, were of the same white limestone, they could not equal the
brilliance of the "Two who Remember," which dazzled the eyes
like burnished metal. I thought that my rowers, none of whom
had been so far downriver before, would wish to take this opportunity of seeing them more closely; but when I suggested that we
should delay our journey for a few hours, they said they would
prefer to keep on, so as to reach our destination by sunset.

Long before we came in sight of the walls of the Royal City the
river was thronged with boats. Pleasure craft skimmed like water-
beetles among war galleys and heavily laden trading-ships. Two
state barges, each of forty oars, held on their majestic course
while sailing boats fell away from the wind to make way for them.
The sails varied from the common red-brown cloth to fine canvas
dyed many different colors and painted with the device of the
owner. Instead of the huts of field-workers, such as clustered
round other towns, the flat landscape was broken only by a few
large estates. Sebek had been here only once before, but he
pointed things out to me as though I were a foreigner he was trying to impress.

"It is sometimes called the 'City of Seven Gates'; and the walls
are so strong that a few men like us could hold it against an army
of barbarians. You will be able to see the pennants flying from the
entrance pylon of the Palace when we get out of the way of that
grain barge." He broke off to shout to the steersman, "Denk!

Look to your oar! If you watch the City we shall never land there!"

The barge passed perilously close, and water trickled down the oars, which had had to be raised in haste, and formed little pools among the traveling boxes at our feet. I cut short Denk's apologies.

"It did us no harm. And if the steersman sees as much to surprise him when he reaches our part of the river, the fish will get the benefit of his cargo!"

The City was on the west bank, which at this point was high and sheer. Rows of shade trees, not yet fully grown, lined the top of the embankment, and about every hundred paces a flight of stone steps led down to a landing-stage. These landing-stages were stone built, and extended far enough into the water for boats to reach them even when the Nile was at its lowest level, before the Inundation.

"Notice how the embankment has been made too steep to climb," said Sebek. "It looks vertical, but really it has a slight overhang, so that even if a man could find fingerhold between the facing blocks it would still be impossible to scale. Only the steps would have to be defended if the City were attacked from the river; and Hanuk thinks there is some way by which the treads can be turned on a concealed pivot so that they too become impregnable."

He told Denk to put in at the fourth landing-stage; where stood a tall man wearing a blue tunic of an upper servant. Sebek pointed to him, saying, "That will be the steward of your kinsman's household. His name is Daklion, and I have heard he is an honest man, though not yet a Watcher. From now we must never forget we are master and servant, for if they hear me speak to you as an equal they will think we are barbarians."

I nodded and turned to Denk. "You all know what to do?"

"I with six rowers am to return to your father, on whose name may Ra shine forever. The four who stay to carry your words which only they of the Horizon may hear, will go to the Street of the Coppersmiths, and lodge at the house of one appointed by Hanuk, Son of Roidahn. One of them, disguised as a beggar, will wait outside the gate of the House of the Two Winds every day, at sunset and an hour after dawn. Should the Young Oryx, or

Sebek his servant, give this man a gift of food and if he finds concealed in it a papyrus on which words are scribed . . . then he who scribed them will know that they will be read in Hotep-Ra within three days."

One of the four men of whom he had spoken said, "The Young Oryx may rest content we shall never forget that we are of the Watchers."

The five rowers on the left of the boat lifted their oars out of the water, moving together as though the oars were the fingers of a hand. I stepped on to the landing-stage, and the men waiting there came forward to make obeisance.

As this was our first greeting we used the words of formality; and as mine was the higher rank I waited for him to speak first. "In the name of Heliokios, Lord of the House of the Two Winds, Holder of the Ivory Seal under Pharaoh, Keeper of the Scales of Justice in the Third Hall of Audience, I bring you greeting. May there be peace upon the house of your father and upon the house of your sons and of your son's sons."

I touched his shoulder with my right hand; a greeting only a degree more formal than that used between equals, and I could see he was pleased at the courtesy. "I, Ra-ab Hotep, Son of the Oryx, bring greetings in the name of my father, Khnum-hotep, Nomarch. May there be peace upon your name, Daklion, Steward of the House of the Two Winds, Keeper of the Seal of Heliokios. Greetings also in the name of Sebek, he who stands beside me and who is to me as you are to my kinsman. May there be peace between you in the name of Ra."

At the top of the steps were assembled the servants who had come to escort us. There were carrying-chairs, each with two bearers, for myself, Daklion and Sebek; and four small asses, on which were tied our boxes and the two carved chests of gifts which Father had sent to Heliokios. We crossed the street which bordered the river and entered another, also lined with trees, leading westwards between the garden walls of houses of considerable size. Where this street was crossed by a much wider roadway we turned north, into what I saw must be the principal way of the City. The surface was of stone chippings, beaten down so as to form a hard pavement, and the central half was raised about a cubit, leaving a lane on either side. Though both side lanes were crowded the central one was empty; not until later did I learn that this was because it was used only by Pharaoh or those heirs of his body from which the next ruler would be chosen. The road was bordered by a double row of shade trees planted in groups of several varieties so that the vista was of receding bands of various tones of foliage. After every seventh tree there was a ram-headed sphinx, resting its forefeet on a stele which recorded the glories of Pharaoh, Founder of the Royal City. This great avenue led to the pylon of the outer courtyard of the Palace; and set in grooves on either side of the bronze gates were the standards of the Nomes, and beside each of these flew a pennant painted with the sign of the Nomarch. A breeze had come up and the pennants streamed on the wind; the yellow Oryx on a white ground, the green of the Tortoise, the blue and violet of the Hare, the green and scarlet of the Leopard, and the blue and yellow of the Jackal . . . standing ranked like mighty sentinels of Egypt.

There was an open space before the gates, and about a hundred paces before reaching this we turned into a side road on the left. It was shaded by date-palms, which must have been preserved when the city was built for they looked as though the smallest of them had more than fifty years. A sudden gust disturbed them, and their heavy leaves rattled like sheets of copper. On both sides of this road were smaller houses, each set in its own garden; later I knew that most of them were owned by minor officials of the palace, though in a few lived the favorite concubine of rich men who for some reason preferred to keep them there instead of in the women's quarters of their own household. At the end of the road, and facing down it, I saw a pair of massive wooden gates, set in a high wall painted a cool, dusty pink, and by their size recognized that they led to a house of more importance than the others.

"You have come to the end of your journey," said Daklion. "This is the House of the Two Winds."

The gate-keeper must have been awaiting our arrival, for as we approached the gates swung open. We entered a paved courtyard, bare of flowers except for those which trailed from four large pottery jars set at the corners of an oblong pool. The house surrounded this courtyard on three sides; the wing on the right contained the rooms of the upper servants, and behind them were the kitchen quarters; in the wing on the left were the rooms of Heliokios's women with beyond it a small private garden used only by them. The central portion of the main block had a second story, and these upper rooms opened on the flat roofs which were shaded by trellis, supported on wooden pillars thickly covered by a vine with yellow flowers, a species I had not seen before.

Daklion told me that these upper rooms were the private apartments of Heliokios, and that those on the right of the ground floor, which we entered through one of the three inter-communicating rooms in which Heliokios entertained his guests, had been set aside for me. He asked me if I would prefer Sebek to have the room next to mine or if he should go to the ser-vants' quarters. I said that I should prefer to have Sebek with me, and after he had asked me to send word by Sebek of anything I needed, Daklion left us alone.

Sebek said he had better have the smaller of the two rooms, which opened on the courtyard. The entrance to mine was through his, and in addition to the two windows it had a door leading to a paved garden, which I was glad to see had a large swimming pool lined with blue tiles. As I knew this was a Day of Audience and Heliokios would not be home before sunset, there was time for me to swim before his return. The water was clear and refreshing, and I wished that Sebek could have shared my enjoyment; I had suggested it, only to be reminded that he was now my servant and that in the Royal City he would not swim in the same pool as his master. When I had finished I found that he had laid out a fresh kilt, two of the turquoise armlets and the hawk pectoral, made for me by a pupil of Neku. Then he left me to join Daklion for the evening meal and I went to meet Heliokios.

I had only seen my kinsman once before, and that was when I was eight years old. He was not so tall as I remembered him; yet must have been very powerful, though now the heavy muscles seemed flaccid under a skin that was a network of fine wrinkles. He was still wearing the ceremonial wig in which he had dis-pensed justice, each of the many plaits tipped with a gold papy-rus flower. He wore massive enamel armlets and a pectoral of pierced goldwork, the design centering round an ape of Thoth holding the Scales of Justice. His lips were narrow, and in his eyes was the look I have sometimes seen in the eyes of a falcon, strong and fearless yet with a glint of cunning.

We exchanged the usual lengthy formalities, in which he inquired after the welfare of my family, and even of those members of my father's household with whose name he was familiar. I replied as was expected of me, for Hanuk had well trained me in the usage of the formalities of the Royal Nomes.

When we were able to talk more freely he said, "As my kinsman you will find many doors open to you, and a young man of your rank will never lack entertainment in the Royal City. As well as banquets, of which you may soon grow weary even as I did at your age, there will be occasions when you will find it very pleasant to let the current carry your pleasure-boat downstream while you listen to singers. When you tire of women's voices you will find plenty of companions to share in other sport, whether you prefer to test the strength of your throwing-spear against a hippopotamus, or to follow antelope or gazelle with a leash of hunting dogs."

I asked him whether I might go with him to hear him giving judgment. He seemed surprised at this request, so I said that my father wished me to learn of his wisdom so that when the time came for me to rule the Oryx I might profit by the experience of my great kinsman. I saw this pleased him . . . at which I was relieved for I feared that I might have spread flattery too thickly.

He ate sparingly, and twice I saw his hand go to his side as though he felt a sudden stab of pain. "Tomorrow there will be many to share our evening meal," he said, "for the younger officials of the Court, as well as the sons and daughters of men of influence, are coming here to exchange greetings with the young Oryx. Soon I shall move to my country estate, the second House of the Two Winds, for it is more pleasant there when the heat increases and is near enough to the City for me to return here every fourth day to administer my office of the Ivory Seal. When we go there you must tell me how it compares with your father's estates. My vines are coming into bearing; for now that I hold seal under Pharaoh it is permissible for me to have my own vineyard."

Forgetting that Roidahn had told me that in the Royal Nomes

all vines belong to Pharaoh, so that even the nobles must pay a royal price for their wine, I said, "In the Oryx any one can have grapes who troubles to plant a vine."

"I have heard that the Oryx has many customs which are unfamiliar here," he said coldly, "and I have no doubt that her son will make a profitable companion even for an old man like myself."

I tried to turn the sharp edge of his sarcasm on the shield of courtesy. "In friendship both must profit equally, for when one profits nothing neither can the other, so it is assured that you will learn from me for you have so much to teach me."

He laughed. "So the boy from the South is not unready with his tongue! I will confess that I asked you to come here because I am an old man without a son and you are nearest to me in blood. I thought you would be a boor, for though your father is Nomarch he keeps the seclusion of a scholar. I even thought I should have to persuade you to change the manner of your dress; but that pectoral you are wearing might have been made for Pharaoh and the linen of your kilt is as fine as my own."

He leaned back in his chair and studied me intently as Father looking at a new scribe's painting. "Yes, you will do very well here, and your friends will not choose you only because they know you are my kinsman. Most of us prefer the shaven head and a wig, but now that the younger prince has taken to wearing his own hair you are in the fashion . . . and won't have to join those who are making trade for the Syrian, who has an unguent which he claims could grow feathers on a vulture's head!"

A Nubian servant came into the room carrying in his arms a gray, female monkey. It chattered with excitement when it saw Heliokios and leaped on his shoulder, rubbing its head against his cheek as he caressed it.

"Mimu," he said pointing to me, "that is Ra-ab who has come here as our guest. You must not bite him or I shall have to punish you. But if you decide that you and he are to be friends he may let you ride on his shoulder when I have to leave you alone."

He split open a fig and gave it to her; she took it very daintily, holding it in one hand and taking small, swift bites until it was finished.

"She will let no one else handle her," he said proudly. "Except the slave whose sole duty it is to care for her; I had to buy him from the trader who brought them both to Egypt, for she had come to accept him and might have pined if they had been parted. When you are as old as I am, Ra-ab, may you be fortunate enough to have a woman who contents you as well as Mimu contents her master!"

In answer to my unspoken thought he went on, "Yes, I have been married. She was a beautiful woman, yet the three years we spent together before she died did not incline me to take another wife. I was more fortunate in my concubines, but even with them there was no fire to cool to ash, only a comfortable habit. There were four of them; for each in turn I hoped to receive a son, but only one felt a child quicken in her womb and that she brought forth dead. They are all old now, and because they are too careful ever to quarrel with me they still live under my roof. They seem content in their own fashion, sometimes I hear them wrangling among themselves but it is seldom they disturb me."

From the tone of his voice, even more than from his words, it was obvious he had no affection for them. I wondered why he still kept them in his house, until I remembered that a man was not supposed to turn a concubine away unless she preferred another man, or wished to live alone, in which case he would have to provide her with the means to do so. Those who wished to remain were treated with the same careless charity that permitted the old hunting dogs to be fed with the others who could still course their quarry.

Heliokios told me that the concubines would take great pleasure at my courtesy if I were to exchange greetings with them. When I was received by them they reminded me of old dogs, who yelp in their sleep as they dream of a lost prowess. Thick cosmetic was strident on their flaccid skins; it seemed to make them unreal, as though wooden puppets had come alive. They wore many bracelets and necklaces which jangled as they moved. I wondered whether their memory of the time they had been given these tokens of affection was still as untarnished as the metal—or had it faded with their beauty?

Heliokios seldom went to see them, and eagerly they asked me for news of him, pretending he had been away on a journey in order to hide from me his indifference. Their power to charm men had been their life; now they were no longer desired, so they vied with each other to warm their pride by any little flame of jealousy they could still kindle. Their eyes were hard and greedy, yet pitiful as the eyes of old monkeys. They were not frightened of death, but against age they fought with an almost savage desperation, refusing his gifts of mellowness and peace as they cried in shrill voices for youth to return. Youth, who had so long forgotten them.

The Heliokios who delighted to play with his monkey seemed a different man to him whom I watched give judgment in the Third Hall of Audience. The Keeper of the Ivory Seal was a figure to inspire awe; with the great wig of ceremony, the purple cloak clasped with the gold lion heads of the Royal Insignia; and in his hand the "flail of the ivory handle," thrice banded with gold.

Petitioners trembled before him, for on his word hung death or freedom. I saw that he upheld the letter of the law, but had not the wisdom to interpret it; so the man who had stolen a loaf because his child was starving received the same punishment as he who stole because he was too idle to work.

On the first day, I heard him sentence a field-worker who had killed a noble's hunting dog which was attacking his child. The law decreed that to raise a hand against an overlord was to die, this also if it were raised against the family or the servant of the overlord.

The steward who represented the owner of the dog pleaded that it had been his master's most faithful servant and should be judged as such. It had been trained to kill, so why should it suffer for mistaking a child for a gazelle?

The field-worker was allowed to bring in his child as a witness. It was crying with fright, and dirty bandages were unwound from its head and right arm to show deep gashes, ragged in the inflamed flesh, where the dog's teeth had torn it before the father had come to the rescue. Surely, I thought, Heliokios must give judgment in favor of the man who protected his child, for in killing the dog he not only protected his own child but other children. It is the noble who must be punished for not already having tried to make reparation. . . .

But Heliokios followed the words of the law and not their spirit. "The hand which held the knife that killed the dog must be cut off."

I only stopped myself from making a protest by remembering how Roidahn had counseled me, many times, that my role in the Royal City was to learn of those whom I met until I knew enough to judge them. Had I needed yet another proof of Roidahn's wisdom, I received it that evening.

Heliokios was trying to teach Mimu to scatter millet for the fish. He turned to me and said, "If I had thought of Mimu while I was giving judgment today, and so had a proper understanding of what the owner of that dog has lost, I should not have been so lenient with its murderer."

"Lenient!"

"Yes, I did not sentence him to death as I should have done, only to lose one hand."

He must have seen my disgust, for he said, indulgently as though to humor a child, "I forgot that you are strange to life outside the Oryx. Is it really true that your father never decrees mutilation and that the heaviest sentence he orders is banishment from that Nome?"

"Yes, that is quite true."

He shook his head in disapproval. "I shall have to teach you wisdom while you are here. I know that your father is a great scholar, but it shocks me that a Nomarch feels so little of his responsibility. If he forgets the Flail there will be a rebellion in his Nome, and if one Nome rebels it endangers the others, just as a single load of diseased corn may spread the rot through a whole granary."

"You are wise, Heliokios, and I will remember your words. If we do not change our ways there may be a rebellion; born in the Oryx to spread throughout Egypt."

Blood Sacrifice

EVEN IN THE TEMPLES of the shadow there were a few true priests, and of these was Tet-hen, whom Roidahn had told me to see as soon as I found a suitable opportunity. The temple to which Tet-hen belonged was to the west of the City, and had been completed the previous year. It was approached by the avenue of the human-headed sphinx, and the entrance to the outer courtyard was through a pylon, forty cubits high, on which were depicted the Royal Family making offerings to Ra and Sekmet. I was not surprised to see the Lord of the High Noon worshipped in conjunction with Set's consort, for Roidahn had told me it was part of the policy of the priests of the new religion to try to direct the traditional veneration of Ra into channels which would make him appear another of the gods of fear.

The great copper-sheathed doors leading into the Court of Tribute had not yet been thrown open, though already many people were huddled in the scanty shade afforded by shadows cast by the pillars of the portico. Even if I had not been warned what to expect from these temples, the faces of those who waited to make their petitions would have been enough to tell me that the tribute they brought was not a free gift, but a bribe which they hoped would evoke respite from Set's flail.

Near me a woman crouched in the white dust, a baby held in the crook of her left arm. Her right hand was swathed in a dirty bandage, and in it she clutched something I could not see. The baby's head rolled helplessly; as though its neck was too weak to support it: and it whimpered incessantly, an unnatural cry like that of a blinded animal. I spoke to the woman, asking if I could do anything for her. She cringed, as though she expected me to hit her.

"Lord, be merciful to me. I am too poor for you to notice me. Have pity, for my child is very sick."

Gradually I made her understand that I only wanted to help her. She was servile in her gratitude, like a beaten cur which crawls on its belly toward an outstretched hand. "I had brought all I had to Sekmet already, but she would not listen to me. Why should she listen to a woman who had nothing of value to offer her? But if she will permit my child to live, he will grow strong and one day be able to pay our debt to her. Set is angry at my presumption. He has crippled the hand of my little son as a sign of his anger."

She drew back the cloth in which the baby was wrapped: its hand was twisted like the claw of a maimed bird. "I have brought Set a token of my humility. Sometimes he will accept payment in blood instead of gold. I would have offered my hand so that he would restore my child's but I had no one to help me. My left hand is clumsy, and the only knife I had was not very sharp."

She held out the little bundle which she had been holding in her bandaged hand. "Unwrap it, O Lord of Pity. Perhaps you will intercede for me with the Gods? They would listen to you, who are a noble. Plead for me that I may save my child!"

Her eyes were brilliant in her thin face, as she watched me unroll the dirty rags. Inside were two fingers; freshly severed at the knuckle joints.

"You do think that Set will accept them? Promise me that you will make him accept them—although I was not brave enough to cut off my hand at the wrist? I was afraid of the blood, and if I had lost too much there would have no one to look after my son."

"I will intercede, not with Set but with Ra on your behalf. I think Ra will do more than heal your child. He will tell me to send you on a journey to a part of Egypt which is far from this city; there you will forget you have ever been afraid. Not your two fingers, but the love which caused you to cut them off has broken the thongs which bound you to poverty and fear. And because of that love, your son will grow strong, and his laugh will ring joyous on the warm air, as though he were a bird singing to greet the sun after long darkness."

"You would not mock me? Please do not mock me, though I have nothing."

I tried to soothe her with my voice. "No one shall ever mock you any more." And I told her to rest in the shade until I returned.

I felt the heat strike up from the black granite steps as I mounted them to enter the Court of Tribute. I knew that I should find Tet-hen in the sanctuary of Ra, on the right of the sanctuary where Sekmet ruled.

"May Tahuti weigh thy heart . . . " I said to the young priest who stood alone by the statue of Ra. And he gave me the answer of the Watchers, "Against the Feather of Truth."

"You are the Son of the Oryx. Peace be upon you whose heart is in the keeping of Ra."

"You are Tet-hen, the light among shadows. The pupil of Ra who works for the sun against the sycophants of the shadow."

Then I gave him the message sent to him by Roidahn.

"I no longer work alone here," he said, "for now there are two others whose eyes are open. This temple will be large for so small a priesthood when the dawn is come, but soon there will be many others who will join us. The Priests of Ma-at will look on the bodies of those who come here, and see if any of the channels through which Ptah sends down his life into man are closed against him. Then will the Priests of Ptah refresh the weary and cleanse those who have a sickness upon them. Those who are in the power of Set shall find that the power of Ra will free them from this bondage. And all who come to the temples shall know that never again will they be without a friend."

"Tell me, Tet-hen, are the high priests strong in the power of Set? Must we challenge their power with yet a stronger, or are they all only men who masquerade as priests and who can be vanquished with ordinary weapons?"

"Only one here is a man with real power; Hekhet-ma-en. He who shall have the honor to break Hekhet's will must be great in magic. If soldiers are sent to take him he may strike them blind, and until his power is broken no one in the temples throughout the Royal Nomes would dare to deny tribute to his master, Set, who gives him strength."

"And what of the rest?"

"Many of them are no worse than courtiers, and no better. It is a pleasant life for a man without ambition, and a father whose daughter proves disobedient can send her here to honor her family by her virginity."

"Virginity?"

"That is a vow imposed on the new priesthood. Perhaps authority found that lonely pupils proved more docile. It is even possible that some believe that priestly powers may be exchanged for temporal pleasures, but this I think is too subtle a reasoning even for their duplicity. They are trying to rule by fear. Love and Fear cannot dwell in the same house. If priest and priestess love each other how then should they continue to sacrifice to Set?"

"During the pestilence it was said that more than oxen died to try to gain the favor of the River Goddess. Is that true of this City?"

"You will find no temple where it is admitted—nor would you

find one where it is not known to be true. I myself had to watch a girl walk into the river. She seemed to be in a trance, whether Hekhet had bound her will or whether she was drugged I am not sure. She smiled when she felt the water lap over her feet. Very slowly she walked forward, with her hands outstretched as though in greeting. But the crocodiles were impatient; she screamed before she drowned."

Then I told him of the woman who waited for me in the outer courtyard.

"Can you arrange for her to travel to the Oryx?" he asked. "For if not, there are ways by which I have already sent many people to Hotep-Ra. Roidahn may have told you that more than a hundred of the Watchers have passed this way to find the Oryx."

"I have a way to send her there: how do you know whom you may trust?"

"There are few who come to this sanctuary, for it is known that Ra is not greedy of tribute and cannot be bought with gold. He is only worshipped here because that was part of the royal decree when the temple was built. To serve in this sanctuary is considered the least important of all the priestly offices, so it was not difficult for me to acquire. Nearly everyone who comes to this temple suffers from fear in some degree, but when I find one in whom love has shown itself to be stronger than fear I know them to be Watchers. To many of these I have been able to teach our ways, but there are some who need more than I can give them and those I send to Roidahn. They travel to the Oryx by several routes; mostly by river. There is a private way from this sanctuary to my house in the priest's quarters. The gatekeeper of the dwelling court belongs to us, and if he was ever questioned he would deny having seen a stranger pass out of the gates. Yet there have been many such strangers, both men and women. Some who came here as a noble left wearing a priest's robe; and some who came here poor as a bleached bone found a curtained litter waiting for them outside these walls."

"Surely their disappearance must have been noticed? A person cannot disappear, even in the Royal City, without their family trying to trace them?"

"One who had ties to keep him here would not go to the Oryx

without telling the friends he knew he could trust. Those who were kept here by bonds they were not strong enough to break without my help—yes, search is sometimes made for them. But if the trail leads to the temple, the hounds say the scent is cold: no one is so foolish as to accuse Hekhet the High Priest, for fear he would demand a second sacrifice."

"You are very brave, Tet-hen. I should be proud if I had a tenth part of your courage. I have not even been tried in battle, but if I had proved myself the victor of twenty battles I should still do you most humble homage."

He laughed. "But why? We are both serving the Watchers, as are thousands of others, and all know that the death which comes to the conspirator who is betrayed is usually unpleasant."

"You are fighting almost alone here, not only against charlatans and knaves, but against one whom you say commands a stronger power than your own. Hekhet would try to destroy not only your body but your soul if he knew you were working against him."

Tet-hen's eyes were young and calm. He touched the statue of Ra caressingly as he answered, "I said Hekhet was stronger than I. . . . I did not say Hekhet was stronger than Ra. He who stands in the sun has the protection of its rays and they who walk in the light need not fear the shadow."

"It was foolish of me not to understand," I said. "But Ra wouldn't stop Hekhet torturing your body? Or could he even do that?"

"Why should he? He does not protect the body of a soldier who dies fighting in his name; why then should he protect my body? You said, Ra-ab, that I am braver than you. If that is true then you must be wiser than I; for it needs more courage to go on a journey along a strange road than to follow a path which is familiar. I do not know round which curve of my road I shall see Death coming to meet me. But I know that the greeting we will exchange will be those of men who have been friends long since; for I have often found pleasure in his company on the long road to the Shining Land."

"I must leave you now," I said, "to take the woman and her child to where they can be cared for until they go to Hotep-Ra."

"Tell her to follow a few paces behind you. There are many

eyes in the Royal City which find satisfaction in spying on things that do not concern them. Here no one would believe you were helping the woman only out of charity."

I had to pass by the statue of Sekmet to gain the outer courtyard. Incense had been lighted in a basalt censer on the offering-table. The heavy smoke seemed to undulate with the purr of a great cat; and the brooding eyes, half cat, half woman, watched me across the room.

The woman followed me, obedient as a dog. I dared not explain what I was going to do until we were alone, lest her gratitude aroused too much curiosity among those who still waited in the courtyard. At the outer gate I stood aside to let a fat merchant pass. Behind him came a Nubian slave carrying the merchant's tribute: two elephant tusks. I wondered what had made guilt weigh so heavily on him that he parted with so much treasure. Perhaps it was Set's promised share of the plunder of some village in the Land of Gold.

The wife of the Watcher who kept the house in Street of the Coppersmiths put the baby in a basket by the window and helped me to wash its mother's hand. The bandage was hard with dried blood, and we had to soak it in water before we could cut it off. When I saw the state of the jagged stumps I asked for vinegar to cleanse the wound. It was difficult to understand how she could have summoned the determination to cut off the first and second fingers of her right hand, with slow difficult strokes of a blunt knife wielded in her left. Sweat made little shining runnels down her thin cheeks, but she made no sound.

I asked her, "Is there any one you would like to take with you on your journey?"

"No one wants me," she said, and there was no self-pity in her voice; it was only a flat statement of fact. "It doesn't matter to anyone what happens to me. The woman who let us sleep in the corner of her byre won't notice if I never go back there. She may think I've moved on, or that we have both died, I and my son. She will say it is the best thing that could happen to both of us. But it wouldn't be better for my son to die. He has got to grow up first, and be strong and happy like his father was."

"Who is his father?" I asked, less from curiosity than to keep her talking while I finished putting the clean dressing on her hand.

"I can't tell you that. I have never told anyone, and I never will." She nodded at the baby, who had fallen asleep. "I might tell him when he is grown up, if he is the kind of person his father wanted his son to be."

"Very soon, when your hand is healed a little and you are feeling stronger, you will be ready to start on your journey. Till then you must stay here and these people will look after you both, and give you new clothes, and anything you choose to eat."

"Could there be milk for the baby?" she asked. "As much as he wants? I can't give him enough any more."

"As much as he wants," I promised her. "As much of everything that either of you wants. And then one day I'll take you both down to the river to a friend of mine who has got a large trading barge. He is going south with a cargo of grain very soon, and has plenty of room for you and the baby. His wife is a friend of mine too, and she will be very kind to you. In six or seven days, perhaps a little more if the wind is contrary, you will come to the place where no one is frightened. The children smile when they see a stranger, and you will hear women singing as they go to the well. That's the first thing you will notice which makes it so different from the Royal City, the people all look happy; that, and the sound of singing. You will have your own room—later you can have a small house of your own if you prefer it; it will be a large room, with a window and a pot of flowers on the sill, and matting on the floor and clean covers on the bedplace. When you are both quite strong they will find some kind of work for you to do, something you like doing. You will always have a home and enough to eat; and there will never be any one of whom you need be afraid."

Her eyes were trustful as a child's; and I realized, almost with horror, that she was not an old woman, but only a year or two older than myself.

"I have heard of that place," she said. "When I was very little someone used to tell me about it. The land where there is no more pain, or being hungry, or frightened. I didn't know it was a real place you could get to by going in a boat. I thought it was the country where the Gods live, and that I should have to die to get there. I'm so glad I don't have to die, so that I can stay and look after my little son until he grows up and doesn't want me any more."

"You will always be wanted," I said. "That's the most important thing about the country you are going to. Once you belong there someone always needs you."

First Greeting

AFTER HEARING HELIOKIOS in audience three times I felt confident in my ability to pass an accurate judgment on him. This I sent to Roidahn by the first of the secret messengers dispatched to Hotep-Ra. I gave a detailed summary of all the judgments I had heard Heliokios deliver, and added certain extracts from our conversations which I considered threw further light on his character. Through Sebek, I had learned that all the members of his household found him a just and considerate master, and it was obvious that Daklion had a real affection for him. So I suggested that although he could not be allowed to hold office after the Watchers came into authority he should be permitted to retain his country estate, or such portion of it as could be worked by those of his servants who might wish to remain with him, where he could live in comfortable seclusion.

By the time I had finished this report, that filled several of the long, narrow strips of papyrus with which I had come amply provided, I wished I had been able to bring a scribe with me; for I found the creation of so many writing-signs exceedingly laborious. I was grateful for the tradition by which no one of noble birth lacked a scribe to translate their messages into the slow medium of reed and papyrus!

As the days passed I began to wonder when I should meet some one else who had sufficient strength of character either to become a Watcher or to deserve banishment from Egypt; for I thought it unwise to let Heliokios guess that my interest was not centered in the entertainment with which he provided me so lavishly.

The first few occasions when I met those who in years were my contemporaries, I found amusing enough, for they were so unlike any people I had met before. The girls were gay and light-hearted, but the moment I tried to turn the conversation out of the channel of flattery they left me to seek someone more congenial to their taste. The young men either belonged to the Royal Body-guard, in which case they were preoccupied with their muscular perfection and could talk of nothing except sport, or else they were nearly as slender as their sisters—and as lavish with eye-paint! Some of these delicate creatures were in high favor with the women, who surrounded them with twittering cries when they declaimed a poem, or would accompany them on the harp when, yielding to welcome persuasion, they consented to sing.

I met several of the younger officials; most of them had only nominal duties which chiefly consisted in providing the back-ground of Court Life. They had been trained to this since they were children, and having from their earliest years been taught the word and gesture suitable to each occasion they seemed almost incapable of thinking as individuals. To watch any such entertainment from a distance would be to see some of the most handsome men in Egypt smiling in the company of her most beautiful daughters. But shut your eyes while you were amongst them, and there would be little to tell you who was speaking, so stereotyped was their conversation even when it was frivolous. Nor would it be easy to distinguish whether the party was today's, or belonged to last week, or was yet another which time con-cealed until the following day. There were so few topics which interested them that when another was added to their little store they were as greedy for it as orphan pigs for milk. It might be the most trivial of happenings, but somehow they would weave it into a net of gossip with which they hoped to catch a few moments' laughter.

I remember how one day they could talk of nothing except the rumor that a red-haired daughter had been born to the wife of the Keeper of the Royal Quarries, a woman who had made her-self unpopular by having a tongue so venomous she had been nicknamed the granddaughter of the sand snake. . . .

"I heard it myself, from the woman who is giving suck to the child."

"Nanu says her mother told her that neither family has the red strain."

Another girl giggled and said knowingly, "I wonder why the

emissary from Minoas noticed her. *I* always thought her *very* insignificant."

"Yes! Of course! *He* has red hair."

"But did she ever meet him?"

Then a fifth girl said, in tones of mock solemnity, "When I bear a child I shall at least admit to have *met* its father."

This was answered by a small woman, whose rounded prettiness held a warning of the fat that time was holding like a cloak to wrap her in. "I expect you will, dear Berikan. You have always been so quick to notice a new man."

This last remark caused great amusement; and I think that if the two women had had the freedom of their sisters of the market-place they would have scratched each other's faces, instead of having to content themselves with an acid smile.

Sebek found those first days more profitable than I, for the servants who came in attendance on our guests were entertained by Daklion, and were apt to speak freely of their masters, especially as Sebek was careful to see that the one to whom he was talking never lacked beer or mead to loosen his tongue. Some of them were loyal, or boasted of the one whose device they wore, for by so doing they enhanced their own prestige among the other servants; but there were others who, finding in Sebek a sympathetic ear, whispered of injustices and said they only worked in the Royal City so as to be able to provide their families with food. Many of them came from the caste who in the Oryx would have owned several fields, and perhaps as many as ten cattle, in their own right. But, for reasons I was to discover later, their land had become forfeit because they were unable to meet the heavy taxes imposed by Pharaoh, and now they had come to have only a little more freedom than the foreign slaves. The information that Sebek was able to gather was fragmentary, but it was sufficient for us to make an additional list of people whom it would be necessary to judge when we knew more about them.

I had been twelve days in the House of the Two Winds when Heliokios told me I had been invited to a banquet at the house of Ramaios, Keeper of the Royal Treasure.

"He holds the Gold Seal under Pharaoh," said Heliokios. "Next to the Vizier it is the most powerful office. Ramaios is respected for his integrity, it is said he is the only man in the Royal Nomes whose favor cannot be purchased—though others say he is a fool not to profit more widely from his opportunities. I am afraid his entertainments have not a reputation for gaiety, though the food is renowned and the wine rivaled only by the finest in the royal cellars; but he has a daughter, Meri-o-sosis." He paused and looked at me quizzically. "From what I have seen of you, you are not interested in women—or have you left your heart in the Oryx?"

Mimu gave me the clue to an answer which would satisfy him: she was crouched over a bowl of fruit, wondering which to snatch first.

"It is not that I am indifferent, it is only that, like Mimu, I am slow in making my choice."

As it was a formal banquet I took Sebek with me as cup-bearer. The house of the Lord of the Gold Seal was beyond the avenue of ram-sphinxes, and its garden went down to the river where Ramaios had a private landing-stage. I knew this because the house had been pointed out to me from the river the day before.

I decided to walk to the banquet, for the shady streets were pleasant after the heat of the day, and I was weary of the inactivity which attendance on Heliokios often imposed on me. It was sunset when I reached the house, and I saw that many guests had already arrived. Litter-bearers were gathered in the shadows of the entrance courtyard, watching their fellow runners set down new arrivals before the three wide steps which led up to the high doorway of the main entrance.

Twelve Nubian servants, so well matched in their magnificent stature that each might have been the twin brother of the man next to him, lined the way to the banqueting-hall. Their kilts were of heavy linen dyed a brilliant yellow, and they wore the sphinx headdress striped in vermilion and yellow, the colors only borne by members of a household of a Keeper of the Royal Seal.

Ramaios was seated at the center of a long table set on a raised dais at the far end of the room. On each side of him were three vacant chairs, in which would sit the principal guests. He wore a wig of the type favored by Heliokios. His eyes were long and narrow, and his unshaven brows were like rods of charcoal, seeming too boldly drawn for that thin, expressionless face, with its high-bridged nose and withdrawn mouth.

On the table in front of him was a gold wine-cup with two handles: from this each guest in turn must drink as he couples his name with that of his host in pledge of friendship; but when the guest is a woman, the host takes the cup and drinks in her name. In accordance with custom, Sebek held the cup for me to drink; a ceremony which commemorated that Pharaoh who had been stabbed by the king of a conquered people while drinking the wine in which the Oath of Fealty was to have been sealed. To the formal phrases, Ramaios added a few words in which he told me that, as the son of my father, I should always be a welcome guest, for they had been friends since as young men they had gone on a famous lion-hunt in which Father had vanquished three lions.

The younger guests seemed to be gathering at the far end of the hall, but as I hoped to meet someone who would prove to be of interest to the Eyes of Horus I avoided them and took one of two stools which were set a little apart from the others and partly hidden by a pillar.

This being an occasion of formality, the host and his chief guests sat at the high table, while the rest of the company chose their own companions and went to whichever of the group seats, ranged on two sides of the room, they preferred; and these groups varied from two to as many as five or six.

The second role of the cup-bearer was to bring wine and food to his master, or rather to tell the servants which of the many dishes would be likely to please him. Of these dishes there was a wide variety; several kinds of fish, bird, and game, and such additions as eggs stuffed with foreign herbs, *paté* of duck's liver, pomegranates split open and soaked in sweet wine, and ripe melons filled with new dates and sprinkled with shredded almonds; and I knew there would be dishes I had never tasted before, for Heliokios was not one who praised another man's cooks without reason.

The great height of the room seemed to subdue the sound of voices, or else there was none of the spontaneity I had found at other houses. I wondered if this was due to Ram-aios, or only because most of the people here were of an older generation than I had met previously. By now five of the six chairs beside Ramaios were filled. I recognized a captain of the Royal Bodyguard, very splendid in his glittering insignia, and beside him his wife, who looked young enough to be his daughter, whose mother was a Babylonian princess. Sebek whispered that another of the guests of honor was the architect who had designed the City and was reported to be close to the Royal Ear, and that the man on the left of our host was the Governor of the Northern Garrison.

To my annoyance the stool next to me was taken by a man only a little older than myself, who, even before he told me, I knew by his insignia to be the Leader of a Hundred from the same garrison as the man who sat with Ramaios. It was of the Royal City I wanted information and it was unlikely he could give me any, but I consoled myself with the knowledge that when the lengthy meal was over I should be free to mingle with the other guests, among whom I had already seen several acquaintances.

The only animation came from the group of young people at the end of the room, and I began to regret I had not joined them. Until then I had only noticed them as a moving pattern of bright colors, but now I saw that Ramaios was looking rather impatiently in their direction. As though he had uttered a command, a girl, who until then had been hidden from me by her companions, walked swiftly up the center of the floor to take her place beside him. She was tall, nearly as tall as I, and her body under its long, pleated dress of green mist-linen was very slender. Her hair was a vivid black and she wore it cut to shoulder-length, held back from her wide brow by a wreath of gold and enamel flowers of most delicate craftsmanship.

I tried to recall where I had seen her before. That I had seen her before I was sure—but where? How could I have confused her with any of the other girls I had seen in the Royal City—she was as different to them as the notes of a night-singing bird are to the screeching of an angry parrot.

The man next to me was also staring at her. "Who would have thought Ramaios had so beautiful a daughter! They say she is very ambitious, and refuses to choose a husband so long as either of the princes has not taken his royal wife."

I tried to stop thinking about her. Why should I be interested in the ambitions of a daughter of Ramaios? I had never been unfaithful to the Girl beyond the River, and no beauty save hers could offer me temptation.

The soldier told me he had just returned from a foray in the eastern desert. By the manner in which he told his story I realized it was only a little band of robbers, twelve in all, whom he, with his Hundred to help him, had killed," to cure them of raiding flocks in the high pasture."

I tried to give him my attention, but my thoughts refused to be withdrawn from the girl who sat at the high table. I was glad I was in the shadow of a pillar for it allowed me to watch her without appearing too obvious. Every gesture she made, every turn of her head, poised like a lotus on the stalk of her neck, made her more familiar to me. I seemed to hear my own voice saying, "Of *course* I shall know you when I see you—I will go to every Nome and every country, look in the fields and in the streets of great cities, until I find you." And a voice which answered, "How will you know me when you don't know what I'm going to look like? I may be old, or fat, or have a squint—how could you love me if I were ugly?"

Certainty came like a sudden shaft of light. I *had* known her almost as soon as I saw her. And I knew her name even before I knew she bore it; Meri-o-sosis, Men, for which the writing-sign is "Beloved."

In some remote distance I heard the soldier recounting yet another exploit, and the few words, in which brevity must have linked hand with discourtesy, which came forth from my mouth in reply. But they belonged to the shell of Ra-ab, for his spirit followed his eyes so that between Ramaios and his daughter there stood a third, though neither saw him.

I found myself united again with the outer Ra-ab only when, at a sign from her father, she came down from the dais to go with him from group to group exchanging a few words with every guest. I noticed that the stool beside me had been vacated, and saw the soldier had joined two other men on the opposite side of the room. They stared at me as though he had been telling them I was either drunk or the biggest dullard it had ever been his misfortune to meet. I looked round for Sebek, to find he had gone to seek refreshment and listen to the gossip of other cup-bearers.

Would she remember my name? She had *promised* to recognize me when we met. What should I say to her to show that I too remembered?

Her father paused to talk with some people further down the room and she came on alone. I heard a woman wish her joy on her anniversary. "How quickly you children grow up! It seems only yesterday I brought you a wooden duck to play with, and now tomorrow you will be sixteen."

I stood waiting for her. She gave me the first greeting, and I could not find words to answer. Then she put her hand to her eyes as though she had suddenly come into a bright light and was dazzled. "How stupid of me," she said, confused. "I have forgotten your name. For a moment I did not recognize you. Surely you have been our guest before? Forgive me for my discourtesy in giving you the first greeting. . . . I am not usually so forgetful. . . ."

"We first met in a great avenue, beyond the River."

"The avenue leading to the Palace? *That* isn't beyond the river."

I wondered if she were teasing me again, as she had done when I became an oryx. To show her I remembered, I said, "Have you forgotten the Oryx?"

Again she pretended not to know what I meant . . . or did she misunderstand? "The Oryx? Of course! You're Ra-ab Hotep, Son of the Oryx. Now I *know* we have not met before, for my father told me you were but newly arrived in the City and I have never been to the South."

Yet the message of her eyes denied her words. And as I gave her farewell my heart was singing; for I had found that a dream could live on *my* side of the River.

The Oryx Necklace

WHEN I WOKE next morning it was long after dawn. For a moment I thought I had been dreaming of Meri, and wondered why I was not reluctant to return to my body. Meri . . . how did I know her name was Meri? The glory of memory poured down on me: we were no longer hidden from each other by the mist of the River. She was *here*, in the Royal City! Yesterday I had seen

168

her, heard her voice, known that although she might not be ready to declare it, she had recognized the link between us.

I shouted for Sebek, and he came through the curtained door-way. "Sebek, I've found her! I knew she wasn't the Daughter of the Hare. . . ."

"Found who?" he interrupted impatiently; and, without wait-ing for an answer, went on, "We went to the house of the Keeper of the Gold Seal, the most important chance we've had since we came here to meet people of whom the Watchers must know—and what did you do! Except for a few remarks to a soldier, and even he found you so dull he left you as soon as decency permit-ted, you sat by yourself and made no effort to speak to anybody. And I had to stand with the servants and watch you waste your opportunities! If the steward of the household had not opened a jar for the cup-bearers, so that we had the chance to drink wine as well as pouring it for our betters, I should not have been able to get even a few poor gleanings of what might have been a plen-tiful harvest. And when I returned to the banqueting-hall it was to find you had already left; so I hurried home, to be told by Dak-lion you had given orders not to be disturbed!"

I was far too happy to be annoyed by his complaints. "Stop grumbling, you dull old man, and listen! Is it of so little interest that I can tell you the name of the woman who is to be the wife of your future Nomarch? You say I wasted our opportunities, yet if you had the wit to realize it you would know that I have found she who one day will rule the Oryx."

"You must still be dreaming, for a more unlikely story I never heard. You never spoke to a woman the whole time we were there, though I suppose even you had to find a few words of courtesy for the daughter of the host!"

"And those few words were enough! Did I forget to tell you the name of she of whom I am speaking is Meri-o-sosis, and that the man on whom I shall bestow the great honor of being grandfa-ther to my heir is the Gold Seal under Pharaoh?"

I laughed at his blank astonishment. "So much for you people who like to scoff at dreams! You thought that if I would only choose a little concubine, as once you so solemnly advised me to do, I should cease looking for a woman who existed only in my imagination. Even Kiyas thought that if I ever found her she would turn out to be the daughter of a fisherman or some other rank which would cause Father to sigh with disapproval."

"It is not suitable for a servant to comment on the choice made by his master," said Sebek, and then added even more dubiously, "I expect when you're fully awake you will find this is only another of your dreams. Though of course if you do marry the daughter of Ramaios I shall be the first to rejoice at your good fortune."

"Why wait? Rejoice *now*, Sebek, never postpone rejoicing."

"Sometimes rejoicing is the Mother of Disappointment."

"Sometimes you remind me of the story Roidahn used to tell us when we were children: of the quail-chick who starved because it dared not eat the worms which it saw its brothers eating, after the wild duck had told it that worms were baby sandsnakes! I am very hungry: go and fetch me honey and new bread and two duck's eggs—and a melon too if you can find one. And hurry, O Father of Disapproval, if your unquiet belly is not too heavy for your withered shanks!"

At which insult he recovered his amiability and tried on me a new wrestling throw he had been practicing the day before . . . and would have thrown me over his shoulder had I not known a counter to bring him down.

While he went to fetch the food, I took the Oryx necklace from the box which Neku had designed. I could give it to her today, her anniversary-of-the-first-breath on which her friends would bring tributes of flowers as a sign of their affection. I decided to go to her house in the evening, so as not to squander the joy of anticipation. I replaced the necklace in its wrapping of green linen; the lid of the box showed a girl stooping to put a garland of flowers round the neck of the oryx, which stood beside her with its head lowered in humble devotion . . . surely it would remind her of the happiness we had found beyond the River? I would hide the gift among flowers which I would choose myself, even if I had to search every corner of the daily market held outside the South Gate.

As I entered the courtyard of the House of Ramaios I saw the soldier with whom I had sat the night before. He looked away and hurried his pace, afraid I might recognize him and seek to impose the further boredom of my company.

Meri was in the garden between the house and the river. Her dress was flax blue, and the fillet which bound her hair had little flowers of pink quartz among amethyst leaves. She was holding court among a crowd of friends, and already the stone bench beside her was piled high with the flowers they had brought. I hoped that if I contrived to be the last to greet her she would find a way for us to be alone, even if it were only for a moment. I had hidden the box among sprays of tuberose and stephanotis in a flat basket of green rushes. She smiled when she saw me . . . but then she had smiled at all the others. She took the basket and set it down a little apart from the rest; at first she did not see the box, and as I noticed that no one else had brought her a second gift I realized I must have broken another rule of etiquette and wondered if she would think it presumptuous.

Then she saw it, and with a little cry of pleasure took out the necklace. "Oh, Ra-ab—Ra-ab Hotep, a thousand thanks must travel to your father for such a splendid gift to the daughter of his friend."

I took my cue and said, "He told me to give it to you on your anniversary; that is why I did not bring it to you when I first arrived in the Royal City."

"Had you done so I should have worn it last night, for I have no other half so beautiful."

She held it out for the others to see and they crowded forward to look at it. "Is it not true what I say? None of you has a necklace so rare in design as this. And look at the box . . . I shall keep my malachite and eye-paint in it, that they may learn of the craftsman who made those clear swift lines and so improve the drawing of my eyebrows!"

I lingered until all the guests had gone and only the four girls who were her personal attendants were still with us. Surely she would make some excuse to speak to me alone? But either she thought it unwise or did not choose to do so. I wished the others were flies so that I might brush them away . . . or leopards which I could kill to show my devotion.

At last I could think of no excuse to linger, and wondering

desperately how soon I could make occasion to see her again, I made my farewell. As though referring to a matter already arranged between us, which to my joy I realized was for the benefit of those who were listening, she said:

"My father instructed me to tell you that when you come tomorrow to deliver those messages for his private ear which you bring from the Oryx, he will not await you here but at his Island Pavilion. He often finds it more restful to work there, and as your own boatmen may have difficulty in finding it, one of ours will wait for you at the third landing-stage. He also told me to tell you that if he is detained on a matter of great urgency you may trust me to repeat faithfully all the messages your father has sent to mine."

If the minutes which kept plodding so slowly past had been slaves in the stone quarries, they would have found their overseer cruel in his impatience to hurry them; but at last it was time for me to go to the third landing-stage. The boat which Meri sent to bring me to her had a prow shaped like a swan, and I sat behind the two rowers on a raised platform. The island was in mid-river, and as I drew nearer I saw that flowering shrubs came down to the water's edge. A flight of stone steps led up the steep bank from the wooden landing-stage, but they were deserted. The steersman made fast, and then told me that if I followed the path at the top of the steps I would come to the pavilion. The path wound through thickets of dense shade. I had a sense of unreality in the green stillness, as though I might see the narrow hoof-prints of an oryx on the powdered limestone I was treading.

I came to an open grassy space and half expected to see Meri running toward me, with hands outstretched as she had greeted me in our dreams; no longer pretending, even though we both knew it for pretense, that we were strangers. In a moment I should see her alone, without need for concealment . . . surely we should be alone? I heard the voices of several women; and disappointment was sharper than a thorn.

The front of the little wooden pavilion was shaded by an awning painted in white and yellow. Under this was a couch whose sides were ebony Hathor cows with ivory horns, and on it lay Meri, laughing at something one of the four girls who were grouped round her must have just said. Sebek had told me the girls were beautiful, but I did not notice them; the stars are not visible when the sun is in the sky.

Meri greeted me as she had done before; with the smiling courtesy due to her father's guest—as yesterday I had seen her greet a hundred others. *Had* she forgotten me, or was it only that for a little longer we must keep up the pretense? She asked me for news of the Oryx, but only as though it were the usage of conversation and not as though the subject held special interest for her. Then she told one of the girls to fetch wine and honey-cakes, but she did not fill my cup herself as she would have done if I had been an intimate friend.

She told another of the girls to sing to the harp, for which I was grateful, for it allowed me to look at her without having to think of trivial phrases to conceal my thoughts. She was wearing a wreath of green corn, and her hair was smooth and dark as the midnight river. Her dress was of finely pleated mist-linen and through it her body gleamed like moon-flowers in the dusk. Her feet were beautiful as the morning, and I envied her scarlet sandals whose gold thongs might clasp them while I must stay aloof. She was very still while she listened to the girl singing, the fan of heron's feathers idle in her hand; a hand that was long and narrow, with gilded nails like almond kernels.

Then I had to feign interest in the lid of a box that one of the others was inlaying with bitumen and pearl shell . . . and listen to yet another song while all I longed to hear was Meri's voice. She sent for a board and gaming-box and challenged me to play. When she leaned forward to move a piece, her perfume was so lively in my nostrils that it was difficult not to cry to her for mercy. Why did she delight to tease me? If she no longer loved me surely she should have the charity to send me away? I pretended to myself that if I had known the greeting that awaited me I should have sent Sebek in my place. She would not have noticed the difference, and he would have enjoyed himself!

The last throw of the dice spared me the need to move pieces on a board. I stood up, searching for formal phrases of farewell to hide my heart; but before I spoke them she dismissed the girls, saying that she would not need them until it was time to return home, and that they might go to the bathing-place at the north of the island.

She turned to me. "My father has told me of matters of importance which I am to discuss with the Son of the Oryx." For a moment she laid her hand on my arm. "There is a flowering tree here which I do not think grows in your Nome. I wish you to tell me if your sister would find its perfume agreeable if the unguents I am sending to her were scented with it."

Disappointment vanished like the mists which used to hide her land from mine. She led me through another clearing which gave on a path like the one by which I had come to her; and when she reached a tree whose opening buds were vivid sparks among the dark leaves, she stretched up to pick a flower that was more fully open than the rest.

She turned and leaned back against the somber trunk. We were tranced in a web of stillness, and then like the song of a silver string I heard her say, "This tree does not grow beyond the other river, but we belong there."

And I answered her, "We have belonged there since first you waited for me at the head of the avenue, to take me to Anubis."

She put her hands on my shoulders. Then she was in my arms; and it seemed as though she had never left them.

While we wandered hand in hand through the green shade, I asked her, "Why did you try to make me think you had forgotten me?"

"I had to be *sure* . . . though in my heart I never doubted you were the one for whom I had been waiting. It is three years since I knew I would meet you, though some of my dreams were not so clear as yours. I didn't remember your name though you tell me I said I should; and I didn't know what you were going to look like. I was always looking for you—among guests that came to my father's house, and among soldiers, among everyone I met. And when I couldn't find you I even searched the faces of rowers, and drew back the curtains of my litter in the streets in case I might glimpse you in the crowd."

"When did you know it was me you were waiting for?"

"I think it was as soon as I noticed you sitting alone and saw that you often looked at me. I pretended I only wanted to speak to you because you looked so lonely and it was my duty toward you as a guest. When I heard your voice I was sure I had seen you before, and had done you a discourtesy in giving you the first greeting. I was confused that I could not remember your name when I seemed to know it so well. Your eyes, only your eyes were as I had always known they would be—that's why I didn't recognize you in the distance. Your eyes held the same recognition which I knew was in mine."

"Then why did you treat me as a stranger yesterday?"

"How could I tell you my heart when people were watching us? O Ra-ab, my love, we are two petals of the same flower, yet as the daughter of Ramaios and the Son of the Oryx we have been taught to speak a different idiom. I have heard of the Oryx and know that you have not had to follow the manifold concealments which have made my life. Sometimes I think that the whole of the Royal Household has no more substance than a painted frieze, as though we were all part of a pattern designed by a long-dead drawing-scribe. When I attended the banquet where we met I thought it would be like a hundred others. The women would wear different dresses, and the food and flowers change with the season, but the pattern would be the same—for if the colors of a tomb painting were altered, the ghosts who whisper among the funerary meats would not change the rhythm of their complaint. Ghosts are jealous of the living, and if they knew that I no longer share their company because you have taken me from their whispering shade, they would combine to get me back. Any one who tries to break the mold in which their lives are cast is treated as an enemy who must be destroyed. I have refused to marry, but that has been forgiven because I am young, and because they suspect my refusal is born of ambition—the younger son of Pharaoh has not yet chosen his royal wife. If I told even the women nearest me, those whom I count most loyal, that I waited for a lover to join me from a dream, they would have whispered that madness had touched me on the forehead; and fire among stored grain travels more slowly than whispers among idle women. My father would have defended himself against the slur of having an afflicted child, by marrying me to a husband of his choosing—and it would never be difficult to find a

175

husband for the daughter of a man so powerful as my father."

"How could he have made you marry against your will? It is against the law of Egypt that a woman should take a husband who is not of her free choice!"

"I should not have been *forced* . . . at least they would not have called it so. I should have been allowed the alternative of going into the Royal Temple . . . in time to become a priestess who followed every design which furthered the power of the false priests, or if I had the strength to refuse to give my will to them . . . well, there are many who die before their initiation."

While she was speaking I realized that as soon as it was known that we loved each other she would share the danger in which I was living; if I were taken as a spy she too would die by torture. I must rescue her at once from these strangers among whom she had been born in exile, and take her to the protection of the Watchers.

I held her close. "We must escape to the Oryx, tonight! As my wife even your father will have lost his power over you. . . ."

Then I told her of the Watchers, and why I had to come to the Royal City. I concluded, "So even if Pharaoh sent an army to bring you back he would have to conquer more than half his kingdom before he could impose his will, for the Watchers will fight if one of their number is threatened and he who joins battle with the Oryx must challenge the warriors of every southern Nome."

While I talked I had been planning our escape. "You must come with me to the house of the copper merchant who is the first link in the chain between me and Roidahn. I think we shall go by river, perhaps in a grain barge or trading-ship. There are several ways by which we could travel in secret; we may have to go from village to village and lie hidden during the day, moving only by night when we shall be disguised as fishermen who cast their nets under the moon. I hope that we shall travel slowly; alone together as I have dreamed of for so long . . . now it will be a dream from which we shall wake to find ourselves together."

She sighed, and my arms tightened round her. Her hair beneath my lips was smooth and fragrant as sun-warm fruit. "Why do you sigh, my heart?"

"Because I want to go with you to the Oryx ... tonight. Because I do not want to return to the stupid pattern of my ordinary life, even for a little while."

"Then there is no need for sighs. You *are* coming to the Oryx; before it is dark we shall have started on our journey!"

She shook her head. "No, Ra-ab, that is a dream which we must wait to share. You cannot betray the Watchers, and for the love of you, and for the Gods, I too belong to them. You have been sent here to discover who must be cut down and who be left to flourish; and who is better placed than I to help you? It is through women that you can best learn of the men, for even the wives of high officials chatter of their husbands as freely as market women. I have a few intimates among them, but in obedience to my father's wishes I am guest or hostess to all the women of importance in the Household. They will find I take a new interest in wifely gossip, and they will smile, thinking it is because I have at last chosen a husband, and so will be eager to enlighten me on how men may be coerced to a woman's will! By their advice to me I shall learn the merit of their husbands ... and if there are any among them whose marriage is as our marriage I shall know it by her silence; for those who are joined by love need no counsel save their own heart. Oh, Ra-ab, my dear beloved, it is going to be so difficult for us to go through the slow formalities of a betrothal according to the custom! I shall have to pretend to be blind to your preference for me, and only gradually must my attendants find that I make excuse to be alone with you. I prepared them today by saying that I had state business to discuss with you in my father's absence. They were not surprised, for it is not the first time I have done this—my father knows that sometimes a man tells more to a girl than he would to a high official."

"How long must I wait for you? How many days must we waste on this shadow of reality?"

"A few weeks, perhaps it may be even less, before I dare tell my father that I wish to take you as my husband. He will not refuse his approval, for he will be grateful that I have chosen someone so suitable as your father's son. Dear Ra-ab, I am so grateful that the Gods did not send you as a fisherman, or me as the daughter of a foreign merchant's concubine!"

"It might have been easier, for then there would have been no need to watch the dead formalities creep slowly forward!"

She laughed and ran her fingers through my hair. "Three days ago we might have measured the time of our meeting in years, and already we are impatient that love must wait on our betrothal! Our marriage may have to be according to the laws of the Royal Nomes, but it shall be your priest who joins us in the name of Ptah when we reach our home in the Oryx . . . it will be the first real home that I have ever known."

Already the river mist was rising to bloom the purple evening, as I kissed my beloved—whom tomorrow I must greet with all formality.

Seal of Ashek

WITHIN A MONTH Meri had enabled me to put the scarlet Scales of Tahuti, the sign that judgment had been given by one of the Eyes of Horus, against eighteen of the names of the list Roidahn had given me.

It was no longer difficult for us to be alone, for her four attendants knew of our secret betrothal and made the rigid etiquette a shield for our privacy instead of a barrier to keep us apart. I had told them of the Watchers, so while Sebek was with them he did not have to pretend to be my servant.

Meri found it even easier than she had foretold to get the wives of the men about whom I needed information to talk freely of their husbands. "They seem to think," she said, "that men and husbands are as different as hippos and crocodiles—and that all husbands are so like their own that when I marry it will be their experience I shall need to help me. Sometimes they are too proud to admit they are unhappy, but they betray themselves without realizing it. You remember Tahu, the wife of the Ivory Seal in the Second Hall of Audience?"

Tahu had come with us on the river three days before: I had wanted to meet her because her husband was so important an official. I knew he was as old as Heliokios, so I was surprised to see she was young enough to have been his daughter, perhaps even his granddaughter. She wore excess of ornaments, and her hair was so stiff with unguents that it looked like oiled stone.

"Yes, I remember her," I said.

"What did you think about her?"

"That she has little to think *with*, and even less to think about. She has much in common with Mimu, Heliokios's monkey, for they are both the indulged playthings of old men. A servant must go to the fruit market at dawn every day to find Mimu's favorite food—green almonds are her greatest pleasure at this season, and I suspect that the packs of the foreign goldsmiths are searched for pretty trifles to put in Tahu's greedy little hands—so that she suffers her master to fondle her; just as Mimu lets herself be fondled when she has got what she wants."

Meri and I were on the island, lying side by side on a grassy bank in the shade of a flame tree. Her head was on my shoulder so I could not see her face properly; but I felt her quiver and realized she was laughing at me.

"What are you laughing at?"

"Because you are funny when you are so dear and pompous! No, perhaps pompous is the wrong word, but you are very *disapproving* sometimes, Ra-ab. What would you do if a man thought of me as you are thinking of Tahu?"

"I should try to pity him for his affliction of madness; but I should probably be sufficiently impulsive to strike him down for blasphemy."

"Oh, Ra-ab, I do love you when you are fierce! But you mustn't practice it too often, or when I have been your wife so long that you've grown used to it you might be fierce with *me!*"

After I had finished punishing her for making such a monstrous suggestion . . . and I found that there is a point under the right shoulder blade where even a goddess may be ticklish, we returned to the subject of Tahu.

"You think," said Meri, "that she's a greedy, over-dressed doll, whose husband, poor silly old man, is eager to load her with presents to try to coax her to smile at him. That's what I thought too, which is why I never bothered to know her any better. But I saw her face when she dropped her bracelet in the water. I know you were impatient when she made such an outcry, and we had to stop while people dived to try to find it. You thought she was boasting when she kept on saying, "If I don't find it he'll give me two more to replace it; and I heard you say to Sebek that she was just the kind of woman who would risk a servant among the crocodiles to fetch a bracelet! But then I saw her face when she dropped it and you didn't. She was frightened, Ra-ab, more frightened than a slave who drops the favorite wine-cup of a ruthless master. She didn't want the bracelet, yet she was terrified of going home without it. Ashek isn't the kindly old man we thought him. He's cruel, and dark with the pride of possession. Envy is the flail which has driven him on; and he wants the salt of envy to sear the mouths of those who must toast the success of his ambition. He took a young wife so that men his own age would envy him; he gives her more jewels than any other woman in the Royal City because they are the seal of his power. Tahu is no more than the box in which he stores his gold dust . . . with his seal closing the lid."

"Meri, aren't you letting a tall tree grow out of a very small seed? Perhaps she *was* frightened; perhaps she is very careless of the things he gives her and was afraid that if she lost this bracelet he wouldn't be so generous in the future. Of course, you *may* be right, but you've got no proof."

"I wouldn't have given my judgment on the Ivory Seal unless I had been sure. Didn't you notice that Tahu was still with me when you left? As her husband was away from the City I asked her to spend the night at my house. . . . I had to find out *why* she was frightened. She accepted eagerly, but said she didn't want a servant to attend her . . . that in itself would have been enough to arouse my curiosity, for she doesn't look the kind of woman who prefers to do things for herself. I went along to her room, and found she was wearing a night-shift although it is the hot weather. She had taken the paint off her face and tied her hair back with a plain ribbon. She hadn't expected me to come to see her; she was startled, for a moment she made me think of a soldier who knows himself cornered when he is without a weapon. I felt as though I was much older than she was, and I said, 'My poor child; I know all about it, you needn't pretend with me.' And she began to cry, slow, heavy tears she didn't bother to conceal.

"It was not a pretty story she told me. It was about an old

man with an estate in the North. It was not a large estate, and when the crops failed three years in succession he was not able to pay the taxes. But he was host, on more than one occasion, to the Second Ivory Seal. And this guest desired his daughter, and the daughter refused him. If you knew this city as well as I do, Ra-ab, you would find this part of the story very commonplace — the daughter who is sold for the benefit of her family. The conventions are observed, of course; the girl is persuaded that it would be very foolish, as well as being most ungrateful to her parents, to refuse this opportunity of family advancement . . . 'She should be flattered at having gained the affection, the most *honourable* affection, of so powerful an official.' It may be hinted that her family would suffer if she were so foolish as to refuse . . . and if she preferred a different husband she would take as a dower to him only disappointment and oppression; for those who incur the displeasure of Pharaoh's courtiers do not prosper in Egypt.

"Had Tahu been the puppet we first thought her, Ashek would have grown tired of her and been content to use her as a living statue which could display his wealth. But she was not a puppet. She had the courage to tell him that though she was his slave by purchase, she was still free, as are all slaves, for man cannot possess another of his kind. She has many jewels. You know the custom when goods are purchased from a foreign trader, that the purchaser sets his seal on the bond of sale? It seems that Ashek likes to adopt the customs of foreigners . . . with certain modifications. Each time he brings his wife another gift he sets his seal as a token of possession. He cannot use the Ivory Seal, for that would not stand great heat. The seal he uses is quite small, about the size of my little fingernail, and it is made of copper. The impression it makes blurs after a time into a deep scar, but the hieroglyphic on those which are fresh can still be read. As she told me this Tahu took off her shift. She said she did not need to open her treasure chest to count her jewels, and had only to count the seals, set in the soft flesh of her thighs."

It was three days before Meri and I perfected a plan to send Tahu to sanctuary in Hotep-Ra. At first Tahu was afraid that if she escaped, her family would suffer, for she had come to accept the idea that her life was forfeit to their safety. She was no longer rebellious, even against her husband—so must the virgins sacrificed to the river have gone unquestioningly to their death. But as we talked to her, hope flickered into her eyes, as though she were a foreign slave who was being promised freedom in her own country.

"I want to escape! Even you can't understand how much I want to escape. But you don't know how crafty is Ashek! Somehow he would find where I had gone. He would invent some story; that I had been kidnapped or lost my wits, and every soldier, every servant of every small official, would be searching for me. Even if I were disguised they would see this scar on my temple."

In answer to my unspoken question, she said, "No, he did not make *that* scar. I fell as a child and hit my head on the edge of a stone step. They thought I was going to die; but the Gods denied me their hospitality and sent me instead to the house of Ashek."

She was trembling; I took one of her hands and Meri the other. "Tahu, you are not alone any more. Ashek has no power over you. No power, do you understand? You belong to yourself. You are free. You are going to the Oryx, and when the Watchers are ready to act, Ashek will be banished from Egypt—and be grateful for banishment."

"How can I go to the Oryx? If the Watchers protected me they might be destroyed. Somehow he will find me. He has spies everywhere; the overseers of the Royal Roads are his creatures and their power extends through every Nome."

"He will not look for you, for we have thought of a plan. Meri told me that Ashek is a man of envy, a man who sets his own value by the envy he can extort from other men. If it were known that you had run away from him he would have to find you and bring you back to prove his strength. But if he could conceal from every one that he is hated by his young wife, even though he tries to buy her favors, he would be eager to do so. On the last count that is what will weight his scales . . . how can he keep envy sharp and bright as an assassin's knife. You know he is not returning to the city for another three days. You must close yourself in your private apartments and see no one. You must behave sufficiently strangely for the women of your household to think, in the light of future events, that you were crazed, but they must have no thought that you are ill or likely to take your own life lest they set a watch on you. On the morning of the day your husband is due to return, you will send for a servant and give her a letter to hand him on his arrival. It will be heavily sealed, and the matter it contains will be brief . . . a few lines to tell him that rather than suffer him any longer you are commending yourself to the mercy of the Goddess of the River, that you will have drowned yourself before he reads what you have written. He will believe you, for he is so sure of his power that he would not expect anyone to dare to give you shelter."

"You make it sound as though it was really going to happen."

"It *is* going to happen; in three days you will be on your way to the Oryx."

"But how, Ra-ab? How?"

"I will arrange everything. You must do just what I have told you. Give the letter to your servant, and then say that you are going to rest in your private garden because you have slept badly, and are not to be disturbed on any pretext until your husband returns. This you must do an hour after dawn. Your private garden has a door which leads into an alley; unbolt it, and you will find me waiting for you outside."

As I waited by the narrow door in the high wall, time seemed to pass so slowly that I began to fear Tahu's courage had forsaken her. Then I heard the bolts drawn back, and a small, cloaked figure slipped through the opening to join me. With a whispered greeting I took her hand and led her by the narrow, winding paths between garden walls to the poorer part of the city. We were both dressed as upper servants, so no one took any notice of us as we threaded our way through the crowded markets. I knocked three times on the door of the house in the Street of the Coppersmiths, and it was opened by one of the Watchers who had come with me from the Oryx.

"The plans have gone smoothly," he said. "A small grain-barge is ready to leave the city for the South. The steersman and the two men who work the sails are all Watchers, and it is not the first time they have carried more than grain to Hotep-Ra. One of them is taking his dead sister's child to be brought up with our people, so I have arranged that Tahu shall pretend to be his wife and look after the baby on the journey."

Clothes suitable to a fisherman's wife were ready for her, and those she had worn were burned, so as to leave no clue that she had been there. I took her out of the North Gate, which was the shortest way to the great stone wharves where lay the trading-ships and barges. The wharves were crowded; Nubians and Asiatics, the tall men of the South and the dark, thin-lipped men of Punt, jostled together as they carried their different loads to the waiting ships. Bales of dressed hides, sacks of grain, cedar logs from the foreign seaboard, squared blocks of red granite from the Royal Quarries, bundles of flax ready for weaving into the fine linen worn by the women of the Court . . . a hundred other kinds of merchandise. Who would have time to notice a woman who hurried along with a blue fall drawn forward on her fore-head, a fall which hid the scar on her temple? The woman reached a small barge whose sail flapped ready to hoist. A man leaned down to help her over the pile of grain sacks, and a baby who had been crying was comforted as she took it in her arms. I stayed long enough to see her safe in the protection of the Watchers; then turned and went back to the city.

Within an hour I was with Meri; and together we leaned on the parapet at the end of the river walk of her father's house. "There they are," I said, "that small barge far out in the stream. You can just see it, behind that boat with the orange sail."

The barge came into view. A flutter of blue showed that Tahu was watching for us; as the North Wind took her on her journey to peace.

The next day Heliokios returned from giving audience, exclaiming at the great misfortune which had befallen a fellow official.

"It is a terrible tragedy for Ashek," he said. "He returned home only yesterday, to find his wife had been struck down by a myste-rious fever. It appears she had been ill for three days, but fearing to distress him she would not permit news to be sent. He is a courageous man, for when he recognized she might have a for-eign pestilence, rather than let any member of his household expose themselves to the danger of contracting the disease he ministered to her himself. To his profound grief she died, and with her last breath made him promise that he would let no priest attend her. Naturally this added to his sorrow, but he could never bring himself to deny her anything. Her body is to be burned; he placed it in the wooden coffin and himself sealed the lid. He said that no one should look on her beauty now it was marred, for that is what she would have wished. It is strange that so noble a man should have shown so much understanding for a vain and foolish woman."

Dark Silence

I HAD BEEN FIFTY DAYS in the Royal City when Pharaoh returned there from his Summer Palace, which he had recently built where the river joins the sea. He announced that he would give audience to the intimates of the Court on the day following his return, and to this audience I was taken by Heliokios.

I found it difficult to visualize Pharaoh as a man; a man whose puny hands were trying to strangle the greatness of Egypt, a man whom the Watchers had condemned. To me he was a legendary figure, almost as remote from individuality as a concept of power. The power of the Gods, the power of Pharaoh; it was the same except in degree, just as the water of the Nile is the same water whether it carries a boat quietly on its course, or breaks down an aqueduct and brings destruction. Ever since Roidahn had told me that this Pharaoh was only a puppet I had wondered how he had borne the magic of the Double Crown, or set on his forehead the uraeus, and yet not perished as a tree would perish that dared the lightning. Did the Winged Pharaohs of the old years know of the imposter who wore the symbols of their heritage? Did they blame him for his foolhardiness, or sigh at the blindness of the descendants of their wise generation, who saw only the regalia and not what it symbolized?

As the son and declared heir of a Nomarch I was entitled to a standard-bearer in the Royal Presence, so it was arranged that when I entered the Hall of Audience Sebek would follow me, carrying the ceremonial Oryx, ivory with gold horns, on a rod of ebony banded with silver. My sphinx headdress was striped with gold thread; belt, pectoral, and the bracelets worn above the elbow, were those designed for me by Neku. Everyone brought a gift to Pharaoh—a conventional sign of gratitude that once again they might be "renewed by the light of his countenance." My gift was a casket of sesemu wood, inlaid with ivory and mother-of-pearl in a hunting frieze of four hounds crying a leopard.

The outer courtyard of the Palace, paved with red granite, was lined with triple ranks of the Royal Bodyguard. They were magnificent in vermilion and yellow, their shields blazing as the sun challenged the burnished copper; each man as physically perfect as years of training could make him, each face immobile as a statue.

In the Hall of Audience, Pharaoh sat alone on a great throne of black granite. His elder son, who although middle-aged had not been made co-ruler, occupied a small throne, a chair with a high back of gilded wood, that matched another on the other side of the dais, in which sat the second prince, a man twenty years younger than the Royal Heir and born of a different mother. Both of these secondary thrones were raised one step above the floor level, but the great throne was approached by seven steps. On either side of Pharaoh stood a fan-bearer; they were Nubians of remarkable height, which was further increased by plumed headdresses. The fans, of twenty-four ostrich feathers dyed brilliant purple, were set in gold and ebony sticks fully eight cubits long. Beside the dais were two leopards in a double leash; one was snarling at its attendant, a boy of about fourteen.

Pharaoh was wearing the Crown of the North; and within the circle of red gold the old head, shaven like a priest's, looked incongruous as an ostrich egg. The flesh was pouched under the little eyes which peered malevolently out from the shelter of overhanging brows, and the high-bridged nose, still arrogant in the encroaching flesh, jutted above lips which were puckered like a miser's purse.

I knelt and touched the Royal Instep with my forehead. He deigned to take my gift, even to open the lid; perhaps he was disappointed to find it empty of gold dust, but he said, "We consider ourselves pleased." Each word rustling past the dry lips like a rat hurrying out of a stubble field.

With head bowed between my outstretched arms, I walked slowly backwards to join the ranks of those who had already presented their tribute, and who were now assembled between the double rows of lotus columns which soared a full forty cubits to the roof. No one was permitted to speak in the Royal Presence, and I realized why Meri had said that the life of a courtier had the unreality of a tomb-painting. A whisper of sandals on polished stone; an almost inaudible soughing of fans; the quick, shallow breathing of a woman standing near me; all served to accentuate the silence, as the sudden rustle of leaves pointed the hush before a storm breaks. The scent of flowers and heavily perfumed unguents lay on the air like oil on water. Yet the courtiers of Pharaoh were well disciplined; no face betrayed boredom; no one stirred or showed fatigue, though some of them must have been standing for more than two hours.

I took a cautious pace to the right so as to increase my view. Now I could see Amenemhet, the Vizier; still very young to hold so great an office, the son of a powerful father whose strength had kept this puppet on the throne. Eyes black and brilliant as a hawk's; the fierce nose of a warrior, the firm, narrow mouth of a law-giver. Would he accept the role that might be offered to him by the Eyes of Horus? Would it be from his loins that a new dynasty was born? Would he or the younger prince rule Egypt? The Vizier was known as a man of strength; the just, the incorruptible. But was he too cold to light his justice with compassion? There lay the only doubt in Roidahn's mind. The new Pharaoh must be strong; the chosen leader of the Nomarch's one whose sovereignty they would freely acknowledge and in whose name they would unite Egypt. What had Roidahn said . . . "Only those who fear their own weakness are cruel."

Pharaoh stood up and like a field of corn bowed by the wind the whole assembly made deep obeisance. Then he slowly descended from the throne. Only when the curtain which covered the door leading to his private apartments fell back into place, did the silence splinter into a ripple of voices.

They were like children released from the dull insistence of a scribe, decorous children who had been told they must not run about in the sun, or get hot, or dirty—but still children. Now the quality of the Vizier was even more apparent: though he used no tricks of pomp or dignity, he was a hawk among sparrows.

Three times during the next seven days I attended some function at the Palace. It did not take me long to see why the choice of the Watchers lay between the Vizier and the younger prince, Men-het, for it was obvious that the Royal Heir was more contemptible even than his father. He had a weak, vicious face; pale, rather protuberant eyes, and a slack mouth with a pouting underlip.

It pleased him to be gracious to me, and I was stupid enough not to realize that if I had been born a girl he would have paid me no attention. So I was surprised when he sent one of his personal servants to ask me to be his guest for the evening. Heliokios said I must accept the invitation, since it was most unwise to offend the prince, especially now it was rumored that Pharaoh was a dying man. I noticed that Heliokios was embarrassed, as though he wanted to tell me something and could not find the right words.

Each of the princes had a house within the palace enclosure, and the one occupied by the Royal Heir was about the same size as the House of the Two Winds. There were no other guests, and the meal was served in a small pavilion which faced down a short avenue of almond trees leading to a large white building that seemed to have no windows.

The prince asked me several questions about the Oryx, but seemed disinterested in my replies. At first I thought he might have heard of the Watchers and was seeking information, but later I decided that his questions were designed to put me at my ease. He seemed to be trying to minimize the difference in our rank, and even dismissed the servants and poured wine for me himself.

"You must not think of me only as your future Pharaoh," he said. "You are my *friend*. You understand that? Pharaoh can deny nothing to his friends. I grow weary of the same faces, the same voices, of the narrow circle of my father's Court. They are so stupid—and so circumspect. But you are different. You are someone to whom I need not fear to speak. We are *men*, and they are only children—or dotards."

I grew still more puzzled. Why should this man, who was

nearly thirty years older than myself, look for a friend in me? Why did he bother to flatter the son of a Nomarch?

"I know I can trust you," he went on. "One must keep secret from the common people, but between us there can be understanding. Being more than half divine, I do not find my pleasures in the way of ordinary mortals. It was my divinity which told me I could trust you, and my divinity is my protection—for if you were to betray me you would die, as others died whom I had to judge unworthy of my confidence." His voice was a little blurred, though of wine he had drunk sparingly. "You will find it pleasant being in the Royal Favor. I think it is doubtful that you will wish to be wearied with office, but if you need the sign of my authority you shall choose your own Seal. Or I will make you the commander of a garrison, if you prefer that . . . though I think it would not be to your taste. You shall have many concubines to rule, and you need fear no rival."

Then, like a petulant child, "You don't believe me! You believe the stories they whisper about me, that I have *no* concubines."

He slid moist, thick fingers up my arm, and his voice dropped to a cunning whisper, "Ah, but that is because I am so clever, *I* keep my concubines hidden. So pretty they are—from Nubia, and some from Babylon, and some from Punt. I will take you to the house where they are so well guarded, safe in the guardianship of the dark silence." He chuckled. "That is my joke . . . 'the dark silence.' Come, I will show you. . . ."

He hurried down the path between the almond trees, his heavy, pendulous belly swaying like the buttocks of an ape which tries to run on its hind legs.

The east face of the white building was also without windows, but in it there was a door, heavily studded with copper nails. He knocked, and it was opened by a Nubian slave.

The prince giggled. "There, Ra-ab, there is my dark silence." And then to the man, "Open your mouth, Mahyiu!"

Between the double row of gleaming white teeth, the mouth was empty of a tongue.

"He's a safe guardian, isn't he, Ra-ab? He can't speak of my concubines—nor can he usurp any of my privileges; for his breechclout is as empty as his mouth!"

He shook with delighted appreciation of his joke; for which I was grateful as it gave me time to conceal my disgust.

When the door first opened there had been a babble of voices; then came the sound of a gong, followed by a sudden hush, broken by running feet.

The prince nodded with satisfaction. "They are well trained. They know they must run back to their cages like obedient songbirds until I summon the ones which will please me today."

From the outer door a passage led into a central courtyard, which, except that it was open to the sky, might have been a large room. On three sides was a row of narrow doors, a barred lattice set in each one. The rest of the walls were covered with frescoes, the chief motif of the decoration being a large eye, a grotesque parody of the Eye of Horus. At the end of the court was the largest of these eyes, high up where the wall projected into a kind of concealed gallery.

The prince pointed up to it. "You shall go into the Eye, from where you may watch unseen. If they knew you were there it might make them timid; but *I* shall know you are there. *I* have nothing to conceal—nothing, do you hear? *Nothing!*" His voice had risen to a scream. Then he controlled himself and said abruptly, "Hurry. Go through that door and up the stairs. Do not make a sound until I summon you."

The stairs led into a little room, the roof so low that I could not stand upright. In the opposite wall there was a narrow door, which I tried, to find it bolted on the far side. At the end of the room, just above the floor level, was the opening shaped like an eye. By lying on the floor I could see through it, down into the court.

Two slaves had carried in a low couch covered with leopard skins. On this the prince was lying, naked, a gold phallus strapped between his thighs.

Beside him stood a Nubian holding a gold-mounted ram's horn. The prince held up seven fingers; and at his signal the slave blew seven blasts. This, as I saw later, was to indicate which of the cells should be opened. There were twenty cells and all of them were numbered.

Into my line of vision came a small, delicate figure, veiled in purple gauze. Her upraised hands were long and tapering; the palms and nails stained a vivid carmine. Slowly she swayed in the intricate rhythms of a ritual dance, a debased version of the Adoration of Min. Always she drew nearer to the gross figure supine in its nest of leopard skins; always the hands were outstretched in supplication. Then as a gesture of surrender she shed her veil. She was an Asiatic, the young face painted in the most extreme of Egyptian fashion. Beseechingly she approached ever nearer the indifferent divinity; at last she touched the golden symbol—and stayed motionless as though rigid with terror.

Only then did I notice the flail hidden in the folds of the leopard skins. Very slowly the prince raised it above his head. The thongs sang through the air: the girl's body seemed to break under them as she slid to the floor.

A slave carried her away. The prince held up three fingers.

Before the third note of the ram's horn had died away, there was a chattering like a furious monkey. Another slave led in a man whose body was covered with a pelt of monkey skins. There was a wide metal collar round his neck, and he pretended to bite the man who led him by the heavy chain. He leaped forward, resting his weight on his knuckles like one of the great apes. He wrestled with his keeper, growling and snarling, and at last managed to sink his teeth in the slave's thigh until the blood spurted.

The prince whistled, like a man calling a dog; the human ape shambled toward him, fawning and slobbering as though in an ecstasy of abasement.

"Down, Niyanga. You are no longer a man; you are an ape! And you were once a prince; do you remember? Your father tried to deny the might of Egypt—but my father was greater than yours. So he was defeated, and you were brought here as a slave. My mother was sorry for you, and said you were to be brought up in the women's quarters of the Palace. But you found out that the Gods were jealous of me and dared not let me beget a son who would be greater even than its fathers—and so greater than they; for I am the equal of the Gods. You dared to pity me—*me* who will be Pharaoh of Egypt, who am divine! But I let you grow up in the Palace; I even let you become a captain in the Bodyguard. You had a wife and three children. They wept when they heard you had been killed in battle; but you had not been killed, had you, Niyanga? You were only wounded, and that for a time brought you a kind of forgetting, for the wound was in your head. When you woke up you found yourself here. It was not until you were stronger that I told you I had caused your *second* wound. . . . I do not like my apes to chatter in too deep a voice. Even if I were to let you go the apes would not accept you into their tribe; you are an outcast from man and beast. You are too proud to go back to me, to see the wife who once admired you, smiling at another husband. Your son is in the Bodyguard now. Remember that if you should become disobedient I shall have him brought here and show him that his father is an ape!"

The ferment of his hatred had risen to a climax. "Down! Down! . . . and drink my spittle from the floor!"

It was only after the next cell had been opened—it must have held two prisoners—and I had watched two Puntite boys go through a dreary parody of perversity, that I realized the first veiled figure was also a eunuch boy, emasculate as were even the guardians of this terrestrial Cavern of the Underworld.

How was I going to prevent the prince from knowing my disgust? If there was a shadow of suspicion in his mind that I was going to compass his death I should never get out of this prison. Somehow I must escape, *now.* I crept down the stairs and found the door at the foot of them was bolted. My heart-beats seemed to hold the menace of distant drums. Then I remembered the other little door. Before I reached it I heard it being unbolted. Another Nubian slave stood in the narrow opening beckoning to me, and by a gesture he adjured silence. I had no other alternative than to follow him. It was no use fighting him; he was a prisoner as much as any of the others. Somehow I must get near enough to the prince to make him suffer a little of what he had wrought. My fingers flexed, and I found I had lost my personal fear in the anticipation of how they would choke the last breath out of that horrid throat.

The passage ended in another flight of steps; and the door at the foot of them swung open. The slave stood aside to let me pass. With a surge of relief I found I was standing in a thicket of trees outside the palace walls. The slave put his hand on my eyes, then on my mouth. For a moment I thought he was going to strangle me, then knew he was using the only means he had to convey a message. . . . "You have seen nothing, you must say nothing."

I nodded to show I understood. He stayed for a moment by the open door, watching me take the narrow path through the trees which led to the Avenue of Sphinxes—and freedom.

Early next morning, Daklion told me that Heliokios was going to his country estate and wished me to accompany him. I wondered if this sudden change of plan had anything to do with my visit to the Royal Heir. Did Heliokios think I was in danger and was making this excuse to get me away from the City? I must make sure of this before I agreed to go with him, so that if necessary I could warn Meri and arrange for us to escape together.

I went upstairs to Heliokios' apartments and found him on the flat roof under the vine trellis, feeding Mimu from a plate of fruit. He did not like being disturbed at that hour and looked surprised to see me.

"You seem worried, Ra-ab. I hope you have not received ill news?"

"That is what I have come to find out. Daklion tells me you are leaving for your country estate this afternoon."

"No doubt you will want to inform Meri that you are going away for a few days. There will be plenty of time for you to do so, for it is only a two hours' journey and we need not leave until the cool of the evening."

"You said nothing to me yesterday about this change of plan. Is it because of me that you have made it?"

"Because of you? Why should it be? Is it so surprising that I should decide to go to the country to see my steward about certain matters which require my ruling, without first consulting you? I know that any time spent away from Meri you consider wasted, but I had hoped you would be willing to spare an old man a few days of your company. Most men would be eager to see an estate which may one day be theirs, and the future husband of the daughter of the Gold Seal should be glad to know that his future possessions will be more numerous than they are at present."

He was annoyed, and ignored me while he peeled a fig for Mimu.

"I must apologize for what must have seemed a most ungracious answer to your invitation. I thought you were taking me away because I had the misfortune to be the guest of the Royal Heir . . . it being probable that such guests find it wiser to put themselves as far as possible beyond the power of their host."

With the fig still in his hand and taking no notice of Mimu's impatience, he said, "Did he take you to the House of Silence?"

"He did."

"I ought to have warned you . . . most certainly I ought to have warned you. Many of us have looked through the Eye, but not usually until we had been his guest on several occasions. He seldom invites a married man to his house, and I thought that as soon as your betrothal was announced he would lose interest in you."

"Have you ever been his guest?"

"Yes, many years ago."

"You have never been endangered by your knowledge?"

"No, for I have been sensible enough not to discuss any details of the Royal Hospitality. Only those who have been sufficiently foolish to talk, have, shall we say, been *unfortunate*."

"I have not discussed it with anyone."

"Then the Eye has not brought you dangerous knowledge. Even I do not know which of my friends have been there, though I know many of them must have. Pharaoh knows the value of his eldest son and delights in stressing his inferiority. It is perhaps largely the father's fault that the boy developed the mind of a monster. His body was injured as a child, a flesh wound in the groin became poisoned and took a long time to heal . . . then it began to be whispered that the Heir was impotent. He was a very cruel child. He ordered his dogs and cats to be emasculated, and once I saw him plucking the feathers from a live pigeon. I think cruelty became an outlet for the normal energies of the body, but even he did not dare to make an open scandal in the City . . . that is why he built the House of Dark Silence. Pharaoh doesn't mind how his eldest son amuses himself so long as it is not made public.

He never allows his son to exercise the powers of co-ruler, that is why the Heir likes to let people know that in his own way he has absolute authority over abject slaves."

"He should be destroyed—and his body burned, for even the vultures would sicken on such carrion!"

"Whatever your private thoughts may be, Ra-ab, you will not make such treasonable utterances while you are my guest. If I were to do my duty as the Ivory Seal, I should have to decree your death for having spoken against a member of the Royal Family. Fortunately I did not hear your last remark, and have already forgotten that you were unwise enough to make it."

Prisoner of Time

THE COUNTRY ESTATE of Heliokios was to the southwest of the City, and we reached it before sunset. It was not so extensive as I had expected, and cannot have employed more than a hundred people. The greater part of the land was given over to pasture, though I saw three fields under flax and perhaps twice as many in which the second harvest grain was already showing. The house was considerably larger than the one in the City, though there was no second story. The women's quarters, in which the concubines lived when they were not at the other House of the Two Winds, were away from the main block and set in their own pleasure-garden surrounded by a wall.

Heliokios was very proud of his oxen, of which he had developed a famous strain. They were stalled in a building of their own and separated from each other by painted wooden partitions. Each stood knee-deep in fresh wheat-straw, and several of them were brought for me to admire. They were magnificent beasts, their brilliant black and white hides shining like highly polished stone, and their long horns tipped with gold. The cows which were kept for household use were of a different breed, much smaller and reddish in color. These were loose in a large enclosure beyond the kitchen quarters, and when I first saw them were being led in to be milked. There was a warm smell of baking bread as we crossed the servants' courtyard, and an old woman who was pounding grain in a stone mortar stared at me, and drew her head-cloth across her face as though she did not want Heliokios to notice her.

The newly planted vineyard was at the back of the house, and beyond it I saw a plantation of sycamores near the ruins of a small temple. The vines showed no signs of bearing, but remembering how I had offended Heliokios over the matter of his right to plant them, I was careful to appear suitably impressed with the small green shoots.

In spite of the estate being a considerable distance from the river, it was well irrigated by a wide canal which afforded a plentiful supply of water, not only for the fields but for a swimming-pool which was at least three times larger than the one in the City.

It was in this pool that I was swimming soon after dawn the following morning, when I saw Daklion come running out of the door which led from my room. I saw something serious must have happened, for usually he was careful and deliberate of movement, never displaying any emotions save those he considered fitting to the dignity of Steward of the Household.

"I cannot wake my master! He is lying as though he were dead, but he is still breathing. What can I do for him? I have sent a messenger to the Royal Physician asking him to come here with all speed. My master seemed quite well yesterday, though he complained of the heat and admitted he was unduly tired. . . ."

I ran to Heliokios' room. When I saw him I knew there was nothing we could do except wait for the physician. In the Oryx I had seen another man whose face had that same suffusion of dusky purple—it was a soldier injured by a fall, but in his case it had been the left side of the body which had gone cold and rigid. The healer-priest who attended him told me that the skull was crushed and part of the brain deeply bruised, and he had also told me that it was possible for the brain to receive a similar injury without any external cause. The soldier had died, and I was sure Heliokios was already dying.

I knew that as I was his nearest blood-relation I should be expected to attend all the rites both before and after his death . . . never leaving his room even to sleep. He did not regain consciousness, though sometimes he tried to move his head as though he were looking for someone, and when the wrinkled lids flickered open there still seemed to be a spark of the old vitality in the eye,. I wondered if Roidahn had known how difficult I should find it not to be biased in favor of a man who had been a kind and generous host, and if that was why he had thought it necessary to remind me on my last evening in Hotep-Ra that my loyalty to the Watchers must take precedence before all the lesser loyalties of hospitality and kinship.

The Royal Physician, with two attendants, arrived soon after noon. I had to pretend to believe his assurances that under his care Heliokios would speedily return to health, and without protest to watch him ply his ignorant trade. Had Heliokios been someone I really loved I think I should have forgotten discretion and sent to the Oryx for a healer; even though during the pestilence I had grown too familiar with the mark of death not to know that nothing could keep him alive for more than a few days. Life I could not have given him, but at least I could have saved him the humiliations which he suffered during his dying.

I asked the Royal Physician if he knew what had caused the illness and told him of the man who had also suffered from a bruised brain. I found by my question that physicians could be as jealous of their secrets as were false priests of their rituals; which was not surprising, considering they were both trying to conceal their abysmal ignorance from the fools on whose credulity they built their power.

He looked at me with covert disapproval, and repeated what he had told me already; that the spirit of Heliokios was being lured away from the body by a demon which had taken upon itself the guise of a delectable concubine.

"Without doubt that is the cause of his affliction," said the physician pontifically. "The demon is keeping him away, and only by giving him a measure of pain can he be made aware of his peril and so restored to life. If you doubt my words you may see for yourself that the enchantress is lying at his right side and draining from it the natural warmth and vitality, that, of course, is why it has become cold and insentient."

He beckoned to his assistant, who handed him a small knife, and I had to watch them score the yellow, wrinkled skin with a network of fine scratches, just sufficiently deep to bead with blood. When this brought no response they rubbed a fiery paste into the wounds; it had a sharp, acrid smell and was streaked with a pale, rusty red. This was continued at intervals from dawn of the second day until noon, and when they had to admit Heliokios showed no change they said they must now employ stronger measures.

They tied up the genitals of the dying man in a bag made from the pelt of a black ram which had been gelded just before being offering as a sacrifice. Even the most powerful spirits, they told me, cannot see whatever part of the human body is so protected. "And so powerful is the effect of this shadow of invisibility that it affects the soul and spirit as well as the physical body. This remedy is only used when other methods have failed, for though it is now certain that the enchantress will release her spell—having no further use for a lover whom she will take to be a eunuch, on his return your kinsman will be forever impotent. Or should he, by powerful spells, be restored to a fleeting virility, any child born to him would be the son of the black ram."

It is almost suffocatingly hot, for the physician forbade the shutters to be opened, and the only air came through a little hole which he had caused to be cut in one of them; in the shape of a mannikin with outstretched arms, through which the soul could return. At the foot of the bed a brazier was kept constantly burning. At night it was fed with bitumen and other resinous gums, to remind the spirit that if it did not return, its body would soon be in the hands of the embalmers. During the day the nauseous things which, had he been able to swallow, the unfortunate man would have been forced to eat, were burned in a canopic jar of the shape most commonly used to contain viscera; for the physicians held that as long as the man was breathing he received in the smoke the same benefit he would have done had his stomach been able to accept them. When I saw of what they consisted I judged his affliction most merciful, in that it had already brought him so near the protection of death that his spirit could not suffer the indignities experienced in the flesh. Every hour of the day from dawn to sunset the brazier was replenished.

At the dawn hour, lion dung moistened with honey; this to give strength.

At the second hour, freshly skinned mice steeped in vinegar; for mice can escape through the smallest crannies.

At the third hour, the larvae of ants in oil; for when their nest is destroyed ants at once begin to build it up again, and the body so strengthened will begin to recreate itself even when deeply mutilated.

At the fourth hour, a bowl of crocodile fat; for crocodiles guard the portals of the Underworld, and he who has eaten of their flesh may return from the Caverns, for the guardians, thinking him to be one of themselves, give him no challenge.

At the fifth hour, the flesh of three snakes stewed in old wine; for the snake keeps in its own flesh the antidote to the most powerful poisons, even its own, and wine increases the vitality of this attribute.

At the sixth hour, garlic in pigeon's blood; for the enchantress will draw back if she smells garlic on the breath of her victim, and the pigeon will give him strength to fly from her at the instant she loosens her hold.

At the seventh hour, a paste made of maggots from the body of a dead vulture, for they consume that which has consumed the dead.

At the eighth hour, dust from the sarcophagus of a mummified cat, black in color, pounded in asses' cream; this will enable him to pass all magical barriers at night, the cream will purchase the aid of the dead cat and strengthen the living one.

The ninth and last hour, the full-time embryo of an ape; to give the power of renewal to the aging flesh. This was the only time they were reluctant to tell me what the jar contained. Was it only an ape? Floating in its amniotic fluid in the dim light of the brazier it seemed the travesty of all ignorant humanity.

The heavy stench was thick as rancid oil, and the gasping breath of the dying man was the only sound in the close stillness. I moved to the side of the bed and leaned over him to lift one of the thin lids; the eye was rolled back into the head and did not quiver. One side of his face was twisted, and from the corner of the mouth a little drool of saliva gathered in the hollow under the sharp collarbone.

I believe that had there been a link of true affection between us I might still have reached him, and brought a measure of comfort to his restless ghost. I tried to pray that he should cross the Great River in peace; the words I used seemed to have no substance, as though they were lying dormant on a papyrus, and I could feel no response flow down to me. I thought how pitiful it was for a man who had been the focus of worldly power to be dying more friendless than the least of his servants.

Smoke from the brazier coiled down like a black snake. I would have opened the windows, but to break the seals the physician had put on them would have exposed me to the charge of deliberately hastening my kinsman's death; the fetid air was not adding to his discomfort and I could continue to endure it.

Soon after sunset the physician came into the room, and in a low voice said that he could no longer conceal from me that his work was finished, and there was nothing I could do save watch by Heliokios until I saw that the time had come to summon the priest who would perform the rites of the dead. His failure had cost him none of his assurance; he seemed confident that he had done everything possible and that the inability of my kinsman to recover was due to his own perversity of spirit.

He said confidently, "You must console yourself with the knowledge that *nothing* has been left undone. When spirits persist in a course that will lead them to death nothing can be done to save them from the results of their folly." His voice changed from the note of formal comfort that he must often have offered to the bereaved. "The priest has been informed he may be needed before dawn; so that there should be no delay he is already in the house, and waits for you to summon him the moment the nostrils are still. Now I will leave you, for it is your privilege to watch alone during the last hours."

As he turned to leave the room he paused and said, "If the warmth of the brazier discomforts you, you may have it removed . . . it is no longer necessary."

The lamps at the head and foot of the bed burned with a narrow, clear flame. The lungs labored for each difficult breath, like weary oxen drawing a load which soon will bring them to a standstill. The silence of the great house waited for this slow sound to join its stillness, only then to be broken by ceremonial lamentations. Minutes shuffled past like the feet of blind prisoners; and the hours they built were heavy as the drop-stone of a tomb.

The curtain over the doorway whispered as though it moved in a sudden draft, and a woman crept forward through the shadows. Her eyes were fixed on the face of the dying man and I think she never noticed I was in the room. She came slowly to the far side of the bed, and I recognized her as the woman who baked bread for the servants. She was withered and old; her dry, colorless lips were puckered over shrunken gums, yet in her eyes was the look of a bride for her lover, and youth lived on in the cavern of her lids. She took the old man's hand between her own and held it against her cheek. Her voice was soft as the skin of a young girl, warm and alive.

"Age has come to release us, O my beloved, and the years cannot divide us any more; for the wall that life has built between us crumbles before the advancing host of death. Death has rent the veil which has obscured us from each other, and we can walk with clear eyes back into that time when the young Heliokios took the daughter of his father's servant, and they found joy together. We are young again! You have just returned from fowling, your body taut as a stretched bow, to bring down the gazelle of contentment with the arrow of desire. Your skin has the sheen of the love of Ra, and your swift thighs and lordly shoulders rejoice in their strength. And I am young; more beautiful than the fairest of your father's concubines. That is what death has brought to us: those hours when you took joy of me and gave me joy; all else is forgotten.

"And what has death taken in exchange? The tears I shed when you had forgotten me, when you no longer thought me worthy to be a concubine, even among many. The years when I had to obey the orders of other women in whom you took delight: grinding malachite that would make more beautiful the eyes which would see you as I once had seen you, laying gold leaf on nails whose hands would know your skin, anointing with perfumed oils the breasts you fondled. . . . I took no other man, and soon grew old. My hands grew clumsy and my feet were slow; I was glad when I was made a kitchen servant, for it was easier to prepare food which you might eat, than to help other of your appetites. Now I bake bread for those who, like myself, are the ashes of your household . . . but death is taking me away. Death has gathered those weary years into his hands, and crushed them into dust your dying breath has blown upon the wind. Time was our jailer, time had brought down our youth and turned your strength to bitter lethargy. Now death has conquered time and bid him go . . . to build round other fools his palisade which death can brush aside like summer grass. . . .

"Come, my beloved. You are returning from the reeds and carry a string of four wild-fowl. You are hurrying, because I am waiting for you under the fig tree which grows from the court-yard of the ruined temple. You have been running, so hard . . . it is only a little further. You can see me now, for when I heard you calling I came out of the shadows and stood waiting in the light where you could see me. . . ."

She took up the lamp and held it above her head while she leaned over him. Her voice rang out, clear and strong, "I am here, Helios, waiting for you. . . . O, my dear beloved. . . ."

She stood up, straight and young, that old, crippled woman. Her hands were stretched out as though she waited for the arms of her lover. Her eyes seemed to see him, standing beyond the bed, beyond the shadows.

Her body crumpled, as the ash of a torch crumbles when its life is consumed. I found myself standing at the window whose sealed shutters I had broken open. The moonlight was very bright; yet I could not see them, though I knew they took a path to where a fig tree had grown by a forgotten ruin.

I saw she was dead before I touched her. On the lips of the dead man lingered the reflection of the smile that lit her face . . . the dead man whom I had thought to see die among strangers.

I gathered her up; she was very light, like ancient wood which soon will fall to dust. . . . She must be saved the indignity of the last rites by which the body is desecrated through the rituals of an ignorant priesthood. She would like to be buried in the ruined temple, so that her body returned to the place where it had found joy. . . .

I wondered whose permission I must obtain to keep her from the common burial ground, and only then did I realize why the household was deferring to my authority: it was because Heliok-ios had appointed no other heir, and so I, who was his closest blood-relation, inherited all his possessions. I was Lord of the

House of the Two Winds; its herds and treasure, its lands and vineyards.

I laid the woman down on a narrow couch under the window and went to find Daklion. He was waiting in the anteroom and must have seen by my face that his master was dead, for he made low obeisance to me, and then knelt to touch my instep with his forehead in sign of fealty, saying, "Your word is my law, above all other law" . . . which were the formal words of the oath of obedience.

I said to him, "There are two funerals to prepare. One tomb stands ready for its tenant and the rituals for the last journey of his flesh are long designed. You, Daklion, have been with Heliokios since he was a youth; perhaps you knew that nearly fifty years ago he was the lover of a woman he seemed to have forgotten. Yet her love was the gold which time does not corrode, for only base metals perish. The voices of the concubines will be raised in lamentation and the women of this household will put ashes on their heads; but the voice of the only woman who loved him will be silent; for at his last breath her spirit left its body also, because there was no longer anything to hold it to Earth. My kinsman's body shall be buried according to the custom by which he lived, but she is free of temporal obligations. Her body was a shackle which has been struck off, and to her the memory of its weariness is a mist that has dispersed before the sun. Though the temple is a ruin, the light there kindled still shines for those who have eyes to see; though the tree is cut down, the voice of the leaves still speaks to those whose ears are open: there shall her body mingle with the earth, in that quiet place where love has laughed at time, and youth has vanquished age with the quick spear of death."

Daklion followed me across the deserted courts . . . deserted because until the declaration of mourning had been given all kept to their rooms. I carried the woman in my arms; her head was turned against my shoulder as though she were weary and slept. The Moon Goddess, who is compassionate to all women who suffer for their love, paved the way to her tomb with silver that the treasure of Pharaoh could not have equaled.

Only a broken lotus column and part of two walls which once had enclosed a courtyard showed where the temple had been; and where the walls joined I could see the roots of a dead tree. Gently I laid her down, wrapped in my cloak. I felt as though a veil were before my eyes and that if I could brush it aside I should see the place as it really was and not as by time's illusion I was seeing it.

I should not be digging in bare earth under the open sky, for here in the shade, grass would be growing, and at this season the boughs above me would be dense with leaves. I worked quietly so as not to disturb the lovers who whispered together in the warm shade. They were the reality and I a phantom who was not yet born, a phantom without the substance of a shadow. The spade dug a narrow trench in the ground; and yet the grass was not disturbed. A phantom lifted the body of an old, tired woman and kissed her forehead before the face was shielded in the folds of a white cloak with the clasp of a gold oryx.

The dry earth rustled down into the hole in the ground, sibilant as water: but the girl who lay with the joy of her lover's head between her breasts did not hear the earth which phantoms moved to fill her grave. For she was no longer a prisoner of time.

If the priest, a middle-aged man wearing a white robe bordered with heavy purple, realized he had not been summoned until Heliokios had been dead nearly three hours, he made no sign; and without comment began rites which were an ignorant travesty of the "sealing of the body" which I had seen performed by Nefer-ankh during the invocation to Ra.

The ceremony I now watched was intended to release the spirit from the body and to protect it during its journey through the Underworld. A white pigeon and a black cockeral were sacrificed on a small altar which had been carried into the room by two acolytes. The blood of the white bird was supposed to protect the spirit during the hours ruled over by the Sun, and of the black bird to protect it when the influence of the Goddess of the Dark Moon was predominant.

With this mingled blood the body was anointed on the forehead, breasts, palms of the hands, and soles of the feet. The oil I had seen used by Nefer-ankh in the temple of the Oryx had been a vehicle of power, but the blood now used was only an empty symbol, for the one who was using it was only a man dressed in the robe of a priest. Then the mouth of the corpse was forced open—it was growing rigid in spite of the heat of the room, and on the tongue was placed a strip of papyrus on which was written the names of the prow and the oars of the Boat of Millions of Years, so that the spirit would know the answers to the challenge given by them on its journey.

"This rite used to be performed before death," said the priest. "The dying man drank the ashes of a similar papyrus in a draft of wine."

Then he began to pray in a loud voice, warning the spirit of Heliokios of the dangers that would beset it on its journey across the Great River, and exhorting it not to listen to the voices of evil demons, who would be sent to lure it to leave the boat so that they could engulf it in the waters of oblivion.

Still intoning, he sealed the ears with little plugs of clay which had been freshly moistened with blood. In the same way he closed the nostrils, telling me as he did so that it was a favorite ruse of demons to disturb the newly dead by making them aware of some perfume associated with the pleasure of the flesh, the unguent used by a loved concubine or the savor of a rich dish, so that the spirit might be tempted to return to its body.

I asked why the demons bothered to resort to such devices, and was told that though the spirit is protected when it first leaves the body, by those spirits whose work it is to attend the dying, if it returns of its own free will it is then open to enslavement by the powers of darkness.

While the priest was carrying out these offices I noticed the acolytes. They were boys not yet fully grown; their eyelids painted like women's, and their ear-lobes and nipples painted carmine. Had I been sufficiently familiar with the practices of the new temples, I should have known them for boys who had been given to the temple when they were five years old, as payment for some special favor granted to their parents by Set or Sekmet. By a gradual process, lasting for two years, they were sometimes rendered emasculate; or else underwent a preparation to increase their sexual ripening, similar to the one which is performed on girls by certain Asiatic tribes.

"There is nothing more for me to do," said the priest. "The body is now ready for the embalmer."

I had forgotten that the body would have to be embalmed, and wondered if Daklion would know who should be summoned. As though in answer to my thought, the priest said:

"Before his departure, the Royal Physician informed me that immediately on his arrival at the Royal City he would tell the Royal Embalmer that his services were needed here. It is probable that his servants will have already arrived to take the body to the embalmer's house."

I was surprised that the body would have to be taken away to be embalmed, for in the Oryx that ceremony, which is only performed on those whose funerary rites are sufficiently elaborate to make it necessary to retard dissolution until they are completed, took place in the house. I asked the priest if he would take wine or other refreshment before he departed. He refused, saying that he had already availed himself of my hospitality during the hours he had waited for Heliokios to die.

He stared at me with curiosity not untinged with hostility; and again I wondered if he knew that he had had to wait much longer than he would have considered necessary.

"No doubt I shall see you again," he said, "now that you are the Lord of the House of the Two Winds. The tribute of this estate is brought to the temple to which I belong. It is less than an hour's journey to the north, and was built twenty years ago, though added to more recently through the generosity of your kinsman. He must be well content that he used his treasure with such foresight, for tribute given to a temple is the only possession which can benefit a man in the hereafter." He paused and looked searchingly at me. "I saw some of your bulls while I was waiting: they are worthy to make the principal sacrifice at our next festival."

"Five shall be given to you," I said, "in memory of my kinsman."

"Five?" he echoed, and then added significantly, "You have a large herd."

"You mistake me. I said ten, not five."

For the first time he smiled. "Heliokios shall rest content. The sacrifice of ten such bulls will make even the Forty-two Assessors very lenient."

After I had watched the priest depart I found Daklion waiting for me outside the room in which lay his dead master.

"The servants of the Royal Embalmer are here," he said. "My master had arranged long ago that his body should be preserved by the one whose skill has no equal. It is usual for the one nearest to the dead man to accompany his body to the embalmer's house, so they have brought a second litter. Will you go with him?"

"Yes, Daklion. I will go with him." And I put my hand on his shoulder, for I saw he was deep in sorrow.

Royal Embalmer

DAKLION TOLD ME that in the Royal Nomes there were two degrees of embalming; the more usual one took four days, but the second degree, performed only on members of the Royal Family, high priests, and a few important officials who had been granted this special favor, continued for forty days. During this period traditional mourning would continue in all households belonging to the dead man, and his property would not pass to his heir until the tomb was sealed.

Tradition decreed that only those whose work it is to attend the dead shall touch the corpse, so the embalmer's servants prepared Heliokios for his last journey to the Royal City. The litter they had brought for him was shaped like a sarcophagus; Nut with outstretched arms guarded each corner, her head resting among the stars which covered the lid.

The litter in which I traveled was closely curtained, in white to signify mourning, for which I was glad as it gave me a chance to sleep. I woke just after we entered the West Gate, and, looking out through a chink in the curtains, recognized one of the narrow streets which lead out of the foreign market. The bearers stopped at a door in a high, unpainted wall, and I heard bolts being drawn before the door swung open. Clipped acacia trees lined the path to a white house, which was similar to those occupied by court officials. Beyond it I saw several outbuildings; they were sunk in the ground and at first I took them to be wine-stores: then I realized they served a very different purpose, for it was to one of them that Heliokios was taken.

My litter was set down at the entrance to the main house, and there I was greeted by a venerable old man, who told me he was

Yiahn, the Royal Embalmer. I had expected him to be a furtive wizened creature, a kind of sorcerer, but he was wholesome as a bowl of sweet butter. He wore a robe of dark blue linen, and though the slant of his eyebrows, and something about the molding of his cheekbones, led me to think he was not of the pure blood, he spoke without a foreign intonation.

He invited me into his house and gave me wine, which, he said, had come from Pharaoh's vineyard. It was heavy in texture and very sweet; as I drank I felt a lifting of the weariness which had come from many hours of insufficient sleep. I wondered if he thought I had come either to spy on him or to make sure that his work was faithfully carried out; so I explained I was a stranger to the city and that in my Nome men did not prepare so carefully for the tomb.

He smiled, the smile of a contented man who is never disturbed by fears or regrets. "Neither do I belong to this city, though I have been here for many years. Pharaoh and the members of his Court are preoccupied with how their flesh may best endure when they no longer inhabit it; that is why I came here after I had added to the skill taught to me by my father, who was also an embalmer. He learned his trade from a kinsman of my grandmother, who was not an Egyptian. Now I am no longer poor; but to cheat corruption has become my craft and I am too jealous of perfection to abandon it while there is still much to be discovered. In the old days I might have become a priest, but the temples of this time make no claim on my loyalties."

He stood up, still smiling, and went on: "The body will be ready for me by now. As he is your kinsman you may accompany me if you wish, and I will not keep any of my secrets until you are gone."

I realized he was doing me a great courtesy so I accepted his offer . . . hoping he did not recognize that I found the prospect disquieting.

"The living must purify themselves before they attend the dead. Come with me and I will show you what you must do to make ready."

I was surprised to find that I had already felt friendship toward this curious man. There was neither deference nor patronage in his manner; he took it for granted that I recognized him for a master craftsman, and he was blinded neither by modesty nor conceit.

His house was furnished with extreme simplicity, though the frescoes in the hall I had seldom seen equaled. Though there was little other decoration I realized that he must be rich to be able so to content his taste, for the floors were of rare stone, white veined with purple or green, and the doors were of cedar-wood, highly polished.

I was shown into a small room where a servant waited to minister to me. Following his instructions, I first washed all over with water in which must have been the juice of many citrus fruits—it was sour to taste and stung like fire when it touched a little cut on my forearm; and then he rubbed me lightly with oil that had a pungent but not unpleasant smell. When he had finished he gave me a robe such as his master had worn, which had long sleeves and covered me from neck to feet. Even my sandals were replaced by others that had wooden soles and thongs of plaited straw.

Then the servant led me back to the room where I had drunk wine with Yiahn, and I found him waiting for me. He was dressed as I was, but the sleeves of his robe left the fore-arms bare and his head was covered with a folded head-cloth of white linen. I saw he had refilled the wine-cups, and, obeying a sudden impulse, I held mine up to the East. Without hesitation he completed the Watcher's toast, "Look to the dawn; and see how Ra returns to those who watch for him!"

"Then you *are* one of us?" I exclaimed.

"The Oryx has already honored my house; for twice Hanuk, son of Roidahn, has found it convenient to wear the insignia of a servant of the Royal Embalmer; and, more than twice, men have left their homes in my litter of the dead only to find their health restored when they entered my door—whereafter my house became the first stage of their journey to Hotep-Ra. It may well be that in the time of the horizon many men who live for Egypt need first to pretend to die just as some may die because they lived against her. None will challenge the servants of the Royal Embalmer, for they believe I hold the secrets of their enjoyment of the hereafter, and it is known that my skill is not for purchase by those who have offended against me. I regret that if you would see me at work there is not time for you first to refresh yourself by sleep; for, especially in the hot weather, the dead will not wait on the patience of the living!"

I followed him across the formal garden; he was so gracious a host that it was difficult to realize I was not to watch him throw millet to the fish in his lotus pool, but instead would see him oppose the law of dissolution. The flight of steps leading down into the ground was longer than I had expected, and at the foot of it we came to a shaft which continued to slope down and led to a narrow room cut in the solid rock. It was lit by four lamps, set on ledges in the walls, and the air was cool as a deep well.

The naked body of Heliokios was lying on a stone table in the middle of the floor, and beyond it I saw a dark opening leading to a further room. The flesh had begun to discolor, and when he saw the extent of the livid patches, Yiahn gave an exclamation of annoyance. Several knives and curiously shaped instruments were laid out on a stool by the body, and beside this were four canopic jars.

Yiahn picked up one of the objects from the stool, it had a handle the length of his palm and at one end were two metal hooks curved like a leopard's claws. In the other hand he took a narrow strip of flexible metal, bent it until it could be inserted into the right nostril of the corpse and then released it so that it held the nostril wide open. Up the nostril he thrust the claw; there was a grating sound of metal on bone; a small sound like a mouse gnawing. To my shame, I felt sweat start on my forehead and the palms of my hands grow chill and damp. I don't know if he realized how I was feeling, but he began to talk, and as I listened the sickness passed.

"Even before I was as old as you are I became interested in the complexities of the human body and there were many questions to which I could find no answer. I knew the body was only the temporary habitat of the soul and spirit; yet I found also that though a philosopher may continue his thoughts uninterrupted if the roof of his house is leaking, he cannot continue to ponder on abstractions when the body in which his soul is housed protests against considerable discomfort. There are some who maintain their soul to be so strong that pain can get no hearing; but though such men exist, and I have seen them deliberately inflict on themselves what to another would be unbearable torture, I have never heard a man who used his vital energy to such a purpose make a statement which has added to the sum of the wisdom of mankind."

He was scraping the brain out through the nose; thick, whitish curds flecked with blood and mucus; and carefully transferring them to the first of the jars.

"I decided that as the soul could be incommoded by the flesh, it was the duty of man to stop its flight from being so curtailed. The priests make a mystery of the soul, claiming that though all men have one, only the priesthood can understand it: indeed I was taught that to inquire of such matters was to incur the wrath of the Gods. But, I argued with myself, if a man breaks a water-jar and has no other to use, he must learn to mend it or else suffer from thirst; is it then unreasonable that if he breaks his body he must mend it also? Yet when I tried to learn, I found that what is under a man's skin is bright with blood and dark with mystery; and I said, 'Is the arrow of an enemy the only thing able to see inside the body? Cannot that which comes to heal have as much vision as that which comes to destroy?' Such questions went unanswered, if indeed I was not actually punished for asking them. "How can I find out what has made a man ill if I may not see what has made him well?' How little we know the workings of this house in which we live! The lungs and the heart, the brain and the viscera, we know of them only because for many centuries they have been withdrawn by embalmers. . . ."

He paused, and with a small knife made an incision under the left ribs. Gently he widened it until he was able to put his hand into the cavity and so draw out the heart. Blood oozed out of it and dripped slowly to the floor. He trimmed it of some of the large blood vessels that still adhered, and then put it into the second jar. His hands were slimy, so he sluiced them in a bowl of water before starting to close the slit in the flesh with swift, delicate stitches, using a copper needle and a strong, waxed thread. While he did this he went on talking. . . .

"Finding that no one would allow a boy to satisfy his curiosity by opening a living body . . . and knowing that to touch a corpse

211

except to prepare it for burial is to court death or banishment, I despaired, until I realized how generous the Gods had been in the choice of my parents. I was the son of an embalmer, so what could be more natural than that I should follow the embalmer's trade? Before he died my father taught me all he knew, and while I worked with him I had to do as he did . . . a hurried removal of viscera and a steeping of the empty corpse in gums and rosins before bandaging. Inside those bandages, in a hundred years there will be only dust and a few poor bones; inside these I now wind, a thousand years from now he who unwraps them will be able to say, 'This woman was beautiful,' or 'This man was proud.'"

He was drawing out the viscera through a narrow slit on the right side of the belly. Winding them slowly on a smooth stick; very slowly, for already they were beginning to rot and might break. The stench of decay and excrement conquered the clean pungent smell of our protective oils. My own belly seemed to twist, like a dog turning round and round to make a bed in the sand. . . .

"I became famous and for this I was grateful; for fame brought me many bodies from which to learn, and I found out many things which others are not yet ready to accept. I noticed that several women who were thought to have died because their unborn child had decayed within them had not in fact conceived but had a growth in their womb—sometimes it was bigger than my fist and hard as stone. What would have happened if this growth had been removed before they were dead? Would they have regained their health? How could I know? There were many healers-with-the-knife, but they only attended one who had been injured by a weapon, or broken a bone so that it protruded through the skin. No one would come to an embalmer until they were dead. So I took to myself a twin brother . . . though he is not known to any of my household save two trusted servants. If anyone has noticed the resemblance between the healer-with-the-knife who has a little house in the poorest quarter of the city and Yiahn the Royal Embalmer none have remarked on it, and I am free to live my two lives without disturbance. It was on a day when I was playing this second role that I first heard of the Watchers. Hanuk was lodging at the house of a woman whose breast I had opened to drain an abscess. It had healed rapidly, and she was grateful and talked of me to all she met. Through her Hanuk came several times to my house, and when he had taken my measure he told me of the Watchers and said I was one of them. Because we were friends, among whom such things are permissible, I played a joke on him, saying I could get the Royal Embalmer to join us; and though Hanuk was doubtful, he at last agreed to come to this house . . . and found that instead of two new Watchers he had only one!"

Through a third incision, in the back, he had taken out the lungs, and the fourth jar was ready to be sealed. A heavy brazier was brought in by a man whom I recognized as one of the litter-bearers, though now he was dressed as we were. Over it was placed a pot of what looked like dark wax, and when this began to bubble it gave off a cloud of steam, the smell suggesting that in it was not only bitumen, but spikenard and myrrh, perhaps septes oil and other things as well. By means of a hollow reed fitted with a plunger, the boiling liquid was forced into the brain cavity, through the nostril that was still held open by the metal strip: and in the same way it was injected into the throat and ears. Then another hollow reed, narrower than the first one, was inserted into a slit in the scrotum; and afterwards the ancient, wrinkled penis was distended with wax until it looked as though it had regained the eagerness of its forgotten youth.

Yiahn paused and glanced at me. "This is the point beyond which I usually work alone . . . but I hope you will stay if you find my work of interest. There is not much more to do, only the withdrawing of the larger veins, but that is slow when the body is old and many hours have passed since the blood congealed."

He opened each arm inside the elbow, and with forceps began to draw out the pallid, knotted cords which once had beat with life. Blood clots slid down on to the table with little soft plops. . . . He treated other parts of the body in the same way; the insteps, under the knees, and at each side of the neck. At each place he closed the small incision with such care that it showed only as a thin line.

Then another pot was put on the brazier; as far as I could judge it contained bees-wax to which had been added certain aromatic gums. When this had sufficiently melted, but before it came near to boiling, Yiahn lightly coated the whole surface of the body with it, using a brush such as a scribe takes for a large wall painting, and allowing one side to dry before turning it over to do the other. At a sign from his master the man who had been tending the brazier came forward and lifted the feet of the corpse. Yiahn took it by the head, and together they carried it through the opening in the far wall which I had noticed when I first entered the room.

As I stooped to follow them, for the entrance was very low, I heard water dripping. The corpse was lying in a narrow depression in the floor, shaped rather like the bath in Meri's apartments, and above it an enormous water-jar was suspended from the roof by strong ropes. At the bottom of this jar a flexible tube led from a spigot, and the end of the tube was joined to a piece of hollow reed about six palm-breadths in length.

"This is not pleasant to watch even when one is used to it," said Yiahn.

I was too proud to admit that I had already seen enough of embalming to last me a lifetime, so I told him I would rather stay to see all he was willing to show me.

The head of the corpse was forced back and the jaws levered open, until the mouth and throat were in a straight line with the trunk. The strong yellow teeth seemed to be trying to crunch on the reed as it was driven down between them . . . at first they seemed to resist the pressure and then it slid on easily. With a sharp twinge of nausea I realized that why it went on easily was because there was no longer anything in the empty trunk to offer resistance. Then up the anus was thrust another short length of hollow reed. . . .

"That is to ensure an even drainage. If it were not there the brine might force its way between the stitches, even past the protective covering of wax, or else it would distend the body so that your kinsman would journey through the Underworld with a paunch. A good embalmer is as jealous of the appearance of those he prepares as is the old woman who bedecks a foreign concubine for the bargaining!"

The great jar was filled with hot brine, which contained various mineral salts used by certain tribes for pickling meat. As the spigot was turned the fluid gurgled down into the corpse. It writhed as though it were struggling for breath, with the chest and belly heaving like a drowning man who fought for life . . . a man *we* were trying to drown.

I forced myself to watch dispassionately. I *mustn't* let Yiahn see how much I want to be sick. . . . The second tube through which the fluid drained away led into a grating at the bottom of the bath. Only when Yiahn had finally satisfied himself that a constant flow was passing through the body without touching any of the outer skin did he say there was no need for us to stay there any longer. "There is nothing more for me to do; the jar will be kept filled for the next seven days and only then will the body be ready for the last stages, when a preparation of bitumen and certain rosins will be applied for the time that must still intervene before it is ready for the bandaging."

I was very glad to follow him up the shaft and to breathe the clean air. I knew I had been underground for a long time, but was surprised to find it was after sunset.

"I hope you will do me the honor of sleeping at my house," he said. "It would be a great joy to talk with one of the Eyes of Horus, and it may not be so easy another time for us to have the opportunity."

When I had washed—this time the lemon-scented water was heated and the servant scoured me with sand to remove all traces of the pungent oils—I joined Yiahn under a vine trellis in the garden, where food and wine had been set for us. I found I was very hungry, and for a time ate in silence; nor did he speak except to ask my preference for a dish or whether I would rather drink a different wine.

He gave me the toast of the Watchers, and said, "I will vouch that the Son of the Oryx has wise eyes and a strong stomach . . . and that is a goodly combination for any man. There are not many who could have watched what you watched today and still done justice to a meal afterwards. Even when the corpse surged with the water you did not flinch. Only two other men, apart from those whose work it is to assist me, have seen that—and one of them vomited and had to be carried out, and the other thought the corpse had come alive and screamed out a confession, in

215

which he told me that he had hastened the death of his uncle by putting into his food putrid meat taken from under the claws of a dead lion. I knew he was guilty, but wanted him to admit it . . . that is why I let him see me at work."

I laughed. "Do you suspect me of my kinsman's death? And if so, do you judge me innocent . . . or too hard with crime for guilt to prick me?"

"Neither; but I live in a city of hypocrisy and it is good to see one who by his actions proves that in the Oryx there are still free men. He was your kinsman, and left you heir to his possessions. In return you are seeing that the customs by which he lived are carried out as he would have wished, but you do not lament his death as others would have pretended to do."

"Why should I lament? Had he been my friend of many lives I should have tried to find the courage to rejoice in his freedom rather than to cloud it with my own grief. As he is not joined to me by affection, but only by relationship . . . though he has shown me kindness for which I am very grateful, why should I lament that he goes one way and I another, any more than if we were two acquaintances who pass each other on the road?"

"The people of this city have so long worshipped false gods and followed the rituals of an ignorant priesthood that they have lost the standard of reality. The false has become their truth . . . and Truth they would treat as a barbarian . . . if they ever met her! That is why I knew you were from the Oryx before I saw the oryx clasp you wear. With you a man is friend or enemy . . . and you hope to teach the enemy to be a friend. You do not suspect others of treachery, because she is a harlot you have never known. Patronage, or the smile of a sycophant, are both strangers to your mouth, for you judge men by their hearts. You know that all men are what you were or what you will become; and knowing this, know also that in them is something which a part of you calls brother. I have seen many dead men, and I learned of them through those who came here as their last companion. Grief and pain; both are enemies of hypocrisy, so in twenty years as embalmer and healer-with-the-knife I have learned much of this city and of these people. I can give you the names of fifty whom I know belong to our company—though as yet they have not heard of the Watchers' and I know of five hundred whom the dawn will blind."

He stood up and put his hand on my shoulder. "Now it is time for us to sleep; you are weary and I too am tired, for five of my temporary tombs are filled with nobles and officials . . . whose flesh should prove to any man that death admits no difference of caste."

PART V

Treasure of Grain

ALTHOUGH the formal declaration of our betrothal was delayed by the death of Heliokios, for no contract of any kind could be undertaken by a member of the household during the period of forty days lamentation, Meri and I were often able to be alone together, since Ramaios had accepted me as the husband chosen by his daughter. His scribes were already making long tallies of possessions which would be hers on our marriage, and I was waiting for similar tallies to come from the Oryx.

Because Ramaios was Meri's father I had expected to find in him an old friend, yet though I saw him many times we remained strangers. He was always courteous, but there was no warmth in him, no fire to kindle acquaintance to affection. I knew him to be a man of meticulous honesty, and it was said of him that his word meant more than the seal of any other man. As Keeper of the Royal Treasure he held the highest office save that of Vizier, and his power extended through every Nome of Egypt. It was he who decided when grain should be bartered for gold and ivory, or when these in their turn need be bartered to foreigners for grain.

Meri told me that until he took office, two years before, whoever held the Gold Seal soon grew so rich that he either became preoccupied with his own vast new estates or else resigned in another man's favor, lest jealousy, or fear of his power, endanger his life.

"The Gold Seal is the most powerful bribe in the Royal Gift," Meri said. "He who holds it can profit himself by as much as a tenth of the wealth of the whole country, and there are none who dare challenge him. It is he who assesses the tribute each Nome must pay . . . so is it surprising that the Nomarchs are content that he should prosper if he sees that the toll on their lands is not too heavy? The one whom Father succeeded was known as the Grandfather of Bribes, and when he died it was said that he had more than five thousand cattle and nearly a thousand foreign slaves, and the great estate he acquired near the Old Capital could accommodate as many as the second city of a Nome."

"Then why did your father accept this office? You say he has not added to his own treasure, nor is he a Watcher to concern himself with the lives of other men. Did he take it so as to prove his own integrity—surely that would be like battering his head against a rock to prove the rock was hard, for he is spoken of as the most honest man in the Royal Nomes."

Meri was curled up beside me, on a yellow floor-mattress in one of her apartments, making a jasmine wreath. "My Ra-ab, how lucky it is that we shall live in the Oryx while Father will continue to be in the Royal City. When I sit between the two of you at a meal it is like eating alone between the granite statues which support the great door of the New Temple! You have never met anyone like him before, have you? You expect everyone to be your friend or your enemy, and you can't understand someone who can be neither. If Father died, no one would be glad and no one would weep; yet they would miss him, as they would miss the great pylon, which marks the northern boundary of the City, if it were to disappear in the night. I've never seen him laugh and I've never seen him admit to anger—though I tried hard enough to make him do either until I found it was useless. He has never been unkind and always treats me with absolute justice. Yet why he ever married I have never understood— neither, I think, has he!"

She paused to consider this matter further, and then went on, "No doubt his mother arranged the marriage, for my mother came of a family whose estates adjoined his, and I have been told she was beautiful. I hope she was like him, cold and without imagination—I don't know, for I have never seen her even in a dream; but if she was like me, though I wept for twenty years I still could not show the measure of my pity . . . for I would know she died of boredom and not of child-bearing! (You told me I picked too much jasmine, but I didn't, for I have enough to make a garland for you to wear around your neck.) That's going to be one of the thousand lovely things of living with you, Ra-ab, I'm never going to be bored. I'll love you, and laugh with you, and fear for you, and cry for you if you have to go away, and hate for you if you have an enemy, and live for you, and of course die for you . . . but I'll never, never, be dull!"

"If the same kind of thing happens thousands and thousands of times—you won't find that dull?"

"What kind of thing?"

"I've kissed your right breast a hundred times, perhaps more, while you've been talking, and your right shoulder about sixty times, and your right eyebrow seventy times. I've forgotten quite how many times I've kissed your ear, and when I kiss your mouth I can't remember to count."

"I'd better come around to your other side, otherwise my left breast and my left shoulder and my left eyebrow and my left ear are going to get jealous; and it would be awkward living in a body when one side was jealous of the other. Think of the way the left hand could pull the bed cover away so that the poor right shoulder would get cold. . . . No, Ra-ab! *Don't*, that tickles!"

"Poor old Heliokios will be safely tucked away in his tomb in another twelve days, and then very soon you won't need a bed cover because you'll have me."

"Not even in the cold weather?"

"Well, it would have to be *very* cold weather."

After a time I remembered to ask her something I'd meant to ask earlier in our conversation. She had given up the idea of plaiting a garland for me, because I had been using the jasmine flowers to make a pattern that flowed down between her breasts into a little avenue across her belly. Then she said they tickled her and sat up. The flowers scattered on the floor and we were both too idle to collect them.

"Meri, you still haven't answered my question: why did your father become Keeper of the Treasure?"

"So as to see if his ideas on barter would really work—it's the only thing in which he's really interested. I've never understood why; it isn't as if he wanted to be richer, or because it gave him power, or even because it made people admire him. He's like the scribe who was content to paint the walls of a tomb though he knew no one was going to be buried in it and it was to be sealed up before anyone saw what he had done. When the Vizier offered Father the Gold Seal—perhaps even Pharaoh gets tired of being cheated after a time and wanted an honest man—it was as though the scribe who had been content to work for his own pleasure found that hundreds and hundreds of people were coming to see what he had done . . . because his work was important after all, important to other people as well as to himself."

"How do you mean he's interested in barter? You can't be interested in barter unless you've got something you want to exchange."

"Oh yes you can, if you're Father. If you and I were poor and had a fish to trade, all that would matter to us was how soon we could find a person who had what we wanted; but Father has got everything he want's so he's not worried by that kind of thing. He hasn't been able to change the barter system yet; he says his plans are not complete and he's busy getting more information on which to base his change. Today all things which do not perish, gold and ivory, silver and malachite, and lots of other things like lamps and statues, only not God-statues of course, we barter with foreign countries when we need things which can only be got from them. Most of this trade is done by officials under Pharaoh's seal, though there are traders in the foreign markets as well. Only nobles have that kind of treasure in their private possession, though some of the merchants and minor officials have some also. But the majority of our people are poor, and what they have to barter are things which perish quickly, fish or fruit, vegetables, milk or eggs, and usually they want to exchange these for grain, except in a very good year when they have been able to grow sufficient for themselves."

"They should always be able to grow sufficient for themselves."

"They can't, Ra-ab, they haven't enough land. How can a man grow enough for himself and his family on a little field, perhaps not more than twenty by thirty paces?"

"Why isn't there enough land? Because Pharaoh and his officials have taken it from the people. The corn is grown, but it does not belong to the grower, it belongs to the man who owns the land. The rulers of Egypt have forgotten that Earth is the estate of the Gods, and that what the earth yields is a gift from the Gods to the man who tills the soil. Of course there is enough land, Meri, more than enough, for every man and woman and child in Egypt to eat their *own* bread. The Nile gives us two harvests, sometimes three, each year: but have you forgotten that only yesterday we saw ninety grain-barges going up-river? They were not carrying grain to the Southern Nomes, they were taking it to Nubia whence they will return with yet more wealth for Pharaoh."

"I still haven't told you what Father wants to do. I keep on starting to but when we're together ideas are as thick as wild-fowl in the marshes—we start to follow one and then see another with even brighter wings."

The walls of the room were painted with just such a scene as she described: tall papyrus reeds, with many different birds among them, growing from a faience-blue river lively with fish.

She pointed to an ibis, standing in eternal contemplation with a frog in its beak. "That's Father, and that's his idea . . . the frog he's holding so carefully. That's why he never laughs, because he's frightened that if he did it might escape him!"

"Think of the frog and forget everything else until you have told me about it."

"All right, I will; but you mustn't kiss me while I'm trying to talk sensibly . . . at least not very often. Father thinks, just as we do, that everyone should have enough land on which to grow food for himself; but he says it's no good taking land away from the rich and giving it to the poor unless there is a new system by which the poor can keep their tenure during a bad year. How do the owners of great estates survive even several bad years, how does Egypt herself survive? This was the first question he asked himself, and the answer was, because they hold treasure so that when their granaries are empty they can exchange some of this durable wealth for grain. If the owner of a great estate lacks something, he gets it by bartering something else, of which he has a surplus, with the owner of another estate. He may lack grain, but have linen, or building stone, or fine pottery . . . and if he has no surplus that year he barters with some of his stored treasures that do not change their value when harvests fail. This is done by one Nomarch with another, and if there is not enough grain in the Two Lands, then Pharaoh's treasure-house is opened and Egypt trades with foreign countries. But the poor have no durable treasure, and if *their* crops fail they lose their lands or else go hungry."

"Why should they? In the Oryx we have had lean years, but we watch the rising of the river and so we know when we shall not be able to fill our granaries and must barter with the North for grain. Father's treasure is used so that his people shall not suffer when Nut is reluctant of her bounty; and if any who live in the Oryx hungered while there was still a single tusk of ivory in the possession of the Nome it would be as though a man ate his fill while his children cried because they were starving."

"If the Two Lands were like your Oryx there would be no need to make new laws, for everyone would obey the laws of the Gods and remember they are brothers. But Father does not know of the Watchers, and even if he did he still would only be able to understand laws which come within his compass of experience. You and your kind of people have a warm humanity, but men like Father can only understand justice which does not need affection to interpret it. There are many people who still need men's laws because they are not yet ready to be free of them. In the Oryx the people are given food if they lack it through no fault of their own, but, except for a few who are given the Royal Bounty, that doesn't happen here. In the rest of Egypt no one gets anything unless he is able to pay for it; if people can't pay in produce they must pay in land . . . and if they have no land they must work for the man who has saved them from starving, until the debt is paid . . . and often this is not for many years, or for a lifetime. How do you think Pharaoh and his nobles build their great houses and other monuments to their importance? By slave labor; and not only foreign slaves, for thousands of our people have to work for them because once they had to beg for grain or see their children starve.

"Grain is the real wealth of Egypt, and grain should belong to free men who have caused it to grow. It should be bartered with foreigners only when our harvests have failed; but now even when the granaries are filled before the second harvest the people do not benefit; rather than they should be free of the fear of famine, and so refuse to work unless they are well treated, the grain is allowed to spoil, unless there are enough ships to take it to the foreigners whose lands border on the Great Sea, or enough slaves to carry it to the trading outposts of the barbarians. When three lean years are linked together, even those who have something to sell cannot get grain in exchange; they blame the Nile, and do not realize that it is Pharaoh who should be called the

Father of Famine. Pharaoh is always reluctant to replenish the granaries when it means that his treasure must go to make the courts of other kings more splendid; for it is by wealth and not by the contentment of his people that Pharaoh judges his power."

"That will be changed when a Watcher rules over Egypt; for then no one will hold authority who does not wield it to bring security to those under his care. So far your Father and I are agreed, but still I do not know the message of the frog he holds so carefully in his mouth."

"Every man should profit according to his work, and he should be protected when this is destroyed by Nut. Under our present system, in a year of plenty a man may grow so many lettuces, or catch such great hauls of fish, that he can find no one with whom to barter them, and in a bad year he goes hungry because he has nothing to trade. He had no durable treasure, and the treasure which should be his, grain which will last for several years, is in the hands of the rulers. Through tradition, a fish has a fixed value in exchange for vegetables; and this value remains unchanged even though the river may have yielded little to the nets while the gardens have given a heavy crop. When this happens the man with the lettuces suffers with the fisherman, for as long as one cannot afford to buy, the other cannot sell. Father says that every Nome should be divided into districts, each small enough for a market overseer to know all the conditions, such as the weather and the state of the water channels, that have affected each particular group of produce. Each of these groups, vegetables, fruit, milch cattle, wild-fowl . . . will have a sliding-scale of values both to each other and within the group. For instance, each variety of vegetable will have a set value in relation to every other kind of vegetable, and these will be adjusted according to how the season has affected each variety. Every thirty days a new scale of barter will be set up in the markets. It will be painted on the wall, in picture signs, not hieroglyphics, so that all can read it. At the top of each scale there will be a circle, meaning that any one of the units painted below it can be exchanged for a unit on any other scale; and below the circle will be the relative value of the things to be found in that part of the market. For instance, in the vegetable market there might be first a picture of an onion, and below it four lettuces, and below that fifteen radishes, and below that a bunch of pot-herbs . . . and so on through every kind. And it would be the same in every other part of the market, so that if you wanted to change a melon for vegetables you would first go to the fruit part and see how many melons were painted below the circle and then in the vegetable part you would see how many circles worth of vegetables you could get in exchange. It would be easy enough for everyone to understand, much better than having to go from stall to stall, haggling and being cheated; and going away discontented because you had seen another woman getting better value, or else feeling virtuous because you had cheated someone who was less shrewd at bargaining! I've often gone to the markets to find out conditions for Father (I went dressed as one of the house servants), and I've seen a woman spend more time haggling over the value of a piece of linen than it would have taken her to weave it!"

"What happens when too many vegetables come to market, or all the women want to buy fish instead of eggs, or fruit instead of honey-comb?"

"They would still be better off than they are at present; but I haven't yet come to the important part of Father's idea. If you have been to many markets you must have noticed the piles of rotting food that no one was able to sell, though at the same time there were people going sadly away because they hadn't got enough to exchange for what they needed. Father can cure all that, and when the Watchers are in power he *will* cure it . . . until then it wouldn't be possible, because it would get too much opposition from those who are profiting under the present system. In the future there will be an official of the granaries at every market; and, after the people have bartered among themselves, everything that is left unsold will be taken to the official and exchanged for grain, and this grain they can keep until they have need of it, as the rich people keep their gold."

"What will the official do with all the things he has taken in exchange for grain?"

"They will be distributed among those who cannot earn their own livelihood. The old people and orphans, the cripples and the sick . . . all those who now have to wait on charity, or starve."

"Supposing there was more food than all the people could use?"

"I don't think there ever would be, but if there was it would be more just that Pharaoh should bear the burden of its being wasted than that this should be borne by the people who had worked to make it grow. If it were found that there was always too much of one kind of food, the people who now produce it could turn to another trade; that wouldn't be difficult to arrange. Think what a difference it would make to you and me, Ra-ab, if we were poor. Say we had a little garden and had worked so hard to make it bear a good crop so that our children should not go hungry. Nut is kind, and we see that there are many basketfuls to carry to the market. What should we feel like if we had to throw it away because no one wanted it? Wouldn't it make all the difference if we *knew* we should get a fair value for all our work? It would mean the difference between being happy and being frightened of the future all the time."

"It's a wonderful idea, Meri! Ramaios is a Watcher even if he's never interested in our philosophies; for a Watcher is only someone who adds to the sum of human happiness instead of taking away from it. His name will be blessed by thousands and thousands of people all over Egypt, and the only people who will wish he had never been born are those who are turning other people's worry into wealth for themselves!"

"Can we stop talking about the frog now, Ra-ab?"

Daughter of the Concubine

WHEN I WENT back that night to the House of the Two Winds, I found Sebek waiting for me just inside the gate of the outer courtyard. Never had I seen him in such a state of agitation, and for a terrible moment I thought the plans of the Watchers had been betrayed.

In reply to my swift question he said, "No, it's not that, but it's nearly as bad. I can't tell you here, where there's a chance of being overheard. You *must* think of something to do, for I can't. I nearly followed you to the House of Ramaios before I realized you would want to keep this news from Meri-o-sosis."

By now we had reached the privacy of my room, and he spoke

more coherently. "You know the house next to this one, the one into which we saw furniture being carried three days ago? Well, our servants have been full of curiosity about who was going to live there; they heard it was a woman. Some said she was a foreigner and some that she was a concubine of one of the princes, who was hiding here because Pharaoh wouldn't have her in the women's quarters of the Palace. I saw a curtained litter going to the house soon after noon today, and decided she could not be a person of much importance because there were only three traveling-boxes with her and no sign of any female attendant. But it was none of my business, and I thought no more about it until one of the boys who works in the garden came to me with a sly grin on his face and said he brought a message from the lady who had come to the House of the Four Acacias, the "lady for whom I was waiting.' I thought he had made a mistake and that perhaps she had come here to Heliokios and had not heard he was dead. If this were the case it was only fitting that it should be by me, instead of by one of the servants, that she should be told that the only concubines in which he was now interested were those painted on the walls of his tomb . . . and, to be honest, I suppose I have the same measure of curiosity as the next man. Anyway, whatever the reason, I did go to her house. I had seen the gate-keeper before, for he had been left in charge of the house while it stood empty. He seemed to be expecting me, and said that the lady was waiting for me in the room beyond the entrance hall. It is a pretty little house; the wall paintings are very light and delicate, but the furniture is over-elaborate . . . perhaps Heliokios used to lodge one of his concubines there. It would be a fitting setting for such an ornament. In the far room, on a couch spread with vermilion silk, a woman was lying, her face hidden by a fan of heron's feathers. I could see her feet and one hand; and her dress, of the most transparent linen, would have let me see much more if I had looked closely. Perhaps I ought to have recognized her even before I heard her voice—"

By now I was highly amused. That the solemn Sebek, whom I thought had never been beguiled by a woman, had after all a concubine whom he had managed to keep hidden even from his closest friend, that was a rich enough jest . . . but that she had followed unbidden to the Royal City! How I would tease him for his secrecy! I tried to conceal my amusement, but felt my mouth losing its siege against invading laughter.

"Sebek, how can you be such an ungracious lover! If a woman had followed *me* from the Oryx, and if that woman was Meri, I should be rejoicing, and would only leave her side to fetch rare gifts for her pleasure!"

"She can't stay here! You must go and reason with her, *now*, and *make* her go away."

He looked so distraught that I fell back on the bed doubled with laughter. "*I* must go—to defend the Captain of my Bodyguard from an importunate woman! Shall I tell her that you are a dullard on whom she wastes her charms; but that in this city even you are as a prince among fishermen, so she had better return at once to the South where men are better able to appreciate her beauty?"

He stood over me, and his voice trembled with anger. "All right, laugh and do nothing! Laugh until you are weary of laughing—for you may not feel like it again for a long time! It is a splendid jest that a woman follows Sebek to the Royal City, and an even greater jest that she will not go away when he tells her to. But till now the jest is an empty cup and you have not yet tasted the real flavor of it—now I will pour the wine of laughter, and you may drink your fill! The woman who waits in the House of the Four Acacias has a name you have often spoken—Kiyas! Or let us give her the name of formality—the Daughter of the Oryx!"

I could not have been more startled if he had poured a jar of water over me while I slept. Now it was his turn to smile. "It's not so funny when you hear the whole story, is it? It isn't *my* sister who is disobedient—though of course as your servant I share something of your embarrassment."

"You should have sent for me at once. Then there would have been time for her to start on the journey home before sunset."

"And if I had, would Ramaios have been so glad to welcome the Son of the Oryx if he had known the new daughter he must welcome also?"

"I must go to Kiyas at once—and you'd better come with me."

"Oh no, Ra-ab—I'm not coming with you! I'm tired of hearing my words fall like pebbles into an empty well. I was persuasive and I was angry, I commanded and I entreated; and all she did was to smile, and ask me whether I thought there was enough kohl on her eyes and if her feet did not look even more slender now that the soles of them were rouged. While I am in the Royal City I keep to my role, and your servant does not argue with your sister."

As I left the room I was conscious that he was nearly as amused as I had been a few moments earlier.

Kiyas was in the same room where she had waited for Sebek. When she saw me she jumped up and ran forward to throw her arms around my neck, "Dear Ra-ab, I am so rejoiced to see you! It has been such a long, long time since you went away, and you have so much to tell me. Letters carry so little news, and yours were far too short."

"You'll have to content yourself with letters until I return to the Oryx with my wife. You must leave the city tonight; but you will not return home by the same way you came. You will have to go disguised, by one of the ways the secret messengers of the Watchers travel."

She lay back on the couch and picked up her fan. "No, Ra-ab, I'm not going away. I have come here to help you, and if you're too stupid to realize it, I shall have to work alone."

"Help me!" I said bitterly. "By bringing dishonor on the Oryx. Help me! By causing a scandal that will make Ramaios withdraw his consent to my marriage with his daughter!"

"Oh Ra-ab, you've grown much more stupid since you went away from me!"

"If I am stupid, then you are the mother of all stupidity; and all the afflicted ones with vacant eyes would consider themselves orphans if you died."

"How courteous you have become, my Ra-ab. It must be a rare delight to hear you exchange praises with your beloved . . . your whispers must be as melodious as two cats challenging each other at the full moon!"

I knew that if I went on making her angry she would only become more stubborn, so I tried to stem my impatience and said, "I'm *sure* you meant to help, Kiyas—though I can't understand how, but this is a thing that I can judge much better than you. The people here are not like they are in the Oryx; many of the women have poison on their tongues, and as they look on each other as potential rivals they are always trying to increase their power by discrediting others. If it had been possible to have you here I should have already sent for you. But Heliokios is still unburied, and during the forty days lamentation no one who was not of the household when he died may enter the gates, save only those who come to prepare for the funeral rites. If they knew I had brought my sister here they would think me a barbarian, and as long as I have to stay in the Royal Nomes I must conform to their customs. Ramaios is the father of formalities, and because it is not customary, he would refuse to ask you to be his guest until the betrothal is publicly announced, even though Meri longs to meet you."

"I know all that, Ra-ab. I haven't asked you to welcome me to the House of the Two Winds, or to the house of Ramaios. Do you think I should have come to this house if I had hoped to be your guest? And do you think I should be dressed like a concubine if I came here as your sister?"

"Then *why* did you come here? And what I can understand still less, *how* did you come here?"

"If you'll stop being cross for a few minutes, and not interrupt, I will explain. And then you can forget how silly you have been and remember how pleased you are to see me."

She patted the cushions beside her and rather reluctantly I sat down to listen.

"I have often been with Roidahn and Hanuk since you went away; I've heard all the news your secret messengers brought to us, and Father showed me all your letters to him as well. I know how Meri has been finding out which of the nobles and officials may become Watchers, from hearing about them through their wives. Hanuk himself said it was a pity that some of the most important men had no wives but only concubines, for Meri wouldn't be able to find out about them because wives, and the daughters of wives, live in a different world to the concubines. But concubines sometimes have more power than other kinds of women. Pharaoh's Royal Wife has been ill for a long time and never leaves her own apartments, and the secondary wife has no intimate in whom she confides. Yet there are two hundred women in the Palace; a thousand intrigues, a thousand secrets, are whispered every day; and there is no Watcher to hear them. If Sebek had had a concubine she might have come here and worked for us, or there might have been a Watcher in the women's quarters of the House of the Two Winds, but there wasn't; you said they were all old and stupid. That's why I came here . . . because I could work for the Watchers better in this way than in any other. Roidahn said he couldn't let me come here without Father's permission, and I knew I'd never get that, so Hanuk helped me to make my plans. I told Father that you had sent for me to come to you as soon as the forty days lamentation were completed, and that until then I was going to stay with Roidahn. Father has just got a papyrus from the Tortoise Nome; it is very old, so old that he gave two elephant tusks and a collar of gold for it, so he is far too occupied with this great addition to his history to be suspicious of his daughter! I *did* go to Hotep-Ra, but Roidahn was away and Hanuk was there alone. Hanuk had already taken this house for me and arranged that clothes, and furniture, and jewels suitable to my new role should be waiting for me. He told me it is not unusual for a rich man to leave a con-siderable part of his treasure to the daughter of a favorite concubine—of course the children of secondary wives rank the same as the children of the chief wife, but the children of concu-bines are a caste to themselves. A concubine's daughter may become very powerful, though it is only rarely she is taken in marriage. They are the only kind of women who live in a house of their own without women attendants, and if they are young, and rich, and virgin, they will soon be asked to every banquet and entertainment, where they will meet the most powerful men in the land, who seek relaxation—and are glad to whisper secrets into an ear which charms them."

"Hanuk must be mad to have led you into this plot! He may be right in thinking that a concubine could find out many things which are still unknown to us, but he should have sent another woman instead of you. Doesn't he realize that if I die without an heir you will be the Oryx? How should we rank among other Nomes if the woman who ruled it had been a concubine!"

"If Hanuk had thought another woman could have done so

much as I, he would have sent her. He knows it is a rule of the Watchers that each shall play the part for which they are best fitted; he trusts my judgment, on which may depend whether a man joins us or is banished from Egypt. You admire Hanuk because he has often traveled in disguise and taken danger for the only companion of his journey; Ra sees my heart and not the color of my eye-paint, and I am as much in his protection as I was when we were children in our father's house."

"Nothing I say will make you change your mind?"

"Nothing, Ra-ab. You can only decide whether I work with your help or without it. Can't we stop fighting against each other and fight together for Egypt?" She slipped her hand into mine. "Can't we, Ra-ab?"

"I would never have allowed this plan—but now it is made of course I'll help you."

She clapped her hands delightedly. "I knew you would when you understood. Oh, Ra-ab, I'm so happy that we needn't pretend to quarrel anymore!"

"You don't seem to have found it so easy to convince Sebek."

"I didn't try. He was horrified to see me, and started to scold me as though I were a naughty child; so I thought it wouldn't do him any harm to go on thinking I'd run away from the Oryx and come here just for an adventure. You'd better go back soon and explain things to him before he does something silly, like sending a messenger to Father. He doesn't know it yet, but he's got to help me. Hanuk says it is quite usual for a woman like me to have a man-servant who goes everywhere with her, a kind of body-guard and cup-bearer combined, who remains within call unless she sends him away. It's not that I think I need protecting, but he might overhear as much as I did . . . and it would be nice to know he was near if I needed him. I shall only take him when I go to the houses of strangers, for while I'm here or out in my litter I shall be quite safe, for the eight who came with me from the Oryx, as litter-bearers and to carry my traveling-boxes, are all Watchers. Hanuk even found one of them who knew how to cook, so I shan't have to employ strangers to look after me. Hanuk thought you might make Sebek the overseer of your household, or give him some other appointment which would explain to the servants why he was suddenly rich enough to visit the House of the Four Acacias. Then he could go on living with you and carry messages between us without arousing suspicion."

And so it was arranged; just as Kiyas had always intended it should be.

Prince Men-het

CONTRARY TO Sebek's gloomy forebodings, Meri had nothing but praise for Kiyas's behavior. As soon as I told her about her future sister, she said that I must at once arrange for them to meet, and though I told her it was most unwise to take the risk of Kiyas being seen with either of us she persuaded me to bring her to the Island Pavilion after sunset that evening.

At Sebek's suggestion Kiyas wore the tunic usual to a household servant and walked a few paces behind me, carrying a basket of fruit as though she were returning from the market. Meri was waiting for us on the landing stage of the island; it seemed a little unreal to me that these two women who were both so near my heart should be meeting for the first time.

Meri held out her hands to Kiyas and said excitedly, "I was right, I did know what you were going to look like . . . though you were younger then. Do you still have Anilops?"

"Yes, I do. Did Ra-ab tell you about him?"

Meri smiled. "No, he didn't tell me."

Kiyas nodded. "Oh, I understand. You dream like he does. I'm so glad, for he would never have been really happy with someone who didn't understand the things he knows about . . . even if she was as beautiful as you are."

Listening to them I was well content, for I knew that between them also there was a golden link.

Later, Meri said, "Till I met Ra-ab, I didn't know any *real* people. You're real like he is, which is the best proof, if any were needed, of the wisdom of the Oryx. You think for yourselves, you *are* yourselves; but most people's minds are like the litter in the streets after a festival—filled with all manner of things other people have discarded or lost. Neither of you would accept an idea without first forming your own opinion of its value. You know where you are going, and *why*. Kiyas, I think, could be quite unscrupulous as to her methods if she were sure she was going to the right goal."

Kiyas laughed. "You've been listening to Ra-ab. He has always said I am unscrupulous; sometimes I have to be, if people are stupid or if it's good for them to be teased a little. You ought to be grateful to me, for if I hadn't teased Ra-ab he wouldn't be nearly such an amusing husband."

"What if you hadn't had him for a brother?" said Meri quickly.

"Oh, then I should hardly have been anybody at all; just a nice, good little girl who was no trouble to look after. And in time I should have been married—probably to Sebek, unless Father preferred the Son of the Hare; and had three children as dull as myself. That's one of the nicest things about Ra-ab, he never lets one be dull, even for a minute. You'll find that out too."

Meri slipped her hand into mine. "Oh, but I have found it out. Long, long ago, on the evening before my anniversary."

I unpacked the basket of food which Meri had brought with her. The lid had come off the jar of honey; we were gay and light-hearted, and ate with our fingers, licking them when they got sticky, like children. Only when we had finished, and had swum together in the little inlet, protected from crocodiles by a row of stakes, did we start planning what Kiyas was going to do. On the way to the island I had told Kiyas about Ashek, about the Royal Heir, and those minor officials on whom I had already been able to come to a decision.

"You don't seem to have found many honest men in the Royal City," said Kiyas. "Even Heliokios could not have been allowed to keep his office if he had gone on living; though I don't expect he'd have minded going to a small house and not being important. I think I should have liked him—you'd better give me his monkey, I expect it misses him, and I like monkeys." She paused and then went on, "I don't think banishment's nearly bad enough for Ashek. Tahu reached Hotep-Ra just before I left. She is going to keep the baby she looked after on the journey. Its uncle is very pleased, because his mother, to whom he was taking it, is getting rather old to be good at playing with a small child."

"What would you do with Ashek?"

"I suggested to Roidahn that he be made to seal himself—with a specially big seal—for every bad judgment he'd given. There wouldn't be enough room on him for all of them at one time, but we could let the skin heal in between."

"What did Roidahn say?"

"He didn't agree. He says the Watchers are to banish fear and so they mustn't create fear even in their enemies. I wonder what the Asiatics will think of the exiles we send them; I don't suppose the Southern Nubians will be very pleased with them either. All those we banish are to have a little brand on their forehead, our sign of the scales, only *unbalanced*, so that foreigners won't judge Egypt by those who betrayed her. What do you think he'll do with the Royal Heir? I do wish I had still been there when your message about him arrived."

"He must have known most of it already. I gathered from Heliokios that nearly everyone at the Court has some idea of what goes on in the House of the Dark Silence, and that I wasn't the only one who'd looked through the Eye. Heliokios had been there himself, and that was why he nearly warned me; he did give me several hints, but I thought he meant ordinary concubines and wondered why he had suddenly become so evasive."

"Why does the Court let it go on?"

"Because none of them will admit to knowing what's happening. Those who have first-hand knowledge would never admit it; they know too well that silence is their only protection. And, apart from fear, I think some of them really believe the Royal Heir is half divine—evil, of course, but strong in the protection of Set."

"What shall we do with him?" asked Meri.

"I wish it was for me to decide, but it isn't. Roidahn will give judgment on him. It will be wiser than what I should do, but not nearly so satisfying to anyone who has seen what that spawn of filth has done!"

"Hanuk thinks," said Kiyas, "that the word will go out to the Watchers as soon as it is sure that Pharaoh is dying, so that we can act before the new Pharaoh is declared. We should have killed Pharaoh if it had been necessary, but as the Gods show every sign of summoning him before the Forty-two Assessors we should be grateful for their consideration; and it only remains for the Eyes of Horus to decide who is to be the new Pharaoh."

"Who is?" said Meri. "Hasn't Roidahn decided?"

"Not yet. He thinks it will be the Vizier, but the Leopard and the Tortoise want the young prince, for if he is chosen we should be more certain of the loyalty of the Northern Nomes. The North has always been against a change of dynasty. Roidahn knows sufficient of the Vizier; and I think, though Roidahn didn't tell me so, that the Vizier knows our plans, but is still undecided whether it would be better for Egypt if he continued as the power behind the throne or took up the Crook and Flail himself. Neither of you seem to know much about the younger prince."

Meri answered her. "He isn't often in the Royal City. His elder brother is terribly jealous of him, and is always trying to influence Pharaoh to send him off on punitive expeditions when any of the neighboring countries get disobedient. I think Pharaoh genuinely believes that it is done in the honor of the Royal House, and sees himself through his son as a Warrior Pharaoh. But of course the Heir hopes Men-het will be killed. He is very popular with the army and they guard him well; if they didn't I expect he would have been murdered by now. He was wounded in the arm only a month ago, that's why he is in the Palace, and I don't think he will go away again until after his father's death. There are many people who think he'll challenge his brother's power as soon as it is obvious their father is dying, and he knows that many people would be only too glad to take his side."

"Is he married?"

"Yes, but it isn't a real marriage, although she has given him two daughters. It was an alliance arranged by Pharaoh, because it was easier than reinforcing the garrison on the Northern Boundary. There is no secondary wife, though he is said to be fond of women."

Kiyas pulled a stem of grass and chewed it reflectively before rejoining the conversation. Then she said, as though giving a carefully considered judgment, "Prince Men-het is popular with the army. Therefore if he is not chosen we may have to fight with swords as well as wits. He is the natural heir, or will be when we have finished with his brother, and yet Roidahn prefers the Vizier. Why? That is one of the things we must find out. The prince has a wife, but they are not fond of each other; she has a house of her own, and it is only to conform with etiquette that he shares it with her when he is here. Another "Why?' He is fond of women, yet he has no secondary wife; therefore what is more natural than that he should be looking for a concubine? Which is the reason, and I can't think why we didn't realize it before, that for the present Kiyas is a concubine!"

Within a few days it began to be whispered that the younger prince was infatuated with the woman who had come to live at the House of the Four Acacias. An hour before dawn Sebek or I watched for the signal of a light in Kiyas's window, and if we saw it we climbed over the wall to hear her news. We always had to leave her before sunrise, for this added precaution had become necessary since she had warned us that Prince Men-het, being afraid she might be imperiled by his enemies, had set a guard of his most trusted soldiers on her house. It was most fortunate that her garden and mine adjoined, for otherwise it would have been most difficult to have visited her without suspicion, there always being two soldiers in the road before her entrance gate and another in the narrow alley which ran at the foot of the garden.

One of Men-het's personal bodyguards, a captain who was also a kinsman of the Nomarch of the Tortoise, belonged to the Watchers, and it was he, acting on Hanuk's orders, who told his master of the beautiful stranger who had arrived in the Royal City and had already become the subject of excited conjecture among the young nobles. This had been quite sufficient to secure an invitation for Kiyas to Men-het's pleasure pavilion, overlooking the river, where he entertained his most intimate friends.

"There were three women and five other men there," said Kiyas. "One of the women was very pretty, with red hair like her Minoan mother, and blue eyes. She had belonged for nearly a year to one of Men-het's captains, otherwise I don't think I should have had much chance of capturing the prince's whole attention. I talked to him on all the subjects I thought most unlikely for a concubine. First I compared the new style of wall paintings with those left to us by the older generations. I think he found this very dull, but he was obviously intrigued by my unexpected field of knowledge. . . . I only repeated what Father says about some of the new drawing-scribes, so it was quite easy to be convincing. Then I asked him if he had used the same strategy in quelling the rebellion in the Land of Gold as he had used against the Puntites. It was Hanuk's idea that I should use this line of approach, which shows he is wiser than a woman at finding the way to a man's heart. By the end of the evening Men-het would not have noticed if any other woman's eyes were blue or brown, and the next morning he sent me a magnicent turquoise necklace and an ointment jar, alabaster inlaid with lapis."

I should have been much less anxious about Kiyas if we had been able to keep to our original plan of having Sebek accompany her as a servant, but this she refused to allow, saying that he was already too well known to risk his being recognized, and reluctantly I had had to admit the force of her judgment. She was fully aware of the dangers she ran, but she was not concerned with the possibility of having to become a concubine in more than name.

She said, "Now it is known that Men-het shows his favor for me so openly, no other man will dare to pay me more than the most formal courtesy. Sebek seems convinced that Men-het will soon grow impatient of my evasions—but then Sebek has always underrated my intelligence. Nearly every woman in Egypt would be overeager to offer the hospitality of her body to the younger prince; and this he well knows and has long grown weary of their compliance. When his eyes grow too warm, I talk to him of the strategies of fighting men; and when he bores me with too long a story of some lengthy campaign I make him remember that I am a woman whom he ardently desires . . . but if he tries to caress me he finds that I have suddenly become colder than the winter Nile. He tried to find out who my parents were; I didn't realize why, until his captain, the one who belongs to us, told me that if it were possible to obtain the Royal Permission he would make me his secondary wife."

This was a complication I had not considered. "What did you tell him? If he connects you with Oryx he may somehow discover who you really are. He would realize that the Nomarch's daughter would never come here as you have done unless she were a spy. He will ask himself, "Why should the Oryx spy on the Royal House?" Never forget, Kiyas, that there have been conspiracies before, both against his father and his grandfather . . . and death, when at last it came, was very welcome to the conspirators."

"Do you think Hanuk didn't warn me of that? Of course he did; and I came prepared with a story to use if necessary. Would you like to hear the story of your little sister's childhood?"

I said I most certainly should, and this is what she told me.

"I do not know who my parents are, for I was abandoned near a little village within the boundary of the Leopard when I must have been less than two years old. I was left at the door of a widow, whose husband and only child had recently died of the black sickness. When she saw me, she thought the Gods had answered her prayers by sending her another child to love. That I was not a mortal child she never doubted, for my clothes were of the finest mistlinen and I lay in a cradle of cedarwood thrice banded with electrum. On each side of me there was a wine-jar, and both were filled to the brim with gold-dust. The widow was afraid that if she told the village headman he would take the child away from her, for he might not believe it was an immortal baby and so would think she had stolen it from its rightful parents. So my foster-mother buried the jars of gold dust under the floor of her house and brought me up as her own child. Only when she was dying did she tell me how I was found and where the gold was hidden. As a child I had fleeting memories of a great house with many pillars, and of a garden bright with flowers in which was a pool where fish swam among lotus. I now realize it must have been my parents' house, but my foster-mother used to tell me they were only dreams, of which I must not speak to other children.

"Men-het was overjoyed when I told him all this, and he is determined to find out who my parents were, for he says it is obvious that I am of noble blood, and as soon as this can be shown he will make me his wife."

"You will have to escape *now*, while there is still time. Don't you realize that as soon as his messenger returns from the Leopard he will know that you have lied?"

Kiyas sighed. "Will you *never* believe that I am not very foolish? Didn't I tell you Hanuk and I had arranged the story? There *was* an old woman in that little village and she had a foster-child about my age. She died, and the child left the village three months ago; no one there knows where she has gone, but it happens that she is a Watcher and is now in Hotep-Ra. The house is deserted, but a most convincing hole, and part of a broken wine-jar, will be found in the floor of the larger room. The girl is not really very like me, but we are of the same height and coloring and the description which fitted one would fit the other."

"Men-het will soon discover there are no noble families whose daughter was kidnapped fourteen years ago."

"I have already hinted that my mother may not have chosen her husband to be my father, and so any inquiries must be made with the utmost discretion lest they bring sorrow or dishonor on the woman who gave me birth. I told Men-het that if he caused her any embarrassment she might kill herself, and then I could never love him, for he would be my mother's murderer."

"Do you realize what all this may be leading to?"

"I have considered the various possibilities. I may be tortured as a spy, and that, if Men-het shares any of his brother's tastes, would be most uncomfortable. Men-het may grow weary of me before I have learned sufficient of his heart to judge its worth, and if this happens we shall be no worse off than if I had never come here. Or I may be able to advise Roidahn that Men-het should rule Egypt."

"Do you love him?"

She looked surprised. "Surely you know that I don't? Do you think that I would act as a spy, even for the Watchers, on a man I really loved? Do you think that if there was a great affinity between us I should take so long to know his quality?"

"If you become sincerely convinced that he should be the new Pharaoh surely you would marry him? It should not be difficult for you to take precedence of his first wife, and with your influence as the Royal Wife you would rule Egypt."

I had not seen her so angry since we were children. "I told you I don't love him, yet you suggest that I intend to become the mother of his heirs. I am playing the part of a concubine and if necessary I will become one; but if I did as you so generously suggest I should be unworthy to mingle with the women who pleasure the soldiers of a garrison!"

Meri told me that all the women could talk of nothing except "she who has captured Prince Men-het's heart."

"Officially they cannot recognize her existence, yet they seem to know just what presents she receives from him, what she wears, even the kinds of flowers he sends her each morning. They know that hers is the carrying-litter with the purple curtains embroidered with silver fishes, and that the four Nubians who bear it belong to the Prince—or did, until he gave them to her. They know that she will drink only the Royal wine which is gathered from the drops the sun draws out of the grapes; that she washes her hair in an infusion of Minoan rosemary; that her unguents are scented with tuberose, not stephanotis as was first thought (this I very well know since I gave them to Kiyas!) even that she has a little mole on the inside of her left ankle. They speculate about her origin, and their stories vary from her being of royal blood, the daughter of Pharaoh's youngest sister who is said to have had twin daughters, one of whom was smuggled out of the palace; to the rumor that she is the child of a virgin princess in the temple of the Great Pyramid, but whether by a priest or through the intervention of a God is still undecided!"

When Meri told me this we were in the little sailing boat I had just given her. It had a green sail with a device of two galloping Oryx painted on it in white. Down-river came one of the smaller royal pleasure-barges. There were ten rowers on either side, pulling leisurely on the long gilded oars. Between the rowers was a raised platform shaded by a canopy; and there, reclining on a mattress of indigo blue, were Kiyas and Men-het.

I spilled the wind out of the sail to let them past. Above the gentle beat of the oars I heard Kiyas laughing. A monkey ran along the narrow deck and jumped on the Royal shoulder. . . . Mimu found herself in distinguished company!

Weighing of a Heart

TO MY INTENSE RELIEF Ramaios had signified his approval when I told him of the Watchers. I had been afraid that his conventional outlook might have prevented his seeing that conspiracy was necessary if the greatness of Egypt were to be restored, but when I told him that under the new authority his dream of reorganizing the barter system could become reality he displayed something more near to enthusiasm than I had thought possible for so dry a man. After lengthy consultation with Meri I decided not to tell him about Kiyas; he might have been able to see the vital role she was playing, but I was afraid of testing his belief too far. Knowing I had a sister, he was a little surprised that she was not coming to the Royal City for the marriage, but I explained this by saying that in my absence she helped our father in the administration of the Nome and he was reluctant to spare her until I returned.

The day of our marriage had been appointed when our betrothal was announced; already the preparations were nearly completed, and immediately after the wedding Meri and I would leave for the Oryx. Ramaios was giving his daughter a magnificent marriage portion; and to do my father further honor the tallies on which this was enumerated were scribed on ivory tablets which fitted into a small ebony casket. As each tablet was prepared he showed it to me. From his estates in the North: five hundred cattle; forty rolls of fine linen; sixty pieces of woollen cloth; two hundred jars of wine; twelve boxes of foreign spices. From his treasure room: eight elephant tusks, each not less than three cubit in length; four collars of gold, two of silver, six of electrum; a hundred ostrich feathers. As personal ornaments to Meri: ten bracelets of various designs; twelve headdresses' eighteen necklaces; six clasps for cloaks. All these of the finest craftsmanship, made from gold or silver, with enamel, turquoise, lapis lazuli, rose quartz or amethysts to further enhance them. Ten chests, to hold her clothes, each painted in her favorite designs, mostly river scenes with fish and birds.

She had a hundred dresses in mist-linen, all finely pleated; forty pairs of sandals, of colored or gilded leather studded to match her bracelets; a great quantity of tunics, shifts, warm robes and winter cloaks. Also sufficient furniture for three rooms, these made by craftsmen who worked for the Royal House. To transport all this he had given her six baggage carts each with two span of oxen. With her would go three of her personal attendants, the eldest of the four was betrothed and wished to stay in the Royal City; two female servants; four litter-bearers; and eight rowers for the little pleasure-barge he had had specially built for us.

I was impatient of every moment which separated me from Meri, and I grew daily more anxious because Kiyas had not come to a final decision about Men-het, for I was determined somehow she must be on her way back to the safety of the Oryx before I left the city.

When I stressed the urgency of this Kiyas seemed to think it unimportant. "I came here alone," she said, "and when the time comes I shall find my way back, alone if need be. Don't spoil your happiness by worrying about what's going to happen. I know Men-het and you don't. Even if he knew I was a spy I think he would still protect me."

"You're not falling in love with him, are you?"

"No, I wish I were. In many ways it would make everything so much easier. I'd marry him then, thinking that my influence would make him a wise holder of the Crook and Flail."

"Then why don't you marry him? It wouldn't be a betrayal if you did it because you loved your country better than yourself. The dynasty would be safe with you; couldn't you, Kiyas?"

"No; but not for the reasons I once gave you. If I thought I could bring tranquillity to Egypt by becoming her queen I should do so even if Men-het were a monster. But it wouldn't be any use, Ra-ab. He thinks he loves me, but he doesn't really, for I don't love him, and where there is a real link it must be recognized by both. I am only the first thing he has asked for which has not been given to him; and that makes me seem terribly desirable. But if I were his wife I should soon have no more power than any other woman. Perhaps for a year he might listen to my counsel . . . and even in expecting so much I may overrate myself. Then, though I were the Royal Wife, it would be as though he ruled alone. And even if I never lost my influence over him, what would happen if I died? No, Ra-ab, it wouldn't be any use for me to marry him. Pharaoh must be fit to rule alone; not just another puppet set up by a power behind the throne. Wife or vizier can never be enough; a mind which is only a channel for another person's ideas is open to false suggestions—the whisper of power, and yet more power for its own sake, even more insidious than the flattery of sycophants."

"Then why do you hesitate to return to the Oryx? You have decided that Men-het cannot rule, that Roidahn is right to choose the Vizier. You must go home at once, for your work here is finished."

"I'm not sure, Ra-ab. I'm not sure. Can't you see that this is a most terrible decision? Men-het is a brilliant soldier and the Royal Army will never falter in their allegiance to him. I have tried to bring him to our way of thinking; and if I fail thousands of our countrymen will die. I shall have killed them because I was not wise enough with words: for what I am trying so desperately to do is to make him see wisdom so that he will recognize for himself that it is better for the Vizier to rule and for him to be Captain of Captains. If I fail you may die, Ra-ab, when you lead the Oryx into battle. Your blood, and Meri's tears, will flow, because Kiyas thought she was more clever than she proved to be."

It was with relief that a few days later I heard a messenger had arrived from Hotep-Ra to say that Hanuk was coming to join me and would reach the Royal City the following day. Hanuk was older and wiser than I, and Kiyas might find more comfort in his counsel than she did in mine.

He came with me when we next saw the light in Kiyas's window, before dawn on the day after his arrival. When I saw them together I was doubly thankful that he was there to help her. She was pale and very tired; in a loose robe of yellow linen, with her hair bound, she looked too young for so great a responsibility.

"I thought I should be able to decide, Hanuk, but I can't. One moment I am sure that Men-het must not be Pharaoh; and then I see Egyptian soldiers killing each other, both sides believing they are fighting for Egypt and that her fields will be yet more fertile when their blood is shed. If Men-het were evil the decision would be easy, but he's *not* evil; he is strong and brave and a magnificent soldier. He is kind, and generous; any of his men would die for him without question."

"Then why shouldn't he rule us?"

"Because he has no wisdom except in strategy; because he will not realize that conquest by the sword cannot bring peace, unless the sword is only the dregs at the bottom of a cup of living wine. It is easy for some to get him to talk of what he means to do when he is Pharaoh. He knows, and therefore hates, the Royal Heir; and is determined to kill him rather than let him rule when Pharaoh dies. Of course I dare not tell him of the Watchers, but I pretended that what they are going to bring about was my idea of how Egypt should be ruled. He agreed that the laws were sometimes wrongly administered and that many of the overseers were corrupt. He said one of his first actions as Pharaoh would be to put many of the officials to death. But he has only one standard by which to judge those he will put in their places: they must be his friends, of whose personal loyalty he is assured. He knows that the greater part of the wealth of the country is held by dishonest nobles, but he says that under his rule the country will prosper and the granaries will never be empty. I told him how people in the little villages suffer when there is a famine, and of how they are oppressed. He listened, and asked me to tell him more. For a little while I thought he might become a Watcher, and wondered why I did not love him. He declared that the overseers should be punished without mercy for what they had done. His justice is all punishments, and only blind allegiance to himself will ever be rewarded. I asked him whether he did not prefer an honest man who was not afraid to tell him when he was wrong to one who offered praise without conviction. He laughed, and said, 'Little Kiyas, I am talking of the future, when I am Pharaoh. How can Pharaoh do wrong?' That is why he must never be Pharaoh. Already he doesn't question the rightness of his decisions, and if he held the Crook and Flail he would consider himself omnipotent, and not even pray to the Gods to give him counsel. He has forgotten the meaning of the Royal Oath, 'With this Crook I will shepherd my people, and with this Flail protect them from their enemies.' If his people feared no enemy but a foreign invader he would be able to keep that oath, but if the enemies of peace were among his friends he would never recognize them. At first I thought he wished for peace for Egypt as a father wishes for the peace of his children; then I found he wished for it only so that the country could grow rich and the armies yet more powerful. He would have every Nome raise five thousand warriors instead of only a thousand. Instead of leading his armies only against those neighboring countries who attempt to violate our frontiers, or fail to pay their just tribute, he would seek to conquer them, bringing their soldiers here to work our fields so that more Egyptians could follow the soldiers' path and set our boundary steles beyond Babylon. I reminded him of 'Those whose name shall never be spoken'; the invaders who held Egypt for more than two hundred years. I asked him, 'Might it not be that if you stole land from foreigners our name in turn would be erased from the monuments?' There can be no comparison. 'Those whose name must never be spoken' were not Egyptians.'"

The next day, Hanuk and I renewed our efforts to persuade Kiyas to return to the Oryx, but they produced no effect. She said:

"I keep on believing that tomorrow—always another tomorrow, I shall be able to make Men-het think as we do. He commands a great flow of energy, and properly used it would be of inestimable value. I feel as though I were struggling to open a sluice-gate which is too heavy for me to turn: if I succeed the water will pour into the right channels, if I fail the aqueduct will be washed away—and destruction come instead of fertility. Egypt has often been threatened by jealous foreigners, and she may be threatened again, even in our lifetime. With Men-het in command of our armies, Fear would never cross our boundaries once we had driven it beyond them. Every man is broken if he tries to carry too much power, just as a wooden pillar cracks if the roof beams are of granite. The name of Men-het as the supreme commander of the garrisons would be honored down the centuries, but Men-het the Pharaoh would become corrupt. I have even suggested that he let his brother rule, for if he agreed to renounce the Crown he might accept the Vizier, saying that Men-het the Warrior would grow weary of the slow routine of Audience; but he would not listen. He tried to comfort me by saying that his divinity would set no barrier between us . . . thinking that it was fear of this which prompted me to speak. There is no evil in him, Ra-ab; it is only that he has not the true humility which takes the full measure of its responsibility but never claims that which it cannot support. He has seen Egypt under a weak ruler, her greatness slowly being strangled by the small, greedy hands of thousands of officials. He cannot be blamed for wishing to be a ruler who is renowned for his strength. May the Gods have pity on him, for not being wise enough to see that the strength Egypt needs is not the strength of arms alone."

"When the time comes," said Hanuk, "we can give him the choice of being Captain of Captains, under the Vizier, or banishment."

"He would never swear allegiance to the man whom he will always consider the usurper, the usurper who gained power by betraying the trust placed in him by the Royal House. Nor will he accept banishment; he will lead those who remain loyal to him to fight against you until he is killed."

I put my arm round her shoulders. "Kiyas, he is only one more Egyptian who may die because he is misled. He is one man, against so many others: think of the slaves you have seen working on the Royal Roads; think of the maimed who shuffle through the dust of village markets, hoping for charity from someone who is a little less unfortunate than themselves. Would you condemn them to continue in their suffering because you are pitiful of one man?"

She tried to smile. "It is difficult to be impartial, and a woman, at the same time. While I am with you and Hanuk I think only as a Watcher. I have only one enemy, and must use every weapon against him until Fear has been banished from the Land of Egypt. But when I am with Men-het it is difficult not to think as a woman, for I see him undarkened by the shadow of a future rank. Today he took me to the marshes to show me his prowess with the throwing-stick. We took no one with us, save his two hunting-cats which fetched the birds he killed. With other people those cats are as fierce as leopards, yet with him they are docile as the white kitten I had when I was four years old. When he had brought down many birds, he went to sleep with his head in my lap. There is a scar on his forehead, made by a Puntite arrow; it felt like a white cord under my fingers. He wasn't a prince then, he was just a young soldier, who loves me in his own fashion. He smiled in his sleep, and looked so young and defenseless . . . how could I remember that ten thousand men waited on his commands? There was a hunting-knife in his belt. I could have slipped it out of its sheath without waking him; I could have driven it into his heart. I should have been a murderess, and worse, a woman who killed a sleeping man who loved her. I had not the courage to do openly what I am doing by more tortuous means. If he had died then, it would have been in peace, with a smile on his mouth. But when he does die, it will be as an embittered man, who knows that I have betrayed him and that he dies fighting against Egyptians .... Those same Egyptians for whom he has so often offered his life in battle."

It was ten days before the wedding when Kiyas told me, "Men-het is going to the Northern Garrison to see the new fortress which has just been completed. The Royal Physician has told him it is unlikely that Pharaoh will live more than a year and may die suddenly at any time. Men-het seems certain that the North will support him against the Royal Heir; I think he is going to consult with some of their captains and that the new fortress is only an excuse to explain his journey. He is reluctant to leave me. He says that I shall become his wife immediately he returns, and that though the marriage must be kept secret for a time, he will declare it as soon as he comes to power. What shall I do, Ra-ab? I tried to put him off, saying that I was not ready for marriage. But he wouldn't listen to any objection, and to tease me he said that if I tried to run away from him he would find me even if I closed myself in the heart of the Great Pyramid. He would find me, Ra-ab. He said he would send his soldiers into every town and village of the eighteen Nomes. When they come to the Oryx how could the Nomarch's daughter hide from them? If they found me the Watchers would be betrayed; and of that I should always be frightened. I must never do that, never bring Fear into the Oryx. I must stay with Men-het, and forget that I was ever Kiyas, who was happy."

"Even if it were true that you would have to bring the Watchers into danger, Hanuk and I would never leave you here."

"You will have no choice if I decide to stay in the Royal City. You forget that soldiers guard this house; you could never take me to the Oryx by force."

I was frightened by the level of resignation in her voice. "Will you come home if I know of a plan by which you would be free without endangering the Watchers?"

"Of course—if there is such a plan. But there isn't; I have thought and thought, and there is nothing I could do to stop Men-het trying to bring me back. If I told him I hated him he would laugh and think it a woman's coquetry. I think it would even increase his desire for me: he is proud of the scar on his hand where one of his cats bit him before he had tamed it."

"There is one place he would never look for you—in your tomb."

"Do you imagine I hadn't thought of that? It would not be difficult to die, but to take that escape while I might still be capable, however little, of helping the Watchers, would be cowardice. I've always tried very hard not to be a coward."

"I did not say that you should die, only that he would not try to bring you back from your tomb. Hanuk and I thought of a plan last night, and it only needs your agreement to put it into action. Men-het leaves for the North tomorrow and expects to be away about fourteen days. In three days, when he will have reached the mouth of the river and it would take four or five days for a messenger to reach him and bring him back, you will be taken suddenly ill; and die before the physicians can be summoned."

Hanuk broke in, "Perhaps it would be better if she was bitten by a cobra. One of the servants could claim to have found it in her bedroom after it had killed her; a dead snake could be kept to show Men-het."

"Yes, that's an improvement on my idea." And then to Kiyas, "Hanuk saw Men-het's captain yesterday, the one who belongs to us, and he is not going north with Men-het. The moment he hears of your 'death' he will send for the Royal Embalmer; that is what his master would wish him to do. You will leave the House of the Four Acacias in a sarcophagus. It will not be the first time that a Watcher has traveled in so curious a litter; there are air-holes in the lid and the bearers are Yiahn's trusted servants. You will remain hidden in his house until Meri and I start on our wedding journey; and as one of our attendants you will travel with us to the Oryx."

Marriage by Ptah

THOUGH IT HAD NOT been difficult to persuade Ramaios to allow us to be married in his house, it was not quite so easy to gain his approval of having the ceremony performed by Tet-hen. He could understand our objection to being married in the New Temple, but as we had to have a priest to hear our vows he found it incomprehensible that we did not wish to have the High Priest.

"I cannot understand," he said rather petulantly, "why you insisted on choosing Tet-hen, when, because of my rank, the High Priest would not have refused if I had asked him to come here to perform the ceremony."

"I know he would," said Meri soothingly. "And if you were not of such high rank you might need to show your power by having your daughter married with every symbol of your importance. But gilding is only necessary when base metal masquerades as gold. Everyone knows you are a great man, so you can afford to acquiesce to your daughter's whims. Surely it is a compliment that I prefer your house to the temple, and it isn't as though you believed in the power of the new priests any more than we do."

"I wish you wouldn't say things like that, Meri." He sounded more than a little annoyed. "Everyone in the Royal City has the right to his own thoughts, but not always the right to speak them. Many of us know the temples are corrupt, but that does not mean they are without power, and a power which if provoked is liable to destroy."

"That will soon be changed. . . ." Meri began, but he broke in:

"Yes. Yes! I know all that. 'The Watchers are going to drive fear out of Egypt and we are to have a new Pharaoh.' You find it convenient to forget there have been conspiracies in the past which failed; and until this one succeeds I prefer not to know about it. It was very honest of you and Ra-ab not to have kept it all from me. I appreciate your confidence, and in exchange I have done everything possible to show my approval of your marriage. If the Watchers come to power I shall be able to put my barter system into operation; it will give Egypt more stability than a thousand societies of idealists who have pledged themselves to bring her peace. But don't tell me any more of your plans; I don't wish to know them; though you may rest assured I pray for their success." He shot a keen glance at me from under his heavy eyebrows, "I am right in thinking your plans must wait on the death of Pharaoh?"

"Yes," I said. "He is already a dying man, and his heart will be weighed by a higher authority than the Eyes of Horus."

"Meri tells me it is probable the Vizier will be chosen. I approve that choice. The Royal Heir, though perhaps I should not say so while he still is the Royal Heir, has certain qualities which are, shall we say, undesirable in a ruler."

I wondered if Ramaios had visited the House of the Dark Silence, and if he knew I too had been there. He went on: "Prince Men-het is fortunately very unlike his half-brother, but he seems surprisingly irresponsible for a man who has proved himself so well versed in strategy. I never listen to rumors, but it has come to my ears that he has been making himself . . . in a man of lower rank one might almost say 'notorious,' with a stranger to the City. You may have heard of it, for you and Meri see more of the people who are not so occupied with affairs of state as I am, and I hear—in my position it is my *duty* to hear as much as possible, that this woman is occupying a house near, if not actually next door, to the House of the Two Winds. If it is true that Prince Men-het contemplates making her the Royal Wife, the Watchers will be fully justified in setting the Vizier on the Throne. It would be unthinkable for the woman of the Court to have to make their obeisances to a—a *person* of most doubtful origin."

I managed not to look at Meri, for I was afraid that if I did we should both laugh. I said gravely:

"Some say she is Men-het's cousin, the twin sister of the daughter born to his aunt; and others affirm that she was born to a priestess of the Temple of the Great Pyramids, through the intervention of Horus."

"I do not believe it," said Ramaios emphatically. "When you are as old as I am you will be wary of accepting such improbable stories. This is hardly a subject to discuss in front of Meri—though by tomorrow what is suitable for her to hear will be your affair and not mine, but I advise you most strongly to look on cases of divine intervention in matters of paternity with the most profound suspicion. The Royal House may be a special case; for I think the most skeptical of us are agreed that the earlier Pharaohs could claim Horus for more than a spiritual father. But when it comes to ordinary people—even if they do happen to be priestesses, claiming that Min, or Ptah, or even Horus himself, has been so enamored of their beauty as to forget the dignity necessary to Godhead, well, I find myself stirred not only to incredulity but to anger!"

"I will remember, Father," said Meri demurely, "and even if Horus should deign to notice me I will send him away disconsolate, telling him that Ramaios will accept only Ra-ab as the sire of his grandchild."

"It is nothing to joke about," said Ramaios severely. "I am sure Ra-ab agrees with me that one must *never* joke about that kind of thing. I must go now, there is a great deal to which I have to attend."

The door closed behind him; and Meri and I were free to laugh.

"Men-het got back to the City last night," I said a little later. "I haven't seen his captain yet, but he told Hanuk that the prince looks ten years older. He must have loved Kiyas much more than she realized, and she is to be buried in his own tomb . . . in the new City of the Dead, half-way between here and the Old Capital. He was agreeable to the short embalming, and did not wish to see the body when he heard it was already bandaged."

"Was it difficult to get a body of the right height?"

"No. Yiahn obtained one without any difficulty; curiously enough it was a girl who really had died of snake bite, the daughter of a small farmer. Men-het had a ushapti figure which had been made for his own tomb included in the bandages, and the mummy bands and both the inner and outer sarcophagus are to be sealed with his own cartouche. All the things he gave her are to be buried with him, and the sacred papyrus which is being put with his own copy of the Book of the Dead, describes her as his Royal Wife, the Keeper of the Heart of Men-het, the Song of Ten Thousand Bowmen. He is convinced that the cobra which killed her was sent by the Royal Heir, so now he is doubly resolved to kill his brother. He has vowed to take no wife and to dedicate his life to the conquest of the Babylonians."

"Poor Kiyas! We must never tell her that. It would make her so unhappy. I believe she was more than half in love with him, perhaps not in love as we know it, Ra-ab, but though it was of a different quality that doesn't mean it had no power to wound."

"I think you are right. She didn't come back to the House of the Four Acacias the night before he left for the North. And the last time I saw her before she went to the Embalmer's she was putting all his presents to her into a casket to be sent to him after she had gone. I could see she had been crying, and she said, "I'm glad I paid a little of my debt.' I wasn't sure what she meant then, but I am now. Do you think she will have a child?"

"No, I'm sure she won't. I told her the "Women's Secret' the first time I saw her. If she had been a real concubine she would have known it herself, but I found she didn't."

"Is that why you haven't been worried?"

"Of course. Didn't you know?"

"Meri, what *is* the Women's Secret?"

She laughed up at me, and then twisted a finger in my hair and pulled me down to kiss her. "That's one of the things you will have to be born a woman to discover. It's not called the Women's Secret for nothing; the magic might go out of it if any man were told. Would you have thousands and thousands of children born all over Egypt just because a man had learned our magic? Think how terrible it would be if women had children when they didn't want them. They would be no better off than ewes that run with a ram! How awful it would be if I came weeping to you and said, 'Oh, Ra-ab, I'm going to have a baby, isn't it terrible!'; instead of being able to say, 'When shall we start having a baby?'; and being able to decide whether we'd like it born in the winter, or the spring, or during the Inundation. I think the Inundation might be the best for our first one, don't you, Ra-ab? It's hot then, but there isn't much else to do except go about in boats."

"Are you *sure* you can't tell me the Secret? You said we should never have secrets from each other."

"I would, Ra-ab, really I would, if it wasn't breaking the Oath, which every woman has to make when first she's told. It's such a very old secret, far older than the Pyramids and *much* more important. Women *must* keep the secret. I don't need it, but other women do; it's their one protection against the superior physical strength of men. Woman is honored; it is through the female line that name and property are handed down through the generations, only because she holds the 'key of life on Earth.' She will not bear children to a man she thinks unworthy to be their father; even Ashek couldn't make Tahu bear him a child, although he tortured her. He didn't know about the secret; very, very few women even tell their lovers there is a secret, so he thought the sterility was in his own loins or else the Gods had robbed her of fertility."

"Can the secret make women have children as well as not have them?"

"No, it can't do that. Some women never have children even when they want them. I don't quite know why; perhaps it is because Min has never blessed them, or that Ptah didn't think he'd made them well enough to hand them on to Min. It must be terrible to be born a foreign woman, like Men-het's wife. She bore him two daughters in less than a year before the woman who told me the secret told it to her too; that's why she hasn't had any more."

"I wonder why the poorest castes have such a lot of children, especially those who are brought here as slaves; they seem to have a child nearly every year."

"Of course *they* do," said Meri surprised. "It's only nobles and the skilled castes who know the secret; otherwise there mightn't be enough people to work in the fields or build roads and things."

"Then why do you call it the Women's Secret? Had you forgotten that 'women' means you *and* the poorest field-worker?"

"I am *very* sorry, Ra-ab. I *did* forget. I was thinking with the small part of me that was made in the Royal City, not with my heart or with my spirit. I shall be your wife tomorrow, and then I'll belong entirely to the Oryx and never say things like that again."

She sat up, looking very purposeful. "It has become the pre-rogative only among rich people and concubines for women to be free of their bodies. *No* woman can be free unless she holds the secret. She would have to stay virgin or else have a child she didn't want. I shall bring the Secret to the Oryx, and woman shall tell woman until there is no one in the land who does not know it by the time she is ready to give away her virginity."

To tease her I said, "I have heard that the barbarians decide not to lie together if they do not wish to increase their families."

"The habits of the barbarians are very terrible; they are always thinking of new ways of making themselves unhappy, which is why they are often so cruel. And how *wicked* of them to be so insulting to Min!"

Even by the laws of the Royal City the man and woman were

alone with the priest who symbolized the Gods when they made
their marriage vows, and so we were able to use the ritual of the
Watchers. We were married in the little sanctuary which had
never been used by anyone save Meri. It was garlanded with
stephanotis; and on the small altar was the statue of Ptah, for love
of whom Neku had given his hand.

It was almost as though Ptah spoke to us through the mouth
of Tet-hen:

"In the name of Ptah, from whom you were first born to enter
the Way of the Gods, which you shall follow until with them you
are united, my blessing be upon your two names which henceforward are as one.

"That which was divided has been made whole, and that
which was lost has been found: the Scales are at peace, and dawn
and sunset meet at high noon.

"Even as the child is born of two parents, so shall that peace
you have not known alone, that wisdom you have not yet experienced, that power which has not yet found you as its channel,
come forth from you at this uniting of your spirit in my Name.

"My voice in your ears; my life in your nostrils; my vision
before your eyes: waking and sleeping, at your going forth and at
your returning, at the sowing and at the harvest. For when two
of my children find the companion of their journey then may I
declare in their new name, 'I have a Son.'

"Go forward together in peace; and remember always the
Father of whom you were born, who waits for your return into
the Shining Land beyond the Sun."

Hanuk was waiting for us outside the sanctuary, and beside
him stood our sister.

"I wanted to be the first to share your happiness," Kiyas said,
kissing first Meri and then me. "Hanuk said it was quite safe for
me to come here, so long as I waited in Meri's room till it was
time for me to go down to the boat. Bringing Neku's Ptah here,
so the room in which he was set would be part of the Oryx, was
Hanuk's idea too."

"Such a beautiful idea," said Meri. "We love you both so dearly."

Hand in hand we entered the banqueting-hall, where the pillars had been twined with ropes of flowers, all of them white, the

symbol of attainment. It was empty, for until we had taken our place on the double throne of gilded wood, set on a dias banked with blue lotus, the guests would not enter to bring us our gifts.

I took Meri in my arms. "You are my wife now, as well as my life. Do you feel the stirring of obedience due from a dutiful woman to her lord?"

"And what laws must the dutiful wife obey?"

"The command never to cease to love her lord."

"That is very easy! Had you commanded me to cease loving you I should have had to disobey you, even if you were to beat me for it twenty times a day. . . . No, Ra-ab! You mustn't!"

"Disobedient already! You will have to be kissed there again— even if I *am* crushing your dress a little."

It was a very beautiful dress, nearly as beautiful as Meri where it was most transparent. The mist-linen was embroidered with many little gold oryx, among ears of wheat; and it was bordered with three rows of gold thread which made it stand out like the bell of a flower. Her skin gleamed as though it had been powdered with silver dust and the buds of her breasts might have been carved from pale coral. She wore the Oryx necklace, and her burnished hair was bound by a fillet made as a wedding gift by Neku, a delicate tracery of leaves with flowers of pearls.

"We mustn't keep them waiting any longer," said my wife.

The great double doors were flung open for the guests to enter. I don't think either of us expected the Vizier to come to our wedding, but he was the first to greet us. In my eyes he was already Pharaoh, and forgetting that his future was known only to the Watchers, I nearly made obeisance to him. His gift was a bow-case inlaid with barks of many colors, the craftsmanship so skilled that it looked as though it had been painted with a fine brush.

"To the Son of the Oryx," he said, "who is the most loyal servant of Pharaoh."

"The most loyal servant of Pharaoh," I repeated. Surely I was right in detecting the emphasis on the final word; meaning that I was *his* most loyal servant. Had Roidahn then already come to a decision?

The Keepers of the Third, and of the Fourth, Ivory Seal; the Lord of the Northern Pastures; the Weigher of the Grain; the

Royal Herdsman; the Commander of the Southern Garrison
were followed by the Sons of the Nomarchs, of the Hare, the
Jackal, the Tortoise, and the Ibex, all of whom had come to the
Royal City to attend the ceremony. As well as these, nearly every
important official of the Court, together with their wives and
such children as were old enough, had assembled to do us honor.

Her four attendants stood beside Meri, and Hanuk and Sebek
beside me, to take from us the gifts as soon as we had given
thanks for them. Hunting-bows; throwing sticks; jars of wine;
quivers; arrows tipped with rare feathers and with shafts gaily
decorated; a set of gold-studded collars for my hunting-dogs
were among the things which I received. To Meri were brought
bales of finely embroidered linen; boxes of spices; jars of
unguents; little alabaster flagons of scented oils; a set of jeweled
studs for a pair of sandals; fan-sticks, both of carved ivory, and
ebony inlaid with silver; a pestle and mortar, inlaid with lapis, for
grinding malachite to make eye-paint; and a lamp for burning
perfume, made in the form of a naked girl lying on her belly and
holding a shell in her outstretched hands.

After the presentation of gifts we went among our guests.
Meri seemed very gay, but I noticed an undercurrent almost of
sadness. Many of those who had been her friends since childhood
she might never see again if they were divided against us when
the time came for the rebirth of Egypt. Many of them would be
happier in the new life, but what of those who could not adjust
themselves to a different Court? Those who were the wives or
daughters of men whom the Watchers would remove from
office, what would they do when they were judged solely on
their own merits and no longer had the background of their
present rank to enhance them? Those who had spent many years
in the rigid steps of etiquette might feel lost in the new freedom.
Or would the Court of the new Pharaoh resemble this so closely
that the scene would appear the same and only some of the play-
ers be different?

The Vizier was seated with Ramaios at the other end of the
room. When next I saw him would he be wearing the Double
Crown? What if Men-het conquered by force of arms and it was
the Watchers who were banished from Egypt?

While Meri and I talked with our guests, I heard snatches of other conversations. . . .

"They say he is stricken with grief. . . ."

"His wife is so angry she has left the City and gone to his estate in the North; some say she is even going back to her father and taking the children with her."

"Yes, I heard that too, it shows how unreliable foreigners are."

"I wish he *had* married her. I should have enjoyed seeing my father's sister making obeisance to the Beautiful Unknown."

And yet another voice, "Do you think it was true that Men-het would have made her the First Wife?"

"All standards of the Prince's army are to bear the white scarf for forty days in sign of mourning. Did you ever see her?"

"I did, once, as her litter passed mine and she drew back the curtains."

"Is she so beautiful?"

"Yes. Even Nefert would have to blame her mirror if she were to remain confident of being the most comely woman of the Court had the Beautiful Unknown been taken in marriage."

"I thought Prince Men-het might have been here today. After all, Ramaios *is* the Keeper of the Gold Seal."

"He is observing mourning as though she had been his wife."

"I think it is a pity she died. At least it would have been a new excitement. . . ."

Ramaios, looking rather harassed, came up to me and said in a low voice, "The Vizier is doing us the honor of staying to watch you set off on your wedding journey. That being so, I think you had better start a little earlier. No suggestion of haste, of course, but it would not be well to keep him waiting too long."

Hanuk joined us. "Everything is ready," he said. "The leading boats left three hours ago, and the servants will have set up the pavilions at the place appointed. If you leave soon you will reach there by sunset and find everything ready to receive you. Sebek and I are going in the second boat with Meri's four attendants."

"Four?" said Ramaois. "I thought one of them was staying here."

"She is," said Hanuk. "But the fourth girl is a friend of Sebek's."

"I see," said Ramaios hastily. "Forgive me for having over-

looked it. I hope you will explain to Sebek that I intended no discourtesy."

Through an avenue of people who strewed flowers before us,
Meri and I walked slowly down to the landing-stage. The little
pleasure-barge was painted in the green, white and silver of a
mallard's plumage, and its figure-head was a white oryx with silver horns.

Petals were showered down on us as we stood together in the
prow. The rowers bent to their oars: the boat drew away from
the bank. Our journey to the Oryx had begun.

The walls of the Royal City were hidden by a bend in the river,
and in our wake the other boat kept to the rhythm of our oars. In
it a girl stood solitary, with her hand on the figure-head.

"That's Kiyas," I said.

"I know," said Meri. "I waved to her but she didn't see me.
Then I saw what she was watching. Look, Ra-ab."

With slow, majestic strokes, a funeral barge beat on upriver.
On a raised platform between the rowers a white lime-stone sarcophagus gleamed like a mist-bird in the dying light.

The steersman wore the full panoply of the Captain of Egypt.
Prince Men-het was taking his beloved to await him in his tomb.

Wedding Journey

WHEN I WOKE next morning, the sky beyond the first of the
eastern cliffs was green as malachite on the eyelids of beauty.
Meri was still sleeping, her head resting in the hollow of my
shoulder. In the dawn light her face gleamed like a white lotus in
the dark pool of her hair. She must have felt me watching her, for
she stirred, and murmured, "Ra-ab, I love you so much." Then,
as I drew her closer, she drifted off to sleep again.

The river had the cold sheen of electrum; two swans, flying
with a somber creaking of wings, were reflected in its quiet surface as though in a mirror. The reeds rustled, and from their shelter a gazelle stepped delicately down the bank; then paused with
head uplifted before she ventured to drink.

Through my love for Meri I had found a new kinship with all the
children of Ra: we were like those two swans, seeking together a

long-dreamed horizon; she was the river of life at which I had slaked the thirst of loneliness. I prayed to the God of Lovers to grant me the strength by which I might forever protect her from sorrow, and the wisdom which could make me worthy to be her husband.

I took her into a deeper embrace. Her mouth awakened to mine: it was as though we lived in one body, no longer separated even by intangible barriers, merging as clouds merge in the fume of sunset.

Later, she said, "I wish we could stay here forever; no other place can possibly hold so much enchantment. We could send everyone else away and tell them to build a wall, out of sight beyond the reeds, so that we should never be disturbed."

"What would we do when we were hungry?"

"You could catch fish, and I'd make a fire and cook them for us."

"Wouldn't you grow tired of fish?"

"Perhaps we should after a while. You could tell Hanuk to bring us a goat and some ducks . . . and some vegetable seeds as well, before he goes back to the Oryx. Then we should have a farm and a garden of our own."

"It would be rather wet during the Inundation," I said, as though this were my only objection.

"Nut is very fond of lovers, magical ones like we are, and she'd turn everything inside our wall into an island, and see that the water level stayed just where it is now. Or shall we have it about a cubit higher . . . so that the papyrus can grow nearer?"

"Not a cubit: I think five thumb-joints would be enough."

"Yes, I agree. You must always be very careful to be sure of exactly what you want before asking Nut for it. Do you remember the story of the farmer who prayed for rain, and forgot to say how much he wanted? Nut washed his farm away to teach him to be more careful in future. I thought it was rather unkind of her, until someone explained to me that it was no use praying unless you know what to pray for."

"I prayed for *you*, Meri, at least three times a day, since the first time I dreamed of the River."

"I prayed for you too. Though when I was very small I didn't realize it was you I was looking for. I wanted to find someone just like me, only nicer. Someone who would always know exactly *why* I did things, even if he knew the things were silly; and with whom I should never be lonely any more. Who would love me all the time, always, not because of what I did, but just for being the other half of himself."

"I wish I had been a poet instead of a soldier, and then you wouldn't need a mirror to tell you how beautiful you are. No other woman gets *more* beautiful every day like you do."

"I'm glad we are beautiful all over, aren't you, Ra-ab, and don't really need to wear any clothes?"

"I suppose we shall have to wear some clothes soon, for Hanuk said the boats would be ready an hour after dawn, and we shall have to start fairly soon if we are to reach home the day after tomorrow."

"Do you think everywhere will always seem so much the loveliest place that we never want to move on?"

"Doesn't moving on become only another adventure to share? Wherever we are will always be the loveliest place because of being together. Think how horrid this place would be if either of us wasn't here."

"Don't, Ra-ab, don't say that even in fun. If you weren't here this would be only a traveling-pavilion of green and white stripes, with green matting on the floor and your box on one side and mine on the other, and in the middle a mattress we slept on . . . and over there the flowers I wore yesterday, looking rather wilted, although I gave them water to drink. And the river would be only a place I couldn't bathe in because there might be crocodiles, and the reeds would be full of leopards wondering when to pounce on me. . . . But I'd be crying so much I wouldn't notice."

"And what is it like when we are together?"

"It is a little Nome of the Shining Land, which Ra has put on Earth specially for us to live in. That's why we are so much happier than any other human beings have ever been."

Hanuk looked relieved when he saw us coming down the path which led to the second clearing in the reeds where he and the others had spent the night. The pavilion, in which Kiyas had slept with the three girls, had already been dismantled, and some of the servants had already left in one of the boats so as to prepare food for us all at the next stopping place.

"Some of our people heard you were spending the night here on your way home," said Hanuk. "They sent a spokesman to me at dawn, asking if they might bring you their greetings. Any large gathering of Watchers would be dangerous, because it might arouse unwelcome curiosity, but only those who live near here have had time to assemble, and even if they *are* noticed it won't matter."

"When will they be here?" asked Meri.

"They are waiting a little further upriver until I let them know if you will see them."

"Of course we will," I said. "What could be more natural than that they should want to see the woman who will rule in the name of the Oryx?"

Meri laughed like a delighted child. "Ra-ab, it will be so much more fun than the guests we had yesterday. Most of *them* came because Father happened to be the Gold Seal, not because they really liked him, much less because they liked me. But these people are coming because they are Watchers, so they are our *real* friends."

Hanuk suggested that the people would prefer it if we received them with a certain degree of formality. I agreed, so we waited for them in our pavilion, seated side by side on a carpet of leopard skins, a present from Ramaios to Father, which Hanuk fetched from the second barge. Only a few of the people we saw had ever been to the Oryx, but Hanuk knew them all by name, describing each one in turn to us as they came forward.

The first was a tall man carrying the staff which denoted the rank of headman of a village of more than fifty people.

"This is Denark, brother of Dardas the fisherman at whose house you stayed when you went on your first crocodile hunt," said Hanuk. "He stayed for a year at Hotep-Ra when he and his brother brought the blind woman to Roidahn, and then he came back to his own village. At first the villagers thought he was a ghost, sent by Hayab to haunt them for having sacrificed her to the river; and when he told them about Hotep-Ra they thought he was describing a dream of a country beyond Earth. But soon he taught them that if they helped him to banish fear from Egypt they too could live in peace."

"What happened to the old headman?" asked Meri, to whom I had told the story of Dardas.

"It was because he was known to be dying," said Denark, "that Roidahn told me to return to this village. The Headman of Five Villages was also of the Watchers, so he allowed my people to make their own choice when my predecessor died."

Then he gave Meri a loaf of bread and a flat rush basket of fish; the symbols of wisdom on Earth and away from Earth.

The next to come forward was a woman, a linen-weaver from the neighboring town. She had become a Watcher because her sister had been looked after in Hotep-Ra. I knew the sister, a woman who had tried to kill herself after both her children had been taken by a leopard; Hanuk had found her and brought her to Roidahn to be cured.

She brought two spans of yellow linen, to be made into a tunic for Meri.

The next was a potter and his wife, both of them old people without children. They had lived in fear of what was to happen to them when they were too old to work, but this fear was lifted when they were told they could come to Hotep-Ra if by then the Watchers did not already rule Egypt. They brought four cooking-pots, of red clay, with an incised pattern of dots and wavy lines. The old woman patted Meri's hand, "Don't let the pots touch the ashes, my dear, and they will last a life-time, even if you live to be as old as I am, which, may the Gods hear me, you will do, and your fine young husband too. You will find you love him just as well even if he grows as old and ugly as this man of mine."

Her husband nudged her, and said in a loud whisper, "You mustn't speak like that of the Young Oryx."

"Of course she must," said Meri. "I'm sure that what she says is absolutely true, and I'll take great care of your presents . . . and may my cooking be worthy of them."

Meri smiled at me, and said, "You like the way I cook for you, don't you, Ra-ab?"

So far as I knew she had never cooked anything in her life, but I said, I hope with conviction, "Your way of cooking blue-fish must be eaten to be believed!"

"Blue-fish?" said the old woman, "I always take. . . ." But to

Meri's relief her husband hurried her away before she could enlarge on the subject.

There was a moment's delay before the next person was brought up to us, and I whispered to Meri, "*Do* you know how to cook blue-fish?"

"Of course I don't. I never even heard of one!"

"This morning you said we could live here forever and you would cook the fish I caught."

"Yes, but this morning we were so magical we could have caught fish already cooked if we had really tried."

Then the widow of a farmer told us how the Watchers had given her an ox to replace the one which had died, and that because of this she had been able to plow her fields and make enough to pay the land tax.

"And the ox that came to us through your father's kindness has calved," she went on, "so now I have a span of oxen as fine as any in the land."

She had her children with her; a boy of about four, a girl a little younger. They stared at us shyly. Then the little girl came forward and climbed on Meri's lap and began to play with her necklace. The mother started to apologize, but Meri said, "Do lend her to me for a few minutes, she likes playing with my necklace."

It was a pretty child, with unusual gray eyes, and black hair so thick that it looked like a little ceremonial wig.

I wondered how long it would be before Meri decided that she would like us to have a child.

Khnum the Potter

IN MERI'S COMPANY Father looked happier than I had ever seen him. He had expected us to want a house of our own, and when she told him we would prefer to have a new wing added to the Great House, he warmed to a deeper affection than he had ever felt for Kiyas and me. I was a little disappointed at her decision, for I wanted us to live in a house we designed together and which had no previous associations. When I told her this she said:

"I would really have preferred that too, Ra-ab. But didn't you see how happy it made him because we wanted to stay here? He has been so lonely, and always afraid of intruding his sorrow on other people . . . that's why he shuts himself away, as though grief were a pestilence which could spread to those who are nearest him."

"I know—and in a way he's right. Grief is a kind of disease which can infect other people. He *shan't* make you unhappy, I won't let him. Can't you say you have changed your mind?"

"And go away without even trying to cure him? The Watchers are to cure people of being unhappy, and Father's sorrow is a kind of illness. He even admitted so to me. To live on hope is almost as bad as starving on fear. He takes no real interest in the present because he is waiting for death to reunite him with your mother. He can't look into the future, so he tries to recreate the past . . . it's only another way of avoiding the present. Haven't you realized that's why he is so engrossed in old records?"

"I don't think you're right there, Meri. He says he searches the past to find a better pattern for the future."

"Then why is he interested in the *age* of a papyrus? The older it is the more magical it seems to him."

"The old people were wiser than we are; it is as though for the last few hundred years the face of Ra had become increasingly obscured."

"We have got to teach him that though he may find much wisdom in the ancient writings, he must not use them to escape into the past but translate their voice into living words. He reads to me every day, did he ever read to you and Kiyas?"

"No, I don't think we ever asked him to."

"When he has finished I say how certain things he has told me remind me of things that are happening now. I think he is beginning to see that the old people were not so different to ourselves, nor so very much wiser . . . it was only that they knew *why* they did things, instead of just *doing* them. He's getting interested in 'whys' like we are. He agreed with me this morning that when a person stops asking questions they are either so wise they need no longer be alive, or else they have forgotten why they were born. That's why everyone is born, Ra-ab, to find out more of the answers. Haven't you noticed signs of his change of heart?"

"He looks happier . . . but so would anyone who had you for a companion."

"It's more than just how he looks. You know that for years he has been preoccupied with the preparation of his tomb, and that most of the rooms in this house have bare walls because all the drawing-scribes are working for the dead? I told him that I should like the rooms you are to build for me to be frescoed, and he said at once that the tomb can wait while the scribes work for you. He is going to supervise their designs himself, and when I left him he was enlarging our plans for the big day-room, so that there shall be enough wall space for the record of our river journey from the Royal City. Now it is to be so large that there will have to be a double row of pillars to support the roof beams, and these are to be decorated in faience-blue and gold. There will be four windows, with shutters which can be removed altogether in the hot weather so that it will be like an open pavilion . . . leading to a garden with a swimming pool surrounded by a wall, so that we can be quite private. Our bedroom is to be made larger too, for until I told him, he thought we were going to have separate rooms. I said I thought that was a most barbarous custom, for if two people don't want to be together all the time it is foolish for them to marry."

"What is the bedroom to be like?"

"The walls are to have another river scene, reeds in the foreground and plenty of fish in the water. I asked him to put in a gazelle coming down to drink, to remind us of the one we saw on the first morning we woke together. It will be *our* river, which you used to have to cross to find me . . . but now we shall always be on the same side of it."

Father agreed most willingly to Roidahn's suggestion that when the Watchers ruled, Nomarchs should be a man and a woman in co-rulership; either a married couple or a brother and sister who would sit in judgment together as had the ancient Pharaohs. In preparation for the time when we should have absolute authority, Meri and I gave audience every seventh day, there being too few petitioners in the Oryx for it to be necessary to dispense justice every fourth day as was the custom in most other Nomes.

Together we made journeys to all parts of the Oryx; in towns we stayed with the overseer, and when in a village, with the headman. In time Meri came to know every rung of the ladder which stretched from us to all our people, and wherever we went we were received as though we were kinsmen. Against this quiet background to our lives the frieze of the coming conflict gradually assumed its final shape. Every day brought fresh news of preparations completed beyond the Oryx, and yet more decisions were reached as to what judgments should be given when the time came.

Roidahn had expressed himself as being more than satisfied with the information I had gathered for him in the Royal City, and it had been decided that if Prince Men-het succeeded in leading the Royal Army against the Watchers, the army of the Oryx, supported by the Hare and the Jackal, under my leadership should be in the van of the battle.

I was surprised that Meri was not pleased when I told her how greatly Roidahn had honored me by his choice.

"How can you expect me to be pleased?" she said. "No woman who loves her husband wants him to gain honor in battle . . . it is *far* too dangerous! Sometimes I wish you were more like your father instead of being a soldier. Couldn't Sebek lead the Oryx instead of you?"

"Would you have people say that while the son of Pharaoh leads his men against the Watchers the son of the Oryx stays in safety and lets his soldiers go forward without him?"

"When you were in the Royal City I have often heard you get impatient with people who behaved in a certain way because they were afraid of what people would *say*. You said it was the most contemptible of all hypocrisies to be whipped on by ignorant opinion. Together you and I can rule the Oryx, but Sebek could never rule . . . he is just, but he has no imagination. He is quite as good a soldier as you are, perhaps a better one. Why don't you let Roidahn make *him* the leader of the armies? You told me yourself there is no better captain."

"When you put it like that it *does* sound very reasonable. But I couldn't let any one else lead my people so long as Roidahn thinks I can do it properly. Sebek is just as good a captain as I am, but he's not the Oryx."

"He is older and more experienced than you."

"None of us have been in a real battle yet, so I may be conceited in thinking that men will follow me better than anyone else."

"Of course they will follow you, who wouldn't?"

"It won't really be me they'll follow, it will be a long tradition of loyalty to the Oryx. It won't be nearly as dangerous as you think. We shall outnumber the Royal Army, unless the five Northern Nomes rise with them. But of course they have had more experience of fighting—none of us have had any, except the Tortoise which sent two small expeditions to the Land of Gold."

"If you go this time you will always be having to leave the Oryx just when it needs you most. What's the good of being a Nomarch if you don't have soldiers to fight for you?"

"The old Pharaohs always led their armies into battle."

"Only in very important battles, not in silly little expeditions against Punt, or when a few ships laid siege to the Cedar Ports to teach them not to send their timber to the Asiatics instead of to us."

This was the first time I had ever had to do something which made her unhappy, and I found it very difficult. I said:

"Roidahn wouldn't have told me to lead the Oryx unless he was sure it was right. I shan't be killed unless I am due to die anyway."

"That's one of the things you believe which I'm not sure about. Though Roidahn believes it and so does Nefer-ankh."

"I don't think it really matters if it's true or not. I shan't die as long as there is work for me to do, and I know there is, years and years of it. I may get wounded, of course, but I shall arrange that if I am, I shall be brought straight home to you, so that you can look after me. I shouldn't mind having a wound if you were there to bandage it."

We were lying on the edge of the fishpool, watching the carp weave slowly in and out of the shadow of the lotus leaves.

"We are very like each other," she said inconsequently. "Your hair is not so dark as mine, but apart from that I am more like your sister than is Kiyas. It won't be so exciting wondering what our children are going to look like, for even Khnum won't have much choice when he has only the resources of you and me to work with. Now if you had been a foreigner, or I had had red hair, there would have been so many more possibilities."

"Perhaps we shan't have any children. Wouldn't they be rather an interruption to us being alone together?"

"Oh, we could have plenty of nurses and things to look after them. And I expect they'll be so specially nice that we'll be very fond of them."

"Do you think parents really *are* fond of their children?"

"We don't know what proper parents feel. Both our mothers died when we were too young to remember them, and your father loved yours so much he was never a real person after she died, and my father loved mine so little that he doesn't really count as a father at all."

"I don't think we had better have any children until the Watchers have settled everything."

"I do," said Meri firmly. "I'm going to have one as soon as I can manage it. You might be more careful of yourself if you didn't want your son to be born an orphan."

Meri always used to say that Khnum the Potter must have been listening to our conversation; for that afternoon he started to spin a new body for our first child.

Women of the Oryx

SINCE HER RETURN from the Royal City, Kiyas had spent most of her time at Hotep-Ra. If she grieved for Men-het she concealed it even from me, and her only interest seemed to be in helping Hanuk further his plans. She took no part in the administration of the Nome, nor did she accompany Meri and me when we went from place to place, staying with overseers and minor nobles. I was still hopeful that the rulership of Egypt would pass into the hands of the Watchers without bloodshed, but Meri seemed to share with Kiyas a foreboding of war.

"The Watchers will triumph; but first there will be clouds over the sun, and vultures will gather over battlefields where the blood of both slayer and slain will be Egyptian."

"Stop imagining horrors, Meri! There may have to be some fighting, but that is something for which we have long prepared. I spent three years at the House of the Captains, would you have me betray all that I learned there?"

"I don't think I should be frightened of battles if they weren't a reason for us being parted from each other. When I make myself see clearly, I know that you aren't going to be killed, and that we shall have a long life together. But even to be parted for an hour is a squandering of our happiness, so how do you expect me not to dread your going to war?"

"You know I find it bitter to leave you. I think the reason why we have fewer of the warrior caste than any other Nome, is because the contented man does not want to risk leaving his family."

"You told me the Oryx had not been to war during your lifetime."

"Nor has it; but the Oryx would have to obey Pharaoh if he should raise a levy. When there was a rising in the Land of Gold it was quelled by soldiers from the Tortoise, but it was only by chance they were chosen and not we. The farmer and his wife can plow their fields together if they wish, the wife of a fisherman can go in her husband's boat; it is only the soldier and his wife who cannot share their work together."

Later I was to wonder if this casual remark had been the spark which kindled a new idea in Kiyas, but at the time I saw in it no special significance. Meri said she wanted to visit Roidahn, and when we reached Hotep-Ra she and Kiyas spent much time together in earnest conversation.

Five hundred young Watchers from other Nomes, whose parents did not belong to the warrior caste, had recently come to Hotep-Ra, asking that they might be trained to follow the Standard of the Oryx. A soldier's village had been built for them on Roidahn's estate and Sebek had gone there to supervise their instruction. Sebek told me he thought it would be best to arm nearly all of them with the mace, which took less time to master than either bow or javelin.

"There are only about thirty of them who are already skilled with a bow," added Sebek. "They used to be wild-fowlers and come from homes in the marsh country."

I approved Sebek's plan, for the need for additional soldiers was urgent. It seemed more than probable that the armies of the Royal Nomes would be loyal to Men-het, and if the North should join him also, the South, at its present strength, would be outnumbered by two to one.

"You say you will have less than four hundred mace-bearers,

and only thirty bow-men, out of the five hundred?"

"The standing army of the Oryx is a thousand on the tallies, but that means less than eight hundred men who can be spared to fight. The rest must be used to carry supplies of arrows, fresh flights of javelins . . . all the many things needed by an army which moves out to war. And after our first battle we shall have wounded to care for . . . even though this will be easier than if we were on foreign territory."

That evening I was thinking over what Sebek had said, and as usual had voiced my thoughts to Meri.

"I'm glad Sebek told you that," she said. "It will make you more understanding of the new idea which has come to Kiyas. She has been working on it for some time, and now her plans are almost ready. She realized before any of us that the army under Men-het may be stronger than ours. She says it is not so much that they are better trained, but they have had practical experience and are greater in number. That is why she has been teaching some of the younger women how to follow the army, to carry supplies and look after the wounded."

"Poor Kiyas," I said. "I shall hate having to tell her that her idea is quite impractical."

"I should hate having to listen to you saying anything so silly!"

I was having a bath, pouring water over myself with a copper dipper, and I was so startled by Meri's last remark that I let it fall into the jar.

"Look what you've made me do!" I said somewhat crossly.

She mocked me gently. "Have I been magical again? It seemed to me that I was sitting at the other end of the room, cleaning my face with almond oil, watching you washing yourself rather clumsily. It only shows that appearances are an illusion . . . for really I was curled up in the bottom of your water-jar and snatched the dipper out of your hand to tease you."

I went across to her, rubbing my hair dry with a towel of unbleached linen. "What have you and Kiyas been hatching between you? Have you decided that men had better stay at home and let women become the warriors?"

She tried to look stern. "Ra-ab, stop dripping all over the floor! You've walked over my dress and spoiled all the pleats."

"I didn't notice it was a dress, after all it *is* on the floor."

"It wasn't a favorite dress," she said magnanimously. "Come and sit down on this stool where I can see you. If you wander about I keep trying to watch you and then I get careless with my face."

She had wiped off the oil and was now rubbing a paste, which had a fresh, slightly acrid scent, into her neck and forehead. I knew from experience that this would be left on for a few minutes before she reached another stage in the curious rites on which she thought the preservation of her beauty depended. I had also learned that when Meri had something particularly important to tell me, of which she was not sure I would approve, she usually kept it for some such time as this, so I was not surprised when, making her voice as casual as possible, she said:

"Kiyas and I have decided that it is quite time the tradition of soldiers' women not being allowed to share their husband's lives came to an end. After serious consideration Hanuk agrees with her, and they have recently been to the soldiers' village, the one near the House of the Captains, to talk the idea over with the wives."

"It's kind of you to tell me of such an important change in my army. After all, I'm only the Captain of the Oryx. I suppose I may enjoy the same privileges as my soldiers, and take you with me into battle?"

"Of course," she said calmly. "That's really why I helped Kiyas with her idea."

"You have concealed from me your skill with the bow . . . or is it the mace or javelin you will choose while you are with me?"

Meri remained unruffled by my attempt at sarcasm. "I shall not take any part in the actual fighting. Kiyas may, for she is very skilled with arrows and has been practicing at a target every day since she came here. I shall command the women, and see they do what they are told and don't quarrel among themselves. I shall also look after the wounded. Kiyas has promised to do that too, which is very unselfish of her. . . . I think only Hanuk could have persuaded her not to be in the first flight of bowmen."

I was relieved, though prematurely. "You mean that you and Kiyas are going to get a house ready to receive the wounded, just as she and I made ready for those who were stricken by the pestilence four years ago? Certainly it is a good idea that those women of the soldiers' families who are not needed to look after small children should be allowed to help you. Ever since I saw the work Kiyas did during the Blue Death, I have been convinced that women should be allowed to play their part in the care of the sick and wounded. I am sure Father would agree to your using the south wing of his house for this purpose, and if you need still more accommodation you have only to ask Roidahn for a house in Hotep-Ra."

"Kiyas has thought of that already. Hanuk has arranged for two healer-priests to be at each place, with as many women as they need to carry out their instructions; but those women will not necessarily be the wives of soldiers, any Watcher who has proved herself suitable would do. Kiyas has already sent fifty women to the Temple of Ra so that the healer-priests can instruct them in what they ought to know."

"Where are you sending the rest of the healer-priests? Nefer-ankh tells me that he now has twenty of them fully trained, and more who are not yet initiate."

"Two will be at home, with Father; two here, at Hotep-Ra; four will remain at the temple to look after our own people . . . that will leave twelve to come with Kiyas and me and the thirty trained women who have sworn to follow us."

"Follow you where?"

"How do I know? If I did I could prepare the strategy of battle for you, as I should know just where Men-het was to be engaged. The only thing I can tell you is that we shall take the same road as the one on which you lead the Oryx. If you insist, I will keep them out of the actual fighting, at least until we have proved that women are not frightened of arrows, or no more than men are. They shall remain out of bowshot while the battle is going on, but be near enough to attend the wounded."

"Who are going to look after the wounded women?"

"There won't be any. Healer-priests still retain their traditional immunity, and can move about, even in the middle of the fighting, to succor a wounded man; and the women who accompany them will share the same protection. It is not even as though we were going to fight foreigners. Kiyas knows Men-het, and she says that none of his soldiers would break the Warrior's Code. So we shall be treated with honor even if we are taken prisoner, and I'm sure Men-het wouldn't refuse to let me share your prison if he captured you. We'd be quite happy as long as we were together, Ra-ab, even if the place they shut us in was rather small and uncomfortable."

I tried to look stern and impressive . . . which is never easy if you have no clothes on and are sitting on a stool beside your wife's toilet chest, while she pretends that three-quarters of her attention is occupied with mixing oil and malachite to the exact shade she needs for eye-paint.

"I never expected Kiyas to infect you with her moonmadness. Do you imagine that I would deliberately take you into danger where, even if you escaped being wounded or killed, you might be taken prisoner and condemned to death or banishment?"

"I should be careful not to be wounded, so that I could look after you. If you were taken prisoner, of course I should make sure that I was captured too. If you were put to death or banished you couldn't be so cruel as to wish me to stay behind? Ra-ab, dear Ra-ab, you couldn't want that to happen to me! If I were to die would you want to go on living? If I were sent to live among the barbarians would you want to go on being lonely in the Oryx?"

I saw that she was so distressed by my apparent lack of consideration that I said hastily, "No, Meri, of course I shouldn't. You know that if you died, every day would seem an interminable exile until I joined you."

She sighed contentedly. "Then we are agreed, and there is nothing more to argue about."

"Oh, but there *is*!"

She came and sat on my knees and put her hand over my mouth. "You may kiss my fingers, but you mustn't talk any more until you've decided not to be silly. I have been miserable ever since I knew there might be a battle, because you might have to go away from me. Now the battle has become only another adventure we can share together. It's very bad for people to be unhappy, especially when they are having a baby. Do you want your son to be born looking like a melancholy little monkey just because his mother was sad?"

"He will probably be lucky even if he manages to look as human as a monkey if his mother goes rushing about getting involved in battles!"

"He will be too small to notice what I am doing for several months yet, and I don't expect the Gods would be so unkind as to let Pharaoh die just when I shouldn't be able to help the Watchers. I could come with you almost immediately after he's born; I have arranged for two foster-mothers in case one can't give him enough milk."

I hoped fervently that if fighting did take place my son would prove more persuasive than his father in keeping Meri at home, but I saw it was no use arguing with her any more at present.

"What if I agree to your scheme?" I said.

"Kiyas and I, with the twelve priests and the thirty soldiers' women who have been trained how to look after the wounded, will follow the army. With us will come other women, who are young and strong and used to field work; they will carry spare arrows and javelins and things, and thus release fighting-men to carry arms. Women can also look after the pack-donkeys, and do the cooking. I have already got the names of two hundred and twelve who want to join us. It was their being able to free men for arms that made Sebek approve of our idea."

"You've won Sebek over too, have you?"

"Oh yes, Sebek was *quite* easy! You mustn't be offended that Kiyas told Hanuk and Sebek first. She had the right to do it because it was her idea—and I thought it would be more of a surprise for you if I didn't tell you until I had arranged the details."

"It *was* a surprise!" I said fervently.

"It was the first idea I've had that I didn't share with you at once, and that was more your fault than mine. You remember we were talking about leading the Oryx, the day when Khnum the Potter must have been listening to our conversation?"

I nodded, and she went on. "Well, that day you seemed so *very* set on leading the Oryx off to war while I stayed behind for years crying among our children."

"Children? Remember what you promised Ramaios to say if ever Horus became importunate!"

"It's not fair to try to make me laugh. This is *very* serious. For hundreds of years, men and women of all other castes have been able to work together, but soldiers have not been able to share their lives with their women. That's why many soldiers aren't very near to their wives; you can't love someone who is living a separate existence that you don't want to share . . . and if they do want to share it and are not allowed to they can't be really happy. If someone's life is cut off from love it must turn in another direction; they have to prove their strength by fighting, preferably against a foreigner. Nearly every animal will defend itself when attacked, but very few, if any, kill for pleasure. The tradition which separates a soldier from his women is gradually making him feel he has so little to lose that he looks for escape either into the role of a hero or into death. The man who loves his wife will fight twice as fiercely in defense of his home, but you cannot invade a foreign country with soldiers who are happy. Think what it would mean, Ra-ab, if we could change the warriors' tradition! Side by side, man and woman would fight together in defense of their security, just as a lion and lioness will protect their cubs, but no man would wish to take his woman into an *unnecessary* war, if he knew she would have to suffer as he did. If the soldiers of Punt and Southern Nubia, the men of the desert and the Asiatics, came to share in this new tradition it might lead to the end of all invaders, and no longer would mankind shed their brothers' blood."

I was surprised to find that Hanuk agreed with Kiyas's scheme and had not been persuaded to approve it against his better judgment. He was a little anxious that I might be offended because I had not been told of it sooner, and as soon as I told him that Meri had informed me of their plans, he said:

"I told Kiyas she ought to have told you about it at the beginning, but she made me promise to keep her secret until she and Meri were ready. I expect at first you thought it quite impractical, as I did until Kiyas made me realize that my first reaction was born of prejudice. Now I consider it as necessary as any other of the Watchers' changes."

"Surely to protect his women from danger is man's most fundamental law?"

"What kind of danger? Pestilence, hunger, pain, extremes of heat or cold, anxiety? Of what use is it to defend her with armed strength when the greatest security can only come through she and her husband living as though they were one? I know, as well as you do, that only a woman who has reached a certain stage of development is ready for such an affinity, but the nearer they can reach to that ideal the greater the happiness they can attain. More than three-quarters of the higher ranks of the Watchers have attained the Marriage of Ptah; they have come from all castes, but the one thing they have in common is that the pattern of their lives is one in which both husband and wife can share. When circumstances threatened to divide them from each other, they came to Hotep-Ra because it gave them sanctuary against separation. Two people who love each other have a dual strength which can give them security even in the stress of danger, but they cannot achieve security if they are living in constant threat of separation."

"You talk as though soldiers were the only people who have to leave their wives. What about traders, or they whose work it is to transport produce from one part of Egypt to another?"

"Why should women not travel as freely as men?"

"They can, until they have children; after that they have to stay and look after them."

We had been down to the soldiers' village to see some of Sebek's new mace-bearers at their exercises, and on the way home we had stopped to drink at a well. Finding it pleasant in the shade, we sat down with our backs against a palm tree to continue our conversation. My last remark seemed to have amused Hanuk for some reason.

"Have you told Meri that?" he said. "I don't see her being content to stay at home and look after your children while you wander round Egypt."

"She's different. She will come with me, of course, she always does; and the baby will be looked after by a foster-mother, and when he is older he will have a nurse."

"You think your company is more important to Meri than that of her child?"

"I know it is; as hers is to me . . . just as my mother was more important to Father than Kiyas or I ever were."

"You agree, then, that if Meri was forced to be separated from you, because there was no one else to look after the children, she would consider it a flaw in the perfection of your marriage . . . and also that it is quite probable she would resent the curtailment of her freedom caused by her child?" I nodded, and he went on, "The Watchers recognize three degrees of marriage, and it is vital that provision should be made for each of them in every caste. First there is the 'Marriage of the Long Years,' the Oath of the New Name, only undertaken by those who, like you and Meri, know that their affinity has come from the past and will endure beyond the span of many lives; the degree second to that is the Marriage for Life, entered into only after two years of marriage of the third degree, during which both are free to leave each other without the priestly decree which is required if people wish to part after having entered the Marriage for Life. Many women who are not yet capable of a more permanent relationship are content to live the greater part of their lives as though they were unmarried, even though they share a house with a man and have borne children to him. The tie which holds such women to their home and children is almost certainly stronger than the link of affection with their husband. When he goes away they would prefer to stay behind, and within the fabric of the present laws they are already well provided for. But those whose links to the husband are stronger than any other should be free to follow him if the work he has chosen takes him at times away from home. There are people, both men and women, whose special talent is for the care of young children. Such people may be childless, or have a small family; a fisherman who catches more fish than he needs himself uses his skill for the benefit of the community; why then should others not look after more children than are born of their flesh, using *their* special talents for the common good?"

"Would women ever consent to having their children cared for by people who did not belong to their families?"

"You had better ask Meri that. Kiyas told me she had already prepared for two foster-mothers for your child, and you should know that is not a sign of unwilling maternity."

"Meri tells me that you and Kiyas went to the House of the Captains to talk to the soldiers' women."

"We did, and never has an idea had a more enthusiastic welcome. It was easy to see which of the soldiers had a woman who really loved him, and which came from a home that had been set up for some reason of expediency. Sometimes it was a wife who wanted to come with us, sometimes it was a sister, or the concubine of a man who was still unmarried. Two hundred and twelve asked to be allowed to join us and to share all dangers with their men. It was a greater number than I had expected from less than a thousand men. Kiyas is having a large house built, next to the two houses where the orphans are brought up, and the children of the women who come with us are going there."

"Hanuk, couldn't the women stay at home and do certain kinds of work which are of direct benefit to the army? They could tan leather for shields, or feather arrows, or weave linen for bandages. Wouldn't that be much more satisfactory than having women with the army?"

"I suggested that to Kiyas, but she told me it would be quite useless. A woman finds little consolation in working for an abstract idea, perhaps because she is usually more of a realist than a man. If you told her she was weaving linen for bandages it wouldn't make her feel any nearer her husband than if she were weaving it for one of Meri's dresses, or the sail of a pleasure boat. If she loves a man she wants to be with him, *needs* to be with him. She can carry his food and spare weapons on the road to battle just as in peace she carries water from the well."

"And what if she is wounded?"

"She will find that pain easier to bear than childbirth. One is apt to forget, Ra-ab, that though men are over-sensitive about exposing their women to the wound of an arrow there are many who consider the travail of birth as a thing of little consequence, over which women make a disproportionate fuss."

"I wish *I* felt that!" I said feelingly. "Meri seems to take it for granted that our child is a son and that his birth will only cause her the most temporary inconvenience. I think that when she was talking yesterday about coming with me when we march against Men-het, she pictured herself as coming up to me just after I had declared the victory of the Watchers to inform me that she had thought the thick of the battle a fitting place for our son to be born . . . and then, while the assembly acclaimed us, she would present me with our son, strong and squalling on a shield! His mother, of course, remaining quite unruffled by her recent ordeal!"

"I expect Kiyas would be like that too."

"I am always afraid of Meri guessing the horrors I sometimes picture. I suppose it's because the most vivid memory I have of my mother is of her dying after Kiyas was born. Meri says I was a woman only two or three lives ago. She says I had a child; it wasn't hers, although she was a man then. I wish I could remember having a child, then I might realize it isn't as bad as I think it is."

"It might seem even worse," said Hanuk gloomily. "I had forgotten your mother died because Kiyas was born. I knew it was soon afterwards, but I thought it was from some other cause."

"You're in love with Kiyas, aren't you, Hanuk?"

"Yes, I always have been."

"I hope she marries you."

"So do I. I would rather be her husband than wear the White Crown!"

Royal Envoy

THAT YEAR WAS A CENTENARY of the dedication of the Temple of Ra at Thebes. The ceremony should have been attended by Pharaoh, as it had been for the last three hundred years, and when it became known that his health was too feeble to allow him to leave the Royal City, it was realized throughout Egypt that the rumors of his approaching death were well founded. I was very glad when I heard that the Royal Envoy who would take Pharaoh's place in the ceremonies was to be the Vizier, Amenemhet, instead of either of the princes; for I thought this sign of the Royal Will might prove sufficient to sway the Nomes of the North into supporting the Vizier against any claim of Menhet's, and so spare the Watchers the necessity of bloodshed.

Amenemhet was to stay with us on his way south; as he was coming as the Royal Envoy he would be received as though he wore the Double Crown, and for many days the Oryx was busy with preparations for his arrival. It was arranged that he should land from the state barge at Hotep-Ra and travel by road to the

Great House where Father would receive him. The roads along which he passed would be lined with our people, wearing the bright tunics of festival and strewing flowers and green rushes before the procession.

Pavilions were being put up in the gardens of our house to accommodate those for whom we had no room within the walls. A great banquet was to be served to the nobles of the two adjoining Nomes of the Hare and the Jackal, who would be our guests for the celebrations. Dancers would perform in the great courtyard, showing us the ritual dances of the Glorification of Ra, and of Ptah's progress from his descent into Earth to his Unification.

Before he knew Meri, I think Father would have resented this interruption of his solitary existence, but now he seemed to enjoy making plans nearly as much as we did. Quite often I heard him laugh, and he used to appeal to me for support against a new demand of Meri's; only a mock protest, for he found joy in giving way to her wishes.

"Need *all* the oxen have gilded horns?" he asked her. "Could not those at the far end of the procession—Amenemhet is very unlikely to notice them—be made sufficiently gay with a little paint?"

"No, Father, you mustn't be mean. Ra-ab has had a hundred bulls brought down from the House of the Two Winds, and their horns are capped with gold, not just gilded. Would you have the Oryx shamed by the riches of the North?"

Father turned to me and said in feigned despair, "You see what she does to me? She is your wife, can't you stop her robbing our treasure-rooms to decorate a festival?"

"Isn't it lucky for you that I'm here," said Meri contentedly. "Otherwise you might be embarrassed at having such a meager display. Oxen with *painted* horns, indeed! As though you were only a minor noble who was trying to impress the Assessor of Tribute with his poverty. I had another good idea I forgot to tell you about. I gave rolls of blue or yellow linen to every village so there shall be no one without a new tunic; and I thought it would be unfair if those who won't be able to watch the procession hadn't a share in the rejoicings, so I arranged for them to be given either three pieces of honey-comb or a jar of beer."

"Where did you get the beer?" I asked.

"Oh, that was quite easy. I sent a message to Sebek's uncle, saying it was your request that he should distribute it as his share."

"And the honey-comb?"

"That is coming from Roidahn's eldest sister, the old one who doesn't live at Hotep-Ra. I noticed she had many bee-hives when we stayed there soon after we were married."

After spending considerable thought on such an important subject, Meri decided to wear the green instead of the white dress she had first chosen.

"You and Father will be wearing white and yellow, because of their being the Oryx colors, and all the litter cushions will be yellow. So me wearing green will be a change. It will be embroidered, of course, with little oryx like I had on my wedding-dress, but silver instead of gold as I'm going to wear it over a silver loincloth."

She was looking at herself in a large copper mirror which had been one of my first gifts to her. "I'm glad that the festival wasn't any later in the year, or else your son might have begun to make me look a silly shape. He seems to have curled himself away so tidily that you wouldn't really know he was there, would you, Ra-ab?"

Her waist was still so slender I could almost span it with my hands, and flowed down to hips narrow as a boy's—perhaps there was a slight curve to her belly, but that only increased her loveliness. "It's difficult to believe you really *are* having a child," I said. "Are you *quite sure*?"

"Dear Ra-ab, how could I be mistaken about anything so important? It will be about the fifth full moon from now when he is born."

"Moon children are often very magical."

"My nurse used to tell me that if I slept with the moon shining on my face Sekmet might catch me. But the second nurse said she was a silly old woman and that Nut would take me under her protection and perhaps give me into the keeping of her sister Hathor so that I should have the water magic. After that I slept with the moon on my face as often as possible, and even opened the shutters when it was cold and I had been told not to."

"Did you ever take any notice of being told not to?"

"Only when *you* tell me. Other people always seemed to tell me not to do things that I knew needed to be done."

"I used to sleep in the moonlight too. Perhaps if we hadn't we should never have dreamed about each other."

Meri was so disturbed by this idea that she put down the kohl stick with which she was lengthening her eyebrows and turned round to look at me. "Ra-ab, how awful! If you hadn't dreamed of me you mightn't have even noticed me."

"I mightn't have done . . . and the sun mightn't rise tomorrow in the East . . . but neither are very likely."

She kissed me, and then went on with the decoration of her face while I lay back and watched her.

"It is surprising what a lot of lovely things there are in marriage which I didn't expect," I said reflectively. "Didn't you expect marriage to be lovely?"

"I knew that with you it would be better than the Shining Land . . . which shows what a good prophet I am. But there are so many *extra* things as well. For instance, how could I have known how your back looks when you are plucking your eye-brows, or the beautiful curve of your arms when you lean forward to comb your hair? Nor had I seen your face in all its various stages, so very beguiling as it is at this moment, with one eyelid green and the other still unpainted. Don't you love talking nonsense just because we are so happy?"

She nodded. "I do; when we were first together we never seemed to have enough time for anything except making love and serious conversation."

"I thought I loved you more than was possible for a human being even before we were betrothed; but if I now met the man I then was I should call him a dullard and a fool for not having the wit to see a tenth of your quality."

"I wonder why other married people aren't happy like we are. Do you realize that of all the women I talked to about their husbands in the Royal City only two of them were really in love? A few thought they were, but it wasn't love as we know it. They seemed to be drawn together by a force outside themselves, like water weeds which become entangled with each other by the flow of the stream. Ptah doesn't make different kinds of animals obey a law which their nature does not allow them to follow in happiness, so why were people ever so stupid as to expect only one kind of marriage to be suitable for all kinds of humans."

"What would have happened if one of us had not been born in the same century as the other?"

"Then we should not have found any one with whom we could have taken the Oath of the New Name."

"Would you have married if you had never met me?"

"I think I should; for the real part of me, the part that isn't just Meri but all the people I have ever been and will be in the future, would have known that Meri's waking must be spent without you. I should have learned to adapt myself to those conditions, like a cat I once had who lost a paw when she was a small kitten and learned to run on three legs. I should have gone on being with you away from Earth, of course, but down here I should have known it was no use expecting our degree of perfection in a husband . . . or else gone on looking for you in the man I married and so always been disappointed."

"It would be terrible, Meri, to be married to you and yet to know that death would set you free to go to the person to whom you really belonged."

"It only seems like that to you because we have a standard by which to measure lesser relationships. If we hadn't grown old enough in spirit to be capable of the greater affinity we should be quite content with one which was not so permanent. Both of us must have many gold links with other people, and those links are not false just because there is another which is stronger. Many marriages, where two friends take comfort in each other's company, are very happy, even though they remain two people in soul and spirit in spite of having borne children together."

"Why aren't more people capable of our kind of marriage?"

"I think it is because they have shut themselves away from unity with the Gods and so cannot hope to find unity with each other. When two lotus have flowered they can become fertile, for they have achieved the winged element. If those same lotus had refused to thrust up their buds towards the light, and been content only to send more and more roots into the mud at the bottom of the river, they would continue to remain separate and uncreative until their mastery of water had given them strength to see the sun."

The evening before the Vizier's arrival, Meri and I went to Hotep-Ra, where those of the Retinue who were not accompanying Amenemhet to the House of the Nomarch would be entertained for two days, until the time came for them to continue their river journey to the point where he would re-embark.

As the colors of the Watchers were the same as the Oryx, all of us could wear their symbol, white and yellow ribbons on the right arm above the elbow, without arousing suspicion among those who did not belong to us. Pavilions had also been set up under shade-trees in fields adjoining the gardens of Roidahn's house, for here also there was a great assembly both from the Oryx and the two neighboring Nomes.

The State Barge was due to arrive in the early afternoon. At dawn the streets of Hotep-Ra were thronged with people, and the houses were being decorated with green boughs and garlands of flowers. Tall poles, painted in bands of white and yellow, flew long pennants every twenty paces of the road, which the procession would take some five hours to traverse, from Hotep-Ra to the House of the Nomarch.

Runners had been posted down-river to give news of the Progress, and at high noon Meri and I took our place beside Roidahn and Hanuk on the landing-stage. Both banks of the river were thronged with people, and among them went water-carriers and men with jars of wine or beer on their shoulders. The air rippled with laughter and snatches of excited conversation. A double row of decorated boats made an avenue to the quay; their sails had been taken down, the masts twined with flowering vines, and the sides hung with brilliantly colored cloths, so that in the distance they looked like small islands on which trees were growing.

The lookout at the bend of the river signaled that the procession was coming into sight. To the beat of a hundred oars the gilded barge of Pharaoh came into majestic view. Uniform as the wings of wheeling swallows, the double banks of oars shone golden as they caught the sun. Now we could see the great plumes of scarlet ostrich feathers as the eight fan-bearers stirred the air in rhythm with the rowers. At last the man who wore the White Crown, the crown he would soon wear as Pharaoh instead of only as the Royal Envoy, could be clearly seen. He might have been a statue, so still was he on the great throne of cedar-wood. In his hands were the Crook and Flail of Egypt; round his neck, the great pectoral of the High Priest of Ra at Noonday, a traditional title of the Lord of the Two Lands. Barge after barge came round the bend of the river; fifty in all, and the smallest of them of forty oars.

The gilding on the State Barge was so heavy it seemed made of solid gold, and in the brilliant sunlight it was almost too dazzling to look upon. As one, the rowers lifted their oars from the water, and so perfectly timed had been the steersman's order that she came alongside the quay smoothly as a swan. The eight giant Nubians who were the Royal Litter-Bearers lifted the throne in which Amenemhet still sat immobile and set it down on the dais which had been prepared for it in the center of the quay.

As the Nomarch's son I was the first to touch his instep with my forehead. Then Meri made similar obeisance, followed by Roidahn and Hanuk, and those other nobles who were with us in order of precedence. I found it difficult to believe that austere face had smiled so friendly a greeting to us on our marriage day only six months before. He was almost too Royal; and again I felt a little flicker of doubt in the background of my mind. Had Amenemhet sufficient warmth of humanity to be Pharaoh of the Watchers? Honor, and dignity, and justice, all of these he had; but were they enough?

The gilded carrying-throne led the procession, and next to it came Meri and I in a double litter. We were followed by the hundred courtiers who were to be our guests, all of them in open litters similar to ours. Every thousand paces the procession halted, for the bearers to rest and Amenemhet to receive homage from overseers and headmen who had come from all parts of the Nome. Wine and cooled fruit juices were handed round, and girls, wearing white tunics and wreaths of moon-daisies, offered baskets of fruit and platters of sweet-meats.

At sunset we were still an hour from our destination, and I was delighted to see how exactly the journey had been timed. While vermilion changed to violet in the West, torches flowered in the gathering dusk. Light seemed to leap from torch to torch, until fire flowed like water to border the road, the links of a necklace on the breast of Night.

A slight breeze had risen, flames streamed from the torches like the hair of a woman running. The warm light shone on the faces of the people who lined the way; white and yellow tunics, garlands of flowers, sparks showering upwards as though, knowing the littleness of gold, they scattered it on the air.

Meri's hand slid into mine. "For hundreds of years Pharaoh has never seen such *happy* people gathered to greet him. After seeing them he will never dare to let crowds in other parts of Egypt stare fearfully at Royal processions which are intended to impress them with the power of the Flail. He must be seeing this as I am, for once I too was a stranger to the Oryx. Only those born beyond our boundaries can know how miraculous it is to see every caste rejoicing together in peace."

The next day Amenemhet sat in conference with the Eyes of Horus. Father did not attend, saying that he must look after our many guests; but Meri and I were both there, with Roidahn, Hanuk, Kiyas, Sebek, and the future Nomarchs of the Hare, the Leopard, and the Tortoise. The Jackal Nome was not represented, for it had been decided that the present Nomarch's son would not prove a suitable ruler; his wounds were healed, but the lameness which he would suffer the rest of his life continued to make him too embittered to be reliable in his judgments.

As I listened to Amenemhet talking, I realized how long and important was the role he had played in the growth of the Watchers, and saw that Roidahn had not overestimated the Vizier's innate authority. Though we all recognized him as being already the rightful wearer of the Double Crown, while in conference there was no barrier of rank between us, it being fully recognized that though outside the Watchers we were all secondary to him, within our order we were valued only by the weighing of the heart, which takes no heed of birth nor office nor gold.

Roidahn had already acquainted him with all the latest developments in our plans, and now the three future Nomarchs gave him news of any changes which had taken place in their Nomes since he had last heard of them.

"Why is the Jackal not with us today?" he asked.

Roidahn then gave him the reasons why the Nomarch of the Jackal had not yet been chosen.

"I decree," said Amenemhet, "though, as always, if any of the Eyes of Horus wishes to oppose this decree he may now declare it, that when I am Pharaoh, Hanuk, son of Roidahn, shall rule the Jackal. And from that day forward, the Jackal shall be united with the Oryx, even as is Hotep-Ra."

The honor done to Hanuk was acclaimed, and I noticed it was to Kiyas that Hanuk first looked to see if she were pleased by the decision.

"I bring news of the North," continued Amenemhet. "The five Nomes are not united as are we of the South. They welcomed the building of the Royal City on the northern boundary of the Royal Nomes, for they took it as a sign that the Red Crown rules the White. My father, the Old Vizier, advised Pharaoh to go north instead of south when he left the Old Capital; but Pharaoh must thank his own wit for building his Summer Palace by the sea, for this move, though I doubt if he knows it, gained him the loyalty of the North. Only the Nomarch of the Ibex, the Nome on the western boundary of the Delta, has joined us unconditionally. The other four will, if it comes to open battle, join with the winning side. All the northern Nomarchs are eager to oppose the Royal Heir; they have all been to the Royal City and so had opportunity to judge him for themselves. Everywhere I found it whispered that when Pharaoh dies the younger prince will reign. Remember, that while the population of the North, if we do not include the Royal Nomes, is not so large as the South, they have a larger army. The warrior caste is more numerous, for it had always been the northeastern boundary which held the greatest threat of foreign invasion, and the Northern Garrison has by tradition been kept three times more powerful than the Southern Garrison.

"As long as I am only the Vizier, I must obey the Royal commands; and it may be that when Pharaoh dies I shall be away from the Royal City. When the time is come we must act swiftly, and so prevent Prince Men-het from appealing to the North for support against us. Once I am crowned they are unlikely to raise a rebellion, for I shall summon the Nomarchs to audience and decree to them that their rule shall be upheld and that under my authority their lands shall prosper as has not been possible for centuries. Their captains may grumble, for they know that under Men-het they would have been led into foreign territory and seen their families grow powerful on the victor's spoils. It will take time before they are content to fight against famine and pestilence instead of against Asiatics; content, not to invade but only to repel invasion. It may take years before the North finds the same tranquillity as the South. I am glad that I am still only thirty years old, for the Gods may allow me to continue to hold the balance of their justice until Fear has lost his last outpost in the land of Egypt."

Kiyas, in a voice which held no trace of her personal feelings, now asked, "What are your plans for Prince Men-het?"

"If I am in the Royal City, when the Forty-two Assessors indicate, by summoning Pharaoh before them, that the time is come for the Watchers to act, I may be able to declare myself Pharaoh without opposition; aided by those courtiers and officials, and certain of the Bodyguard, who have already given me the Oath of Allegiance. As fast as news can travel, my name as Pharaoh shall be declared in every Nome. It is to be hoped that Men-het can be persuaded that it would be useless to attempt action against me; even though it may mean his having to suffer imprisonment until he has agreed to uphold the Watchers. Thereafter he shall be restored to his rank of Captain of Egypt and enjoy even greater privileges than he did under the rule of his father."

"What if you cannot take him?"

"Then he and those who follow him will have to be overcome by force of arms."

"What if Pharaoh dies while you are here, or acting as the Royal Envoy on some other journey?"

"It is to be hoped that will not happen. If it does, I think it probable that Prince Men-het will pass judgment on the Royal Heir and then declare himself Pharaoh. The South will still proclaim that I am the rightful wearer of the White Crown; I hope the North will follow the South rather than join with the Royal Nomes. If they go against us, then for a time the Two Lands will be divided against each other, and the sign of the Watchers be painted in blood."

Then he addressed us all: "Some of you have waited for the Dawn nearly twenty years. The Watchers were born of Roidahn, who saw that the wise laws decreed by the grand-father of Ra-ab Hotep could bring peace not only to the Oryx but to all Egypt. Yet Roidahn saw that we needed a new authority; for laws in themselves are not enough until men have been taught how to administer them wisely. He has named his estate in truth, Hotep-Ra, 'the place where men learn the peace of Ra.'

"Roidahn saw that Egypt suffers from a pestilence, a pestilence born of famine. This pestilence flourished as well in fat years as in lean; for it was not food for their bellies that men lacked, though there were many who starved in the flesh also; it was truth for their spirit for which they hungered. Like a man carrying loaves into a famine village, Roidahn gave truth to all he met. He saw that those who had been starving grew strong, and in their turn took the bread of truth to others, who until that time had known no respite. Gradually the sores on the body of Egypt began to heal; the Oryx became the heart of her renewed body, and from it flowed fresh understanding, the Blood of Ptah, through channels which had long been dry. Roidahn is a wise physician; he knew that if a scab is pulled from a sore before the flesh beneath it is nearly healed, it will cause a fresh wound, and so he knew it took time for such a long-established pestilence to be cured. The famine victim must eat slowly if he is to recover; but now the time has almost come when the scabs can be shed, to show that the body of Egypt is clean.

"When I was nineteen, at the age I first met Roidahn, I thought Pharaoh was the cause of the pestilence. I had been brought up among old men, who were blind to the sorrows of the people they ruled and let the spiders of complacency spin shrouds which further obscured their narrow vision. If Roidahn had told me then that the Watchers had a plot to kill Pharaoh, I would have gladly joined them. I saw Pharaoh and his sycophants as the chains which held Egypt prisoner, and I longed to strike them off. So I told Roidahn he was only an impractical idealist, who, with the people he had gathered round him, pondered on abstractions while false priests waxed powerful and corrupt officials deprived our people of their rightful heritage.

"Roidahn told me that an idea could be stronger than a mighty phalanx of bowmen, surer than ten thousand mace-bearers, swifter than javelins. We had been together on a lion hunt near the Old Capital; he had killed two lions and I a third, and afterwards he came back to my father's house to be my guest." He looked at Roidahn and smiled. "I can see you as you were then, my most honored friend, sitting on the steps which led down to the main courtyard; still hear your voice saying, 'You think it is *only* an idea? Give me twenty years, and of that short span I have already worked for five. Tell one man the truth, and it will flow down the threads which join him to the friends of his long years; and from them it will flow through other threads, further and further. Yet, however far it travels, its strength will not diminish; no matter how many drink from the Jar of Truth the living water never grows less, though thousands grow strong because it has quenched their thirst.'

"Do you remember, Roidahn, how you picked up a stick and drew a pattern in the dust. You drew the outline of a man, and radiating from him were lines which joined him to his friends both past and future, and from them other lines to other men. You showed me those were the threads from which a united Egypt could be woven on the loom of peace. Then you made some dots, and said they represented people who have severed the threads through which their affection should flow. You told me they were like the thorn I was taking out of my arm—dead wood which must be cut out of the body of Egypt lest it cause corruption.

"I asked you, 'How do you find your Watchers?' And you replied, 'Only when love flows through a man can truth enter him; only when he recognizes truth can he know love. When I meet one in whom love is stronger than fear, I know him to be a potential Watcher, ready to be trained how best to use his strength to free others from Fear's dark domination.'"

Then, again speaking to us all, Amenemhet said, "That is how Roidahn found one of the Eyes of Horus. Think of him for a moment as he was then; a young man sitting in the courtyard of the house of the Old Vizier, talking to a boy and drawing in the dust a pattern for Egypt which in fifteen years has spread through every Nome. His idea has divided the living from the dead, the

clear-sighted from the blind, and many of those who were imprisoned it has set free.

"The stick which Roidahn then held has become the Crook
and the Flail of Egypt, and had he decided to keep them in his
own hands I should have counted it a great honor if he had made
me his vizier. But for reasons known to all of you he has put
those symbols of authority into my hands: may I be a channel of
sufficient love to be worthy of them."

PART VI

Torch-Bearer

FOUR MONTHS HAD PASSED: the preparations had been completed. Each man and woman was ready for the role they would have to play, and everywhere Watchers were waiting for the word to go forth, the word which would herald the rebirth of Egypt.

There were those within the Royal Palace who were sworn to the cause of Amenemhet, and so news of the slowly declining strength of Pharaoh reached us every few days. Amenemhet had twice been to the North since he had been with us in the Oryx, and was now there again, receiving tribute at the Summer Palace in the Royal Name. That he should be in the Royal City or, if not there, in the South when Pharaoh died, seemed essential to the smooth working of our plans, so we were always anxious when he had to go to the North.

In another twelve days he would be back at the Royal City, and as only yesterday a report to Roidahn had said that Pharaoh seemed stronger than he had been for some time, and the Royal Physician had declared that it was probable his master would linger into the new year, it seemed likely that the Hour of the Horizon would not come until Meri was no longer prisoner of our son. It was with relief that I told her this news, for as the time of the birth grew nearer she had become increasingly anxious that it might prevent her being able to come with me if the Oryx marched against Men-het.

It was now the third month of the Sowing, and the heat was not intense even at midday. During the morning we had been watching the scribes completing the fresco on the walls of the nurseries. It was a frieze of animals belonging to the South; first an oryx, followed by a hare, a jackal, a tortoise, a leopard, a gazelle, and the other standards of the Ten Nomes of the South . . . the oryx leading the rest into a river meadow, where grew the plants and fruits of our country. After we had talked to the scribes for a little while, I sent for our double litter and for a runner to tell the sailing-master to have ready the smallest of our boats, the one we used when we wished to be alone without a crew.

The airs were light, and we drifted down-stream until we found a place where trees grew down to the water's edge and I could tie up in the shade.

Meri, who had been drowsing in the bottom of the boat, yawned, and said contentedly, "When we are alone like this it is difficult to remember that the Hour still belongs with tomorrows instead of yesterdays. I have grown so used to living among happy people that the fear and cruelty which are the background of the Royal Nomes seem unreal as a nightmare; a dark dream which I am no longer dreaming."

"A dream does not cease to exist just because you are no longer dreaming it, any more than a dream becomes a reality just because you believe it."

She sighed. "I know. But sometimes I wish we could live within the Oryx and forget the rest of Egypt."

"Father used to think that would be possible, until Roidahn made him realize that to see oppression and be content to turn away, making the excuse that as it is beyond your immediate authority it is not your concern, would be like a fish in a trap, which tried to pretend the wicker basket was the cave it had chosen and not a prison, and that as long as it could forget the rest of the river the fisherman would never come. If the Watchers allowed power to remain in the wrong hands, we might continue to enjoy the peace of the Oryx for a few years—perhaps only for a few months; but eventually our indifference would return, just as swallows return, and they would have grown new feathers on their journey, gray as fear and black as a statue of Set."

"I know that too, Ra-ab. Egypt, as you once told me . . . or did I tell you, I forget? Egypt is like a human body; no part of it can know real tranquillity if another part of it is in pain."

The tone of her voice made me wonder if she herself was in pain, and I said anxiously. "You said you think he'll be born in about twenty days from now; are you sure it won't be sooner than that?"

"No, he's not ready yet." She curved a long, slender hand round her belly. "Oh, Ra-ab, I *do* wish women didn't have to become such silly shapes! The rest of me is the same as it always was, but the curve of my belly would match a sickle! I wish having a baby didn't take so long; I wish it didn't make me feel clumsy; I wish. . . ."

"Do you wish you weren't having him?"

"No, I never wish that; especially now he's so nearly finished. I dreamed of him again last night, not a very clear dream or I should have remembered to tell you about it before. It was as he used to be, not as he is now. You were in the dream too, and I think we were all women. The country we lived in then looked rather like Egypt, but not a part of it I have been to. I know he's going to be someone who is a friend of ours."

"I wonder if we shall recognize him as soon as he's born?"

"It will be funny seeing someone we know well, someone who perhaps used to be older and stronger than we were, suddenly wrapped up in a little body, that can't even walk or make intelligible words. It will be very exciting when he can tell us what he is thinking about; especially if he can remember being with us before."

"He should be grateful for all the bother you are going through for him."

"No, he shouldn't," said Meri decisively. "That is the one thing no mother should ever expect from her child, gratitude for the trouble of bearing it. It is the mother who should be grateful, or apologetic; and do everything she can to help her child to find sufficient wisdom for it not to be a waste of its time being born as her child."

"I wonder if a child knows whether its parents want it? In spite of the Women's Secret there must be many women who have children unexpectedly."

"Of course it does! If our son was unwanted he would feel as we should do if we were suddenly banished to live among hostile foreigners. Even if the foreigners tried to be kind to us we should probably hate them; even though, because we were hopelessly outnumbered, we should have to conceal our feelings under a pretense of gratitude, or even of affection. When I was very small I used to have a dream of walking through a meadow, picking white flowers and singing to myself because I was happy. Suddenly a great vulture swooped down and carried me off in its talons. Black clouds covered the sky and there was nothing but an awful roaring of wind. The vulture took me into a cave, narrow and dark; and then it turned into a black moth which wrapped me around and around in a kind of cocoon. That part of the dream wasn't very unpleasant, for quite often I dreamed myself back in the meadow. But I always woke up from there to find myself a prisoner who must struggle to get free. Then the bird came back and took me out of the cave; again I heard the wind roaring, and talons dug into my head and shoulders and hurt me. Then it dropped me, and there was a terrible feeling of falling which went on for a long time. I seem to be tangled up in the cocoon again, and there were faces looking down at me, faces of strangers I had never seen before. They leaned over me and their eyes looked as big and stupid as white stones. I screamed at them to go away, screamed for someone to come to set me free. They didn't understand what I was talking about for they were all foreigners who spoke a different language. There was no one there to whom I was linked with love; if there had been they would have understood, for the link would have carried thoughts between us. When I was older my nurse told me I was a very naughty baby because I cried so much. . . . I suppose she had forgotten what it was like to be a prisoner among strangers."

For almost the first time since I had been with Meri, I was resentful of the barriers imposed by time. I wanted to have been there when she was born, to take her away from those stupid, unthinking people and bring her up in the love which should be the natural protection of every child.

"No child could feel itself a stranger," I said, "if it is born to parents who love each other as we do. I don't expect our son will mind being born."

"He won't mind because he *isn't* a stranger. A child born to people with our degree of affinity never is; that's why if no one except people like us had children, being born wouldn't be called 'going into exile.' That's another thing we must teach our people, Ra-ab, that children should always be born of love and never for expediency."

That evening, those who welcomed Ra to his home after his day's journey carried banners of flame and coral-red. Pennants of cloud streamed up from the West, until, with the rising of the North Wind, the last fires of sunset were quenched in the wine-dark sky. The sail curved out as though it tried to reflect the curve of the new moon. Meri leaned back against my knees as I sat at the steering-oar. The water was smooth and cool as black linen, and the whisper of the boat against the current was gentle as the wings of a night-bird in the stillness.

As we rounded the last bend of the river the boat lay over a little to meet the wind. The moon was brighter now, and I could see the shape of the trees beyond the landing-stage. I saw a torch moving along the path to the water-steps, and idly wondered if someone was going down to spear fish.

A man stood waiting for us to come in, the torch held high above his head as he leaned forward, trying to see into the darkness. I shouted to him; and he waved the torch three times . . . the signal agreed on by the Watchers. It meant, "Pharaoh is dead: the Hour of the Horizon is come!"

It seemed as though the Ra-ab who was traveling to Hotep-Ra as fast as relays of runners could carry him, was not one man but two. The Lover, for the first time, parted from his wife; her kisses still warm on his lips, her voice still so much more real than the padding feet of the litter-bearers who were carrying him so swiftly away from her. The Captain, eager to prove his powers of leadership, thankful that the hour for which he had trained for seven years was now at hand.

Meri had stood at the gate to watch me go, looking so small and valiant in the flickering light of the torch held by the gate-keeper. Her farewell had been, "Remember, Ra-ab, that my heart and all of me that is real goes with you. It is only my body which must stay here, and until you return it will be no more a part of me than the kilts which will stay folded in the cedar chest until your homecoming."

So much had happened in the last two hours. . . . When Meri and I had reached the Great House it had been to find a scene of controlled excitement. The message of Pharaoh's death had arrived early in the afternoon, and immediately Kiyas had left for Hotep-Ra, the place of assembly for the women under her command as it was for all the soldiers of the Oryx. From village to village the news had been sent throughout the Nome; during daylight by columns of smoke, after dusk by torches. Those who could reach the Great House in time would gather there to hear

my father declare Amenemhet, Pharaoh of the Two Lands. Elsewhere I knew that people would be streaming into the towns to
hear the same pronouncement made by their overseer, at dawn,
the traditional time for announcing a new Pharaoh. In every
Nome of the South similar scenes would be taking place; and
many thousands of people would hear also that henceforward
they were to be ruled by a new Nomarch as well as by a new Pharaoh. Only in the Gazelle was there any fear of disturbance, but
the Old Nomarch, an uncle of the man chosen by the Watchers,
had long been in his dotage and if he refused to abdicate it was
unlikely that any would offer him serious support.

I wished that I was one of those who have the faculty of looking on water and seeing it as a window to another part of Earth,
but as Ra-ab I no longer had that power; the North had not yet
revealed her intentions and I must wait on a messenger to tell me
if the Oryx must go to war. Every two thousand paces the bearers were replaced by fresh runners, and so well were they trained
that they hardly slackened speed as the poles moved from one
man's shoulder to another's.

Before dawn I came in sight of the torches of Hotep-Ra; other
lines of torches were converging there, so I knew that many had
arrived before me. I met Sebek where the path from the soldiers'
village joined the road; he told me that three hundred men had
already reached him and that by noon we should be ready to
march.

"Kiyas's women are all here," he said. "Either she got a signal
to them first, or else they are more eager even than the men, for
they are all here, two hundred and twelve of them. They are
camped in the field adjoining the house Roidahn gave to Kiyas.
You had better go down and see her as soon as Roidahn knows
you've arrived." He looked up at the sky. "No, you won't have
time before he makes the formal declaration that Amenemhet is
Pharaoh. I was on my way to hear him, so we can go together."

In the great square, around which the town of Hotep-Ra was
built, more than two thousand people were assembled. Standing
on the plinth of the statue of Ra, was Roidahn, surrounded by the
great concourse of his pupils who with him waited for the Dawn
he had long promised them.

Light flooded up from the eastern cliffs; and the Watchers saw Ra, in whose name they asked for power, ascending into his majesty. Then did Roidahn speak to them:

"In the name of Ra, the Hour of the Horizon is come! Your eyes are open; and now you shall see the fulfillment of your work. Your ears hear the Word; the sound of tribulation shall cease and where there was weeping now shall there be laughter. The mouth of Fear shall be dumb, for Egypt listens to the silver voice of the Goddess of Truth. Her voice shall be echoed out of your mouth; it shall command tyranny into exile, and summon peace and wisdom to be the Twin Rulers of the Two Lands. Love is the knife which cut the shackles that made you a prisoner; now you are free, ready to go forth to loose those who are still bound. Ra is the Lord of Love, and Will is the power of Horus, his son. Father and Son together have made you strong: in their name send Fear to dwell forever in the tomb that soon will enclose the body of he who was not Pharaoh. Pharaoh is dead; and in the name of the Watchers, Pharaoh is born again. Hereby I declare to you his name: Amenemhet; who will rule as Iss-hotep-ab-Ra— wisdom in peace by the love of Ra."

I was standing, as were all the others, with my hands upstretched in prayer. More than ever before, the Life of the Gods, by which all things are made to live, flowed down into me. Thus should be the Egypt of the future, with hands upstretched to meet the sun; never again to cower like a slave beneath the flail.

As the crowd began to disperse I saw Hanuk and made my way toward him. "There is no more news yet," he answered to my eager question. "There has not been time for a runner to reach here from the Royal City, though Father hopes for one by this evening. Amenemhet must still be in the Summer Place, and it was arranged that if the death occurred while he was there he would declare himself Pharaoh without waiting for our support. He thinks the North unlikely to offer serious opposition, though they will not lend armed force against Men-het. I think we should march before noon, to meet the Hare on the northern boundary of the Jackal. We must not enter the Royal Nomes until we hear what Men-het intends to do."

Suddenly I realized that now he *was* the Jackal. "You are a

Nomarch now," I said. "Why are you here instead of in your chief city?"

"I can depend on the loyalty of the old Nomarch's son; I was afraid he might feel bitter toward us, but he wants to join the Watchers and says he is glad not to have to spend his life patiently administering our laws. Last time I saw him he was busy on the plans for a new aqueduct and had little thought for anything else. He appreciates my trusting him to declare me Nomarch when he gives out the news of the Royal Death to the people. His father was willing to let the succession pass to me and has been impatient to abdicate for some time."

I knew that Hanuk would have been in the Nome which now belonged to him had it been necessary, but I also knew that only the wish to be with Kiyas would have kept him away. I wanted to see her, and found her busily engaged in apportioning loads among the women.

She was saying, "I know that ten javelins are not so heavy as fifty arrows, but they are more unwieldly to carry and so I consider that a fair division. If you are not satisfied you had better go into the other court where the loads of food are being given out. They're not too heavy; three days ago I carried one of them ten thousand paces, during the noon hours, to make sure."

As soon as I got her alone, I said, "Why did you keep Hanuk here? It was his hour of triumph, when he should for the first time have entered his city as Nomarch."

"It isn't my fault," she said. "As soon as the news reached us I told him he ought to go; but he said he didn't approve of unmarried Nomarchs and wanted to make his formal entry with his wife beside him."

"Meaning you?"

She nodded. "I told him he might have to wait a long time. I love him very much, but I'm not going to marry him while I still keep thinking about Men-het. That's why I really made Hanuk promise to let me come to the battle . . . if there is one. I have been haunted by the thought that it is partly through me that Men-het will fight against Egyptians. Though since I've seen Amenemhet I know he's the right man to be our Pharaoh."

"Amenemhet would have been chosen without you, Kiyas.

What you told Roidahn only made the choice still clearer."

She was testing the thong which held a bundle of arrows. Her hair swung forward and hid her face. "I know it had very little to do with me," she said, "but I still feel responsible that Hanuk and Men-het will be fighting on opposites sides. That's why I want to be there, so as to be sure of my heart."

"And what if Men-het doesn't fight?"

"I'm praying for that. Then I should know he hasn't even the kind of courage I loved him for; he would be like a dream from which I would be thankful to have wakened. Oh, Ra-ab, I have prayed so hard that when the messenger comes it will be to tell us that Men-het has fled the country . . . then I should be free to love Hanuk with all of me."

"It must be hard for Hanuk."

"I know it is. I wish I didn't love him so much, for then I needn't have been so honest with him. I've never lied to Hanuk, even in the little things. When I found I couldn't, even though I knew the truth would hurt him, it showed me I loved him."

As the Jackal adjoined the Reed, most southerly of the Royal Nomes, it was at the Jackal's soldiers' village, about six thousand paces within their northern boundary, that the armies of the Oryx, the Hare and the Jackal, had agreed to foregather. The Leopard, the Gazelle, and the Tortoise, would hold themselves in readiness to join us, and the four smaller Nomes, in the extreme south, were to wait until events showed whether they were needed to come to our assistance or to repel any attack made by Southern Nubia, which for a long time had refused to pay tribute to Egypt and might take this opportunity either to attack the Southern Garrison or to invade those parts of the Land of Gold which acknowledged Pharaoh as their Overlord.

The army of the Hare was taking the West Road, so although they would pass through part of the Oryx, we should not join them until we reached the meeting-place. The captains of the Jackal were all well known to Hanuk, so they had agreed with enthusiasm to acknowledge him as Captain of the Nome as well as Nomarch. Although Hanuk, myself, and the new Nomarch of the Hare were of equal rank, each being Captain of a Nome, I was the only one who had held the rank during the old reign, and it was because of this that Roidahn had put me in authority over the others.

An hour before noon, marching at the head of the column between Hanuk and Sebek, I took the road to the north. Sebek had trained his men to keep in step, and to the rhythm of their sandaled feet they sang the traditional warrior songs. After the soldiers, who march four abreast, each Hundred under its own leader, came Kiyas with her following of women. They were singing the same songs as the men, and I was amused to see that she had taught them to keep even more precise ranks than my soldiers. When I commented on this to Sebek, he grinned, and said:

"By the time she's finished with us we shall all be trained as dancers! I pretend that I don't know she has been teaching some of them to use a bow. Many of them learn more quickly than men, though of course they can't fly an arrow so far."

"If Men-het looks like defeating us," I said, jestingly, "we can call on them instead of sending for reinforcements from the Leopard."

"You wouldn't have to call on them, they'd not wait for the asking! If we get hard pressed they will do more than *carry* arrows, and the knives they have been whetting so carefully will slit more than a duck's throat. It's lucky for the husbands that their women have followed them out of love, else they would have found one of Kiyas's soldiers a rough bedfellow!"

"Do you think Men-het will fight?"

"If he doesn't I'll barter my captain's armlet for a sickle, and cut down corn instead of rebels."

"Aren't *we* the rebels?"

He looked startled, and then said, "For a moment I thought you were serious. *Us* rebels! We're loyal Egyptians who refuse any longer to see our country being ruled by imposters. Driving out the invader, that's what we're doing. What does it matter if they are Egyptian born or belong to the people 'whose name must never be spoken'? By the way, it's such a long time since their name was spoken that I don't know who they were! Do you?" I shook my head, and he went on, "As I was saying, it doesn't matter whether the usurper is a foreigner or an Egyptian, if he can't use his power properly he's got to go . . . personally I hope we'll have a chance of hurrying his flight! Many's the time I'd have liked to kill Men-het, and now perhaps I'll have a chance to do so."

He lapsed into silence. Hanuk seemed to be lost in his own thoughts and I wondered if he would have found Sebek's comments interesting. Kiyas would not lack for champions in the coming battle!

When we reached our destination it was to find that the army of the Hare had arrived before us. Quarters had been arranged in the House of the Captains for Kiyas and her women, and the rest of us were sleeping in the open. On long marches, each soldier carried a blanket as well as his cloak, and these were now set out in orderly rows with their owners' weapons beside them; the Hare on the west of the practice ground, ourselves on the east. Fires had been lit, over which small cattle were being roasted on spits, and by each fire were baskets of loaves, lettuce and onions, and jars of beer.

Ever since we had entered the Jackal, the roads had been lined with crowds who had come to acclaim Hanuk; and it was easy to see there was widespread rejoicing that he was now their Nomarch. Next to the House of the Captains a large pavilion had been set up in which an informal banquet would be held in his honor. Before this began, he received the Oath of Fealty from the overseers of near-by towns who had taken this opportunity to greet him. Kiyas sat next to him as though they were already formally betrothed, though she was wearing a plain yellow tunic, which, except for the gold oryx clasp on her shoulder, was the same as those worn by her soldiers; she looked worthy to rule not only a Nome but to have been the Royal Wife.

None of the other captains had women with them, so at the banquet Kiyas was the only woman present. All of us gave the same consideration to her suggestions for the strategies we might adopt as though she had been a man; but I think few of them forgot that she was a woman, and beautiful. I drank a silent toast to Ra, asking him that she might marry Hanuk. Each was a perfect complement to the other, like enough to have been brother and sister, though he, the tallest man in the Oryx, had nearly a cubit more in height.

Soon after we had finished eating there was a shout outside, taken up by many voices, "A messenger for the Captain of the Oryx!"

A panting runner came into the pavilion and gave the message into my hand. I read it aloud. "The younger prince stabbed his brother to death and has proclaimed himself to be the Lord of the Two Lands. Many of those loyal to Amenem-het have fled from the Royal City, and Men-het has given orders that all those captured are to be killed as traitors . . . though there is news that the Royal Nomes are letting many of them escape to the South without hindrance. Men-het has raised his standard in the Royal City and the whole of the Royal Army has declared itself loyal to him, except for a few who have either been massacred or managed to escape. It seems that Men-het has not yet decided whether to march North or South, and his army is encamped near the Royal City. It is thought he is waiting for news from the North, as he still hopes that it will join him. Amenemhet asks that you bring the Royal Army to battle, for the North is waiting to join the winning side and if you delay they may decide against our Pharaoh . . . and so the Red Crown and the White will once more be divided against each other."

I raised my wine cup, "I give you Amenemhet, Pharaoh; under whose rule Egypt will be reborn. I give you the Watchers of the Horizon, who march to battle at dawn!"

The Oryx Marches

AFTER CONSULTING WITH the other captains I decided that our armies should enter the Reed in three columns, not only to protect us from surprise, but so that the spies which Men-het was sure to have posted on all the roads leading north might find it more difficult to estimate our full strength. There were three available roads; the central one, a Royal Road, was broad and in most places paved with stone; the western road was little more than a wide track, linking the villages on the edge of the desert; the third followed the western bank of the river and passed through the Old Capital. The three roads were seldom separated from each other by more than a few thousand paces, and if any of the columns were warned, by one of the Watchers in the villages near which they would pass, that Men-het's army was disposed in force ahead of us, there would be time for us to close our ranks before the battle was joined. I decided to take the central road so as to keep more easily in touch with both the other armies: the Hare took the western road and the Jackal that on our right.

If it were true that Men-het was waiting for news of the North before taking any action, it was unlikely that we should find serious opposition during the first day's march, but as a precaution we adopted the formation considered the safest while passing through hostile territory. Where the width of the road permitted, the soldiers went six abreast; each Hundred under its leader, who at the first sign of danger would deploy into a depth of three ranks. In front would be the javelin-throwers, who after their attack would crouch down to allow free aim to the bowmen, and behind these again stood the mace-bearers, who would pass through the other ranks to enter the fight at close quarters as soon as the javelin-throwers and bowmen had played their part.

I told Kiyas that her women must henceforward move in double file, with a file of mace-bearers on each side of them, whose first duty would be the protection of the women; and instead of their coming at the end of the column the women were to move up to allow of a rearguard of two Hundreds.

Once we had crossed the boundary of the Jackal it was easy to see which villages had suffered under the old rule and which had been protected by a kindly headman; those who had been oppressed hurried out of their houses, or came running across the fields from the scattered farms, to shout greetings to us or to bring gifts of bread and fruit to the marching men; while the others were suspicious of any change in their accustomed system of rulership. It was evident that news of our coming had preceded us, for people had gathered at the wells, which, as on most of the Royal Roads, were spaced at intervals of about six thousand paces. At a few points there were demonstrations of open hostility, but the only weapons they used were stones, or clods of earth, which were easily deflected on our shields. No one was hurt except a mace-bearer, who was cut over the eye by a stone flung by a small boy, who, seeing what he had done, scuttled to his mother for protection. The mother, when she saw the mace-bearer had no intention of pursuing the child but instead shouted to him, "You throw so straight it's a pity you aren't old enough to join our army!"... ceased to stare sullenly at us and began to smile and wave, at the same time administering a sharp slap to her belligerent offspring.

Toward evening we came in sight of the Old Capital, and here the Jackal joined us, to avoid passing through a thickly populated part of the Nome. Hanuk said he had told his men to scatter among several near-by farms, all of which he knew to be owned by people friendly to us, and to wait there until he sent them further instructions. They would provide a rear-guard in case any attack developed from the south, and as soon as we had found a suitable place to spend the night a messenger would be sent to tell them our location. Soon afterward a runner from the Hare arrived to tell us they were encamped as planned, in the gardens of an overseer who had long been a Watcher.

As we drew nearer to the Great Pyramids we saw a herd of five bulls being driven along the road ahead of us. They were in charge of a temple servant, who, by the color of his tunic, we knew to belong to the Temple of Sekmet which had recently been built outside the Old Capital. Two priests belonging to the same temple were following the herd, and when I drew level with them they pretended to be engaged in earnest conversation and not to have noticed the approach of the column. I asked the elder of them in whose name the bulls were to sacrificed, and he answered, "Sekmet," in a harsh and arrogant voice.

Priests, even false priests, enjoy immunity from armed interference in their duties, but I considered myself fully justified in replying, "As Sekmet is no longer to be worshipped in Egypt, by Royal Decree of Amenemhet, Pharaoh, she can no longer command a sacrifice. Therefore your five bulls are to be driven in the wake of my army, for I have no doubt that Ra will be pleased that they should be eaten by the soldiers acting in his name."

The priest began to curse me in monotonous tones. Had he been a vehicle of power his words might have blasted me like a stroke of lightning, but as he was only an ignorant man relying on a ritual he did not understand, we were no more affected than if his voice had been the whirring of a grasshopper.

An abandoned country estate, with much of its garden walls still intact, lay to the east of the road, from which it was concealed by a small wood. Had not Sebek known from a previous journey, that it was there, I might not have seen what an ideal place it was for us to camp. It was already dusk, and after two days of marching the men were in need of a night's rest. I more than half expected Kiyas to tell me that many of her women found the pace too hard and wanted to go home, for I myself was weary after marching almost continuously from dawn to sunset. When I questioned her, Kiyas told me, rather scornfully, that her women were less tired than the men. As though to prove the truth of her words they were already hurrying about, getting food ready and gathering fuel for the cooking-fires.

As we did not wish to make our presence too conspicuous, only small fires were lit, and around these the men gathered, to roast, on the points of their daggers, collops cut from one of the slaughtered bulls. The men slept in the garden, with their women beside them; but Kiyas, Sebek, Hanuk and myself, unrolled our sleeping-mats in the only room of the ruined house which had a roof still partially intact.

I was the last to fall asleep, and for a long time lay watching the moon through a hole in the ragged thatch. A large rat ran across my feet, and disappeared through the opening that had long forgotten the door which had once closed it. There was a slight breeze, and above my head a decaying palm-leaf flapped languidly in the draft. Kiyas was half turned toward me, the moon shining on her face, which looked calm and aloof as the silver mask of a mummy.

I woke once during the night, disturbed by another flurry of rats. Kiyas and Hanuk had moved together in their sleep. His left arm was round her and she was curled up beside him. I tried to pretend Meri was beside me, but it did little to assuage my loneliness for her. I argued with myself that I should be thankful she was safe in the Oryx, yet all the time I knew that we should have both been so much happier if we had been together, even though there should be danger as well as rats to disturb our sleep.

The previous day I had arranged for two of my best scouts to travel in the litters brought with us for the wounded, so that at night they would be fresh to seek such information as I might need. They had gone to the Old Capital as soon as they had shared the evening meal, and at dawn returned to report to me.

The first scout said that all seemed quiet in the town, though he had heard that the High Priest of Sekmet's temple had made a solemn declaration to the people that Men-het was the Pharaoh appointed by the Gods, and that any who followed the Vizier who was attempting to usurp the Double Crown would be condemned to a thousand years of torment in the Caverns of the Underworld. This condemnation he claimed to have been personally authorized by Set. He had then exhorted the assembled people to do everything in their power to hinder the progress of the "rebellious South." He also told them that as the army of their Nome had followed Men-het to the Royal City the time for armed resistance by the populace had not yet come, and that they must be patient and wait for the rebel armies to be annihilated by the forces under the command of their rightful Pharaoh. The High Priest then went on to suggest that in spite of the need for patience there were other means by which they could help their country; such as poisoning the wells at which we were likely to drink, and leaving baskets of fruit by the roadside in which small snakes or scorpions had been thoughtfully concealed. He added that this might prove especially valuable as it would make us suspicious of accepting further offerings such as had been given by those misguided enough to make us welcome.

When the first scout had finished his story, I asked him, "Did the High Priest tell the people that this too was Set's advice?"

"I don't know," he answered. "But, from whispers I heard, most of them think he had no right to tell them to poison the wells. They reminded each other that if they were caught doing it they might be condemned according to the law, and die the Death of the Two Vipers. I don't think we need worry about the wells, and if we have any doubts we could always make the well-keeper drink first, and see if he was frightened."

"On how many houses did you see our sign?"

"About one in every three had the twisted rope, and on about every fifth door I saw our scales, in the form which means 'he who dwells here has been condemned to judgment of the Watchers.'"

"Did you hear of any disturbance when Men-het was proclaimed?"

"There was a good deal of muttering, and some said that as he
wasn't the Royal Heir he must have murdered his brother and so
wasn't fit to be Pharaoh. There were a few who shouted for the
Vizier, but the overseers' whipmen were swift to quell those protests."

He pointed to the scout who had not yet spoken and said, "He's
got an idea there is trouble hatching, though he's got no real
proof."

"What have you seen?" I asked. "It doesn't matter about proof,
an instinct often gets nearer the truth than a fact does."

"It isn't exactly what I've *seen*, nor rightly what I've *heard*. The
army leaving the Old Capital and going to the Royal City . . . it
doesn't seem natural to me. Why not stay and do battle here
instead of letting us pass unhindered right through this Nome
and into the next one? An army's first duty is to protect its own
Nome, Pharaoh or no Pharaoh. The army of the Reed was
famous for its courage, and doubly particular of its honor since it
was slighted by the capital being moved to a rival Nome. Yet at
Men-het's orders they marched out of their quarters, leaving
them empty as a barn floor in a famine. Marched through the
town and took the road to the North, every one of them, meek as
a flock of sheep! Only three old store-keepers left behind, and
two of them are blind in one eye. Now there's another thing; you
would think this would have made the people resentful, and keen
to transfer their loyalty to us. But are they? No! I hung round the
market-place, and I've been in six taverns . . . not to mention con-
versing with several young women who aren't particular about
being free in their talk to strangers. Nearly every one of them
wants Men-het to keep the Crown; and when I said I thought it
was funny his taking their army away, they shut up quick and
wouldn't say any more."

"You think they have left the barracks only to hide somewhere
else in the town?"

The first man answered this question. "No. They marched out
all right, one of our people counted them as they passed, seventeen Hundreds of them; more than half of them bowmen and the
rest mace or javelin."

"Do you think they came back into the town after night-fall?"

"Not into the town they didn't. I had a friend posted at every entrance pylon and no one passed through except a few women frightened by rumors of war, who thought they would be safer in the town than on isolated farms until things were peaceful again."

The other man said stubbornly, "He's right enough there, but I still think they came back after it was dark."

"Where could they be hidden?"

He scratched his head reflectively. "That's what I've been trying to puzzle out. Trees, now . . . you'd want a lot of trees to hide seventeen Hundreds, and what's round this house is the biggest wood for a long way. They need a building, a nice, large, *unsuspicious* kind of building."

I realized what he was groping toward. "The Temple of Sekmet! Soldiers hidden in the priests' quarters, waiting to attack our rear as soon as we'd passed. That's why we've been allowed to come so far without any attempt being made to stop us. Men-het thought we should be defeated before we reached the Royal City, and that when the North heard we had been beaten without even being engaged by his main army they would think the South was finished and transfer their allegiance to him. Are you too tired to go out again immediately? If so I can send another scout."

"No, let me go," he said eagerly.

"Rub ashes into your hair and wear only a loin-cloth; pretend you are wandering in your wits. Go to the temple and beg for alms, try to get into the inner court, and if you can't do that find out which gate leads into the priests' quarters. If they turn you away that will help to confirm your suspicions. A crowd of soldiers makes a noise even if they have been ordered to keep quiet. Keep as close as you can to the wall where they may be hidden, and listen. Come back to me as soon as you have anything to report, and be sure no one follows you. You had better have something to eat before you go, and then be as quick as you can."

I went to tell the others what I thought might be Men-het's strategy, and Hanuk and the rest agreed with me.

"I will send a messenger back to my men," said Hanuk, "to tell them to wait at the village south of the town. The main road doesn't pass through it, and it is one of the few places in this

Nome where everyone is a Watcher. One of the Royal Granaries adjoins this village, and I know that it is more than half empty. All the Jackal can hide there until they are needed and the village people will supply them with food and water. I will tell them to converge on the granary from several directions; most of them will manage to avoid being seen, for the water-channels in this part of the country are especially deep and afford good cover for anyone crawling along them."

"A few of them are sure to be seen," said Kiyas.

"It doesn't matter if they are, for they would probably be taken for soldiers deserting from Men-het. I don't think anyone would try to stop them, for the field-workers are nearly all in favor of us and it is only in the big towns that Men-het can hope to find many enthusiastic followers."

"Although we are fairly well concealed here," said Kiyas, "Men-het must have had spies on the road and know where we are encamped; even if we've been lucky enough to conceal the whereabouts of your men and the Hare. As we entered the Royal Nomes he must know we want to join battle with him. He also knows we have been told he has withdrawn to the Royal City, and will expect us to follow him there with all speed. It's no use our making a feint march and coming back here after dark like the others did. We must keep them where they are until we have completed a plan for their defeat; but we mustn't let them suspect we have any idea they are still here or we shall lose all the advantage of a surprise attack, which they at present think is going to be theirs."

"They know we have come a long way in two days," I said, "and therefore would not think it suspicious if I decide to rest my men before going on."

"It's a risk we can't take. For some reason we don't yet know, they want to give battle somewhere north of where we are now. It must be a good plan, otherwise they would have attacked us last night. Therefore they won't attack us as long as we stay here *unless* they suspect we've got wind of their plans. We must have time to send scouts ahead to find out if there is another army between us and the Royal City; hidden as this one is, so as to make a surprise attack on both the front and rear of our column."

"We'll have to risk their suspicion."

"No, we needn't. I suggest that some of my women go to a few of the outlying farms, especially to those we know are disloyal to us, on the pretext of trying to get milk or eggs. They run a slight risk of being attacked, but I don't think it at all probable. They must pretend to be disgruntled with the hardships of the march, and boast that they have managed to make such a nuisance of themselves that you have had to promise them several day's rest. They can also say you are trying to decide whether it would be best to send them home with a small escort to protect them, or whether to insist that they continue to follow the army. The word will soon go around that most of the soldiers of the Oryx are women, and dissatisfied women at that!"

"Why make us a laughing-stock?" objected Sebek.

"Because if the enemy is scornful of us it will give us an easier victory; and so make it easier to prove that all who go against us are fools."

Warrior Frieze

INFORMATION WAS FLOWING through our prearranged channels even more smoothly than I had expected, and by late that afternoon enough news had been received for us to be virtually certain that there was no army between us and the immediate vicinity of the Royal City. Reports brought in by the scouts I had sent out earlier in the day had been sufficient to confirm my opinion that the army of the Reed was hidden in the priests' quarters of the Temple of Sekmet. There were traces that a large number of people had recently passed along the paths leading to the north gate of the temple enclosure, and the very fact that an attempt had been made to obliterate these traces made their presence doubly significant. The discipline of the hidden soldiers must have been excellent, for the scout, in spite of having managed to keep close to the wall for nearly two hours, had heard nothing but a low murmur, to which, had his suspicions not already been aroused, he would have paid no attention.

Six of the women who Kiyas had sent out had each brought back stories which were curiously similar. Though they made no secret that they were following the army of the Oryx, and we knew that the owners of all the farms they had visited regarded the South as rebels, they had everywhere been made welcome and given the food for which they asked. When they began to retail their grievances they found a sympathetic audience, which, after exclaiming against the injustice of making women behave like soldiers, urged them to refuse to go any further until they had had several days rest . . . always the *several* days were stressed.

"It is quite obvious," said Kiyas, "that those people had all been warned what to say. The enemy must have known we have women with us, and therefore thought it probable we would send them out to forage for us. Why do they want us to delay here?"

"Perhaps Men-het's strategy needed time to ripen," suggested Hanuk.

"Then why don't they make a surprise attack on us here?" I said. "Dawn this morning would have been the best time for that, and would have found us comparatively unprepared."

"As they *didn't* attack," said Kiyas, "I think it proves they want to fall on us from the rear when we have gone further north."

Here Sebek joined the conversation. "By now Men-het knows of the Watchers, and he must be beginning to realize how widespread is our power. He may even know that Horus has a hundred Eyes born of one man's vision, and that with them there are more than ten thousand Watchers. He knows that if one of us, especially one of the Hundred of Horus, remains alive, this same fire we are now kindling may flare up again. We are not only an army he must defeat, we are individuals whom he must kill, or else wait for us to compass his postponed destruction."

"Sebek is right," said Hanuk. "But I think Men-het, with his superior strength of arms, must feel confident of his power to destroy us in battle. His renown as a soldier has been justly earned: remember how he defeated the Puntites when they outnumbered him ten to one, and how he put down the rebellion in Nubia with only three hundred men when they must have mustered nearly five thousand untrained troops against him. But if he only defeats us as an army he must know there will only be a lull before we rise again. That's what the hidden army is for, to see that none of us get back to the South. He will decree that as we are rebels we have renounced the honors of war, and then neither our wounded nor our women can hope for quarter. He will reaffirm his father's decree that anyone who raises a hand against the Royal House is condemned to death by torture; and that anyone who may shelter or succor us, even if it is only to give water to a dying man, shall receive the same punishment. By that means Men-het will find an excuse to destroy not only ourselves but any other Watcher; anyone who has rendered us assistance, in however trivial a degree, will come under the edict and be put to death." He turned to Kiyas, and asked her, "What do you think? Am I being unjust?"

She paused a moment before replying, and then said slowly, "Men-het has never broken the Warriors' Code, and his soldiers would never dare to kill a wounded enemy or to treat captive women and children except with honor. But while you were speaking I remembered the tone of his voice when he said to me, 'You forget, I shall be *Pharaoh*. Pharaoh can do no wrong.' He thinks he *is* Pharaoh; and therefore has the right to destroy without pity anything which imperils the security of his rule. He will think of himself not only as Pharaoh, but as Egypt herself. All who oppose him will cease to be Egyptians; they will be the foreign invaders . . . and his family have never been merciful to foreigners. If it is true that he himself killed his brother, the fear of the blood-guilt may have made him cruel."

"Why should it?" I objected, "I would have killed the Royal Heir myself, and felt no compunction."

"You would," she said. "You knew that he was only a man, depraved and insane. Men-het has hated him since they were children, but he still believes his brother was half divine. He couldn't help doing so, for if he denied it he would have to deny the power of the royal blood, and so cease to believe in his own omnipotence. That's why he would have been so dangerous as a ruler: he believes, with the most profound sincerity, that his power over his people should be absolute, not because he is divinely inspired but because he is himself divine."

"Then you agree with me?" said Sebek. "He will try to destroy us, however dishonorable the means?"

"That is true of everything I know of his character . . . a brilliant piece of strategy which he will carry out ruthlessly because he believes it is serving a rightful purpose."

"Shall we wait here and besiege the Reed, or send an envoy to challenge them to give battle?" asked Hanuk.

"Besieging them is no use," said Sebek. "As soon as Men-het found what we were doing, he would come down in a flank attack, sending a strong force, either by river or by the desert road, to bar our line of retreat."

I then put forward my opinion. "This is more than a conflict between armies. Of course if all else fails we shall have to kill as many of them as are needed to force them to surrender; but I have a plan which may give us a victory with little bloodshed, and may even turn the Old Capital and its soldiers into our friends. If we can prove to them that Sekmet can give them no protection, then they may become loyal children of Ra and so be of our company."

"Are you suggesting that our priests should go and talk to them?" said Sebek a little scornfully. "They would gain no entry to the temple, still less a hearing."

"Our priests do take a part in our plan; or at least three of them do, the Horus priests, Ptah-aru, Ptah-atho, and Kepha-Ra. I have consulted with them, and they say that what I suggest is in accordance with the great tradition; they have instructed me to tell you that what I propose to do has their entire agreement; it now only remains for you to approve the plan."

After they had listened to what I had to say, my plan, with a few minor alterations, was adopted; and immediate preparations were begun to put it into effect.

Hanuk sent a messenger to his men, telling them to join us as soon as darkness had fallen. Another messenger went to the Captain of the Hare; who was also to advance under cover of the first darkness, but not to come nearer than two thousand paces of our present encampment and to lie hidden in a long-dry watercourse, which once must have carried an overflow from the Great Lake in the time when the Lake was much larger than in our day. Kiyas made preparations to receive the wounded; for she and her women would remain in the encampment on which I ordered a guard of a hundred mace-bearers.

I spent the day in giving detailed instructions to the men for the exact role they would have to play in the coming operation, and in superintending the construction of a hundred scaling ladders; each of these being strong enough to bear the weight of four men and of a length to reach the top of the outer wall of the temple, which was fourteen cubits high. Fortunately we had a quantity of rope among our stores, and the trees surrounding our camp afforded all the other necessary material.

I had come prepared for an attack by night, and each man had been provided with a dark blue loin-cloth which made him far less conspicuous than he would have been in his white-and-yellow kilt, and the higher ranks had dark cloaks to wear until they reached their objective. All of us wore a twist of our colors on the left arm, so that even in the heat of battle friend and foe could be immediately identified.

Since sunset a strong wind, laden with dust and sand, had been blowing from the desert, and the moon was frequently obscured by clouds; the weather could not have been more ideal for our purpose, when, two hours before dawn, we began our silent advance on the temple.

The main entrance was on the east side; the gates of the pylon were closed from an hour after sunset to an hour before dawn, and one of our scouts had reported that the larger outer courtyard was deserted and that only two temple guards were posted at the gate. This gate was in the charge of Sebek, who had with him a hundred javelin-men and two hundred mace-bearers. A smaller force, of a Hundred under one of Hanuk's captains, concerned themselves with a small door in the south wall, which was hidden by thickly planted bushes and was obviously used as a private means of leaving or entering the temple. I thought it possible that the Sekmet priests might attempt to escape that way, in which case their reception had been provided for. The west wall was free of any opening, and the north side had only the gate leading into the priests' quarters. It was here that a foray in force was most probable, and I gave its security to Hanuk, who had with him all our soldiers not already appointed elsewhere, except for the men I kept under my immediate command, two hundred bowmen, and two hundred javelin-men.

I gave the other three leaders time to get their men into position and then led my force forward. We advanced in files of four, made up of two bowmen and two javelin-men, and each file carried a ladder. Behind me came the standard-bearers of the Oryx, wearing, as I did, full regalia concealed under the long hooded cloaks which hid our sphinx headdresses.

I knew the darkness on either side of me was thick with armed men, but so well did the sound of the wind conceal their movement that I might have been thrusting alone through the heavy curtain of night. A shadow loomed up; someone touched me on the arm, and the voice of one of my scouts whispered, "There were only two guards on each gate and it was easy to get them before they had time to cry out. I had to be a little rough with one of them, but I think he will wake again tomorrow, to wonder what gave him his head-ache! They are all tied up as neat as mummies and will give no further trouble."

About seventy paces from the west gate of the temple I halted while the rest of my men took up their positions. Then we continued our silent advance. Every four paces a scaling-ladder was in position; mine in the center of the west side and the rest covering three sides of the priests' court; the fourth side being cut off from the rest of the temple by the wall of the sanctuaries. The men climbed the ladders; each leader waiting with his head just hidden by the top of the wall, the other three pressing close behind him. When we were all in place on the ladders the leaders stretched out an arrow which was grasped by the next man so that there was an unbroken chain of contact; three jerks showed when the chain was complete. I and my standard-bearers had already dropped our cloaks; the wind had swept the last cobwebs of cloud from the face of the moon, and the silver horns of the Oryx standards shone like white flames.

By breaking the chain of contact I gave the signal. The men poured up the ladders and took formation on the top of the wall. I stood with a standard-bearer on each side of me. The walls had grown living battlements: a frieze of alternate bowmen and javelin-men; arrows notched to eager strings; arms poised to launch the flying shafts.

Between the priests' houses, thirty in all, lay row after row of sleeping men, their cloaks drawn over their heads to protect them from the sharp wind.

317

A great shout echoed around the walls. "The Oryx! The Oryx! Surrender to the Oryx in Ra's name! In the name of Pharaoh, Amenemhet, we bring you peace!"

Like an anthill disturbed by a hippopotamus, the courtyard burst into frenzied activity. Men leaped up groping for their weapons. Most of them were still half asleep and seemed to think that attack had come either from the outer gate or through the portal which led into the sanctuaries.

"You must look up to see Ra!" I shouted to them. "Look up, and see the men of the Oryx watching you from the sky!"

Some one loosed an arrow at me. It sang past my ear, but I could not see the direction from which it had come.

"Let one more arrow against us and *my* bows shall sing. Each of my men has had time to select his mark; you are an easier target even than a cow plodding to turn a grindstone! Send forward a spokesman so that from him I may receive your formal surrender!"

I saw a man, almost hidden by shadow, climb stealthily on the roof of one of the houses. He was notching an arrow at me; I was lucky with my aim, though it had to be swift. I saw my arrow quivering in his shoulder; he dropped his bow and fell back with a scream of pain.

"Got him!" said the man beside me. To my surprise I discovered there is more satisfaction in killing a man who is trying to kill you, even than in killing a crocodile. I found I was enjoying myself; though I knew that if Meri could see me she would have said it was childish and ridiculous to have made myself deliberately conspicuous. I knew that if she had been with us she would have insisted on being beside me or else made me change my plan. No, she *would* have been beside me, enjoying it as much as I was!

There were sounds of furious activity at the gate, and then shouts of, "The Oryx!" A few of the enemy must have been trying to make a sortie and had found an avenue of mace-bearers to greet them. In a few moments the sound of battle ceased, and a voice shouted, "We surrender to the Oryx with the honors of war!"

A man, who by his insignia I saw to be the Captain of a Nome, followed by a torch-bearer, came forward into the center of the open space below me.

"The Reed speaks with the Oryx; not as a loyal soldier to a rebel, but as Captain to Captain. I surrender rather than allow my men to be massacred. You have outwitted me by a trick, and set upon sleeping men without warning of battle. Do rebels follow the Warrior's Code?"

"We follow the laws of Horus!" I shouted back. "All men are free save those who have made other men slaves. We fight for Egypt, and for the return of her greatness under Amenemhet, Pharaoh!"

"I acknowledge no usurper to the throne, nor will I join with rebels."

"You thought yourself safe in the protection of Sekmet. Do you still think she can protect her own? It seems the Eyes of Horus can see more clearly, even though she should have the cat-sight!"

"Her curse upon you, for blasphemy!" he shouted back.

I pretended to stare up at the sky and cried out mockingly, "So powerful a curse, and so little result! Surely Sekmet's priests have more power in her name. Tell them to come forth from the holes where they hide like rats; then your men and mine can watch while my priests, the Horus priests, challenge yours to prove their powers. Three against three, as though three bowmen were champions for their kings!"

"Why should I ask my priests to let you mock them?"

"Mine is a challenge, not a mockery; and if your priests refuse it, then are they self-condemned as sly imposters. Did not your High Priest declare that Set himself in his dark majesty had told him Men-het should hold the Crook and Flail, and so be Sekmet's governor, of this, a province of her husband's kingdom? He speaks bold words; now let him be more bold—and try to prove them!"

"If our priests triumph, as they must, what then?"

"You shall go free, to let the issue between us rest on an equal combat. A Hundred on either side, and all picked men. Will you allow your priests to prove that you had not the courage to chance a fight with the Oryx on equal terms?"

"What if they lose?"

"When you have seen the victory in Ra's name, by the power of the true priests who follow Horus, his son; when you have seen the pride which upheld *your* priests running like sand out of a child's stuffed toy, then will I still give you two paths to choose. Either you swear the Warrior's Oath to bear no arms against us or our cause for forty days; or else in honor you may join our ranks and live for peace while Amenemhet rules."

"I take your challenge," he shouted back. And this was acclaimed both by his men and mine.

Trial by Magic

THE CAPTAIN OF THE REED informed me that the High Priest of Sekmet had agreed to the Trial of Will being held at noon. This surprised me as I had expected them to demand it be held at sunset; the hour dominated neither by the sun nor the moon.

The Captain added, "The High Priest, Hekhet-ma-en, has chosen the noon-hour because his strength is such that he can afford to give you every advantage. He will even allow you to decide whether both sides are to employ the aids of ritual magic or stand alone."

While he was speaking I tried to remember where I had heard that name before: then I realized that Hekhet-ma-en had been the high priest of Sekmet whom Tet-hen had spoken of as possessing great power.

"Is your priest the same Hekhet-ma-en who used to be in the new temple of the Royal City?"

He told me this was so; and I knew that though I had issued the challenge because I thought it would give us the opportunity of exposing the Sekmet priests as impotent imposters, it had become a challenge to battle between mighty magicians: Light against Darkness, Ra against Set; personified in the power of their priests.

Ptah-aru had already instructed me to allow the Sekmet priest the advantage of ritual magic, so that after their defeat they would not be able to claim that we had denied them the full use of their powers.

When I told Kepha-Ra, who being the greatest of our three Horus priests would be opposed to the high priest of Sekmet, what Tet-hen had told me of the one who would be ranged against him, he displayed no disquiet, and answered:

"If I am true to the name of he whom I follow, then he will

make me a vehicle of his power, and even if Set himself should challenge me, still would I triumph. Only if I have left undone that which I should have performed, or allowed the arrow of my trained will to grow blunt in the quiver of my body, shall I be destroyed; and so show myself to be an unworthy servant of the Lord of the Hawk."

"Tet-hen said he would not dare oppose Hekhet on equal terms."

"The strength of a country lies in the wisdom of its priesthood. If we, the priests of the Oryx, are overthrown, then, until others of our brotherhood have proved the strength of the priests of the Watchers, we are not ready to rule Egypt. Warriors can break the power of armies; warriors can protect their country from invasion: but unless a people have a living priesthood the worm of conflict will be in the fruit of victory; peace will be found to be rotten at the core, and the gold of conquest turn to bitter ashes. I now wish that I and my two brothers be left alone until the time of the testing of our strength, so that we may prepare ourselves according to our tradition."

After saying this he joined Ptah-atho under a nearby shade-tree and appeared to sleep.

Though I trusted the Captain of the Reed, I thought it possible that Sekmet's servants might try to disturb our champions, so I posted a strong guard, at a distance sufficient to protect them and yet not disturb the contemplation into which they had withdrawn. To have left a guard on the temple itself, or even to have set scouts to watch the movements of the Reed, would have been to deliver an unwarranted insult to an honored opponent, so, as it was still three hours before noon, I led the rest of my men back to our encampment. They were in great heart, laughing and joking among themselves, and all seemed confident that in a few hours they would be enjoying the humiliation of the followers of Set. Hanuk was beside me, and I took this opportunity to tell him about Hekhet-ma-en.

"Your strategy has proved brilliant up to now," he said. "But need you have set victory in the balance again when it was already won?"

"If the power of Hekhet is broken it will do more to lift the shadow of fear than anything we could have achieved by arms alone. Few of the Sekmet priests have real power, and they feel profound awe for those who possess it. To them Hekhet is more than a high priest; he is the living personification of the dark powers. Let them see him broken and they will be free. Some of them may hope to learn how to join Ra's priesthood, and the rest will no longer be the prisoner of a false temple but will be able to employ their lives for Egypt."

"Do you think Tet-hen exaggerated the power of Hekhet? From what I know of Tet-hen he is not given to overstatement."

"I share your opinion of Tet-hen; but I pray that you are under-estimating the power of our priests."

"Then your prayers and mine are the same. For if the news spreads that our champions were defeated it would be a sorry blow to our cause. All those who are still undecided which side to join, who are kept away from us because they are blinded by superstition, would declare immediately for Men-het. It might well be enough to sway the North away from us, and once they were convinced that the protection of Ra had proved violable they might even dare to put Amenemhet to death."

"You forget that even if our priests were defeated, the Captain of the Reed must still acknowledge the challenge of the Hundred. Do you doubt that we should be victorious in that battle?"

"If we had fought it this morning I would have been confident of success; but if our soldiers have to fight after seeing what they will take for a sign that their Gods have already been defeated . . . . Well, men cannot fight unless they believe in their Gods. Show me an army which does not believe in the virtue of its cause and that the Gods fight with them, and you will have shown me an army defeated before they have loosed a single arrow."

I began to wish that I had earlier revealed the whole of my plans to the others. When I had started telling them what I pro-posed to do I so intended; but for some reason, not even clear to myself, I had stopped short after explaining how the plan of attack would take the enemy by surprise. Certainly Kiyas had asked me what part the three priests were to play; at which I had looked mysterious, and said she would know that when the time came, and for once her curiosity lay dormant. I tried to imagine that Meri was beside me, giving me the courage of my decisions; and almost immediately I began to be scornful of my unspoken fears. Was I, Ra-ab Hotep, no better than a superstitious fisherman, ready to run away from the powers of darkness rather than to challenge them?

By the time we reached our encampment I had recovered my peace of mind. Only four of our men had been injured, for when the enemy had rushed out of the narrow gateway they had found themselves between close ranks of mace-bearers, who had knocked them down as though they were rats bolting out of the door of a granary. The wounded were being well cared for, and had already been attended by a healer priest and bandaged by Kiyas. One man had a dagger wound in the shoulder and two had a broken arm, of which one had had a bone protruding through the skin. The fourth man was still unconscious from a blow on the head, but the Ma-at priest, who had used his trained sight to find out the extent of the injury, reported that as there was no bruising of the brain, or crack in the skull, he would recover without any permanent ill effects.

Though I had never seen Trial by Magic, I knew that both priests would concentrate the power available to them into a thought-form, which on its own level would be as effective as though it had been brought down to the physical. These thought-forms would, of course, be invisible except to those who had been trained to use the sight which is not limited by the three dimensions of Earth; so I asked the priest of Ma-at to accompany me to the temple to describe what was actually taking place, and this he agreed most willingly to do.

After we had eaten, we proceeded to the Temple of Sekmet. The column now consisted of the full muster of the Oryx and the Jackal, except for three women who had offered to stay with the wounded, and the guards which I posted around the encampment. The men of the Hare remained in concealment, for Hanuk thought it wiser that a portion of our strength should be undeclared so as to guard against possible developments.

News of what had happened had spread through the Old Capital, and it was evident that people knew there was to be a Trial by Magic, for the huge crowd which had already assembled kept a discreet distance from the temple gates. They seemed to think that magical power had a strictly limited field, and that as long as they kept outside this they would be safe from the forces they feared, but of whose nature it was obvious they had no understanding. By common consent they seemed to have decided that magic was only dangerous within the length of two bowshots, and at this distance they had collected, pressed together as though leaning against an invisible rope.

I deliberately marched my men close to them before wheeling the column to approach the temple gate, for I thought a close sight of us might dispel the illusion that the South were a pack of disorderly rebels. The majority of the crowd were hostile, but a small boy waved to me and cried out, "Nice soldier!" for which he was soundly cuffed by his mother. A few girls smiled back when our men called out to them, but the majority only stared with apprehension or sullen curiosity.

"You will soon be marching through the Underworld!" cried one old woman. "There will be a fine sizzling in Sekmet's kitchen tonight! Tender young blasphemers please her even more than sacrificial bulls!"

Here a man near her joined in, "Greedy for bulls, too, is Sekmet! Three bulls I gave her last year, promised them to her I did if my wife should bear me a son. So the old woman did; but not for seven years, when I'd forgotten the bargain. But the priests are good keepers of tallies, and they were quick enough to see I paid my debt. Three bulls my boy cost me . . . and an idle, silly child he is too, not worth the tail or the hooves of one of them!

This crowd, half frightened, half ribald, seemed a strange background to an ordeal which might well be the decisive factor in the future of the Two Lands. In the great outer courtyard, the soldiers of the Reed were ranked twelve deep against the north wall; and we took our places opposite them.

A black basalt statue of Sekmet, about twice the height of a man, had been placed at the foot of the steps leading up to the sanctuaries. In front of it was an altar made of the same basalt; and on this was a large gold chalice and a silver bowl.

In the center of the open space were six circles, drawn in black on the stone pavement; two rows of three, ten cubits apart.

They were large enough for a man to stand in them, but if he collapsed he would fall across the line; and the first to do this was held to have been defeated by the man opposite him. To render the opponent unconscious was the effect most usually attempted, but there were many other ways of making him break the circle. Such Trials of Will were not unusual in Sekmet temples, but nearly always the person set against the priests had no magical training and soon found himself as powerless to resist as though he were a bird in the eye of a snake. Once this influence had been established, the victim would have to do exactly as he was told by the one who had attained dominance over him. Tet-hen had told me he had seen a man running around a courtyard in terror, trying to escape from an invisible dog which he thought was snapping at his heels; another man had gone on all fours, and tried to lap water from a bowl which wasn't there; while a third had drawn a knife from his belt and obediently severed the toes of his left foot. There was usually a crowd to watch these demonstrations, which proved most useful in keeping the people in the power of the priests; for they thought that if they disobeyed him, he could, even at a distance, make them behave in any humiliating or criminal way he chose. Tet-hen had also told me that sometimes this belief was so strong that people obeyed without question any command of a priest whom they had seen display this sorcerer's trick, and would even let themselves be made an instrument of murder, so long as it was not against one with whom they had a strong link of affection.

Our priests went forward and sat cross-legged behind the circles in which they must stand their ordeal; their eyes were closed and they seemed entirely disinterested in their surroundings. A line of acolytes, boys with heavily painted faces, wearing tunics of purple linen and necklaces of crocodiles' teeth, filed out of the sanctuary and took their places on either side of the statue. They were followed by the priests who were not taking part in the ordeal; of these there were twenty, wearing leopard skins which partially concealed their purple robes and carrying long staffs, headed either with a crocodile of the Underworld or with the cat which symbolized the dark sight. Most of them were fat, and one of them had breasts which hung down like the dugs of an old hound bitch. They wore gold amulets, various symbols of Set or Sekmet, and several had rings on their thumbs. Their nails were long and ragged, and their hands deeply grimed with dirt.

Kiyas noticed this when I did and whispered, "Why are they so dirty?"

"Because they want to be as different to us as possible. Our priests perform a ceremonial cleansing before prayer, but dirt is their symbol of the grossest aspects of the Earth, and so of their channel with the Underworld."

A black and white temple bull, its horns wreathed with ivy, was now led in. Two of the priests stepped forward, and while one caught the animal by its horns, the other slit its throat, letting the blood gush into the silver bowl he had taken from the altar. Then two black goats, a male and a female, were sacrificed. After this, two pigeons, whose plumage had been smeared with bitumen, had their heads bitten off by a third priest, and their blood, together with some of the blood from the silver bowl, was poured into the gold chalice, which, after being offered to Sekmet, was placed in the center of the altar.

From somewhere within the sanctuary came a sudden shrill scream, quickly stifled.

"What's that?" whispered Kiyas.

"They are trying to bribe Sekmet by every means in their power. She is known to be fond of human blood, but even *her* priests dare not make a human sacrifice in public. I think they have killed a virgin in Sekmet's sanctuary . . . if I'm right another bowl of blood will be brought out in a minute."

A priest came down the steps. He was trembling, and a single scarlet gout spilled from the bowl he held so carefully between his hands.

"The bull, the goats, the pigeons . . . and now the virgin," I said to Kiyas. "We shall see Hekhet come out now."

The robe of the High Priest was purple and white in wide, vertical stripes. His pale, shaven scalp gleamed in the sunlight, and the tendons of his dirty hands stood out like the bones in a bird's claw. His lips were intensely red; they seemed to glitter like metal in his pallid, mask-like face. He had no eyebrows, and the skin was stretched so tightly over the forehead bone that his black eyes were cavernous as a vulture's.

He intoned a long evocation before the statue; a string of unintelligible words. Then he lifted the chalice of blood; not to pour a libation as I had expected, but to drink from it deeply, like a man who is very thirsty. Now I knew why his lips had been that glistening scarlet; they were wet with a draft he had already drunk while in the sanctuary.

The other two priests who were to take part in the ordeal now followed him in the making of evocation; but I noticed that both of them only touched the chalice to their lips and did not drink. Then they moved forward to take their places behind the circles which they would occupy on each side of Hekhet when the signal was given; although they would not begin their ordeal until the High Priests had decided the first trial. Though it was unusual, the two second priests had been known to flee from their circle rather than wait for their defeat to follow that of him whom they knew to be more powerful than themselves; and sometimes they had been tempted out of their circle by the wish to succor a fellow-priest who was struggling in torment, or even dying.

Our priests had risen to their feet, and were standing with their arms upstretched toward Ra, calling silently on his name that his power might flow down into them through the channel opened in the name of Horus, his son.

The signal was given, a long note blown on a ram's horn, and the six priests stepped forward into their circles. Behind our priests was the bare white wall of the courtyard; behind the Sekmet priests brooded her statue, the eyes baleful as a stalking cat. The rows of acolytes were now swinging censers which gave off clouds of incense.

Kepha-Ra against Hekhet; Ra against Set.

Hekhet stretched out his right hand, the first two fingers extended, the thumb and the other two fingers joined in the palm. I knew this method of directing a flow of power was often used, both for healing and for destruction. Kepha made no movement; but in his stillness was the temper of a fine dagger: I could see nothing super-physical, yet I was aware of power streaming from him.

The Ma-at priest was standing on the other side of me, and he began to describe the form the battle was taking, as each priest drove his will against his opponent.

"Kepha is creating a personification of Horus; in the form of a hawk, not the man with the hawk's head. It is forming about a cubit above Hekhet's head. . . . Now it is almost complete, perfect as the gold hawk made by Neku. Into it is flowing the power from Kepha, and also life from the level of the Gods. If he can only gather sufficient power into it, then it will strike down and destroy the will of Hekhet."

Suddenly I saw Kepha flinch as though in great pain.

"What's happening to Kepha?"

The eyes of the seer-priest were still fixed on a point above Hekhet's head, but at my voice he turned, still with his hand over his eyes, to stare toward his fellow-priest.

"Hekhet is indeed a powerful magician! He has thrown a serpent of Apep about Kepha; three of its coils are around his legs and thighs, and its fangs are buried deep between his shoulders. Its mouth is wide open, flat against the skin. It is sucking the life out of him . . . draining his strength with every second."

I saw with horror that Kepha no longer held his upright position. His knees were slightly bent, his back curved, the elbows braced back as though he were trying to resist a desperate pressure which was driving him relentlessly forward. Sweat was pouring down his body . . . it was almost possible without being a seer to know what was forcing him into such an unnatural position.

"The hawk, tell me of the strength of the hawk!"

"It's growing larger . . . No! Now it is swaying . . . it looks as though it were going to fall. Now one wing has grown a little blurred."

Even those who saw nothing except two men standing opposite each other in the brilliant sunshine, must have been conscious of the tremendous manifestation of power. Nothing visible touched the two priests; they made no sound—yet the sweat of extreme exertion was sluicing down their bodies; and one of them was curiously contorted, looking as though he must have fallen if something invisible that had closed him in its coils was not supporting him while it completed his destruction.

The seer-priest was whispering to himself, "Horus, let him triumph! He is trying to build up *your* Hawk. Help him, in the name of his Father! Make the Hawk live in your power. . . ."

Then his voice grew louder. "It's getting stronger! Look! Look! It's towering to strike!"

All eyes were fixed on Kepha who seemed about to collapse. Suddenly, as though with an almost impossible exertion of strength, he drew himself erect. He stretched out his hands; then brought them down to his sides, like a hawk folding its wings before it plunges on its prey.

Hekhet screamed; the high, frantic scream of a hare in the talons of a hawk. With one hand he plucked at this throat, while with the other he seemed to be trying to defend his eyes. He screamed out, "I shall be blind! Blind!"

Again I heard the seer's voice, "The Hawk's got him by the throat! Its talons are buried deep in his flesh . . . he will never find the strength to tear them out! It's pecking at his eyes. He believes it is blinding him; so it *will* blind him. He will never see again, and with his sight so has his power been taken from him! Look! The power of the serpent is already broken!"

Hekhet staggered frantically backwards, trying to beat off that which was attacking him. Even without a seer to tell me the form in which Kepha had personified his power, I should have known the Hekhet fought against some great bird.

The High Priest of Sekmet was now only a man; blind and powerless, stumbling for shelter, screaming for his fellow priests to save him. The habit of obedience was strong in them. They ran after him, and so left their circles.

Tomb of Sekmet

I SHALL ALWAYS REMEMBER that scene in the courtyard of the Temple of Sekmet as though the time in which it was being enacted had the quality of dream time and was not concerned with the arbitrary divisions of hours; for I was able to observe things simultaneously as though they were in a sequence spaced sufficiently far apart for me to give them undivided attention.

Hekhet, no longer the medium of dark powers, but only a

man, old and brutish, beaten to the ground by the Hawk of Horus; his screams dying down to a shrill whimpering, as he crawled on his belly toward the sanctuary of the Goddess who had been powerless to protect him.

A few of the acolytes still swung their censers to and fro, but the ordered line of priests had broken. They were huddled together, staring in horror at he who for so long had held them under his domination.

I gave an exultant shout which echoed along our ranks.

"Horus has triumphed in the name of Ra! The Oryx has put the servants of Set to flight. Great is the power of Ra in whose name we live. Honor to the champions of the Oryx!"

With wild enthusiasm they acclaimed Kepha, who except for extreme exhaustion showed no sign of his terrible ordeal. It was not until late in the evening that he showed me the scarlet furrows where the fangs of the serpent of Apep had been powerful enough to score not only the *Ka* but the khat, the physical body as well as its life-bearing counterpart.

The soldiers of the Reed had kept their ranks, and I went forward and spoke to them.

"Men of the Reed, you have seen how Ra has conquered Sekmet, and the light triumphed over darkness. It is not you whom we of the South are fighting against; we fight against Fear, the secondary title of the Goddess whose servant Hekhet we have overthrown. Our enemies are those men who desire to leave authority in the hands of Fear; who desire that the child shall flinch from the father, and the woman from the man; the village cringe before its headman, and the headman quail at a word from the overseer. If you wish men to work only because they are driven by whip-men, and the granaries to be empty because Pharaoh fears his power will grow less if his gold is bartered with the Asiatics; if you wish Hatred the Harlot to be the most honored of your women and Truth to find no lodging in your homes; if you wish to live as blind men plodding in shackles. . . . If this be what you wish for Egypt and yourselves: then continue your fight against us! Try to make Men-het your Pharaoh, so that Sekmet may rule! To your Captain I have given my word that even in defeat you still have a choice to make. Let the Reed join with the

Oryx and the South; to live in peace while Amenemhet rules, and Fear and Sorrow go down into the tomb of a dead Pharaoh. Or take the second choice: for forty days, sworn by the Warrior's Code, to raise no hand against us or our cause. If there are those among you who would join us, come forward; as a sign that you know Amenemhet to be the rightful ruler of the Two Lands!"

The Captain of the Reed came forward and put his hands on my shoulders, the greeting given between brothers. "My men must judge for themselves," he said. "But henceforward the Captain of the Reed is under your command."

Rank after rank his men surged forward, cheering as they came, "The Reed and the Oryx!"

"For Amenemhet and the South!"

I had posted a strong guard at both the other entrances to the temple, so I knew that none of Sekmet's servants could have made their escape. Tet-hen had told me that in the Sekmet temple of the Royal City there were underground rooms to which only the high priest, and those who worked in closest collaboration with him, had access. If there were similar rooms here I thought it advisable that the Captain of the Reed should accompany me in their discovery; and so be able to tell his soldiers, who in their turn would tell the townspeople, the value of the priesthood who until today had held the Old Capital in subjection.

The Captain of the Reed asked that the Oryx and the Jackal should be the guests of his soldiers in their barracks, and to this I agreed most willingly, for there can be no better way of bringing peace to a city than by conqueror and conquered entering it side by side in friendship.

I decided to keep with me only a hundred mace-bearers, and of these twenty accompanied me, together with Hanuk, Kiyas, Ptah-aru, and the Captain of the Reed, while to the rest I gave the task of destroying the statue of Sekmet, and was glad I had had the foresight to include in our equipment hammers and wedges suitable for such work.

Immediately beyond the entrance at the top of the steps was the sanctuary from which the statue had been brought. Beside the plinth on which it usually stood were the rollers which had been used to move it, and I saw there were three other doors, one on each side, and a third opposite the main entrance. I opened the door in the south wall and found it led into a smaller sanctuary; which was lit by a small opening in the roof and lined with slabs of black granite. It contained a statue of Set in his human form, flanked by two smaller statues of the crocodiles which guard the Underworld. There was a partly consumed black kid still smoldering on the offering table, but apart from this the room showed no signs of recent use.

In the sanctuary on the north side, the statue of Sekmet was in the form of a cat. On the plinth was a bowl of milk and a basket of fish; though I didn't notice this until later, for what occupied the offering table held my whole attention. It was a girl, perhaps a little younger than Kiyas. Her body was bent backwards; the shoulders and loins supported on the altar; her hair, a beautiful dark red, hanging to the floor. So grotesquely had her body been tied that it looked like a travesty of the position in which Nut is sometimes depicted as Goddess of the Sky. The girl's eyes were open, as though she were watching for death to come to release her from the torments of the flesh. Her belly had been ripped open, downward from the navel; and between her legs had been set a bowl, now nearly full, to catch the blood as it drained down.

"She screamed only once," said Kiyas. "That wound wouldn't have killed her instantly. She must have been in pain a long time. . . ."

The girl's mouth was distorted; the jaw was not yet rigid and it had fallen open. I looked more closely and saw that a wad of rags had been thrust down her throat. To Kiyas I said:

"That's how they stopped her screaming."

There was a sound of retching; one of the mace-bearers was being sick outside the door.

"May Ra blast the soul of the man who killed her," said Hanuk.

Kiyas was breathing rapidly and her hands were tightly clenched; yet she managed to keep her voice controlled and dispassionate.

"Ra would . . . if the man had not done so himself. He has blasted his own soul, so why should the Gods interfere when their laws are already in operation?"

The door at the back of the central sanctuary led into a gallery from which several rooms opened. The doors were sealed, but when they had been forced we saw that in the first three the temple treasure was stored. On wood shelves were a large quantity of valuables of many kinds, tusks of ivory, collars of gold and silver, women's ornaments varying from the most rare jewels of the wives of rich nobles down to a single carnelian bead on a leather tong, perhaps the most cherished possession of a woman of the very poor.

In another room were thousands of tallies; some on clay tablets, others on papyri, others on wooden panels, which recorded the particulars of all bribes offered to Sekmet by petitioners. I remembered the man who had paid his three bulls after a lapse of seven years; he was right in saying that the priests of Sekmet were careful of their tallies.

In another room were many small rolls of papyri, which, when they were later examined, proved to be lists of discreditable activities of nobles, officials, and merchants; used as a threat to exhort additional tribute. This information had come from many sources; sometimes a household servant had been allowed to pay no temple tribute if instead he could reveal something, such as an appropriation of taxes due to Pharaoh, that was punishable by death or torture. There were also many records of women who had been unfaithful to their husbands, and who ever since had lived under the fear of exposure if they failed to fulfill the demands made on them by the priests.

At the end of the gallery a door gave on to another running parallel to it. At one end was the entrance to the priests' courtyard, and at the other were the two rooms which had been occupied by the High Priest. Rather to my surprise these rooms were empty, so we went on to the courtyard, thinking Hekhet had hidden in one of the priests' houses.

Houses and courtyard were equally deserted. I went to the gate and asked the guard I had set there if any one had passed through. He was emphatic that no one had left the temple, either by the gates or over the wall, since we ourselves had entered before the Ordeal.

"They must all be hiding in an underground room," I said to Hanuk. "I was prepared to find that Hekhet and the priests nearest to him had disappeared; but I thought they would have left the others to feel the first edge of our anger."

"The sanctuaries are above the level of the courtyards," said Kiyas. "I expect the rooms will be under them."

"Yes, we'll look first for the entrance there; it probably leads out of one of the sanctuaries. Tet-hen told me that in the other Sekmet temple there was a sliding stone, at the back of the plinth of the statue itself, which could only be moved by one who had the secret of the exact place where to exert pressure."

We started a long and careful search. All the floors were squares of polished granite of uniform size, and though we banged every one of them with a mace, to see if it gave off a hollow ring which would betray a hidden cavity, there seemed nothing to distinguish one from another. They had been well laid; even a thin knife blade could not be driven between the blocks and to prise up the whole floor would have taken days.

When we had finished in the sanctuaries we started on the store-rooms, but though we went over both walls and floor several times they yielded no result. It was Kiyas who noticed that the sleeping-mat on the bed-place in the inner of Hekhet's two rooms was crooked. She pulled it off and stamped on the stone. It sounded as solid as the rest of the floor, but she cried out excitedly," I believe it's under here! I think I felt the stone shift, but it was so little that I can't be sure." She pointed down, "Look where the stone joins the floor! The crack between it and the next one is no wider than the others, but it is free from dust."

Something on the wall caught her attention, "Look, look! There's a smear there, like the print of part of a hand. It's still wet, either oil or blood. . . ."

She leaned forward to test the origin of the smear; in doing so she slipped and the whole of her weight came on her outstretched hand. Hanuk leaped forward and pulled her back; as, almost noiselessly, the stone on which she had been standing sank down to disclose a square opening.

"That's the way they've gone!" exclaimed Hanuk.

"Look, there are grooves which we can use as steps cut in the shaft."

I started forward to climb down, but Hanuk pulled me back.

"Not so fast, Ra-ab! I have heard of these places before, they are as disagreeable to unwelcome guests as a tomb to a tomb-robber. You must test every stone before you trust your weight on it. You and I will go first and keep hold of each other in case the floor gives way."

I sent for two of the altar lamps, which gave off a steady light. Holding one of them in my right hand I lowered myself carefully down from foothold to foothold. I noticed that the grooves had been made to take the ends of planks, which, when in place, would have made the descent quite easy. I was glad to reach the bottom of the shaft, for, while climbing down, I should have been an admirable target for anyone waiting at the bottom.

The shaft led to a narrow passage, too low for me to stand upright and sloping gradually downwards. Without any warning a stone on which I had just put my weight gave under me. Had it not been for Hanuk's grip on my arm I should have hurtled down into a vertical shaft, for the slab which had given way was about eight cubits long and had not moved until my full weight was on it. By the light of the lamp I could see, about thirty cubits below me, the glitter of water.

"And there wouldn't have been only water to greet you," said Hanuk. "There are probably spikes under the surface to impale anyone who is unfortunate enough to fall in . . . just to make sure they have an uncomfortable death!"

As the cavity was too wide to jump, we had to wait until two poles, which once had supported the roof of a priest's house, were brought to make a bridge. Kiyas rather reluctantly agreed to wait for us at the top of the shaft, with Ptah-aru and most of the others, but in addition to Hanuk and the Captain of the Reed I took ten mace-bearers.

The passage turned to the right and then appeared to end in a blank wall. This I guessed to be a drop-stone, and in a few minutes we managed to raise it, with the levers we had brought for the purpose, sufficiently to crawl underneath. There was another short flight of steps, and then the passage ran level for about twenty paces before turning again, this time to the left, after which it was closed by a massive wooden door.

I hammered on the door with the hilt of my dagger, shouting a command that it be opened in the name of Pharaoh. It was very thick, but with my ear pressed against it I could hear a confused murmur of voices. When my second command brought no response, I told my men to break it down, which they did, though not until they had used a pole for a battering ram.

The bolts which had been holding the door burst from their sockets with a loud crack. I was looking into a room rather larger than the central sanctuary. The low ceiling was supported on four square pillars and the walls looked like the sides of a natural cave. In the center of the room crouched Hekhet; his arms folded on his chest like a sick baboon. He had the wide vacant eyes of the blind, and spittle drooled from his mouth to course down his body like the slimy track of a snail.

Around him were huddled the other priests and among them the acolytes. The boys were silent, but the old men cried out in a quavering chorus, "Mercy! Have mercy on us!"

"Would he have had mercy?" I said, pointing to Hekhet.

"That quivering travesty of a man!"

"We thought his was the only power; we knew of no other!" protested the priest of extraordinary fatness whom I had noticed earlier in the day. When he saw I was not impressed by his excuses, he went on, still more shrilly, "How can we be blamed for being ignorant? We have all been here since we were children, like these our sons."

He pushed forward one of the acolytes, saying to him, "Boy, tell him we have been good to you, that we could not help obeying he whose power is now broken."

"But you haven't been good to me," said the boy sullenly. "You flatter me when you want me to pretend to be your woman, and that's not the only thing you want me to do. But when you are tired of that kind of play you pinch me and make me beg for enough food to keep me alive."

The boy turned to me, "He said he was Sekmet on Earth, and that if I disobeyed him in *anything*, or tried to run away, he would make snakes come out of my mouth until I died of a screaming madness." He held up his head defiantly, "I'm not going to stay here any more. You and the other men are soldiers. My father was a soldier when I lived outside the temple. He wouldn't have kept his promise that I should be given to the temple if my mother recovered from the pestilence if he'd known what was going to be done to me."

The child, for he was little more, shook himself free of the fat priest's hold on his arm and ran to stand beside me. "You can trust me, noble lord, because now you're here I'm not frightened. Before you came I would have lied, or stolen, or killed people if they had made me, because I was too frightened to disobey. It's easy to say you'll be brave when you don't know what they can do to you; but I've seen an acolyte beaten to death, and another one was taken out to the river at midnight and given to the crocodiles. They gagged him so that he wouldn't scream. He was my friend, and I saw his face as he was pulled under the water. His eyes were open, asking me to do something to help him, but I couldn't because I was too frightened. When you're obedient they pet you and feed you with food from their own bowls in their dirty fingers. But I think they're sorry when you're obedient, unless you cringe a lot, for they enjoy thinking of new punishments."

"Don't listen to him! He lies, he lies!" screamed the priest.

"Have no fear that I shall be deceived," I said. "The Eyes of Horus have been well trained to see the different shades of truth and falsehood. You shall suffer no pain you have not inflicted. What you have done shall be done unto you.

"No! No! Be merciful, merciful!" He flung himself groveling at my feet.

"I find it interesting," I said, "that one who professes kindness should be afraid, should beg for mercy from the consequences of his own acts. Is it true that you have whipped boys and suffered them to undergo other indignities?"

"No, no! Never have I done that, never!"

By way of answer the acolyte tore off his tunic and showed me his back. It was marked like a grid, barred and counter barred, with welts long healed and welts that still were raw.

To the cringing priest I said, "It seems that your kindness has been a little rough. But you shall receive it in the same measure. I have heard cooks say that flayed meat is more tender, and no doubt the crocodiles will be grateful for my consideration of their appetites."

"But it wasn't only me! It was him, and him, and him!" he shrilled, pointing around the room.

Others of the acolytes had taken courage, and were now crowding forward to show me their scars; while the priests in terrified voices kept trying to foist their guilt on the shoulders of another, so giving me the opportunity to judge that they were all equally base.

To the man who was still groveling at my feet, I said, "Mockery of a man in a welter of fatness! A woman has been murdered in the sanctuary. How came that woman here . . . for it seems that Sekmet is too jealous of her sex to admit of priestesses."

"I know nothing of any woman—a woman dead? Perhaps Sekmet killed her, for she is impatient of women."

"Answer me quickly, spawn of a toad in a vulture's belly. A woman was sacrificed. Where are the others you keep in Sekmet's larder?"

He tried to set his forehead on my instep in token of humility. I ground down my heel on his fat fingers, saying, "A little foretaste of what you are shortly to feel. There is only one way to escape, only one way for any of you. The first to tell me where your prisoners are hidden may get less than he deserves."

In unison they shouted, each eager to betray their fellows, "They are under here!" And they all pointed to the same corner of the room.

The stone which hid the entrance had no counterweight, and was lifted by an ordinary ring-bolt set in the slab. A wooden ladder led down into the darkness.

Three girls, none of them more than fifteen, were there. None of them answered my shout that I was coming to set them free. How could they when they were all hanging by the neck from a beam which ran across the fetid cell?

I touched one of them and her body was still warm; but when we cut them down there was nothing we could do, for they were all dead.

"The priests were afraid they would talk," I said to Hanuk. "They have been here a long time. Their hands cannot have been untied for days, look how the ropes have eaten into the flesh."

I turned to the Captain of the Reed. "I cannot say I find any of the habits of your priesthood attractive."

He answered me, "Never again while I live shall any of my soldiers give tolerance to Sekmet."

I stood facing him, the dead women laid in a row between us. Very solemnly he said to me. "The Oryx has conquered the Reed by arms and by magic. But the Reed does more than honor a brave adversary. She thanks the Oryx, and the Gods of the Oryx, for her soul."

"If we are speaking as Watcher to Watcher, it is for me, as an Eye of Horus, to make the decision. If we are speaking as Captain to Captain, then, because this crime had been committed in your Nome, it is for you to give judgment. Which shall it be?"

"Your judgment shall be mine."

"Before Hekhet was conquered I thought that when his will was broken his fellow priests would be freed. I even hoped that some of them might learn to become real priests and the rest be able to lead useful lives. Now I know they are too corrupt for anything but death to cleanse. If one maggot-ridden fruit is placed next to another which is sound, soon both will stink. Therefore these priests cannot be allowed to mix with other men, and they are too far gone in the disease of evil to be kept apart until they are healed. The acolytes are young; some of them may have learned vice from the way in which they have lived, but they have many years before them in which their cure may be effected. I suggest that they are sent to Hotep-Ra, where we are used to curing the afflicted. Is that agreed?"

"Most certainly."

"Before I give judgment I will ask the acolytes if there be any priest who in their eyes deserves a second chance."

"And for the rest?"

"I can think of no more suitable tomb than this room; in which three of their victims have not yet grown cold in death."

Carefully we carried the girls' bodies into the upper room; they would be buried with a ritual which would ensure that the soul was unmarked by the memory of the violence through which it had quitted the body for the last time.

I did not tell the acolytes what was to be done to the priests, I only asked them, each in turn, whether there was a priest to whom they had reason to be grateful for any act of kindness however trivial. Of these there were two; both old men who had been little more than temple servants. Only one word of affection did the others need to save them from death; but this word no one would give them.

I sent the acolytes and the two old priests, in charge of a mace-bearer, to wait for us in the sanctuary. In spite of the certainty of my justice it was not a pleasant task which I undertook, with Hanuk, the Reed, and the mace-bearers to help me. But it was quickly over.

The beam across the lower room sagged under the weight of twenty-one bodies, which still swayed at the end of their ropes, even when they no longer danced with death.

The floor had been covered with filthy straw. To this was added thatch from the priests' houses and over it a jar of oil was poured. Now the bodies were waist deep in litter, like stalled oxen.

I threw down a blazing torch: and left the dead men to the cleansing fire.

Broken Basalt

ON MY WAY UP from the tomb of the Sekmet priests, I counted my paces so as to find out how far beyond the temple enclosure the underground passages extended. After telling Kiyas and Ptah-aru what we had found it necessary to do, I went through the small south gate to see if I could see smoke which would show me if my calculations had been correct, and if the fire was still burning. In the direction I had anticipated I saw a clump of trees, and on entering it found they surrounded what looked like a disused well. Smoke was rising from it in an oily column, and by peering down I could see the mouths of two ventilation shafts which entered it just above water level.

On my return I saw that the crowd outside the entrance pylon had enormously increased. They already knew that their High Priest, whom for so long they had feared, had been defeated in a magical battle; but having taken this as a sign that the Reed was vanquished they were mystified at having seen their soldiers marching amicably with ours under a single command.

I suggested to the Captain of the Reed that he would be the

best person to remove any lingering hostility they might feel toward us, so he sent a herald to tell them to come into the courtyard to hear what he had to say to them.

Meanwhile the bodies of the three murdered virgins were laid on an improvised bier at the foot of the steps leading to the sanctuary; their pitifully distorted beauty covered with soldiers' cloaks. The people of the Old Capital came pouring in through the gate, jostling each other in their eagerness to be in the front ranks.

Then their Captain addressed them:

"People of the Old Capital, I speak to you as the Captain of your Nome. In the old years this city was the capital from which wise Pharaohs ruled. You have suffered under false Pharaohs, who had lost the traditional divinity which would have made them more than men who wear a crown. You have seen the Two Lands ruled from a new city, and listened to false counsel from new temples built in the name of Sekmet.

"Yet none of these things were new; they were old as the fear on which they were founded. Hekhet the high priest has been destroyed, and those of the priests who were his brothers have followed him into the Underworld. Those who were the prisoners of this temple have been set free; and in time shall be healed of the corruption they learned here, even as a man with many lice may be made clean.

"A true temple is a place where everyone may come who needs counsel from one wiser than himself; it is a place where people receive comfort and the sick are healed; a place where the lonely find a friend, and the orphan both father and mother. This is what a temple shall again be to you, when you have built it on clean ground.

"This temple of Sekmet was a flail you gave into the hands of the Lords of Darkness, that they might scourge you with the whips of superstition and poison you with the scorpions of fear. You have been content to give bulls for sacrifice to Sekmet; black goats you have also given and pigeons closed in wicker cages. Did you know, people of the Old Capital, that Sekmet was not content with the blood of animals? Did you know she was greedy for the blood of virgins?

"Hekhet, whom once you honored, did not let her thirst. This morning there were four girls, kept as prisoners in rooms below the temple. This morning they were alive; we could have set them free to find happiness under the sun. Yesterday, I and seventeen Hundreds were within these temple walls: we thought our enemies were the soldiers who had come from the South, and that those for whom we fought were the priests from whom we had claimed sanctuary. Yet it was the men of the South who had marched to set us free; we, the soldiers of the Reed, were as much prisoners of superstition as you were; we were shackled by fear which bound us more securely than the fetters of slaves who labor in the quarries.

"Today we are free; and our jailers are dead. But four of their prisoners were put to death before we came to release them. They died to prevent them speaking of what they knew; but they have died so that you shall live, for I speak for them. When you have seen them I think there is not one among you who will ever again give your power into the hands of Set, or his dark consort.

"Come forward; see if any one of you can tell me the names of those who were murdered on the day that you regained your freedom!"

He turned back the cloaks so that the faces of the dead girls could be seen. Silently the people filed past the biers. A woman dropped on her knees beside the girl whose belly had been ripped open.

"She is my daughter, my daughter! Six months ago a priest told me she had been to the temple, bringing with her a man from the South to whom she had made the oath of marriage. The priest said he pitied me, because my daughter had proved that she gave me no affection and had gone away with her husband without a thought for her parents. I wept because I was lonely for her, but I thought that one day she would come back to me."

Tears were running down the woman's face. Then she stood upright, stretching her hands to the sky, "Ra, in the name of your son avenge my daughter! Let the temple of Sekmet be broken down and her priests die in torment! Torment!—as though their bowels writhed with serpents and white ants consumed their brains until their skulls are bare. Yet let their souls live on in their skulls, so that their pains continue for a thousand years!"

Then she turned and harangued the crowd.

"Hekhet is dead: or I would claw out his eyes and crush them between my hands like serpents' eggs! But his temple still stands. Help me to tear it down! For while one stone stands on another, until the sand has hidden even the outline of its walls, it will be here to remind of us how we have been led into dishonor because we were afraid."

A roar went up from the crowd. "Destruction to Sekmet! All that was hers shall be burned to the glory of Ra!"

The Captain held up his hand, and the crowd quieted to listen to him. "Return here in an hour and the temple is yours to destroy. Bring hammers and wedges; bring oil and fire. And let no stone, nor particle of stone, be taken beyond the enclosure; for evil can live even in a grain of dust. When all here has been destroyed, for fifty years this place shall be set apart as unclean; and none shall enter it save at their own peril."

Then I sent heralds throughout the Old Capital to proclaim that on the morrow I, with the Captain of the Reed beside me, would sit in audience to pronounce the names of those in authority who would continue to hold office under Amenemhet, and those who had been judged unworthy. By my decree also it was proclaimed that those who knew by the weighing of their own hearts that the Watchers would send them into exile might leave the city without molestation if they did so before the third hour of the following day. These might take with them sufficient to maintain them for sixty days; but they must whiten their heads with ashes, as mourners had done under the rule of Sekmet, to signify that they were penitent of their sins. By this sign they would be known, and at the villages they must pass through on their way out of Egypt they would receive food and shelter sufficient for the needs of their journey.

The Captain had an estate close to the Old Capital, and this he said I was to consider as my own so long as I remained in the Nome. It was here that the four wounded men were taken, together with the two old priests and the acolytes, who would stay there until they were ready to start on their journey to the Oryx.

Of the fourteen boys, only three had been made into eunuchs. One of these, who told me he was eleven years old, was grotesquely fat, and the other two had the wizened faces of old men. They were pathetically anxious to please me, and, with each in turn, I had some difficulty in convincing them that they had no sexual interest for me. They had been drilled in harlotry, and at first thought that because I refused to accept their offers they had in some way offended me. Each refusal increased their fear; and I discovered that when a priest whom they had been trying to amuse had been too satiated or too senile to find satisfaction through their antics, he had vented his thwarted brutality by giving them a merciless whipping.

Under their purple tunics the boys' half-starved bodies were crusted with dirt; their faces were layered with paint and they reeked of rancid unguents. They were too pathetic to be repulsive; midway between crippled children and forlorn, imprisoned monkeys. I had asked Kiyas to help me with them, for I thought they might be less frightened of a woman than a man. She sent for three of her women to help us, and together we washed the acolytes and dressed their running sores.

One of them put his skinny hand on Kiyas's arm and whispered, "I'll try to help you escape. Sekmet is thirsty at the full moon, but I won't let her drink your blood. I know that's what women are for—to be given to the Gods to stop them from being angry with men. But you are kind, and not frightened like the other women I've seen. They cried all day, and battered on the walls of the room they are kept in till the bones of their knuckles pierced through the skin. I used to take their food to them; sometimes there was so little of it that I was ashamed. We sometimes got a big meal, because Sekmet doesn't mind if we eat the meat she has finished with, but the women who were being kept for her were always hungry."

I shall ever remember that scene. The bath was a stone trough in the floor and in this the boy was lying, trying to comfort Kiyas who knelt beside him as she scrubbed off layer after layer of ancient dirt. She talked to him as though he were a very young child who had just wakened from a night terror.

"Sekmet is dead. She has got no more power than a dead crocodile or a drowned cat. Tomorrow you are going on a journey to a place where you will forget all the things you have learned and

be taught how to be happy. You will have to wash twice a day, but
you'll soon get used to that, and you can eat as often as you are
hungry, and sleep when you are tired. Instead of watching bulls
being sacrificed you can live on a farm if you like, and milk the
cows when they come in from their pastures and collect the eggs
before the ducks are let out in the morning."

He stared up at her through eyes still heavily ringed with khol.
"That doesn't sound like the heaven the priest promised me,
where I would go if I was obedient to him all my life. He said that
I could have ten acolytes, or even more if I was very obedient,
from whom no secret of desire was concealed. I didn't think it
sounded a very nice kind of heaven, because I might have
remembered to be sorry for the acolytes."

"Ours is a much better kind of heaven," said Kiyas confidently,
"and you won't have to bother to die to get there. Tomorrow, or
perhaps the next day, you will go in a litter for several days, sometimes you can walk if you want to for a change, and then you will
come to a place called Hotep-Ra."

"And won't there be any old men whom I have got to make
whimper with excitement?"

"There are no old men like that in Hotep-Ra; because in our
country we are not afraid of Min . . . we don't fear anything at all."

That night there was rejoicing in the Old Capital such as it had
not seen for centuries. The soldiers of the Oryx, the Jackal, the
Hare, and the Reed, went laughing and singing through the
streets and the townspeople ran out of their houses to join them.
All around the city, fires had been lit; jar after jar of wine and beer
were opened and everyone had as much as they could eat or drink.

The Reed had given a banquet for us in the old Hall of Audience; and to it came all the captains and leaders of Hundreds, and
those nobles and officials who were Watchers. We toasted Ra, and
Horus, and Amenemhet. We toasted each other and the South.

I saw there was truth in the legend that the heads of soldiers
are thicker than other men's, or perhaps the wine of the Reed
was not so potent as that made in the Oryx; for though we
feasted until half-way between midnight and dawn there was not
one of us who could not still have walked a rope bridge without
overbalancing.

The Captain's house was only about two thousand paces from one of the city gates, so we decided to walk home. Kiyas linked arms with Hanuk and me. As we walked through the streets, which even at this late hour were still crowded with people rejoicing in their freedom, I saw a soldier, whom I recognized as one of my bowmen, carrying a girl up the street. She, with her arms around his neck, was planting kisses all over his face. Through the half-open shutters of a little house came the sound of an exchange of passionate endearments. Hanuk smiled. "Khnum the Potter will be kept busy marking his tallies tonight!"

"What does it matter, since the children will be born into freedom," said Kiyas. "Yesterday they were all slaves, though they didn't realize it; slaves of superstition, of caste, of jealousy, of ignorance. Fear was their whip-man, and we have set them free."

We passed through the pylon of the west gate. "Look, Ra-ab," said Kiyas, "look Hanuk! Sekmet has lit a torch for us that will never go out."

From the ruins of the Temple of Sekmet rose a pillar of fire. The darkness was giving forth light in the name of Ra.

Siege of the Royal City

SINCE I HAD TOLD the Captain of the Reed the history of the Watchers, what they had already accomplished and what they hoped to do for Egypt in the future, his only concern was to further our cause by every means in his power. To him also Amenemhet was Pharaoh, and so Men-het had become the usurper who must be overthrown so that the Two Lands could be united in peace.

He sent a messenger, who pretended to be a fugitive from the Reed, to tell Men-het of what had transpired, and that the allegiance of the most southerly of the Royal Nomes had been transferred to Amenemhet. I sent messengers to Pharaoh, and to each of the five Nomarchs of the North, whom I felt confident would now feel nearer in their allegiance to us than they had done before.

The Captain of the Reed sat with me in audience while I gave the judgments of the Eyes of Horus in the name of Pharaoh; and at the end of the audience I proclaimed him to be governor of the Old Capital until Pharaoh should decide whether he wished the Royal Nomes to continue under the direct authority of the crown or to have their own Nomarch. I had already told the Captain I was virtually certain that when Amenemhet heard what he had done to bring peace to the Old Capital he would be confirmed in the office of Nomarch of the Reed.

For five more days we stayed at the Old Capital, until messengers arrived from the North with the news for which I waited. I had hoped that when Men-het heard of the secession of the Reed he would accept the terms offered to him by Amenemhet; which were either to go into exile while his men went free, or else to swear allegiance to Amenemhet, in which case he would be made Captain of Egypt and retain all his estates and privileges. But the Royal messenger told me that Men-het had refused these terms, and had sent an insulting reply addressed to the "Traitor and Usurper, sometime Vizier."

Amenemhet had decided to stay in the Summer Place, as from there he had more opportunity to influence the North. It appeared that though the five Nomarchs had provisionally accepted him as the rightful wearer of the Red Crown, they would not continue to do so if it meant their having to take any part in the shedding of royal blood. If Men-het were deposed they were willing to join with the South, but the traditional jealousy between the Two Lands was still sufficiently strong to make them view with suspicion any plan which had originated in the land of the White Crown.

Messengers from the outskirts of the Royal City, and some from the city itself, reported that Men-het was preparing to stand a siege. Not only had he withdrawn inside the walls, but he had stripped the surrounding countryside of grain and a large part of the herds and fodder. It was estimated that he could survive without any outside supplies for half a year, or even longer. I was sufficiently familiar with the fortifications of the Royal City to know that to take it by assault would be impossible while it was so strongly held. In time we could starve them into surrender, but time we could not afford. At any moment the old antagonism of the North might flare up. For several centuries the Red

Crown had been stronger than the White; they would not forget that Amenemhet had been born at Thebes and that the Watchers who had given him the Crook and Flail came from the South. Until they were convinced that there was no longer any rivalry between the Two Lands, they would be afraid to further any plans which might involve the waning of their supremacy.

Hanuk, Sebek, Kiyas, the Reed and I were discussing this problem when another messenger arrived, to say that grain-barges were being allowed to proceed up-river to the Royal City and were adding considerably to the powers of resistance already held by Men-het.

"We must surround the city immediately and cut off further supplies from the North," I said. "The quays at which they are unloading are well protected from the landward side so we must attack from the river. Simultaneously we must advance on the City from all sides and post such strong guards outside the gates that nothing can leave or enter without our permission."

Sebek suggested, "If Men-het is convinced that he is hopelessly outnumbered he might surrender. Shall we send for reinforcements?"

"No. We have already a force equal to his, and we do not require extra Hundreds to convince Men-het that our forces are much greater than they are."

"How can we do that?" asked Kiyas.

"The main road to the North runs in sight of the watch towers, but it is out of bow-shot. Columns of men passing along the road will be fully visible; their numbers can be counted and their standards easily identified. Columns will march north until they are out of sight; then they will leave the causeway and return on the far side of it, ready to march northward again under different standards. There is only one place where the causeway is not high enough to conceal a man standing upright, but at that point the road runs beside a deep irrigation channel which will provide ample cover for men crawling along it. At night we will light many more cooking-fires than are needed—it is very discouraging for the besieged to think they are watching a force many times greater than their own who have nothing to do except wait and eat while they themselves grow increasingly hungry!"

"How many do you think are still with Men-het?" I asked the Reed.

"The Lotus Nome used to muster two thousand, but of these I think less than half stayed with the prince. The majority of the Royal Bodyguard have remained loyal to him, but I doubt if he has more than thirty-five Hundreds in all."

"Then we have outnumbered him already, now that the Reed has joined us," said Kiyas. "Why should our soldiers play games like children, creeping along water-channels and hiding behind causeways, so as to pretend we are stronger even than we are?"

"Because we dare not let Men-het stand a siege . . . and this he knows better than we do. Already the North is restive; it may remain uncertain for a few more days, perhaps longer, but after weeks of inactivity the Nomarchs would begin to doubt Amen-emhet's strength. They would think it was to their advantage to be the rescuers of Men-het rather than to acquiesce in the plans of the South."

"Somehow we must make a real marriage between the North and the South," said Kiyas. "At present the North is like a vain and jealous woman, who must be continually cajoled by her husband to prevent her setting the house in an uproar by her tempers!"

While the greater part of the four armies proceeded north-wards to encircle the City from the landward side, four Hundreds, under myself and Hanuk, went downriver in a fleet of twelve war-galleys, which had been waiting on the boundary of the Jackal until they were required.

The townspeople of the Old Capital lined the banks to cheer us as we started on another phase of what was now their cause as much as our own. I was surprised to find that Men-het had made no attempt to hold the bank opposite the Royal City, for though it had never been fortified there were several big houses beside the river which would have provided excellent cover for a large number of soldiers. The scouts who had gone ahead along the east bank reported that all was quiet; though the larger houses were deserted the work of the fields was going on as usual.

Lack of opposition on the east made our progress much easier than I had anticipated, for the river was wide enough for us to remain out of bow-shot of the city so long as we kept in to the further bank. I saw that Hanuk had been correct in thinking that the treads of the steps leading up from the landing-stages could be turned so as to add to the defense; they were now smooth stone runnels, no easier to scale than were the walls. The parapet at the top of the embankment had been heightened at several places to provide additional protection for bow-men, and it was obvious that any attack from the river could be repelled without serious difficulty.

Beyond the City we saw several barges tied up to the quays. One of them was being unloaded at full speed under the protection of a Hundred of bowmen. To my demand for surrender they replied with a flight of arrows which hissed into the water just short of the leading galley in which Hanuk and I were standing. As our rowers were protected by wooden shields they were able to bring us nearer to the bank without endangering themselves, and at the same time my bowmen returned the assault from the quay.

When Men-het's men saw the strength of our force and that further resistance was unlikely to produce a result in their favor, they retreated rapidly, though without disorder, leaving the cargo still remaining in the barges to fall into our hands. These cargoes proved more useful than I had expected, for in addition to grain they included a quantity of arrows of excellent workmanship and four hundred jars of wine.

The next three days produced little of interest. Any approach to within bowshot of the walls produced a swift and accurate rain of arrows; and repeated challenges to come out and give battle received in reply only derisive laughter from the sentries.

From Kiyas's estimate of Men-het's character I was sure he was not motivated by cowardice; if he preferred to stay inside the walls instead of coming out to fight it was because by doing so he was producing a situation more favorable to himself even than a decisive victory against us would have been.

"He wants us to stay here," said Kiyas. "If he didn't he would try to drive us away."

I turned to the Captain of the Reed and asked him, "Did he tell you *when* he intended to join battle with us?"

"No. We were to cut you off when you tried to retreat to the South. It was part of his original plan that you should besiege him here."

"Do you think he has a plan by which he hopes to influence the allegiance of the North?"

"I do. He seemed certain that the North would come over to his side, but he gave me no hint as to how he hoped to bring this about."

What Men-het's plan was I did not find out until later, but I will state it here as though I had the light of future knowledge.

He had sent a bribe to the chief of one of the largest Sinaitic tribes, saying that if the chief made a feint attack on the Royal City from the northeast he would find himself joined in friendship by Pharaoh, and from him receive rich gifts and the right to graze his herds for fifty years on the eastern uplands without tribute.

Men-het then intended to send messengers to the Nomarchs of the North, telling them that a powerful force was invading Egypt, and that he, their warrior Pharaoh, was going forth to drive it out of the country. He was confident of being able to leave the City when he wished, by crossing the river in grain-barges at night and breaking through the ring of besiegers. He would then march against the invaders, who, as they would offer no resistance, he would find no difficulty in "expelling."

Thus he would be in a position to tell the North that while they were trying to make up their minds, Pharaoh, and by that he meant himself, with only the Royal Bodyguard in support, had saved Egypt from being overrun. He would emphasize that he had allowed himself to be besieged rather than shed Egyptian blood; and that when Egypt was threatened it had been Pharaoh who saved her while the North and the South quarreled among themselves, having been made the dupes of a usurper.

I think Men-het had underrated the influence of the Watchers when making this plan, but even so it would have had a chance of succeeding. He was already renowned as a leader of men, and if he had been able to proclaim himself Pharaoh, not only by the right of blood, but because he was worthy of the Crook through having refused to kill fellow Egyptians even when they rebelled against him, and at the same time by the power of the Flail had driven off the invader single-handed. . . . One must not forget the effect of popular imagination: soon Men-het's three thousand fellow soldiers would have been forgotten and the "invader" shared in the reputation of "those whose name must never be spoken."

But I repeat, we did not know this plan until much later; for us it was sufficient that Men-het wished to be besieged, and therefore it was vital for us to end the siege as soon as possible.

Three times we made a simultaneous attack on all the seven gates of the City; but from every attempt we were driven back without inflicting any injury on the defenders, though our own men were beaten down under a hail of arrows, like grain in a summer storm. If we could not get into the City we could at least ensure that they should not come out. As it might have been possible for a man to slip through our lines under cover of darkness, I caused encircling watch-fires to be kept up from sunset to sunrise; and behind these were posted bowmen, who would find anyone an easy target who attempted to cross the belt of firelight.

It was Sebek who first suggested driving a tunnel under the walls; and this work was begun on the third day of the siege. As it was essential that the besiegers be taken by surprise, the tunnel had to be started from a place which was hidden from any vantage point of the enemy. A small group of trees, surrounding a well, afforded the nearest available cover, and it had the added advantage that men going to and from it in daylight would be thought to be going there to draw water.

It was about five hundred paces from the center of the west face, and, as nearly as I could judge, the tunnel would come up in the garden of one of the houses in a road leading off the Avenue of Sphinxes. As I knew these houses were occupied by minor officials of the Court, it was possible that we should find ourselves under the protection of one friendly to Amenemhet, which would make a secret entry in force considerably easier. I expected the tunnel to be completed in about seven days, but though I hoped to get many men through it before we were discovered, I knew I must be prepared to lose many killed and wounded.

As my country estate, which had come to me at the death of Heliokios, was only two hours from the Royal City, I decided it would be the best place for the wounded to be taken who were strong enough to stand the journey. I had not seen Daklion since my marriage, more than a year before, and he was overjoyed to welcome me. In spite of Men-het's soldiers having raided the surrounding countryside for grain and other supplies, I found every-thing much as I had left it. The famous strain of oxen had been sent to the Oryx to improve our herds, but there were still a few milch cows which would be useful for our needs. Experience gained during the pestilence made it easy for me to judge what we were likely to require for the care of the wounded; and under my orders Daklion soon prepared suitable accommodation for five hundred. Many of the women wished to remain in the encampment with their men, but the rest were eager to help Daklion and the household servants to make ready; and on the following day, twenty-five who had been wounded in the skir-mishes before the gates were sent there by litter.

The work on the tunnel went on unceasingly, but by the fifth day I saw that its completion would take far longer than I had hoped. The ground through which it was being driven had at first been either sand or loose gravel, which made it necessary to shore up the sides with timber every five cubits to prevent caving in. Later there came rock; which meant that either the tunnel had to be considerably lengthened so as to avoid it, or else the two men working at the face had to pick laboriously at the stone, which slowed their progress to a few thumb-joints an hour.

It was after the third of these delays that I received another messenger from Pharaoh. In spite of the capitulation of the Old Capital, the faction in favor of Men-het was daily growing in strength. Amenemhet could count on absolute loyalty only from his personal bodyguard, all of whom were Watchers, although the Nomarchs still extended him the courtesies due to the Holder of the Crook and Flail. He stressed the fact that if a decision could be reached while they still maintained this outward friendship they might well rally to our cause with genuine enthusiasm; but if they had begun to show their dissatisfaction openly, even though we found means of suppressing their activities against us, we should have lost their willing cooperation, perhaps for many years.

I had never before realized that a cat at a rat-hole is as much a prisoner as the rat itself. The walls between Men-het and myself bound us both the slaves of time.

As the moon grew toward the full I began to be increasingly

anxious about Meri. By now I had hoped to be victorious, and so to reach home before the ordeal of birth came upon her. I had news from her nearly every day; yet though I knew I joined her when we slept I remembered only her presence and not what she told me of her waking life.

Then came another messenger from Pharaoh. "To the Captain of the Oryx, commander of my army of the South. Know that you, our most loyal servant and our Brother in Horus, have worked with strength and subtlety for the cause, and that this you continue to do by every means in your power. Now must I tell you, both for your sake and my own, and therefore for all the peoples of Egypt who are so dear to us both, that Time, on whom we have waited for twenty years with every courtesy, now is begun to declare himself our enemy. With every day, through the impatience of the Nomarchs of the North, he gives increasing strength to Men-het. In the name of Pharaoh I counsel you to call up Ra to give you the guile of leopards, the strength of lions, and above all the swiftness of the Oryx, so that, by whatever means or strategy may come to your hand, you may bring Men-het, prince of the dead dynasty, to battle. If you should fail in this supreme endeavor, then that prince may receive the Red Crown; and though I still wear the White there will be tribulation from the East to the West, from the sea to the Lane of God, for Egypt will once more be a house divided."

Voice of the Dead

ON THE EIGHTEENTH DAY of the siege, I had been down to see the wounded, and when I got back to the encampment I found a message from Kiyas saying that as she was very tired she had gone to bed without waiting to see me. Sebek joined me as usual for the evening meal, and when I commented on the absence of Hanuk, told me he had gone off on some business of his own and did not expect to return until late.

When Sebek went on his round of the sentries, I accompanied him as far as the ring of watch-fires and then walked on alone. By night the walls of the city looked even more impregnable, as though they were strong as the cliffs on the eastern boundary of the Oryx. The moon rose, and silver light flooded the fields like a ghostly Inundation. There was no wind, and the silence was profound as deep water. Yet I was conscious of menace in the silence, which seemed taut as a stretched bow. I tried to think of something which needed doing, so as to break the uneasy circle of my thoughts. Even to check over the stores would have been a relaxation, but the men had settled down for the night. I could hear the sentries moving to and fro beyond the firelight. I said to myself, "Anxiety spreads like a pestilence, and they must not know that with every hour which passes I imagine armies from the North mustering to outflank us. The best leaders have calm minds, and though I cannot attain such detachment I can at least conceal my lack of ease."

I went back to my tent and lay very still, so that the sentry would not know that I was restless. I must at last have fallen asleep, for I woke with a start to see two cloaked figures, hoods drawn forward to hide their faces, standing beside me.

Kiyas's voice: "It's only Hanuk and I."

I slipped my dagger under the edge of the sleeping-mat so that she shouldn't guess the tension which had made me snatch it up. "Has anything happened? Is there any more news?"

"Good news, I think," said Kiyas. "We shall know for certain at dawn, less than an hour to wait. I think Men-het will send a challenge to battle."

"How do you know? How can you possibly know?"

"Because he would not disobey the voice of the dead!"

"What do you mean? What voice?"

"Mine," said Kiyas. "You won't be able to understand unless you make yourself believe that *you* are Men-het. Lie back and shut your eyes ... You are not Ra-ab; you are Men-het, who believes himself to be Pharaoh."

I did as she told me; perhaps it was because I was so sleepy that the scenes she evoked seemed to be taking place before other eyes than mine. . . .

"Although you know it suits your strategy to stand siege in the Royal City, you find it irksome. You try to pretend you are here of your own free will. Are you not a warrior Pharaoh resting between conquests? When you were only a prince, your favorite place in the City was your pleasure pavilion, built overlooking the river. It has a narrow terrace on the top of the river wall, and it is here you always liked to be when you have a difficult problem to consider. It was here you so often sat with Kiyas, the woman who died before you could marry her. You often think of her, perhaps that is why you come here every evening. You don't know that you can be seen from the opposite bank, or that it is known to your enemies that no one else ever uses this terrace. You are looking toward your tomb, where she is buried. . . .

"The moon has just risen, and her light on the water is as a bridge to carry your thoughts to the woman you loved. A moment before, the path was empty as your heart; now there is a boat gliding down-stream. It is the color of moonlight, silent as death. Who stands at the steering-oar? A man with the head of a jackal. Anubis, steersman of the Boat of Millions of Years! Is he coming for you, Men-het? See, the boat comes straight toward you; quietly, so quietly. Why don't your bowmen loose their arrows? Have they fled, or are you the only one who can see the boat?

"There is an open sarcophagus which gleams like silver in the moonlight. Has Anubis brought your coffin to you, Men-het? You wonder if you are dreaming; but your hands gripping the parapet are real enough . . . you can feel the grain of the stone under your fingers. Further along the wall a sentry calls to his neighbor that all is well, He cannot see the boat: why should he, when it has come for you? Now you can see down into the sarcophagus. In it there lies a woman. She whom you love is come back from your tomb to speak with you.

"Slowly, very slowly, she rises up. She is pale as river mist. Her hands are outstretched to you: you hear her voice. . . . 'Men-het. Men-het. The spirits of the warrior-dead are mocking you. They are saying the man I wait for is afraid. They say I lie when I tell them Men-het is greater than they. They are whispering, Men-het; surely when the evening is quiet, you have heard them whisper-ing? They say Men-het hides in his Royal City because he dare not go out to fight! Tell them, Men-het, that I do not wait in vain!'

"The woman sinks back into her sarcophagus. Not daring to move lest the vision vanish, you watch the boat slowly turn and glide on down-stream."

It seemed that Kiyas had evoked the soul of the dead. It might have been I who stood on the wall of the Royal City, straining my eyes to catch a last glimpse of a boat which returned into the darkness.

"Was your dream so real," I asked, "that you are sure Men-het will remember it?"

"It was no dream," said Hanuk.

"What do you mean?"

For answer they let their cloaks fall. Their bodies were white as salt. Kiyas smiled at my bewilderment. "We painted ourselves white, then rubbed the skin lightly with oil and dusted it with silver."

Hanuk showed me what he was carrying under his arm; a mask made like a jackal's head. "I was Anubis, and she the woman who returned from the dead."

Admiration for a brilliant strategy ran in conflict with anger that Hanuk should have exposed Kiyas to such danger. Anger won; and I said, "Hanuk, you had no right to let Kiyas do it! She is my sister, and you should not have dared so desperate a plan without my permission."

"It was *my* permission she needed: and I gave it to her with my heart."

"Since when has a kinsman more authority than a brother?"

Hanuk put his arm around Kiyas's shoulder and smiled down at her: the look on her face should have been enough to tell me what his next words would be, but I was still dense with sleep.

"Since when has a brother more authority than a husband?"

"A husband?"

"Yes," said Kiyas. "And, dear Ra-ab, you mustn't be angry about it. Last night we made the Oath of the New Name, before Ptah-aru, and swore him to secrecy."

"Why didn't you tell me? You know I have always wanted Hanuk for a brother."

"Because you would have made us tell you why we wanted to get married so suddenly. Do you remember that I once promised you I wouldn't marry until I found the man with whom I could make the Oath of the New Name? Well, three days ago I discovered that Hanuk was the person whom I'd been looking for all

EYES OF HORUS

the time. It happened just after I'd told him my idea for playing on Men-het's superstition so that I could make him believe I had come back from the dead. Hanuk said, 'Do you love the Eyes of Horus so much that in their name you are willing to betray the man you love?' I knew then that I didn't love Men-het, and never had, and that however important it might be for the Watchers, even if it had been the only way of saving Egypt, I still wouldn't do anything against Hanuk... because he would always be far, far, more important to me than anything else. I told Hanuk that I was very sorry for having wasted such a lot of our time; and when I asked him to marry me at once, so that we shouldn't waste any more, he said he would."

"That's all very interesting; but I still don't see why you couldn't have told me about it."

"What Hanuk and I were going to do was very dangerous. You would have been sure to try to stop us, or else insist on sharing the danger. We couldn't let you do that, because the chance of our succeeding seemed rather small and you had to stay to lead the armies. It didn't matter Hanuk and I going into danger together, because we should either both go on living or else both be dead... nothing matters to us except being separated. If we didn't return, then you would have heard what had happened to us from Ptah-aru."

"How *did* you get back?" I asked Hanuk.

"We had with us a large black cloth which could be pulled right over the boat, making it practically invisible from the bank. The current was strong enough to carry us downstream, and when we were out of sight of Men-het we crossed over to the other side of the river, using short paddles which we could wield lying down."

"What would you have done if Men-het hadn't been there, or you had been seen by sentries who were not so easily deluded?"

"That was one of the risks we had to take. I admit that I was not nearly so hopeful as Kiyas that we should manage to deceive him."

"You take your responsibilities as a husband very lightly! Don't you realize that if you had been taken prisoner, Men-het would have known that Kiyas has always been no more than a spy and that her story would make him a mockery? He would have had her tortured; slowly and terribly . . . she might have lived for several days."

"Kiyas is not only my wife; we are both Eyes of Horus: therefore we are pledged to take any risk which we believe is to the furtherance of our cause. We were both fully aware that our marriage night was likely to be the only one we should know together. I took every means I could of protecting her; we had arranged that if an alarm was given we would both dive off the boat and try to swim to the east bank, where some of my men were waiting for us."

"I should judge your chances of reaching the bank to have been about one in a thousand. Had you forgotten the crocodiles?"

"No," said Kiyas. "Crocodiles guard the Underworld for Set; but ordinary Egyptian crocodiles would have sent Hanuk and me to somewhere where we should still have been together . . . and that is all I ask of my heaven."

Suddenly she ran forward to pull aside the tent flap. "Listen!" she cried. "Listen!"

Across the mists of the morning came a trumpet call. "It's a herald," said Kiyas. "Men-het's herald . . . coming out to bring a challenge to battle."

Prelude to Battle

THE HERALD was conducted to my tent by two sentries. In an expressionless voice he delivered his message:

"I speak in the name of Men-het, Pharaoh. Hereby do I challenge the army of the rebellious South to a Battle of the Six Hundred. All those who are not of the number appointed must swear to take no part. When the surrender has been sounded, then shall the defeated army suffer itself to be made prisoner without resistance. Hereby do I promise in the Royal Name, that prisoners taken shall not suffer violence in their persons and shall be set free after forty days; if by that time they have experienced a change of heart and are once more loyal Egyptians. The battle to be joined at dawn tomorrow; in the Field of Hathor to the south of my Royal City. Given under my seal on this, the twenty-second day of my reign."

"Tell the Prince, your master, that we accept his challenge of six Hundred against six Hundred. Tell him also that by tomorrow he will have learned that his message was wrongly phrased: it is Men-het who is the usurper and we who fight for Pharaoh."

The herald made no answer, and I assigned four soldiers to escort him back through our lines.

Kiyas had remained hidden while he was there lest she were recognized; now she joined me with Hanuk beside her.

"Tomorrow at dawn, Ra-ab! Men-het has proved an obedient servant of the dead!"

"Do you think he will lead his men himself?"

"I am sure of it. Remember that he thinks the shades are mocking him . . . he would not let them add another taunt: that Men-het was afraid to fight and asked his men to restore his honor for him!"

"Yet I doubt if his pride will outweigh his judgment," said Hanuk. "In such a battle the leaders do not wear distinctive dress, for if they did they would soon leave their army without a leader."

"It has long been arranged," I said, "that if I am killed Hanuk takes command. The six Hundred will be drawn from the Oryx, the Jackal, and the Hare; each two Hundred under the leadership of myself, Hanuk and the Captain of the Hare. It is possible that both Hanuk and I will be killed. I decree that if this be so, you my sister, wife of the Nomarch of the Jackal, will command the three armies until such time as Roidahn or Pharaoh choose to make other provision. You have proved yourself to be wise in strategy, and Sebek will be at your side to advise you and to see that your orders are carried out. Of this decision all the Leaders of Hundreds will be informed. And if it be that tomorrow Hanuk and I are summoned before the Forty-two Assessors, you at the same time will be receiving the oath of allegiance from the warriors of the South."

A challenge such as Men-het's had many precedents in antiquity: though the number of combatants might vary from a few champions, sometimes only three, to as many as five thousand. The battle always began at sunrise and would continue either until a decision had been reached or until dusk; when there would be a truce until dawn of the following day. The immunity given to all priests under the Warrior's Code held even in the thick of a skirmish, and those who tended the wounded might do so without danger save from a chance arrow.

The Field of Hathor was a large meadow where temple bulls used to be pastured, and was about a thousand paces square. I talked with those sent by Men-het to make ready, and it was agreed that they should take the north side of the field and we the south. I caused tents to be erected on the southern boundary of the field, where our men could rest if the battle lasted into a second day; for the combatants were not permitted to leave the scene of battle until a decision was reached. On the western side, midway between the two lines, an enclosure was marked off by poles flying blue pennants. Here the wounded of both sides would be taken and accommodated in their respective tents. No one might enter the enclosure except those engaged in the care of the wounded. Wounded men of the defeated army were not taken prisoner, and would be treated with every consideration and given a safe-conduct to their homes.

Since the acceptance of such a challenge meant that no offensive action would be taken by either side until the time appointed, I was not surprised to see several groups of people leaving the City to come and stare at the preparations being made on the field. Two shallow trenches, less than a cubit wide, were dug across it; and these were separated from each other by a distance of five hundred paces. These trenches marked the area in which the fighting was to take place, and the rival armies would try to drive each other back over the line furthest from their own side. The army which was first to have no man left alive within these limits was declared defeated, and their trumpeters would immediately sound the surrender.

A man was allowed to leave the field to have his wounds dressed, or to get other succor or fresh weapons, and could then return to join in the fray. If men could be temporarily spared during a prolonged combat it was not unusual for the commander to order several to take a short rest so that their vigor be renewed. The responsibility on the individual soldier was greater than in any other form of battle, for after the initial stages the lines broke into separate groups and twelve or more fights might be going on at the same time in different parts of the field.

At noon I had our full strength assembled to tell them the laws under which we would fight. Then I asked that those who wished to take part should raise their arms. They responded as one man; so I told them that I should leave the choice to the Leaders of Hundreds, who were the best judges of those most proficient to serve our cause. I told the Leaders that I wanted in each Hundred an equal number of bowmen, mace-bearers and javelin-men, and that only those who were specially skilled both in wrestling and with the long dagger should be selected.

Later in the afternoon I took the six Hundred to the Field of Hathor and outlined to them my strategy. "At the first trumpet the mace-bearers will dash forward so as to occupy as much of the intervening ground as possible before we meet the enemy ranks. Behind them the javelin-men will advance, though at a slightly slower pace, and when they can be sure their shafts will not be wasted they will launch them; but not until they receive my order, at which the mace-bearers will crouch down to let the javelins pass overhead. The javelin-men will then make way for the bowmen, who will aim high so that their arrows rain down on the enemy. After the battle is closely joined, half of all the javelin and bowmen will throw down their first weapon and fight on with shield and dagger. The rest will withdraw behind the melee to pick off any enemy who can be aimed at without endangering our men. When their turn comes to fight at close quarters they too will exchange their weapons for the dagger."

Though I was almost certain that Men-het would obey the Warrior's Code, I had the watch-fires lit at dusk, yet posted only half the usual number of sentries. I had oxen slaughtered to provide all the men with extra food, and allowed a jar of beer to every twenty men. They laughed and shouted warrior songs in their warm, rough voices. I overheard many fragments of conversation when I walked down the lines, but not once did I hear anything to suggest they entertained the possibility of defeat. To them the battle was already won, and so strong was their faith in our cause that they would not have been surprised if Ra had struck down Men-het should he show any signs of winning.

I wished that I shared their certainty. Part of me was confident of victory, but my shoulders were bowed with the weight of responsibility. The men under Men-het would be veterans, strong in the confidence which comes from a series of victories. They would be used to seeing friends killed beside them, used to the cries of dying men, immune to pity. On the practice-ground my men were a match for his, but it is a terrible test to meet the supreme endeavor when men are still untried. Had I been unwise in refusing the offer made by the Captain of the Reed to allow me to choose among his picked men as well as my own? Then I remembered the relief which he had tried to conceal when I said it were better that men who so recently had been comrades in arms should not be asked to fight against one another.

I was unlikely to escape injury; perhaps tomorrow Kiyas would be leading a defeated army to the South. If Meri were dead I should be glad to follow her, but my death would condemn her to many empty years. I wanted to be alone with my thoughts of Meri, and I knew that Hanuk and Kiyas would wish to be with each other. The path I took led down to the river. The water chuckled against the bank, a safe, comfortable sound. Perhaps I wasn't going to be killed: soon I might be hearing that same sound while Meri and I lay together in our pleasure-boat. Did I wish that she was here with me?

Again I was of two minds; for my own sake I wished that if this was to be my last night on Earth I might share it with her, yet I did not wish her to suffer the torture of anxiety through which I knew Kiyas must be passing. At dawn I would have no time for anxieties, but Kiyas would not be so protected from her thoughts. She would watch the press of men swaying to and fro, trying to see if Hanuk and I were still safe. She would look up at the vultures, wheeling slowly and patiently over the field as they watched a feast being spread below.

For so long I had been impatient of Time: in the House of the Captains; during my training as one of the Eyes of Horus; while I awaited marriage to Meri; during the siege of the Royal City. Always had I been Time's impatient servant; now for a little while he had become my friend. His hours were a shield between my body and the dawn. He allowed me to feel strength flowing along my smooth muscles, and to appreciate the bliss of being without pain. He counseled me, "Dwell on this peace which I have vouchsafed you; enjoy to the full these moments which pass so slowly . . . and if tomorrow you receive a grievous wound, do not rail against me to speed my pace."

The Field of Hathor

AS THE NIGHT PALED with the coming of the dawn, I spoke to my men assembled on the Field of Hathor.

"Men of the South, I speak to you in the name of Pharaoh. This day may be remembered in the history of Egypt, not only as that which marked a great battle or as the day when Pharaoh was no longer challenged in his rightful powers; but as the day when Fear went into exile and the Watchers of the Horizon brought peace to the Two Lands. Each one of you is the symbol of a thousand men. If you triumph they will be free; if you fail they may be enslaved. Fight not for glory, though your name will be imperishable as pyramids: fight that your fellow men shall not be betrayed: fight until defeat or victory is ours. Call on the name of Ra to give you strength. Ask Horns to bless your weapons that they may be thirsty for the blood of Men-het and his followers. The Dawn is come! Peace be upon you; and through you on the Two Lands!"

Long shadows were stealing across the field as I took my place two paces in front of the first rank. On my right, at the head of the men of the Jackal, stood Hanuk; on my left was the Hare. On the other side of the field the enemy were assembled; their breechclouts vermilion, the Royal color, their leaders wearing no insignia of rank to distinguish them. Hanuk had been right; Men-het was too wise a soldier to wear the headdress of a warrior Pharaoh, as he would have done had this been an ordinary battle.

The heralds raised their trumpets; both lines of men crouched for the dash forward. Everything was very quiet; then the fabric of the morning was torn by the blare of trumpets. Like hounds slipped from leash we leaped forward; fast, but not too fast, for we must not be breathless at the first encounter.

My shouted command was echoed down the ranks; the men who held unbroken line with me flung themselves down to let the javelins speed over our heads like a flight of wild-fowl.

Up and forward! The shield was already on my left arm, the

dagger naked in my hand—another safe in its sheath hanging from my belt. With a crash the waves of men broke against each other. Arrows were no longer falling. The man opposite me threw down his mace and drew his dagger. Almost before I realized my hand had struck at him, his eyes opened with inarticulate surprise. I jerked out the dagger, buried nearly half to the hilt under the angle of his jawbone. He was dead before he hit the ground. I was glad he was beyond further pain; for I heard his ribs crack as men surged over him. . . .

The man I was fighting was the only thing of which I was conscious. I might have been alone with him on an empty plain instead of being surrounded by a press of men. I was on the ground and he was trying to strangle me. He had kicked my dagger out of my hand and somehow I must have made him drop his own. I locked my legs round his thighs and tried to pull him down. Part of my mind had a curious detachment. I noticed that the man who was killing me was a little older than myself. The lobe of his left ear was missing, and his eyes were a light, clear gray. There was a roaring, louder than floodwater, in my ears. I tried to shout, but my tongue had swollen too big for me to move it. I plucked at his hands. Nothing, nothing could ever be strong enough to pull them from my throat . . . Suddenly there was a curious red flower on his forehead. I could breathe, though it was an agony to draw each breath. He put his hand up to his head. The red flower has white stamens. No, I can see better now: they are slivers of bone in pulped flesh. I was still gripping his body with my legs. I rolled aside and he fell backwards. The mace-bearer who had killed him for me grinned and looked for another on whom to test his skill.

The main focus of the battle had swept past me, and I was able to regain my breath and look around. I saw Ptah-aru and the other healer priests going calmly about the field; kneeling beside fallen men to see if they were dead or only wounded. I remember thinking that if only Men-het had priests who followed him to battle ours would not have had so many to look after. He was quite dead, the gray eyes already losing their luster, like the scales of a dead fish.

I saw that my policy of keeping some of the bowmen back had

been justified. An enemy who broke through our ranks was allowed to run on unhindered until he provided an easy target. One of them was still running, trying to pluck an arrow out of his side. A priest hurried over to him and led him away.

The battle had not long been joined, but already there must have been two hundred dead. I thought, "I must find Men-het; it is he, not his men, whom I must seek out to destroy." Though I had seen him only twice while I was at the Royal City his face was sharply defined in my memory. Once I could get to grips with him, Horus would give me the strength to kill this tyrant who was trying to enslave my people. . . .

My heart had steadied to an even thudding and it no longer hurt me to breathe. I was impressed to see how deeply the Warrior's Code was ingrained in the soldier's character; two men engaged in a desperate fight were endangering a wounded man whom they had not noticed. I knew they were blind to everything except their immediate enemy; yet when Ptah-aru commanded them to cease while the wounded man was moved to safety they fell apart as though suddenly cast into statues of fury. They stood motionless while Ptah-aru and another priest carried the man away; only when they heard the priest tell them they were free to go on fighting did they fall upon one another again.

There was a brief lull; both sides, as though by mutual consent, fell back a few paces and began carrying their dead back to their own lines. After they had laid down the corpses they sluiced water over themselves, some rubbing the palms of their hands with powdered rosin to improve their grip on the dagger-hilt. There was no way of telling man from leader except by personal recognition; all were rennelled with sweat and dust, and most were smeared with blood, either their own or an enemy's.

All down the line fighting flared up again. At the entrance to the enclosure of the wounded I saw a woman standing, and knew it was Kiyas. She would be able to recognize Hanuk even when he was at the far end of the field, for no one could match his height. He was fighting on my right; a smile on his face, and at his feet two men he had just killed. I saw an enemy bowman aim at him and shouted to him to duck. He did not hear me. The arrow struck in his right shoulder, and while he was trying to pull it out two men attacked him. They must have recognized him as a leader; five more of Men-het's soldiers dashed toward him.

"I can still fight!" he shouted to me as I ran up to join him. "Keep your back against mine and watch their eyes."

The first man to rush me slipped on a patch of blood; as he did so my dagger caught him in the belly and ripped it up. He crawled away, a loop of bowel protruding between the fingers of the hand with which he was trying to close the rent.

There was a stifled cry from Hanuk, "They've got me Ra-ab!"

For a moment his weight was supported against my shoulders, then he slid down at my feet. "The Oryx! To the Oryx!" I shouted; and saw that two of my bowmen were already running toward me. I straddled Hanuk's body, trying to protect it. I realized that they meant to take me prisoner, else why did they try to grapple instead of using javelin or mace? A man sprang on my back; I was lucky, and caught his arm so that I was able to throw him over my head in the wrestling hold Sebek had taught me. Three of the five remaining men turned to meet the bowmen, who dropped their bows and drew their daggers. I felt Hanuk move; he wasn't dead. "If only I can keep these two off a little longer he will be saved for Kiyas." One of them drew back and I saw him pick up a mace. I lunged forward to catch the other man around the waist. "If I can lift him I can use him as a shield." The mace descended. . . .

I was falling down a black well-shaft and could see the water far away at the bottom. What was it Hanuk had said? "There are spikes under the water so that death shall be unpleasant." . . . The Sekmet priests have beaten me at last. I thought I was too clever for them. Surely Hanuk pulled me back when the stone turned? Then why am I falling? I must have hit my head.

They shouldn't have let Kiyas come on the field. I can hear her voice. My eyelids are so heavy I can't open them yet. Kiyas ought not to be here. Her voice is steady; she can't know about Hanuk yet; I shall have to tell her. She is talking to Hanuk: doesn't she realize he's dead?

"Lie quite still, my very dear. The shaft of the arrow is broken and they've got to cut the head out of your shoulder. Your left arm is broken at the elbow: Ptah-aru set it before you regained consciousness. Oh, my dear, it's hurting you so terribly."

"No, it's not at all bad."

Hanuk's voice! With a great effort I opened my eyes. I was lying on the ground in one of our tents. Kiyas was kneeling between Hanuk and I. His left arm was in a splint, and Ptah-aru was cutting an arrow-head from the other shoulder. I saw Hanuk's lips tighten as he tried to keep back a gasp of pain. Blood dripped down in slow, heavy drops. Kiyas's forehead was beaded with sweat, but her hands were steady as she poured cane-spirit on a pad of soft linen and helped Ptah-aru to bind it over the wound.

"How is the battle going?" he said between his teeth.

"I don't know, but we're sure to be winning," answered Kiyas. "Over a hundred of their wounded were brought in before you were hurt, and they have lost twice as many dead."

"Are you sure Ra-ab's all right? I should be dead if it wasn't for him, Kiyas."

"He'll be all right. He's not hurt so badly as you are, though he's still unconscious."

I raised myself on my left elbow, "No, I'm not. But there's not enough wine in Egypt to give me another headache like this one! Though by tomorrow we shall all have one nearly as good— through drinking to our victory. I'll have the first drink now and then go back to the battle."

"Lie down, Ra-ab," said Kiyas firmly. "I'll bring you some wine, though you mustn't have too much, for you've been hit on the head. You've got a huge lump over your right ear. Ptah-aru said it was a miracle your skull wasn't staved in . . . anyway you can't go on fighting, because you've got a bad wound in your right arm."

For the first time I noticed there was a thick pad of folded linen covering my right arm from elbow to shoulder. I flexed my fingers and found they still moved freely. "There doesn't seem much wrong with my arm," I said. "What's happened to it?"

"You'll know soon enough when Ptah-aru comes back to put in some stitches. He said he was going to do it as soon as he finished Hanuk."

Ptah-aru came into the tent carrying a shallow dish in which were several electrum needles and lengths of waxed linen thread. When the sodden dressing was removed I saw I must have lost a lot of blood: the flesh had been sliced in a thick flap from the point of the elbow nearly to the shoulder.

"It looks as though I had been fighting cannibals who tried to steal a collop off me," I said, trying to pretend I thought the wound trivial.

"The tendons have not been severed," said Ptah-aru. "In time there should be no more than a scar to remind you of the wound."

He shifted the loose flesh into place and began to draw the gaping edges together as calmly as though he were a fisherman patching a sail. For one awful moment I thought I was going to be sick; and tried desperately to think of a joke, however feeble. "I'm surprised that even Sekmet is greedy for human sacrifice. I should have thought one taste would have been enough to make her prefer temple bulls, or even goats burned to a cinder!"

He put fourteen stitches in my arm, and each of them seemed to hurt more than the one before; feeling was flowing back into the numbed shoulder and the cane-spirit in which he soaked the bandages lapped like fire on the wound.

"Lie quiet now," said Ptah-aru, "or you will unpick my careful work—and then they'll set me to sewing loin-cloths for field-workers instead of letting me repair Ptah's tunics!"

Kiyas went out every few minutes to get news from Sebek. For a time the tide seemed to be flowing in our favor, but about noon I realized her cheerfulness was forced.

"You've got to tell me the truth, Kiyas. Sebek's worried?"

"He's not exactly *worried*. Things are not going quite as well as they were."

"Ask him their losses and ours as near as he can judge. I order you to tell me exactly what he says."

In a moment she was back. "He says they have about two hundred still fighting, and he is almost sure Men-het is not wounded. That, more than anything else, is giving them the advantage . . . though they have more men left than we have. The Hare has been killed."

"I must go back."

"No, Ra-ab! You mustn't, you can't!"

I struggled to my feet; then realized to my shame that I was going to faint.

From a dark vortex came Hanuk's voice. "We'll both have to lie here and do what Kiyas tells us. The best bowman can't fly an arrow when the bow-string is broken."

I lay still, and thought miserably, "For the full use of my right arm for an hour I would lose it for a lifetime. If only my brain didn't feel as though it were loose inside my skull; it makes it so difficult to think properly."

For a time fortune turned again in our favor. Our men were fighting even more fiercely now they had heard that Hanuk and I were still alive, and the men of the Hare were avenging their Nomarch with great ferocity.

At last I could bear the suspense of inactivity no longer. I got slowly to my feet, and found that after a moment or two the ground no longer seemed to be swaying about like a boat in a high wind. The entrance to the enclosure was only a few paces from my tent. Sebek was standing there, and by his face I saw that things were very serious.

"We have only sixty men left," he said, "and they still have at least a hundred. Our men are fighting like Gods, but some of them have already been wounded. It is so terrible to have to stand here watching them and not be allowed to do anything to help! The enemy have still got Men-het to lead them; when men are very tired it is difficult for them to think for themselves. We have not even got a Leader of a Hundred left on the field."

"I will go out to them."

"No, don't Ra-ab. Kiyas says you have lost too much blood, and fainted again a little while ago. If you go out and they see you fall it will take the heart out of them."

"How many wounded have we?"

"Three hundred. And of those nearly a hundred are likely to be dead by this evening."

"Are there any with only slight wounds?"

He pointed to the field. "The slightly wounded are out there."

"There must be others no worse than I am. I'll go and see them."

"The least seriously wounded are in the first tent, and the dying are in the one beyond. Their men are in the tents on the far side of the enclosure."

The men were so closely packed together that there was only a narrow path down the middle of the tent. They tried to cheer when they saw me, and I said to them:

"Men of the South, whatever the outcome of this battle, you will be remembered as mighty warriors. All of you here are badly wounded and the priests say you should not be allowed to return to the battle. You have played your part; whether we or Men-het wins you will still be given safe-conduct to your homes and will not be made prisoner. You have gained your wounds with honor, and I have no right to ask more of you. Yet I do ask more: that all of you who are still strong enough will follow me back to the fray, even those who can only pretend that they are able to fight. We have less than sixty men on the field and they have more than a hundred. If you come with me and give a great shout, 'For the Oryx and the South,' the enemy, who must be nearly as tired as we are, may lose heart ... thinking I have deliberately kept some of you back to throw against them when they are almost exhausted."

The man beside me pulled himself upright by one of the tent poles. His left foot was swathed in heavy bandages. "I'm with you, Captain; though if it were with a snail I had to race it would be doubtful on which to wager! It's a bowman I am, and I can still sight an arrow, for all that one of Men-het's barbarians has stolen three fingers off my right hand. I'll have to get this bandage off though, so as to get my thumb and first finger free."

All who could stand joined me—a hundred and thirty of them, men who had already shed so much of their blood and earned the honors of war; yet who for a chance of victory were very willing to die.

"We will go forward slowly; keeping an unbroken line. Each of you take the weapon you can best use."

I took a dagger; and was grateful that long ago Sebek had made me learn how to use it with my left hand as well as my right. In spite of their bandages the men made a brave show: sweat and blood had been washed off their bodies when their wounds were dressed, so they looked as though they were less seriously wounded than they were. I prayed to Ra that Men-het would think I had withdrawn these men to rest so as to launch them on him at a favorable moment.

We shouted our battle-cry, "For the Watchers and the South!" and the cry was echoed by the men already fighting so desperately.

Men-het was now easily recognizable as he rallied his men around him. The wounded bowman who was still beside me knelt down to take careful aim. I saw blood pouring from his hand; but he was whistling a marching song through his teeth. I heard the twang of the bow-string.

Men-het spun around; swayed . . . and then crashed to the ground. An arrow was sticking out between his ribs.

In an awed voice the bowman said, "Think of me being the one to kill Pharaoh's son . . . and my father was not even a soldier, he was a fisherman."

A cry went up from the ranks of the enemy, "Pharaoh is dead! Pharaoh is dead!"

Our men surged forward again; and the enemy broke before them.

As though from a great distance I heard their trumpeters sounding the surrender.

I saw four men run to Men-het and kneel beside him. They had brought a rough litter with them, on which they lifted him. To my surprise they carried it slowly toward the enclosure of the wounded; and I realized he was not dead.

A wave of sound rippled across the field, "The Oryx and Victory! The Oryx! The Oryx!"

I realized they were cheering me, and that the South had triumphed.

I wondered why they were taking Men-het to the enclosure instead of back to the Royal City. Then thought, "It must be so that he can claim immunity from being taken prisoner. It is for Amenemhet, not I, to give judgment on him. There need no longer be enmity between us: now we are only two soldiers wounded in the same battle."

I saw his men took him to the small tent which I had shared with Hanuk. The men came out and I passed them at the entrance to the enclosure. One of them, whose old scars showed him to be a veteran of many battles, had slow tears running down his face.

I asked him, "Is he badly hurt?"

"He is dying. He made us promise that he should never be taken prisoner. That's why we brought him here. He shall be free until he dies."

Men-het was unconscious. Ptah-aru, who had just finished examining the wound, said to me, "The arrow has gone through the left lung and I think it has severed one of the large arteries. To try to remove the arrow would only hasten his death. I do not think he will ever come back to feel the pain his body is suffering."

The lips of the dying man moved. "Kiyas. . . . Kiyas . . . I will keep you waiting only a little longer. I died on a victory . . . the spirits of the dead can no longer mock me, can they, Kiyas?"

She was kneeling beside him, and leaned forward to kiss him on the forehead. He opened his eyes, and as he recognized her, the lines of pain and bitterness seemed to be smoothed out of his face. His voice was stronger now. "You always told me that death was a little thing, but I never really believed you. I am so happy to be dead. . . . I have found you again."

He turned his head to kiss her hand. His eyes slowly closed, as though he were too sleepy to keep them open any longer. There was a smile on his mouth: still there even when the blood had gushed out of it; and he was dead.

I walked slowly out of the tent. Ra had nearly ended his day's journey, and the western sky was flooded with green and scarlet; as though banners were flying to welcome his warriors home.

I heard someone come out and stand beside me, then Hanuk said, "I have left Kiyas alone with him. His spirit may linger for a little while and she will be able to comfort him."

"You ought to be lying down."

He took no notice, and went on as though speaking to himself, "I have been jealous of Men-het because I love Kiyas; and I have hated him because I love Egypt; yet now I feel almost as though my brother had been killed."

"I am glad that neither you nor I flew the arrow: his was a brave heart."

"This morning I hated him; I wanted to kill him and destroy his false divinity—to kill him with my bare hands. How could I have wanted to do that to a brave man who loves Kiyas . . . and only died in peace because he thought he went to join her?"

"That is the bitterness of war, Hanuk. An enemy ceases to be a man; he has become a symbol of an idea which cannot live with the ideas in which we believe. Twelve hundred men today were consumed with one idea—to kill each other. All of them thought they were dying to save Egypt. We knew why we were fighting, but did they? They fought for Pharaoh—and if tomorrow they acknowledge Amenemhet, they will still be willing to die for something they do not understand."

"How can they understand each other when they do not even understand why they are willing to die?"

"That is what the Eyes of Horus must teach them. Teach men to know themselves so that they can recognize the brotherhood they share. If Men-het had known himself, even as well as Kiyas knew him, he could have lived for Egypt instead of dying that she might live. Seven hundred sons of the Two Lands would not be dead, nor would nearly another three hundred perhaps be crippled. The women who now weep would have been rejoicing, and children would not have been left fatherless. A big price for Egypt to have paid . . . because one of her children did not realize the true value of his qualities."

I saw Sebek walking rapidly toward me through the gathering dusk. "I have been talking to the Captain whom Men-het appointed to command after him. He asks that their surrender may be postponed long enough for them to follow Men-het to his tomb as free men. Men-het left orders that no funeral rites were to be performed, nor was his body to be embalmed. His sarcophagus is open beside the one in which he thinks Kiyas is buried, and he decreed that nothing be put in it with him except the presents he gave her."

"Tell the Captain of the Royal Bodyguard that they need not surrender until dawn of the day after tomorrow; when he, and all who followed Men-het's standard, shall assemble on the Field of Hathor to hear what I have to say to them."

When I saw the bier which was brought for Men-het I wondered if he had expected to be killed, for I doubted if there had been time to fetch it from the Royal City. It was covered with gold-leaf, the carrying-poles inlaid with turquoise and electrum, and to each of the four poles there were seven bearers.

I went into the tent: "They are coming to take him away, Kiyas."

She folded the hands of the dead man on his breast; and I saw that in one of them she had placed a lock of her hair. She kissed him on the mouth, and then stood up. Brushing away the tears which were sliding down her cheeks, she said, "I have prayed so very hard that Ra will take him under his protection . . . so that he goes to the one he really loves—of whom I must have reminded him."

"You must leave him now; his men have come to fetch him away."

The path leading from the Field of Hathor was lined with our soldiers in honor of the dead. Very serene did Men-het look as he lay on the bier; the smile still lingering on the quiet mouth.

Ahead of him went torch-bearers; and the men who followed him, rank after rank in triple file, also bore torches.

Slowly the ribbon of fire wound across the plain; past the Royal City where for twenty-three days he had ruled as Pharaoh. Then the funeral procession took the Royal Road, to the tomb of the last of a dark dynasty.

Dawn over Egypt

I WAS STILL WATCHING the now distant torches of the funeral procession when Sebek's voice broke the thread of my thoughts. "I have had Hanuk's tent pitched beside your own, just beyond the enclosure—I thought you would both wish for privacy and yet to be near the wounded. Ptah-aru is waiting to dress your arm again."

I put up my uninjured hand to find that blood had soaked through the bandages. "Is there nothing else I ought to do? Have messengers been sent to Amenemhet? Is everything being done for the men?"

"There is nothing else you need worry about; everything is being attended to."

"I wonder how long it will be before the news of our victory reaches Pharaoh?"

"In a few hours; for soon after the battle was joined a messenger arrived from him to say he had left the Summer Palace and was now at the house of one of the Nomarchs, not far to the north of the Royal City. Our message, by relays of runners, will reach him by dawn."

"Ask Men-het's Captain if he agrees that the dead, both his and our own, shall be buried in this field. They are all warriors of Egypt, who have died to bring us peace."

I swayed on my feet, and Sebek put out his hand to steady me. "Ra-ab, all that shall be done. But you've got to go and rest now."

It was good to be able to lie down, and let Kiyas help Ptah-aru to put a fresh dressing on my arm. Some of the stitches had broken, and the new ones seemed to hurt much more than the first ones had done. I was so tired that the pain—though I kept on telling myself it wasn't really bad pain—was almost unbearable.

Kiyas was holding my hand; and suddenly it seemed as though we had both become children again and that I was trying to comfort her while a deep cut on her knee was being washed by Niyahm.

Then someone, I think it was Kiyas, was making me drink spoonfuls of broth which smelled of poppies. I protested, "You mustn't give me a sleep-drink. There may be something I have to do, and I can't think properly when I'm drowsy."

"It will make you think all the more clearly tomorrow," said Ptah-aru.

"All right . . . if you're sure it will."

Far away I heard Kiyas saying anxiously, "He's very cold. Shall I get a hot stone to put at his feet?"

"No; two extra woolen covers will be enough."

I felt them being tucked around me, but I was too lazy to open my eyes.

"You're sure he's not going to die?"

"Quite sure. He's lost a lot of blood, but he's young and will soon heal."

"I'll tell his servant to stay just outside the tent so that he can hear if Ra-ab moves. I'll be with Hanuk, but I'll hear if I'm called. You ought to rest, Ptah-aru, you look very tired."

"Don't worry about me; Ptah is a most considerate master to his servants. You look after your husband and your brother, and send for me at once if either of them needs me again."

I heard them both go out of the tent. Pain was a small black boat, drifting further away from me on the tide of the sleep-drink: I could still see it, but it didn't really matter any longer. . . . Perhaps Meri is in much worse pain than I. The last message from her said our child wasn't going to be born yet, not until I got home. Funny she should have been wrong about the time—she seemed so sure. Very soon I shall be home with her. . . .

I stretched out my left arm and tried to pretend she was lying beside me with her head on my shoulder . . . Meri, my heart, my love.

I was caught in a nightmare. I was trying to staunch the wounds of the men I had killed, while the women who loved them stood by in silence and in tears. Mothers and wives, sisters and children . . . all weeping because I had killed their men.

I tried to wake myself; and suddenly I had slipped into a safe, happy dream. Meri had come back to me. She was lying with her head on my shoulder just as I had imagined. I said firmly, "I mustn't let myself wake. If I do I shall be alone in a tent with pain, instead of being happy with Meri. Don't wake up, or Meri will go away. Don't wake up!"

"You *are* awake, my very dear; and I am still with you. I'm never going to let us be parted any more."

"No, Meri. You mustn't let me wake up. You're in the Oryx and I'm in a tent outside the Royal City—but I'll be coming home very soon because Men-het is dead."

"I know, my love; but I'm not in the Oryx. I'm here in the tent beside you. I'm not only a dream Meri, I'm my down-here self as well. Do dream kisses feel as real as these?"

Suddenly I realized I *was* awake and Meri was lying beside me. Yet I was dazed by the poppy drink and said, "You oughtn't to have made the journey. Oh, my love, I'm so glad to see you . . . it has been so lonely without you. . . . But what would have happened to you if the child had been born on the journey."

She took my hand and ran it down her body. I was bewildered. "I don't understand. The message which reached me two days ago said he wasn't ready to be born yet."

"That was the only lie I've ever told you; and I don't expect I'll ever have to tell you another. Your son is eight days old—I found I was much better at having a baby than I thought I'd be, and in four days I found traveling in a litter much more enjoyable than staying in bed. Niyahm grumbled a good deal when I said I was bringing him to you . . . she seems to think he's as much hers as mine!"

"You brought him *here?*"

"Yes, he's in Sebek's tent with Niyahm."

"No man ever had such a beautiful and bewildering wife! You bear me a son, and long before any other woman would think of leaving her bed, you set off on a long journey without even being sure of your destination. Is he all right, does he like his foster-mothers?"

"He didn't have the chance to find out. I think your father was rather shocked; anyway he tried to explain to me that the wives of nobles were too delicate to feed their children. I told him that nobles' women being different to other women was just another of the silly ideas which the Watchers have got to stop people believing in. He must have approved of his grandson, even if he was cross with me, for when he found that he couldn't make me change my mind about coming to you he sent his own litter-bearers with me and his own body-guard. He gave me an impor-tant message for you: 'Tell Ra-ab that his son is the Young Oryx: he'll understand what I mean.'"

"It means that we are the Nomarch."

"Ra-ab, I love you so much! Your shoulder must be hurting too badly for you to be able to enjoy all the lovely things which are happening to you. We are together—and that will always be so much more important than anything else; you have a son; you are the Nomarch of the Oryx; and because of your victory thousands of other men and women will be able to be happy together . . . and have specially lovely children who are born of love. Would you like to see your son now, or wait until the morning?"

I knew she wanted me to say I was impatient for my first sight of him, so I said, "See if you can borrow him from Niyahm. I wouldn't dare to try—I'd rather take its cub away from a leopard!"

Meri stood up: naked and very beautiful. "Oh, Ra-ab! It is so wonderful to be a nice shape again! But having a baby is well worth the trouble: we'll have some more later on."

She put on my cloak and went out of the tent. I heard my son before I saw him: he was protesting vigorously at being wakened in the middle of the night. Meri held him in the crook of her left arm while she lit a second wick in the lamp.

My son continued to express his annoyance, although his mother tried to reason with him. "I do think it's tiresome of you to be so cross: it makes you look so crumpled, and you're really very handsome when you're good."

Gradually the yells faded to a whimper and then ceased. Meri put him down beside me. He looked much the same as any other baby, yet I felt ridiculously proud of him. "Niyahm says he looks *exactly* like you," said Meri, as though paying me a supreme compliment.

The Young Oryx stared at me: for a moment his eyes looked very wise, as though he was trying to tell me something. "I think he knows he's a long friend of ours," I said.

"Of course he does; and we'll show him that it can be very nice to be born, even when one's still a child. We shall make him very happy, so that he will be a wise Nomarch when his turn comes to rule the Oryx."

"Meri, we have worked so long for the Dawn; yet it is only the beginning of the day in which we of the Horizon shall see peace over Egypt."

Then Meri lay down beside me: to sleep between two who had loved her down the centuries.

The next day I found myself extraordinarily willing to be obedient to Meri and Ptah-aru; to doze, and on waking to take the broth, the raw eggs, and wine which were given me. At dusk Sebek brought me the long-awaited message from Pharaoh:

"The North has proclaimed Amenemhet to be the only rightful wearer of the Double Crown. Seven days' feasting has been declared, and in three days he will make his triumphal entry into the Royal City. He sends greetings to you, calling you 'his most beloved servant and Brother in Horus.' To honor the Oryx and Roidahn, to whom he has given the official title of Lord of the Horizon, he will make a Royal Progress through our Nome; there to bestow honors upon you and also upon these others who have seen peace born of their wisdom brought to Egypt. Pharaoh further decrees that you are to be the sole judge of those who followed Men-het, saying that whatever you decree shall be as though he had set it above his own seal."

At dawn next morning nearly three thousand of Men-het's followers were ranked on the Field of Hathor. They were in ceremonial dress; the Leaders of Hundreds in front of their men, and, in front of them again, the Captains, each with a standard-bearer beside him. Where Men-het would have stood was the Captain of the Royal Bodyguard.

Many of them must have been thinking that this would be the last time they would be allowed their panoply. The man they had called Pharaoh was dead; now he against whom they had rebelled was in authority. They must have expected to be sent into exile, or to labor in the quarries . . . even if they were not sentenced to death. Would they be given the honors of war; or be treated as rebels? They must all have known that rebels did not die an easy death; yet all of them were calm and proud, for they were true Egyptians.

I stood between Meri and Hanuk, and beside him was Kiyas. Behind us were the standard-bearers of the three Nomes who had vanquished the power of a dynasty.

Then did I speak to them:

"Look to the Horizon, O men of Egypt, and see the Dawn is come! The shadows of yesterday are forgotten, for Ra has returned into his majesty and there is peace throughout the Two Lands.

"We are no longer enemies, for together we have done honor to Men-het the Warrior; and together we have sent Fear, our common enemy, into exile. Long have the Crook and Flail been a sign of tyranny: now in the hands of Amenemhet they have become the symbol of kinship with the Gods. The Flail is no longer a sign of oppression; nor shall it be echoed by whip-men in any Nome.

"Today the order has gone forth that there are no longer slaves in Egypt. Power has been taken from the hands of the oppressors, and Authority has become a wise counselor to befriend those under his protection. The people of the villages shall go to the headman as to a father, and the word 'overseer' shall become the title of a friend. No longer shall Egypt pay tribute to the Gods of Fear, for the peace of Ra has returned. The statues of Set and

Sekmet have been overthrown, and no blood sacrifice shall be made on any altar, neither in the North nor in the South. No man shall be called upon to give more than his just tribute of the tenth part; of which not an ear of wheat nor a grain of gold-dust shall swell the private treasure of any man. All that is given by the people of Egypt shall be shared among them for their common welfare; and during the lean years there shall be no famine. No one shall go hungry or be without shelter: in sickness they will be cared for in the temples, nor shall they be without a friend during their lifetime.

"I call upon you, who love Egypt, to join with me in freedom to keep the Two Lands forever safe from Fear. You have shown yourselves to be mighty warriors; the foreigners shall hear of you, and the cruel, the greedy and the jealous-hearted. They are your enemies, and it is your strength which shall protect your people from them.

"I do not demand allegiance from you; I set you free of all loyalties which your mouth has spoken and of which your heart is now unsure. If you do not wish to stay with us to live for Egypt; return to your homes, free men, to dwell in Egypt whom other men protect.

"Those who wish to stay; keep ranks. Those who wish to go; depart, to dwell in the peace we made."

Not a man moved; then a great shout echoed along the ranks, rolled like a wave to cleanse the land from fear, "Amenemhet! Pharaoh is born again! Pharaoh is born, and we are his bodyguard!"

One by one, the Captains and the Leaders of Hundreds came forward to make their oath of fealty to me in Pharaoh's name.

Then they who had been our enemies, wheeled and took the road back to the Royal City; to wait for Pharaoh to return to them.

The End

ABOUT THE AUTHOR

JOAN GRANT was born in England in 1907. Her father was a man of such intellectual brilliance in the fields of mathematics and engineering that he was appointed a fellow of Kings College while still in his twenties. Joan's formal education was limited to what she absorbed from a series of governesses, although she felt she learned far more from the after-dinner conversations between her father and his fellow scientists. At twenty, she married Leslie Grant, with whom she had a daughter. This marriage ended soon after her first book, *Winged Pharaoh*, was published in 1937—a book which became an instant best-seller. Until 1957 she was married to the philosopher and visionary Charles Beatty. In 1960, Joan married psychiatrist Denys Kelsey.

Throughout her life, Joan was preoccupied with the subject of ethics. To her, the word 'ethics' represented the fundamental and timeless code of attitudes and behavior toward one another on which the health of the individual and society depends. Each of her books and stories explores a facet of this code. As Denys Kelsey wrote, "The First Dynasty of Egypt once knew the code well, but lost it and foundered. Eleven dynasties were to pass before it was recovered, but those were more leisurely times when the most lethal weapon was an arrow, a javelin and a club. We feel that in the present troubled days of this planet, these books must be presented."

Joan Grant's books, with their unique mix of ethics and 'far memory', continue to inspire readers today. They are the teachings of a woman of compassion, humour, and extraordinary psychic gifts. In their time, her books were treated as fiction, respected for their historical authenticity. But in her autobiography, *Far Memory*, Joan publicly acknowledged that they were recollections of lives threaded like beads on the same string as her own. In her personal life Joan was by turns poetic, inspirational, down to earth, challenging, funny, and wise—never conventional, always to be relied on to think for herself, and ever ready to help others. She left important messages for us all, especially in this

time of extraordinary global ethical challenges. As a single example we offer this statement, found in one of her notebooks, which
speaks volumes in the current time of financial crisis: "Money
should be a symbol of how many people you can protect."

Who was Joan Grant? She says it best: "I am all the others
whom I have loved, no matter who they were or who they now
are, down all the ages since I started to enter the Great Dance. I
am the rocks, the plants, the animals, the humans and also those
who are ahead of me on the Great Creativity…"